How to HELP a HUNGRY WEREWOLF

ALSO BY CHARLOTTE STEIN

When Grumpy Met Sunshine

How to HELP a HUNGRY WEREWOLF

CHARLOTTE STEIN

ST. MARTIN'S GRIFFIN
NEW YORK

First published in the United States by St. Martin's Griffin, an imprint of St. Martin's Publishing Group

HOW TO HELP A HUNGRY WEREWOLF. Copyright © 2024 by Charlotte Stein. All rights reserved. Printed in the United States of America. For information, address St. Martin's Publishing Group, 120 Broadway, New York, NY 10271.

www.stmartins.com

The Library of Congress Cataloging-in-Publication Data is available upon request.

ISBN 978-1-250-35233-0 (trade paperback)
ISBN 978-1-250-35234-7 (ebook)

Our books may be purchased in bulk for promotional, educational, or business use. Please contact your local bookseller or the Macmillan Corporate and Premium Sales Department at 1-800-221-7945, extension 5442, or by email at MacmillanSpecialMarkets@macmillan.com.

First Edition: 2024

10 9 8 7 6 5 4 3 2 1

For the girl who dreamt of a
world where all of this is possible

Dear Readers,

While this book is very much a cozy, heartwarming, and hilarious paranormal romance—with a full-on proper HEA—it does contain some sensitive, heavier topics. These include brief references to parental neglect, bullying, and an incident that includes fatphobia, plus brief mentions at a few points of the effects that fatphobia can have.

Hopefully, this will help you make an informed choice before reading! I've done my best to handle all topics with sensitivity and love.

Take care of yourselves,
Charlotte xx

How to HELP a HUNGRY WEREWOLF

PROLOGUE

Cassie wasn't sure why he was suddenly being kind to her. But though she hated the way she'd responded—like a flower opening up at the first sign of the sun—she couldn't deny that it had felt good. Or that she was already starting to wonder if she could have her buddy back.

Maybe he's tired of those jerks now, maybe he's starting to remember what they did to us, maybe he wants movies and Mario Kart and swimming at the quarry with me again, she thought, as she wheeled her little cart up onto the stage. The one he'd suggested she use, so she could do her talent for this show.

"You'll be great," he'd said. "People are going to love watching you spin sugar."

And he had sounded so sincere. Like her best friend again. Instead of the friend of those bullies who'd made their lives hell for the better part of their school lives. The ones he'd grown cool enough for, and now spent all his time with. The ones he was standing with right now, when she glanced to where the staging area was, about a second before the curtains opened.

Oh no oh no oh no, she found herself thinking.

But of course it was too late now. And anyway, this couldn't be a trick.

Because, yeah, sure, he was their friend now, instead of hers. But he'd never actively joined in with their cruelty. He just didn't talk to her hardly at all anymore. He just looked away when he saw her coming down the hall. And that wasn't the same as being an asshole, was it?

No, she told herself firmly, as what looked like the entire high school was revealed, sitting in folding chairs, ready to clap for her cake-decorating tricks. Or at least they were ready to clap if she did them right. They would probably boo if things went wrong.

They might even laugh, she knew.

But truthfully, she didn't think that was going to happen. She knew what she could do. Sometimes she could almost feel it, deep down in her bones. A sense of calm and surety. And it was here with her now as she unveiled the plain, tiered cake, and giggled through her introduction. A little snarky, a little self-deprecating, a little weird. The way Seth used to love.

But she didn't think he loved it anymore. Because just as she was about to start, there was a whine from a microphone that wasn't hers. And someone's voice—frantically high, but still completely recognizable. Seth, it was Seth. It was Seth who shouted those two words. The ones the Jerks used to use all the time, but she had never thought he would.

"Fat ass," he said.

And that would have been fine. She could have shrugged that off. She'd been waiting for it from him for what felt like a decade now—but was really only a year or so. Just that small amount of time to turn him from the boy she loved into this. A near-man who would yell that insult at her.

But then her cake suddenly toppled over, spreading all the way down the front of her body. And now everyone was laughing. They roared as frosting slid to her shoes in great clumps. One of them threw something. Another echoed what Seth had said.

And she couldn't shrug that off.

She couldn't be Carrie getting a bucket of pig's blood on her head, without at least some fury. In fact she could feel it now, boiling and burning and brightening inside her, until it genuinely felt like she might do something unhinged. She turned and looked at him, surrounded by his laughing buddies, and found herself thinking of that line from some book. The one about chests and cannons and shooting your heart at someone.

Then she had the strangest feeling, for a second, that this might somehow happen.

That she could do it. That she could kill him that way, if she really thought about it hard enough. And the idea was so terrible, and so strange, she didn't hesitate. She ran. She went straight through the double doors at the side of the stage, all the way out to the parking lot. Fast, so fast she almost didn't hear him call her name. She nearly didn't stop.

The burning bright feeling was enormous now.

It felt as if she might burst because of it.

Then she felt him reach for her. She got a hint of his hand, barely brushing over her right arm. And she had to do something. It was too much to have him touch her, to have him protest, to hear him say something like it was just a joke. She couldn't stand it.

So she did the only thing she could.

She turned and yelled:

"You're a beast, Seth Brubaker!"

Then she shoved him away with both hands. And she ran again, as thunder rumbled across the sky.

CHAPTER ONE

Cassie's first instinct on seeing him approach the house was to murder him, then bury the body in the backyard.

Until it occurred to her that this would involve a lot of digging, and dragging of his gigantic body, and finally tamping down of dirt—and frankly all of that seemed like way too much effort. Plus she'd probably get crap all over the place if she tried, and she really didn't want that to happen.

She'd only just managed to scrub away seventy years of grime from the ramshackle remains of her grandmother's old home, after two days back in a place she hadn't visited in years. At least thirty cobwebs had violently threatened her during the course of her cleaning spree. She'd found things in closets that no human eyes should ever see, unless they maybe wanted to unleash an ancient curse on a small, unsuspecting New England town. And her kneecaps were about to fall off from all the kneeling.

There was no way she was letting Seth Brubaker undo all her good work. If she was going to kill him, she was going to have to do it tidily. Maybe get a bath of acid ready first, to dissolve him in. Or hire a wood chipper to chop him into pieces.

Both seemed like pretty good ideas.

But maybe not quite as good as just refusing to open the door to him in the first place. After all, he had no decent reason to be here. And she had every reason in the world to never want to see him again. He was responsible for the most devastating series of events of her high school life.

In fact, they were so devastating that they still haunted her now, at the big old age of twenty-seven. She found herself lingering on the bright brilliance of having been friends with him for most of their childhoods. Defending each other from the Jerk Squad who had tormented them. Then the brutal sting when he had gotten too hot and cool for the likes of her, somewhere in the middle of high school, and started hanging out with the very boys who'd stuffed her into lockers and called the two of them losers for liking cringe things.

And of course anything had been cringe to Jason Kirkpatrick and his buddies. So everything had become cringe to Seth, too. Starting with the things Cassie and he had treasured together, the things they had shared, and ending with that fateful incident.

All of which made it perfectly justifiable to ignore his now insistent knocking.

Hell, maybe she could even pretend she wasn't home. The door was thick and nothing but wood. And she'd been in the basement for the last hour, so he couldn't have seen her silhouette through any downstairs window. *Stay quiet and he'll just go away,* she told herself—which seemed like a reasonable thing to imagine.

Only then he started hollering. And even more bizarrely, it wasn't her he was hollering for.

"Adeline, are you there?" he called out, and Cassie's stomach seemed to drop three feet. *That was her grandmother's first name.* A name that she herself had barely spoken aloud. In fact, she wasn't sure she *ever* had. The woman was Gram or Granny to her, and nothing else. So what the heck was Seth Brubaker doing, using it like that?

He'd hardly known the woman. Even back when Cassie and he had still been friends and hung out at her house together— which had not been often, the occasional bout of board-game playing or begging for milk and cookies aside—he'd always called her Mrs. Camberwell.

Because he'd been a polite dork. Instead of the asshole big shot he grew into.

"Come on, Adeline, open up," he said. While Cassie stood on the other side of the door, horrified. But also completely baffled.

And in the end, it was the baffled part of her that won. It made her grab the door's handle and fling the thing open before she could think any further about it.

Though she wished she had, once it was done.

Now not only was she abruptly face-to-face with her mortal enemy; she was face-to-face with him while being the absolute worst possible version of herself. Most of her dark hair was almost gray with dust. And she'd made the mistake of covering the rest with a red scarf—one that she'd found at the bottom of a box labeled "garbage." She looked like a reject from a Rosie the Riveter photo shoot. Doubly so when you factored in the overalls she had foolishly chosen for this cleaning spree. They were far too short in the legs, and so worn you could probably breathe on them and make a hole. And even worse: they were very tight over her butt.

Which wasn't a problem to her.

She loved how that clinginess made her curves look.

But the trouble was, she knew he didn't feel that way. Oh yeah, she knew his feelings on that all right. And she had zero desire to hear any of those feelings ever again. She didn't even want to be reminded with some sort of surreptitious glance down or pointed lip curl. Because if that did happen, she knew she would most likely do something very inadvisable.

Like try to attack him somehow.

Even though attacking him was never going to turn out well for her.

The gawky boy she had known looked even cooler and tougher now than he had during those final high school years. His shoulders were the size of boulders; the hand he had on the door resembled a shovel. And, oh god, the clothes he was wearing. He had on an actual leather jacket. Over an honest-to-goodness Henley. Paired with boots that looked like he'd killed a biker for them.

And all of this was before she even laid eyes on his annoyingly handsome face.

Because even though she hated the very sight of it, even though it turned her stomach, even though she would have done anything to have back the boy with the too-big-for-his-mouth braces and the milk-bottle-bottom glasses, she had to admit: it was handsome. That jaw like the side of a knife; those wide-set, caramel-colored eyes that seemed constantly starved for something you didn't want to consider.

And that *mouth*. How did he have a mouth like that? His upper lip was as plush as a peach. However, his lower was almost *mean*. It made him look like he was three seconds away from murdering you at any given moment—but in such a soft and seductive way that you'd be really happy about it when he did.

And then just in case all of that wasn't enough, there was his hair. That black hair, stalking angrily over his eyes and swirling in thick waves across his jaw and forever settling in a perfect swoop just above his broad brow. *Like a raven's wing*, she'd once thought, back when it had been thicker and shaggier and less immaculately coiffed.

And she'd been allowed to have such thoughts about it. Heck, she'd been allowed to touch it back then—and without so much as a second of worrying about the consequences. Because her milk-bottle-best-friend wouldn't have had any consequences to dole out. He hadn't seemed to even know what consequences for things like affection *were*. He just wanted to play Mario Kart or watch horror movies until they screamed themselves hoarse.

But that boy wasn't coming back. This man had shed him, like a skin he no longer needed. And he'd discarded her along with it. In fact, the only sign that he'd been that boy was the slightly crooked incisors he'd been unable to completely fix. The ones she saw when his mouth dropped open, the second he clocked that it wasn't Adeline on the other side of the door.

"Cassie," he said, in a voice she'd never heard from him before. It was so faint it barely qualified as a voice. It was more like he'd just let out a slightly heavy breath. As if he'd seen a ghost, she thought—which she supposed was true, in one way.

He had pretty thoroughly murdered her in high school, after all.

She just hadn't completely died. She had kept going, with all the dead parts stored inside. And now she had to somehow pretend those dead parts weren't there. Even though that was much, much easier said than done. It took almost every ounce of effort she had just to look him in the face, never mind be cool and calm and collected while she did. Then somehow she was supposed to say something to him, without her voice shaking all over the place? *Impossible*, she thought.

Until suddenly it was just happening. Words were blurting out of her.

Though, god, they were not good ones.

"I have no idea why you're looking for my grandmother, but no matter what the reason is you're out of luck. She died of a heart attack," she said, and knew she had made a mistake the moment it was out. Bad enough that Seth Brubaker was getting to see her looking a mess. But now she'd also filled him in on the reason she was *feeling* like a mess. She had given him more ammunition. And felt pretty sure he was about to open fire. *Any second now*, she thought.

Then didn't know what to think when he looked concerned.

"Died of a heart attack? Just like that? With no sign of it being anything else? When?" he asked. As if somehow, inexplicably, he really wanted to know. More than that, in fact. It was like he was frantic to know. Like the very idea of not knowing made him lose his shit, just a little bit.

Even though she couldn't for the life of her think why. He had long since stopped caring about her—never mind her grandmother. Heck, she couldn't think of *anybody* who cared about her grandmother. Even her parents hadn't thought much of her—mainly because they agreed with the rest of the town about how weird and antisocial her Gram had been. The woman would have done anything for anyone, but she didn't suffer fools. And she wasn't one for gossip, or too much time spent in company.

So when Cassie had told her parents she was going back to Hollow Brook to settle Gram's affairs, they'd seemed at first dismissive, and then annoyed. *Just sell the house as is and put the money to good use,* her father had said. *Maybe you can finally get your act together and go to college, like you should have done years ago.*

And Cassie had come pretty close to doing that. But then she'd thought of her grandmother wanting her to have the house, and one particular soothing summer she'd spent with her, and she just couldn't sell it. She couldn't throw that away. She had to at least pay her respects and swim in a few treasured memories.

And now here she was, paying dearly for that sentimental choice.

"Cassie, answer me. Are you sure she died of a heart attack? Did anything cause it to happen so suddenly?" Seth repeated. Only now he was getting pretty close to yelling. And she wasn't about to stick around for that.

"I don't think that's any of your goddamn business," she somehow managed to bark out. Then even better: she was closing the door on him.

Actually closing the door on Seth Brubaker. Captain of the swim team. Homecoming king. Guy voted most likely to succeed at being extremely handsome. It was amazing—even if he wasn't about to go down that easy.

He put a hand out to stop the door. And though it shouldn't have been very hard to push against him, it really was. In fact, it kind of felt as if she were trying to force a large boulder up a mountain. Instead of just closing her door on a single outstretched arm.

Man, he got strong, she found herself thinking.

It wasn't just his strength that was startling, however. He was also significantly taller than he had been in high school. She had to tilt her head all the way back just to meet his gaze, and once she had, she wished she hadn't bothered. He looked weird. Almost like he was having human feelings. About her grandmother, apparently.

"It is my business," he said. "She was my friend."

He even made it sound convincing. Like sincerity.

Despite the fact that it couldn't have been.

"My grandmother would never have been friends with the likes of you," she said, and it felt true when she did. True enough to get him to stop, at any rate. But he didn't. He kept going.

"Hey, just because I made a mistake in school doesn't mean I'm beyond help."

"Probably not. But calling the abandoning of your best friend and then betraying her in front of said school a 'mistake' sure does. I mean, hey, I got that we weren't buddies by that point. The fucking Jerk Squad were your buddies, despite all the bullying they subjected you to before you turned cool. But I never thought you'd stoop so low as to yell insults at me in front of an auditorium full of the people I had to face the next day. And especially when you only did it to impress those assholes." She pictured the episode. The talent show, the cake, the icing she'd made with her grandmother that changed colors as you applied it. Then the way it had looked all down her.

They rigged it to topple on you, she told herself, for the umpteenth time. *They turned you into something from a Stephen King novel. You know they did, because Principal Sykes found the contraption they used to do it and suspended them for hardly any time at all.*

And now she wanted to close the door again. But Seth was still protesting.

"I told you—I didn't do it to impress anyone, okay?"

"Dude, you didn't tell me *anything*. You just yelled an apology, one time."

"Right. Right, and that was wrong. All of it was wrong, I know that. I fucked up majorly and you hate me and you're never gonna stop and that's fine. But if you could please just set that aside for one second, because I really need to know what happened to your grandmother. Like, if I could just hear some of the details."

Fucked up majorly, she thought, and felt her heart lift a little bit.

But then she digested the rest of what he'd said and forced it back down. Because quite clearly, he was only doing this to get something that he inexplicably wanted. Something probably bad. And so now she had to find out what that bad thing was, before he could somehow hurt her with it.

Even if she had to be a little hyperbolic to do so.

"I see, so you can use those details to torment her too," she said.

Much to his probably fake incredulity. "You think I'm so awful that I can somehow bully someone from beyond the grave? What do you think I'm going to do, dig her up and give her wedgies and a wet willy?"

"Well, *now* I do. Christ, I don't even know how you came up with that."

"I came up with that because there aren't any other options."

He nodded, like he was satisfied with his answer. Though she had no idea why. There were a million things he could have said. And now she was going to stick him with all of them. "You could have gone with pissing on her grave."

"That's almost as bad as what I suggested."

"Or insulting her ghost."

"Ghosts aren't even real."

"That is not an excuse for poking your soggy finger into my dead grandmother's ear," she said, and oh, his outraged expression was a peach. In fact, it almost made all her anxious sweating worth it. Until he started arguing with her again.

"Oh my god, don't say it like I've already done it. Or would actually do it. It was just an example, because you said that thing about tormenting her," he blew out. Like *she* was the bad one here.

"Yeah, and now you're tormenting me."

"I'm just asking you a question."

"While trying to ram your way into my house."

She knew she was exaggerating wildly, even as she said it. He wasn't trying to ram his way into her house at all. In fact, that hand he'd put on the door had begun to slide down ever since she'd first started tearing into him. And she was pretty sure one good shove would have put paid to it entirely. But here was the weird thing: he didn't act like that was the case. Instead, he seemed to jerk when he registered what he was doing. As if the body parts responsible didn't actually belong to him. Someone had attached them in the night, while he was sleeping. Now they were roaming around, randomly holding open doors and making him seem really tall.

"I didn't know. I didn't realize I was doing that. I just. I thought," he said, as if he'd forgotten how to finish sentences properly. He kept putting periods where they weren't supposed to be, and trailing off in the strangest places.

She had to prompt him. "You thought what?"

Though in response he just shook his head, like a dog trying to get dry.

"That I gotta go," he answered.

Then he suddenly started backing away. He stepped off her grandmother's front porch. Or more accurately, he stumbled off it. He almost went flat on his ass, and probably would have done if he hadn't managed to grab the railing that lined the steps down.

And even after he'd righted himself, he didn't seem steady. He kind of staggered away, drunkenly. Lost his footing again, and regained it.

None of which should have been that shocking. But it was, because Seth Brubaker was the one doing it. Seth Brubaker, who had grown into the kind of guy who never put a single foot wrong. Who had started walking down hallways as if his feet were made of wheels, with hair that was never out of place and swimsuits that didn't disappear into the crack of his ass, and the kind of cool life that she could never have hoped to follow him into.

He'd left her behind, utterly and completely.

Yet here he was, practically making a disaster of his exit. In fact, he was making so much of a disaster of it she came close to asking him something very strange. Something she could never have imagined saying to him in a million years. *Are you okay?* she thought. *Are you okay, mortal enemy of mine?*

And was grateful that he was gone before she could.

CHAPTER TWO

She tried not to think too much about Seth Brubaker. After all, she had plenty of other things to contend with. Like all the junk her grandmother had accrued over the years, which turned up in the most ridiculous places.

There were coins in the toilet cistern. Weird coins, from countries that no longer existed. Or maybe hadn't ever existed, if Google was any indication.

And that wasn't even the strangest thing she found.

There were also boxes full of dolls—and not the good kind. No, these were the kind that she'd screamed over when watching a movie about them with Seth. The kind with glassy eyes that followed you around the room, and too little hair on their weird shiny heads, and bodies made out of sacks someone had discovered on a haunted farm.

She honestly found herself wondering if they might eat her in the night.

Which was ridiculous, she knew it was ridiculous. Yet if she was being honest, it kind of fit with the theme of this place.

Because it wasn't just all the weird objects and spooky crevices that she was almost constantly stumbling across. There were other unsettling things about her grandmother's old home. Like the fact that the whole house made a ridiculous amount of noise. Pipes knocked even when no water was flowing through them. Floorboards creaked despite the fact that not a single person had stepped on them in hours. And the less said about the staircase, the better. The night before, she'd been pretty sure that she'd heard something thumping up them to the bedroom she'd been sleeping in. She'd wound up shoving her grandmother's ancient dresser in front of the door.

Not that this had made things any better, however. Instead, the noises had just started coming from the room she was in. She'd had to stay up for the rest of the night, glaring at the possibly alive rocking chair in the corner with narrowed eyes. And then of course she'd been so tired the next morning that she'd accidentally buttered a sponge.

She was still picking bits of yellow fluff out of her teeth when dinner rolled around.

So it was almost a relief when she finally found something normal. Something that she remembered from her time here with her grandmother. Specifically, the time right after the whole school had laughed at her getting Stephen Kinged, when she'd needed a distraction desperately.

The journals. The ones her and Gram had filled with mad recipes, in her ramshackle kitchen.

Every one of them disgusting and ridiculous, but all of them imbued with meaning she still remembered so clearly.

Like the potato pie she'd declared a cure for aches and pains, when her Gram had told her the weather was biting. And how her Gram had enjoyed pretending a slice of it had worked, just to make her happy. Or the one for plum cake that supposedly made it rain. Then the laughter when a downpour had hit, just as they threw a handful of crumbs up into the sky.

Coincidences like that had felt almost magical.

And so much so she had never wanted to stop. In fact, it had only been her own lack of skill that had made her. *You should really quit cooking before you give someone food poisoning*, her grandmother had said. And she had quit, too.

She wasn't even sure about getting too engrossed in the journals again.

Until she came across one particular recipe.

"Feel Better Soup," it was called. Even though she couldn't imagine it ever making anyone feel better. It sounded completely bananas. You had to simmer everything for twenty-four hours. And the main ingredient seemed to be garlic.

Seventeen cloves, it required. But for what reason, it didn't say. It just instructed whoever was cooking it to throw them all in, skins and all, then add a few other things in amounts that made no sense. There was a "speck" of rosemary, and a "whiff" of chili oil—and then for some reason it suggested thickening this unholy brew with ground-up beans. It was mystifying. And yet at the same time Cassie had the strongest, strangest urge to give cooking a go again. Like maybe this time she might make something good. This time, it would work. She wasn't going to poison anyone, she was sure of it.

So she checked the stone-floored and stuffy pantry for ingredients.

And when that yielded very little, she searched through the ancient bulbous refrigerator. But aside from the necessities she'd stacked in there, she found next to nothing. There was just a collection of jars inside—none of which had labels on them. Heck, two of them didn't even have visible contents. A strange gray murk clung to the insides of the glass, obscuring whatever was in there from view. So god only knew what it was.

And she wasn't about to check.

She shoved the jar back among its equally unsettling siblings, and made her way down to the shed at the bottom of the garden. And sure enough—there was her old bike. Still where she'd left it, and not even covered in cobwebs like she'd imagined. In fact, it was almost in as good shape as she remembered, shiny as a star and so well-oiled that it barely made a sound when she wheeled it out. All she had to do was recall how to ride it.

Shakily, at first. Like she'd forgotten how.

But then faster and faster, until she was barreling down the final hill that slid into Main Street. Hair a black streamer behind her, those tarot cards her grandmother had put between the spokes clicking away, furiously. And all the sights and sounds barely more than a blur of color and a few snatched details.

Though she knew what all of them were anyway. Nothing

seemed to have changed much in the seven or so years she'd been gone.

There was the old movie theatre, somehow limping on despite a million multiplexes and streaming services—and the fact that they were still spelling all the films wrong on the awning outside. She caught a glimpse of the words "Classic Horror Month," and then underneath: *Scram, The Winches of Eastlick, Candyland.*

And was that Mira Parvati unlocking the double doors, and wearing Mr. McKellen's old manager's waistcoat? She thought so, but went by too fast to say for sure. All she got was a glimpse of that shaggy black hair before she was past the place and on to the library, the tiny town hall, the office of the *Hollow Brook Gazette.* Each of them as familiar as ever, even though she knew they were mostly run by entirely different people now.

The mayor was no longer that red-faced blowhard Arthur Dollard, according to her mother. It was some tough old lady called Kathy Yates. And Tabitha Kendall—who Cassie remembered from a million story hours at the library, sitting at the head of a circle of kids with her soft brown hands clasped in her lap, telling tales she never needed the book for—had finally managed to oust that permed and pearled sourpuss Mrs. Vernon.

Or at least that was what Cassie had managed to gather from the online version of the *Gazette* that she'd read that morning. "So-Called Committee for a Clean Town Behave like Clowns Again," the headline had hilariously read, over an actually pretty serious report on Vernon's involvement with said committee, and all the ways their book-banning activities had led to her downfall. Which made sense, considering the kind of person Vernon was.

And who the writer of the article had been.

Marley Maples had been the byline appearing underneath the headline. Marley Maples—smart as a whip, sassy as a sexy cartoon cat, and the person Cassie had most wanted to make friends with in high school. But of course had never dared to go anywhere near.

She'd have probably written a headline like that about me. *"Loser Makes Fool of Self During Hollow Brook High Talent Show,"* Cassie thought, as she slowed just enough to see the curve of one winter-pale cheek through the window and knew immediately it was Marley. Then she sped up, pushing harder on the pedals, like going faster would somehow leave that idea in the dust.

Even though more reminders of miseries past were coming up.

There, outside her little bookshop, was the one other friend Cassie had almost sort of managed to have in high school. Still as cheery looking as ever, still all snub-nosed and pink-cheeked and so much like someone who wouldn't let you down.

And honestly, Nancy hadn't.

After the talent show, she had come calling. Sent Cassie flowers, said she was sorry about how awful that whole thing had been. But Cassie had been too sore and embarrassed to respond, and that had felt like the end of that.

Yet when she passed, Nancy looked up. And she grinned and waved like a lunatic.

I'll have to call her, Cassie thought to herself—though of course as soon as she did, she started thinking of all the ways something like that could go wrong. The ways she could be rejected, hurt, embarrassed. How she could end up relying on someone, only to have them let her down.

No, no. It was better to be as she was.

Always moving on, before anything got bad. Temporary acquaintances, temporary jobs, temporary time here. Even if here wasn't just about the people and the places.

There was also the loveliness of it.

The trees that lined the street were beginning to shed their sunset-streaked leaves—some fluttering in the air as she sailed past, others collecting in heaps so tidy they almost looked arranged. And though it was well into a crisp, bright morning, the fairy lights strung between the trees still glowed brightly. Like those deep October nights lingered, far longer than they should have. The darkness hung on, giving everything a spooky air.

Though the decorations everywhere definitely helped. She spotted pumpkins of all sizes, crammed into every nook and cranny of the bandstand in the center of town. Cobwebs swirled from every roof and awning, catching people as they strolled past. There were skeletons peeking from shop windows, and creepy lettering advertising all kinds of things, and finally there was that scent.

That Halloween is here, fall vibes scent, all bonfires and burnt caramel and something deliciously spicy. Mugs of cider spiked with cloves, she imagined. Or maybe cocoa infused with cinnamon and nutmeg. Or possibly whatever was in those donuts from the new donut place.

She almost stopped there, at the gaudy window. The man behind the counter, absurdly tall and gawky looking, waved. But she pressed on. She pulled up outside the much less appealing Stop and Save, intent on getting what she came for. After all, old man Hannigan had probably bent enough to sell something like garlic by now.

Then she pushed open the door that still stuck a bit at the bottom, and there it all was.

The store that even the Amish would have balked at.

Only somehow even worse than it had been back when she was a kid. Now it looked like he didn't even sell the licorice he had once allowed, with the salt in it. There were just rows and rows of cabbages. Then yet more rows of potatoes. Followed by some sacks of stuff that she *hoped* was flour. But was more likely to be the grain you had to grind to make it.

Because that was Hannigan's MO.

He had always been a big believer in the idea that everyone had everything easy these days. And he was an even bigger believer now, if his position as head of the clean-town committee was any indication. Not to mention every sign inside his shop. *Produce fondlers will be prosecuted*, one of them said. *All skirts must be knee length or you shall be asked to leave*, another proclaimed.

And then there was the man himself.

He looked just as terrifying as she remembered. Gaunt enough to pass for a skeleton in the right light. So tall he seemed to loom over her, even from all the way behind his enormous counter. And when he smiled, it looked more like a grimace than anything else. Partly because of his teeth, which were the size and shape of tombstones. But also because it never seemed to reach his eyes.

They stayed as flat as two old coins as he watched her coming toward him.

And they got even flatter when she asked her question.

"Garlic?" he spat. As if she'd just requested he sell her heroin. Then sure enough he spelled it out. "We have none of that filth here, Cassandra Camberwell."

Though it was really more the last part that disturbed her, over the first thing. He remembered her name, even after all this time. He remembered both names, in fact. And he deployed them like some kind of weapon. *A switch*, she thought, *that he intends to whip me to within an inch of my life with.*

She decided to beat a hasty retreat before he could.

After all, there were other places in Hollow Brook to get what she needed. There was the market on the outskirts, where she got herself not only garlic but some crusty bread, and a wheel of cheese, and about ten other items that would help her live like a wanderer in a seven-thousand-page fantasy novel. And once she had all those things, she rode back to Gram's house with something like satisfaction in her heart.

Things were okay.

She was okay—or at least, she was getting there. She'd spent a whole morning focusing on things other than her grief. Plus she hadn't once thought about Seth Brubaker doing nefarious things. In fact, she still wasn't thinking about Seth Brubaker doing nefarious things when she wheeled her bike around the side of the house.

And there was Seth Brubaker.

Actually doing nefarious things.

In fact, if anything, the word "nefarious" was far too kind a way to describe his current behavior. Nefarious sounded more like something a cartoon villain would do, in a kiddie show that played on a Saturday morning. But this was full-blown, prime-time adult nonsense of the very highest degree. He could have stepped straight out of an episode of *Criminal Minds*—and not just because he had the moody clothes and the angry mouth and the permanent scowl.

Because he was totally being a criminal.

He had one whole leg inside the living room window. Even though the living room window was about four feet off the ground. He had to have really struggled to get it all the way up there, she imagined—and in a way that was very bad for him. Firstly, because it meant he couldn't immediately detach himself and run off into the woods. Or even just saunter away casually while she gawped like a guppy at whatever this was.

And secondly and more importantly: because it gave him no possible way to explain.

There was no excuse he could give. No claims of accidents that could realistically have put him in this state. He had nothing, and his expression said he blatantly knew it. Though god knows he tried all the same.

"Oh, hey, Cassie," he said.

And to his credit, his voice almost hit breezy. He even managed a little hand wave. Like they'd just bumped into each other on the street.

"Seth, do you realize that your foot is inside my grandmother's house," she said. But even after she had, he still tried to maintain that casual, cheery manner.

"I do realize that. In fact I was just about to remove it from said house."

"That's good, that's really good. But you know what would be better?"

"I feel like I do, but probably you should fill me in anyway."

"*Not* having your foot inside her house in the first place."

"Yep. That's about what I imagined."

He nodded, then. As if to underline what he'd said. But she could tell just by the tone of his voice that he knew he was beaten. An audible wince ran through it. And a healthy dollop of resignation. And when he finally managed to meet her gaze, those feelings were visible in his eyes. *Go ahead and finish me off,* they seemed to say.

So she obliged. "Then I guess now is where you tell me what possessed you to go ahead and do this batshit thing. And lemme tell you, the reason better be incredible," she said. Though truthfully, she didn't expect him to come up with anything. And boy, were her instincts correct.

"All right, that's fair. But I mean, first I have to know what constitutes incredible to you in this situation. Just so that I have some idea of what I'm working with," he said, like the bullet-dodging bastard he was.

The worst part was, though, it worked.

She went with his flagrant attempt at changing the subject.

"Aliens abducted your feet while the rest of your body was still attached to them, and forced them through my grandmother's window," she suggested, then instantly regretted it. He almost smiled to hear her say it. Bare minimum, his eyes sparked with something like delight or triumph.

"Okay, how likely is it that I can get away with saying yes to that?" he tried.

Then somehow she just couldn't help answering him. "About as likely as me declaring you incredibly trustworthy and kind."

"Fuck, that is the most impossible thing I could ever imagine happening."

"Yup. It's very high on the no-fucking-way scale."

"I'd believe the aliens thing before that one."

"I guess you'd better come up with something better then."

She said it as flippantly and dismissively as she could. With an added eye roll at the end.

But here was the thing: he seemed to take it seriously. Like a challenge, of the kind he really wanted to put his back into. His brow furrowed; he looked skyward for inspiration. Then after what felt like a thousand years, he snapped his fingers.

"Got it. How about: I sleepwalked here. And then unconsciously climbed in the window," he said. And to be fair, he worked hard at making it sound plausible. She almost let herself consider it, for a moment. Then she remembered that all of this was ridiculous.

"That would be great. Really great. If it wasn't one thirty in the afternoon."

"Hey, maybe I go to bed super early."

"What, like noon?"

"Yeah," he tried to say.

Though she could tell he wasn't even convincing himself. His whole face was creased. And he was already bracing for her response. Which she duly gave him. "Even the elderly don't go to bed at noon, Seth."

"Okay, but I could be much older than I look."

"Dude, we were friends. Who went to the *same high school*."

She said the last three words the same way people tell children that they can't eat crayons. However, it didn't really seem to sink in. Instead he almost immediately jabbed a finger at her.

"So did Edward and Bella. And he was, like, a hundred years old."

"I see. So you're going with you being a secret vampire, who unaccountably has some sort of narcolepsy that makes you sleepwalk in the afternoon."

"Yes. No. Hold on." He shook his head, almost desperately. "Go back to the part about school. I got all turned around."

"You got turned around because you were always incredibly terrible at keeping your story straight when forced to lie. And have apparently gotten even more terrible at that since we last spoke. I mean, holy shit, how do you ever get out of anything? Wait, don't tell me. I don't want to know that you told your mom your high school girlfriend got pregnant via divine conception."

He looked genuinely confused by that. Though she wasn't exactly sure how she could tell genuine from not, considering how thrown he seemed by all of this. He hadn't even taken the time to maneuver his leg out the window—that was how flummoxed he was.

And he continued to be, massively.

"What are you talking about? I never got my high school girlfriend pregnant. I didn't even really *have* a high school girlfriend," he said. As if she were describing a real scenario, instead of just flat-out making fun of him. Though she supposed it made sense that he didn't grasp that, considering who she was dealing with.

He probably hadn't had anyone roast him in years.

"See, I know that's true, and yet you're so bad at lying I'm kind of doubting."

"Well don't, because I'm being completely honest with you."

"About everything except why you're climbing in my grand-mother's bedroom window," she said, and he looked at it then. Like he'd never seen it in his life before.

Though he had good reason to be shocked. To ask incredulously, "This is your grandmother's bedroom window?"

Because mostly she was just being a sneaky asshole now.

"No. I just wanted to see if you reacted like you knew that."

"Why would you want to do a thing like that?"

"Because I'm honestly starting to suspect you were sleeping with her."

That got a real reaction out of him. Or at least the kind of re-action she'd been expecting since he'd first rolled up to her door. So far he'd gone really softball on things she would have thought he'd hammer her over. And there was a strange quality to his be-havior, too, that she couldn't quite place. A kind of vulnerability, she wanted to call it.

Even if that seemed silly.

"I wasn't sleeping with her. The age gap would have been out-rageous," he exploded. Voice almost high and way too loud, eyes flashing, body suddenly battling hard with the window he was still half caught in. And once he was free he didn't immediately get in her face.

He didn't do anything, in fact.

He just glared at her. But even that reaction seemed to quickly die. He took a couple of calming breaths, and it was gone. And once it was—once that flare of anger had dissipated—he did some-thing even stranger. Something she couldn't fathom but under-stood all the same.

"You know what, just forget it. Forget it," he said, and she could hear it in his voice. She could see it in his face. This was weary resignation, plain and simple. Like he was too exhausted to keep fighting. Even though fighting someone like her should have been a cake walk. Not even just a cake walk—it was supposed to be something he enjoyed.

But boy did he seem to be doing the opposite of enjoying this.

He looks old somehow, her mind suggested.

And even though that was a bizarre thing to think, she couldn't help acknowledging the truth in it. His pallor was just a little bit grayer than usual; there were dark circles under his eyes. And his expression had sagged just a bit farther than an expression on a twenty-something face should. All of which made her go easier than she really wanted to.

"I can't forget it when you haven't told me what *it* actually is," she said.

But either he didn't hear the gentleness in her voice, or he was too distracted to care. "Nothing, okay? There was just a book your grandmother promised I could borrow. But you were justifiably never going to let me have it. So . . . ," he said, with such despair in his voice that she couldn't doubt his claim. Even though it was about books, and promises, and other things Seth Brubaker had long stopped giving a shit about, she could hear that he was telling her the truth.

And that shook her a little.

It made her want to ask, *which book?* Then of course her mind automatically went to the ones with Gram's recipes in them. *Maybe he wanted to make Feel Better Soup too,* she found herself thinking, and kind of wanted to laugh.

Only here was the thing: she couldn't laugh. It wasn't possible.

Because that thought felt true. Right in her bones. Deep in some weird part of her. It felt completely and wholly true. And oh man, she just did not know how to deal with that in any way whatsoever. It was too at odds with everything she knew about him, and all her own feelings about how this was supposed to play out, and by the time she'd managed to process both issues enough to ask him about any of this, he was halfway into the woods. Like he knew his cause was lost, so felt no need to continue talking to her.

Even though for the first time in years . . .

She actually wanted to talk to him.

CHAPTER THREE

Cassie wasn't sure how she managed to get to sleep after her last encounter with Seth. But she knew why she jolted awake at what had to be the darkest depths of the night. It was the sounds, again. The haunted house kind of sounds, that she still couldn't quite shake off as nothing. A thud on the stairs, she thought it had been.

Then it came again, louder this time. Louder, and clear enough that she knew it wasn't a ghost. Or a demon. Or something from the fifth dimension. There was someone in the goddamn house. There was a whole intruder, clearly—though she tried to tell herself otherwise for a second. *You're just inventing new threats now that you've almost gotten over the terror of spooky things*, her brain calmly informed her.

But it didn't work.

It couldn't work, because there was the noise again.

And this time, it was loud. It was massively, preposterously loud. As if someone had dragged a massive piece of furniture across the floor. Or maybe not even something as innocuous as a piece of furniture. It could have been a terrible thing, like a dead body. Or a sack full of body parts. Or possibly a big weapon that someone was going to use to turn her into mincemeat. *He has an axe*, she thought, *and it's so gigantic that he can't lift it all the time. He has to just trail it behind himself until he's ready to swing it.*

Then all she could think about was it being swung at her head. While she just sat there in bed. Waiting to be murdered.

Get up, she instructed herself. And somehow she made a start. She slid out from underneath the covers, as stealthily as she could make herself be while also shaking with terror. Then once she dared to put her feet down on the floor—a difficult process at the best of times, considering her constant fear of what was under this giant brass bed—she tiptoed across the room to the door.

And ended up banging into the table that stood there. She had to fling out her hands and catch it before it fell. But even that made a noise. She froze. Breath held. Body tensed. Every inch of her suddenly icy with sweat.

Yet there was no relief when she got nothing.

Now she had to keep going. She had to actually go out into the hall, without so much as a big knife or a baseball bat to protect her. All she could think of was the hatstand in the corner, and it wasn't ideal. It was so heavy she could barely pick it up. It almost toppled her over, as she swung it out in front of herself.

But it was long. And it had prongs at the end.

It would keep anyone who attacked her at a distance.

And that thought kept her going.

She crept along with the thing held out, every bit of her braced to suddenly see the intruder's shadow looming in the endlessly gray and gloomy hall. Then she got to the top of the stairs and braced again. Because now there was moonlight filtering up from the kitchen window. And she was certain moonlight would reveal his hideous visage.

In fact, it took almost everything she had to peep down into the foyer. She held her breath, and tried to keep as much of her body back as possible.

Only to see absolutely nothing.

No axe murderer. No axe. Not even a sign anyone had been there. She even went to breathe out, with relief. Sagged back against the nearest wall, let the hatstand drop a little. Started to gather herself together, to get back to bed.

And that was when she glimpsed it.

Just out of the corner of her eye, barely anything at all. Merely a stretch of floor that looked a little blacker than it should, lying between the archway into the kitchen and the archway into the living room.

But of course she knew what it was. The hatch that led down into the basement. The one whose trapdoor she had definitely closed before she'd gone to bed. But which was now as open as the maw of a starving beast, about three seconds from a long-awaited meal.

Fuck, she thought.

Because, yeah, okay, if the intruder was down there she could probably get to the front door. Maybe even make it to her bike and pedal to the nearest place with a phone signal.

However, she had to maneuver *around* that hole to do it. And that was terrifying. So terrifying, in fact, that she had to force her foot onto the top stair. Then force the other to follow suit. And even though the next steps came faster, it took her five full minutes to get to the bottom. And another five to start edging around the hole. And all the while she was getting sweatier, and shakier, and oh god now her grip on the hatstand was starting to falter. Another thirty seconds of this and it was going to fall right out of her hands.

Then he'd leap up the stairs, suddenly.

Right when she had nothing to defend herself.

Just run, now, her mind insisted. And it was tempting, it was. The front door was right there. He was definitely down in the depths. It made sense to try. She could even slam the trapdoor closed before she did, and maybe shove the dresser over it too.

But before she could, she took one terrified glance down, beyond the jutting rim that hid the basement beyond. And saw the light on down there, illuminating the very thing she should have guessed. Because of course it wasn't an axe-wielding maniac at all. Or even a garden-variety burglar.

Oh no no no no.

It was Seth Brubaker.

Somehow, it was Seth fucking Brubaker. Just down there, in her grandmother's basement, in the middle of the motherfucking night. Rummaging around, clear as day, as if that was an incredibly normal thing to do. When it was the opposite of normal in every single way. In fact, it was so not normal she couldn't even bring herself to believe it was true.

She had to creep down a few of the rickety basement steps to confirm.

Though all that did was make the situation worse. Now she could see him in the highest-possible definition. Like someone had jammed a telescope between her eyes and his face, entirely against her will. And that only revealed a bunch of other things she wasn't really braced for.

For some reason, he looked sick.

Seriously, horribly sick, in a way that was making him perspire.

In fact, no. It wasn't just something as slight as perspiration.

This dude was *sweating*. He was leaking buckets of the stuff, from what looked like every pore. She could see it running down the nape of his neck and gleaming all over the space between his nose and his top lip. Hell, she could see it gleaming on weirder places—like the backs of his hands. Even though she felt sure that the backs of hands didn't sweat.

And god, he seemed gray. Actually *gray*—not simply ashen or pale or whatever else people usually said when someone was sick. Like he'd just stepped out of a black-and-white movie, she thought, and was fairly alarmed at how well that fit.

But she was even more alarmed by his left leg.

It just did *not* seem to want to stop jiggling.

Massively jiggling, like someone was setting off firecrackers inside of it.

And as she watched, said firecrackers seemed to spread to other parts of his body. Now his right leg was jiggling too—which honestly just made it look like he really badly needed the bathroom. She almost wanted to tell him he could go if he had to.

But she was glad her brain saw sense, and forced her not to. Because (a) it definitely wasn't the need to pee that was causing this to happen, and (b) he had broken into her home, in the middle of the night, and was now doing god only knew what. Really, she should have been whacking him with the hatstand. Not politely inviting him to use the facilities.

And especially after he seemed to clock her standing there, in the middle of that rickety staircase. He actually jerked as if struck. As if *she* were the wild, unexpected thing here.

Then even more unbelievably, he said *this*:

"I swear to god, I am not down here looking for drugs."

Instead of anything more reasonable, like an apology. Or an explanation for breaking in. Or even an excuse for something she had actually accused him of. Which of course only made him look more guilty of the very thing he was trying to deny.

"I feel like you *totally* just confessed to being here looking for drugs," she told him.

But weirdly, he didn't seem chastened by this. He actually sighed in an exasperated way instead. And waved an impatient hand at her. Like *he* simply didn't have time for *her* nonsense.

"No, I said the opposite. The opposite. You need to listen better," he said.

And that meant he was going to get it both barrels now.

"I'm honestly trying to, but the thing is you just broke into my house in the middle of the night, scared the absolute shit out of me, made me creep down here with a hatstand for a weapon, and are now talking to me through gritted teeth for some reason I probably don't want to know," she said, and was proud of herself for doing it. She had spelled everything out. And sounded calm as she did so. In fact, the words had almost come out a little dry and deadpan.

Even though she was practically boiling alive inside.

Honestly it was a miracle she hadn't breathed fire on him. Or at the very least hit him with the hatstand she was still clutching. But he didn't seem to care. "Okay, for starters, my teeth are not gritted. I'm just clenching my jaw really hard," he said.

As if that was the part that mattered.

"How does that make *any* of this any better?"

"I'm not trying to make things any better. I'm trying to tell you the only reasonable things I can. Like the fact that I am just here for my medication, and as soon as I get it I swear to god I will be out of here."

"Yeah, but that does not sound reasonable at all. It sounds like medication is a polite way of describing something completely weird or illegal or possibly terrifying. Like maybe a great big bunch of cocaine."

"You can't possibly believe that your grandmother was a coke dealer."

"Well, I didn't five seconds ago. But I'm sure starting to rethink that now."

Another exasperated sound came out of him. Only there was an edge to it this time. A desperate sort of edge that she didn't like. Especially when it only got keener in his words.

"Cassie, she was eighty-seven years old. Her favorite show was a crafting thing about making macramé toys to give to a dog she doesn't have. The very idea of her doing anything like that is impossible and ridiculous."

"Yeah, but until right now I thought it was ridiculous that Seth Brubaker would know my grandmother's first name and all of her hobbies and then break into her house at three in the morning. And yet here you are. Doing just that. Probably to torture me, again."

"Cassie, I'm not trying to torture you. I have never tried to torture you. The torturing just keeps happening, against every bit of my will and sense," he groaned, and god he sounded sincere.

Hell, he *looked* sincere. His brows had drawn together into a fraught peak over the bridge of his nose. There was actual anguish in his caramel eyes. And the hand he had out—well, it was very convincing. If he'd been any other person, it would have been enough to assure her that his motives were pure.

But he wasn't anybody else.

He was the guy—or at least one of the guys—who made her have to be homeschooled for the remainder of her last high school year. The guy who had proven that wanting anything good in your life—that believing in anything good—was just courting disaster.

And that meant he got this, instead.

"So get ahold of your will and stop. Leave now, before this gets any worse," she said, and oh the terror she got in response. He practically clutched himself.

"I can't do that. Not without what I need."

"Then you had better explain exactly what that needed thing is."

"I swear to you, it's nothing. It's not illegal, it's not horrible, it won't make you want to kill me. It just might improve my . . . condition."

Condition, her brain moaned despairingly.

Probably because her brain knew this was one more thing that would make her lower her guard. And sure enough, she could feel herself letting the hatstand drop a little. She took two more steps down the stairs. She was almost on the earthen floor now. Plus she was saying things. Things that sounded too sympathetic and helpful. "And what exactly is this something?"

"Just a kind of herbal remedy. Or maybe the recipe book your grandmother used to make it. Though I would need that last one fast, because you know the longer I go without it the more likely it is that I'll get . . . that things will be . . . that I might just—"

"You might just what? Do something wilder than sweat through a leather jacket?" she asked, and was pleased at the level of sarcasm in her voice. But less pleased about it when his hands immediately fisted into his hair.

"Oh fuck. Oh Christ. Please tell me I'm not at that stage already."

"Honestly I kind of want to, but your soaked clothes are making it hard."

"Okay cool. Cool cool cool cool. But nothing else is wrong, though. Right?"

He gave her such a hopeful look on that last word. So hopeful, in fact, that it was hard to say yes. Instead, she found herself wincing. And prevaricating.

"Uh. Well. That depends on what you mean by nothing else."

"I mean, like. My face is a normal color."

Fuck, she thought.

Though she went with the truth anyway.

"Hoo wow, no. No, not even slightly."

"Kind of looks like I died five days ago and just don't know it, huh."

"Honestly that would be putting it in a polite way. The more realistic one is death occurred sometime last year. Because you drowned in gray paint," she said, and did it as lightly as she could. But it didn't matter. His face still seemed to collapse into despair on hearing this news. She actually got to see his mouth turn down at the corners, in some cartoon parody of pain and disappointment.

Though he seemed to recover quickly. He shook himself. And clapped his hands together. Like some sixty-year-old dad who was about to tackle a problem with real, practical gusto. Then sure enough: "Great. Okay. Well, here's what we are going to have to do right now. Or more, what you're going to have to do for me right now. Whether you like the idea of doing it—or not."

"I'm gonna guess I'm really not."

"Yeah," he conceded. "I suspect the same thing."

"You should, considering the last time you suggested I do something, it turned out to be a ruse designed to humiliate me in front of the entire graduating class of Hollow Brook High."

"I know, I know. And frankly, I'm panicking really severely about the fact that you can't trust me because of that. Considering that your life kind of depends on you being able to," he said, and though she wanted to immediately scoff, she couldn't.

Because, god, the anguish in his voice. And the way his eyes were almost begging her to listen. It was seriously convincing—to the point where it was starting to unsettle her. Really unsettle her, in ways she wasn't ready for. Her hands were suddenly sweating so much that she had to set the hatstand down.

Then once she had, she kind of wished she hadn't. *You might need it soon*, some scary part of her whispered. Though she tried to stay calm and cynical when she spoke. "Okay, fine. Let's hear this probable bullshit."

And thankfully, he followed her lead. He kept it light.

"Well, it starts with you going back upstairs."

"Right. I see."

"Then shutting the hatch."

"Honestly, that makes sense to me. I mean, who would leave it open?"

"And once that's done, you drag something heavy over it."

"Okay, that's slightly less understandable. But I guess I could."

"Oh, and did I mention? You do all of that while I stay right here."

She was still almost smirking when he said that last little part. But that dropped pretty quickly once she'd processed it.

Because he meant . . .

He meant that . . .

"You want me to trap you in this basement," she said, all in a rush. And in a voice that sounded like a spooky ghost's impression of her. But even more terrible: he was already nodding.

"That's *exactly* what I want you to do."

"And you're not even gonna explain the reason."

"Honestly, we do not have time to get into it. I have about thirty more seconds here before a lot of things happen that I really do not want you to experience in any way. And to be honest? You're really not gonna want to experience it either."

"Why? Is some weird part of you about to rupture out of another part?" she asked, and was kind of half joking when she did. Or at least she thought she was half joking. However, she could hear the rising panic in her voice.

And his answering expression did absolutely nothing to quell that.

He just stared, and stared. Before finally telling her what her thundering heart and churning stomach already knew. "That is so eerily close to the truth I don't even know how you guessed it," he said, to which she really wanted to reply that she didn't either. But she couldn't, because the truth was—she kind of did. Even though it was weird and impossible and like something out of a horror movie, she could feel it.

Heck, she could see *evidence* of it.

"I guessed it because you look like you're trying to hold your guts in with your bare hands. Honestly, Seth, if you press your fists any harder into yourself you're gonna push your spine right out of your back."

"Well, about that . . ."

"Oh dear god. What do you mean 'well, about that'?"

"You know what I mean. It's why you're backing away."

I'm not, she wanted to say.

But when she looked down, sure enough. She was farther away from him than she had been before. And by the time she looked back, whatever was happening to him was definitely happening more. He had started sort of slowly curling over, until he was practically hunched in a ball on the floor. Like someone who had been stabbed and simply could not stay standing. He needed to hug his wound, even though in this case there wasn't one.

There was just that nightmare thing he'd said.

The one that now seemed a hell of a lot more believable than it had before.

"Oh my god. Is this exploding spine thing seriously that bad?"

"I want to say no, but honestly this is only about one-tenth of it."

It was the *way* he said the words that made her formulate her next move. It was barely a human language. She wasn't even sure if she'd deciphered what he'd said correctly, in the middle of all the teeth-grinding and growling and drooling.

Really drooling, too. Like animals did when they had rabies.

So she just made the call, without thinking anything further about it.

"Okay, that's it. I'm gonna get an ambulance here right now," she said. And she turned to do it. But the panic in his reply stopped her. Hell, the fact that he managed to reply *at all* stopped her.

"No, you can't. You can't do that," he choked out, even though his face was starting to turn purple. Almost like he was fighting something, she thought, then tried not to think about what that *something* might be. Because whatever it was, it looked enormous. And horrible. And he was definitely losing the battle against it.

As she stood there—frozen in fear and dread and complicated feelings about her former friend—he finished curling all the way up. Now he was a tight ball on the floor, face pressed into his knees, arms around the back of his head.

And after a minute, she realized something else: he'd gone really quiet.

Spookily quiet. No more grunts, no more growls. Not even the sound of his breathing. Like he'd died, she thought, then couldn't help taking a step forward. She got a little closer, just so she could find out for sure if he was breathing or not.

And when that still didn't tell her anything, she leaned down. She reached out a hand. A shaking, hesitant hand. In fact, she almost touched him. She got within a hair's breadth of him. She could actually feel the heat of his body.

Then his head suddenly snapped up.

And oh. Fuck. No.

Because holy *fuck* his *face* when he did.

She had never seen anything like it. She came close to screaming over it. Because even though it was impossible, even though it was ridiculous, *his face simply was not his face anymore.*

Those caramel eyes she'd once known so well—they were suddenly near white. As if they'd somehow been drained of all their color. And the smooth brow that had once sat perfectly normally above them? It was suddenly thicker and heavier, in a way that shouldn't have been possible.

Because, sure, eyes could sometimes shift shades.

But you couldn't spontaneously grow bigger bones. That wasn't a thing, it just wasn't.

Yet it had happened nonetheless. And not just to his brow, either. Every part of his face was bigger—his jaw, his cheekbones, his nose. They all protruded now, in so significant a manner that his skin looked paper thin. Like it had been stretched to tearing point, by whatever this was.

All of which was bananas enough on its own.

But then there were his teeth. Those too-crooked incisors were now no longer crooked. They were perfectly curved, just beneath the rising snarl of his upper lip. And oh, they were bigger. They were bigger, and they were thicker, and they were sharp, god they were so sharp she wanted to call them razors, knives, broken glass. Anything that would slice you in two the second they made contact.

And if that low growl was anything to go on, they were about to, pretty soon.

It was the reason she took a step back. Why she held up her hands and said his name: Seth. Though truthfully, she didn't know why she bothered. He hadn't even been willing to listen to her *before* whatever this was. There was no way he was going to listen to her now, in this state.

She wasn't even sure if he was *capable* of listening anymore. That part of him seemed long gone, at this point. And now something else was in its place. Something beast-like. Something that growled louder, at the sound of a name it no longer knew. Then it took one more terrible step toward her, and she did the only thing she could. The only thing that made sense.

She swung the hatstand.

And the second she felt it make contact with something, she ran. She ran faster than she ever had in her life. It barely felt like her feet touched the ground. She all but flung herself up the stairs, and when that didn't seem fast enough, she actually grabbed at individual steps to haul herself up. Splinters bit into her palms; she ripped a nail enough to sting. But she kept going even so.

Yet still, it didn't save her.

Three steps from the top she felt something snag her by the ankle—hard enough that she knew it was only a matter of time before it had the rest. There was no way she could haul herself out of its grip, clearly. Though god knows she tried. She threw herself left, away from that feverish touch. And she yanked her foot toward herself with as much force as she could manage. Then when that didn't do a single goddamn thing, she kicked with the other.

Pathetically, she thought. Like someone trying to blow a truck off themselves after it had run them over. But she made contact with something. And this something didn't like it either, because it grunted and went sideways.

She saw the banister beside her shake. Dust sifted down from it onto the side of her face.

So she kicked again. She kicked, and screamed at the thing. *Let me go you motherfucker*, she tried. And oh god, oh god, it let go. It let go. She didn't know how or why or what she'd hit with her bare foot. But the iron bar around her ankle was gone, and she was free, and the exit out of this basement hell was *right there*.

She just had to reach for it.

And she did. She grabbed the edge of the hatch and pulled herself up. All in a mad scramble, desperate and breathless, and even though she immediately wanted to collapse in the blissful cool safety of the hall, she didn't pause. She scrabbled for the trapdoor and slammed it shut.

Then padlocked it, just for good measure.

Only apparently it wasn't good measure enough. Something slammed into the wood from beneath, about ten seconds after she snapped the lock shut. And it did it so hard that she heard the trapdoor splinter. Hell, she heard something *screech*. Metal on metal, like the padlock was actually giving.

Then she remembered what he'd said.

About the heavy thing over the trapdoor.

She got up off the ground. Even though she was shaking and every muscle was screaming, she forced herself to get up. She staggered to the dresser that stood by the entryway to the living room. And just as wood and metal screamed again, she shoved it. She shoved, and shoved, thinking, *oh god I'm not strong enough, oh fuck it's not going to move, he's going to get me he's going to get me I'm going to have to stare up into my former friend's face as I'm brutally murdered.*

Then suddenly it gave.

It slid.

And there was nothing but silence.

CHAPTER FOUR

She didn't know how she'd managed to fall asleep. She just knew that she had when she woke to find herself curled up on the floor, by the dresser she'd shoved over the hatch. And that she'd done it quite a long time ago, because sunlight streamed through the windows in the kitchen. Good, bright sunlight that warmed her cold skin and her stiff limbs.

And more importantly: it made everything look so *normal*.

There were her shoes, by the door. The ones she'd worn to pedal into town the day before. She could see the pot she'd cooked the soup in, still on the stove. Her apron, tossed over the kitchen table, smeared with the usual mess she made whenever she tried to cook anything. Bits of garlic skin scattered across the floor; chili oil splashed all over the place. And all of it so mundane that she could barely believe what had happened the night before. *You must have imagined things*, she told herself. *Maybe he just wigged out from wanting weird drugs, and because he's so big now, it scared you enough to make you see things.*

And that all sounded really true and reasonable, it did.

But she still screamed when she heard a thump from below.

Then when the thump turned into the sound of someone obviously climbing the stairs, she couldn't help it. "You stay down there, Seth Brubaker," she yelled. And got a satisfying silence in response. No more shuffling, no more coming closer to where she was. Just complete quiet for what felt like a pretty long time. Before finally, finally, it was broken.

With the most ridiculous opener of all time.

"Cassie? You're still up there?" he called to her.

For reasons she couldn't even begin to guess. At the very least, he should have started with whatever the fuck happened the night before. But he hadn't. He had asked an absurd question. So now she had to get into exactly how absurd it was.

"Of course I am. This is my goddamn house now."

"Well, yeah, sure it is. But I figured after I terrified the bejesus out of you, probably you had fled to someplace you felt safer. Like maybe the other side of the planet. In a steel-lined bunker. Under the ocean."

"I don't even think that would do it, to be honest, Seth."

"Right. And that makes sense. But you know, if I could just explain."

"Is your explanation going to be that I did not see what I totally saw?"

Silence then. And even through the wood, she could tell it was an awkward one. She could almost hear him shuffling, in a way that said yeah, that was totally what he had wanted to go with. Then sure enough, a moment later: "That depends. What do you think you totally saw?"

"You becoming some kind of hideous thing."

"Hey, I think 'hideous' is a little strong."

Well, at least he's not denying it, she thought. But she couldn't be pleased about that. Mainly because she was too busy sweating over the fact that he'd confirmed it. He'd confirmed that he was some kind . . . of creature. And he'd done it in the most annoying way possible: with his fucking vanity leading the way. "I cannot believe *that* is the part you're objecting to."

"Well, I don't see why you can't. The other part didn't hurt my feelings."

She snorted, loud enough that he'd be able to hear. "So as long as your ego doesn't get dinged, you're fine being some weird whatever that tries to eat people."

"Okay, first of all: I didn't try to eat you. I'm just not used to juicy humans being right in front of me when I'm in that state," he said, and she could almost see the irritation all over his face. And the firm lines he was probably drawing in the air, to indicate how completely unreasonable she was being. Even though all he had to add was this: "So certain grabbing instincts very briefly took over. But I swear, I would not have sunk my teeth in. And if I had, I definitely wouldn't have done anything beyond a little light nibbling."

To which she couldn't help throwing up her hands.

"A little light nibbling? Seth, have you *seen* those teeth you somehow grow?"

"Despite trying very hard to not, yes, I have. And I accept that they look bad."

"*Bad?* They look like Freddy Krueger's fingernails, you dingus."

"Oh come on. They're not that grim."

"I bet your bottom lip doesn't say that after being whatever that was," she said, and meant it as a bit of snark. But the problem was, she had started picturing it now. And picturing it was not funny. It was terrifying. It made her shiver and want to grab a weapon again.

Doubly so when he wasn't in any hurry to reply.

He could be down there planning his next grisly attack, she realized. About ten seconds before he replied, "One time I woke up, and the bottom half of my face was gone."

She couldn't help it after that. She shuffled away from the hatch. Then grabbed the hatstand that still lay beside her, before she responded. "And yet you're trying to downplay what I saw last night."

"Well, I don't want you to be scared of me."

"I think that ship has fucking sailed, Seth."

"So let me do what I can to bring it back to dry land."

"There's nothing you can do. And even if there was, I would know that you're only doing it so I'll let you out," she said, and more silence followed. Pretty telling silence. That was broken with what sounded like a lot of throat clearing.

It seemed to take him an age to stumble out words.

"Uh, yeah. Yeah. That's totally the only reason I want you to not be scared of me and trust me. So you will let me out of here," he said. She didn't know why, however. It didn't do a single thing to help him.

"So tell me how that's enough for me to believe you're not gonna eat me."

"All right. How about: I'm totally normal and human again now?"

"Yeah, I'm gonna need more than your word on that."

"And what other word do you want me to give? It's not like there's a committee down here to vouch for me," he said, then paused. During which time she could practically hear the cogs in his head turning. "Well, unless you count the creepy dolls. But I'm kind of hoping they don't have the ability to speak."

She almost laughed. "Maybe they do. In fact, maybe they're about to burst out of that box and chew your face off."

Then, oh, the sound he made in response. It was almost a moan of terror.

And his voice when he spoke again was a haunted whisper.

"Holy shit, why would you say something like that to me?"

"I dunno, Seth. Maybe because you're my mortal enemy. And also because you broke into my house in the middle of the night. Oh, and finally there's the fact that a man with the ability to shear through a metal padlock with his supernatural strength shouldn't be fucking afraid of evil dolls."

"But I *am* afraid. Because you dragged me to that movie where they do all that weird stuff I've never been able to forget."

She thought of it then.

Not just the movie itself, but how it had felt to do things like that with him. Both of them scrunched together in the falling-apart seats of the theatre, popcorn usually forgotten by halfway through. The smell of the aftershave he'd pinched from his dad because he figured it made him seem older than eleven. Those plaid shirts he'd always worn, soft as butter against her cheek.

And sometimes, just sometimes, his hand tight around her own. That little sense that maybe, just maybe, he liked her in *that* way.

Though of course she had never *wanted* him to. And she certainly didn't now.

So she shook herself. She shed that sudden bloom of warmth. Then made herself as snarky and cold as he now required. "I see.

So it's my fault that you're about to feel them touching your face with their tiny porcelain hands. And biting you with their tiny porcelain teeth. And licking you with their weird porcelain—"

"Cassie, stop, please. Just let me out."

"I told you, you're gonna need more than begging."

He let out a desperate sound. And she could hear him shuffling around down there. Almost like he was pacing. Or running a frantic hand through his hair. Before he seemed to gather himself together. "Okay, okay. How about if I prove that I'm human again?"

"And how are you gonna do that? Pass me a recent DNA test?"

"My phone still has some battery. I could FaceTime you."

"There's no signal in here, Seth. Probably because it actually is haunted."

Another pause, filled with what she suspected was him checking up on what she had said. It certainly sounded like tapping on a screen at any rate. And then there was a huff of frustration, and some further rustling, and what might have been an *aha* kind of sound, before finally, finally, a very breathless Seth gasped out, "I saw a Polaroid camera down here. I think it still works."

"Well, that's great, but I don't know what good it's gonna do you."

"Because I could take a snap and slip it to you."

And okay, she had to concede. That was a good plan.

"Fine. Go ahead," she said.

Then she heard him thump down, down into that dark space. The one which could actually hold all kinds of horrors now, in a way it hadn't been able to the night before. Back then it had been spooky, sure. But just a basement. Now it was potentially something else.

Like a portal to another world.

And even though she didn't like him, it bothered her. She didn't enjoy hearing him thumping and rustling and wrestling with whatever was down there. Twice he made a sound so stricken she almost called out to ask if he was okay, and only managed to stop herself when she remembered she was not supposed to be concerned about him.

And even then she held her breath.

And she continued to, on and off, until a picture slid through the crack between the trapdoor and the hole it filled, and skittered across the floor. At which point, she tensed up for a whole different reason. Because he'd promised and he'd said and he'd sounded startlingly sincere. But what if it was all a ruse? What if he'd taken a picture of something horrible, as a prank?

It could be, she thought, as she reached for the face-down Polaroid.

Then she turned it over, whip quick, and there it was.

His perfectly normal face, pushed into the goofiest, broadest grin she'd ever seen him make. It was so goofy and broad, in fact, that she could see both of his crooked, too-big-for-his-mouth incisors. The ones he'd never been able to wholly fix with the braces. The ones that had made him stop smiling sometime after he'd gotten the braces taken off, in case smiling gave away that he wasn't really cool.

But apparently, he didn't care about giving that away now. He'd even given her a thumbs-up in the picture. As if for this brief moment, her trusting him mattered more.

And it was this idea that got her up, off the ground. That made her shove the dresser until it slid off the hatch, muscles protesting all the while. Then she dealt with the mangled but still movable, padlock, and lifted the trapdoor. Heart in her throat, but holding.

And there he was. As human as she could imagine anyone being.

More human than that, in fact. Because, man, he looked wrecked. Exhausted. Maybe even a little vulnerable—to the point where it probably *would* have affected her. It *would* have played on her heart strings. If it hadn't been for one other tiny detail about him that she simply had to focus on instead. "Are you actually wearing one of my grandmother's nighties?" she asked.

Because god, he was. He totally was. And it wasn't even one of the simpler ones either. It was a huge, flowery tent, with ruffles on the ends of the voluminous sleeves. Then more ruffles on the hem, and around the middle.

He looked like a display in a cake shop window.

And he obviously knew it. His sallow face flamed red the second she spoke. "Don't say it like it's nuts. It was either this or emerge completely nude."

"But you had loads of clothes on last night. There must be some of them left."

She waved in the direction of where the clothes should have been, as he clambered out into the hallway. But he just sighed and rolled his eyes. "All that tells me is that you haven't fully grasped what just happened."

"I totally have, okay? Your face went weird."

"Yeah, and the rest of me followed."

"So your whole body grew fangs?" she asked. And, okay, she loaded it up with deadpan. But she was pushing it now, and she knew it. Worse: he knew it too.

He gave her such a withering look.

"Oh come on, you can guess better than that. You've seen this movie a million times before. Heck, you're an *expert* on movies like this. You once told me the entire plot of one of them, when my mom wouldn't let me watch."

She pictured herself telling him, even more strongly than she had envisioned the memory of the movie theatre. She saw his face getting increasingly more disgusted as she went into all the gory details. Saw him trying to scoff as if he wasn't scared, even though his eyes had always given the game away.

Then later on, he'd snuck up to her window. Like in the movies, where the guy comes to cop a feel. Only instead of anything like that, they'd hidden in their usual place: her closet. Before falling asleep while talking about all the ways they'd save each other, if the plot of *Ginger Snaps* ever happened to them.

And now it was, kind of.

But she wasn't doing half as well with it as she'd thought she would.

"Right. Yeah. But that's when it's not real. And if I say it out loud now, then it's very real. It's extremely real. It's too real for my apparently fragile brain to cope with," she said. But he just shrugged. And plowed on.

"So then I'll just say it."

"Okay, but break it to me gently."

"There's no way to gently break this."

"Sure there is. Use some nice-sounding euphemisms."

"What, like once every full moon Uncle Hairy comes to visit?"

He said it in the same slightly desperate, kind of exasperated tone he'd been using for the last five minutes. But the thing was, he'd gone with those words. And those words were funny, she couldn't deny that they were funny. So now on top of trying not to put too much trust in him, and going all soft over flashbacks to their once-was-friendship, she had to force her immediate response to that down.

She pressed her lips tight together. And when that didn't work she glanced away. But it was too late. It was too late and she knew it. She could see it all over his face. He looked *delighted*.

And he sounded delighted too. "Hey, you're almost laughing," he said.

Damn him. "I am not. This is my horrified face."

"You may be able to get away with claiming that with other people. But not with me. I was your best friend for like ten years, remember? I know your amused expression when I see it."

"Well, maybe it's changed since then."

He shook his head firmly. "Nothing about you has changed since then."

"Wish I could say the same for you right now."

"Because I became the kind of person you can't ever like?"

Fuck, she thought. Then almost had to clutch at her stomach, it hit that hard.

She couldn't fault him, however. It was the truth. He *had* become the kind of person she couldn't ever like, and that was how she felt, and there was no getting around it. And yet somehow, at this moment? She kind of wanted to.

And that felt so weird and so mixed up that she didn't know how to deal with it. For a moment she was split—between the resentment she knew she should still feel toward the man he'd become, and the urge to go easy on this seemingly vulnerable creature in front of her.

And it made her cock one eyebrow. Voice as dry as the Sahara somehow. "Well, that," she said. "And the fact that you're apparently a fucking werewolf."

CHAPTER FIVE

The silence spun out endlessly. And to the point where she was really starting to feel the cold. Though she had to imagine he was too—his nightie was even more flimsy than hers. She could see his very human but very hairy ankles and feet sticking out the bottom.

But he wasn't hurrying this along.

He just stared, and stared, like he was waiting for something from her. Even though she was the one who needed some kind of response. She even knew what response it was supposed to be.

So she decided the best course of action was to prompt him.

"You're not saying, 'Oh my gosh, of course I'm not, Cassie.'"

And got flat nothing for it. No immediate agreement. No laughter.

In fact he just looked pained for a second.

"Believe me, I want to. But then I'd be lying to you."

"You never had problems with trying to lie before."

The pain on his face deepened. "Yeah, and I'm turning over a new leaf."

"And this is what you start with?" she asked. "Being a whole-ass supernatural being?"

"Well actually, werewolves aren't classified as supernatural beings. They're in the creature category. You're thinking more of vampires and fairies and even ghosts, I'm pretty sure ghosts are considered . . . more like . . . they. . . ." His words simply dried up. And she knew exactly why too. She could feel it happening before he even explained. "Okay, I'm gonna stop there because your eyes look like they're about to fall out of your head."

"Of course they are. You just made my every childhood nightmare real."

"Your childhood nightmare wasn't vampires or fairies or ghosts."

"Maybe it should have been, if they fucking exist. Are you telling me they exist, Seth? Answer me now, immediately," she couldn't help saying. And she couldn't help the rising panic in her voice either. Honestly it was all she could do not to grab him and shake him, because holy fuck was he seriously confirming there was *more* than werewolves? As if werewolves alone weren't impossible enough?

It certainly seemed like it. But she needed him to spell it out.

Even if he quite clearly did not want to.

"Maybe I can answer you later," he said. "Much later."

"No, there's no later, Seth. You're gonna tell me now."

"But I think maybe you need to calm down first."

"And exactly how am I going to do that when you just dropped a bomb on reality? Because you get that you've done that, right? Like, you can see how completely wild this all is. One second everything is ordinary, and the next your mortal enemy is confirming that the supernatural stuff you last laughed at in an old episode of *Buffy* actually exists somehow."

She spread her hands, like she was waiting for him to fill them with answers. But all she got was a sigh. And an *eye roll*. An actual eye roll.

"Okay, for starters it's *nothing* like *Buffy*," he said, in this withering tone.

As if scorn for the verisimilitude of an old TV show was what mattered, instead of anything more sane. And of course, now she had to go with him on this absurd media-based scale of how fucked things were. "So what is it like? *Underworld*? *Chilling Adventures of Sabrina*? That movie where all the vampires eat everybody and then they turn into vampires and eat the people they just ate?"

"You mean *Daybreakers*."

"Don't tell me what I mean. Just tell me how frightened I should be."

"Well, I mean, not constant vampiric cycle of cannibalism frightened."

Thank fuck, her brain said. About thirty seconds before she realized that he'd kind of hedged there. He'd left things open to other levels of being frightened. And the way he was trying not to meet her eyes confirmed her suspicions.

"But I'm guessing not *The Addams Family*–level of relieved, either."

"Probably not, no. I mean some of them are pretty scary," he said. And then he saw what was undoubtedly her face falling three feet, and rushed on. "But honestly? Their scariness is really nothing you should worry about. I mean, vampires in particular don't really interact with humans at all the way they usually do in movies and shows. They just . . . go about their own business."

"Yeah, but their business is occasionally drinking blood."

"True, but any blood will do. And it does, as far as I know."

"As far as I know doesn't fill me with confidence, Seth."

He raised a curious eyebrow. "Then what would fill you with confidence?"

"Well, for starters, you could warn me about where their nearest castle is."

"They don't live in castles," he said, and honestly she had no idea why that was the thing that stopped her dead. But it did. In fact for a whole thirty seconds she stared at him, waiting for him to say "Psych." To tell her all about their fancy halls and floofy blouses and goblets full of probably murdered people.

But all she got was him looking at her, with the same level of matter-of-factness that he'd had in his words. Like this was just obvious, and how didn't she know. Even though she could never have known. Not only were vampires apparently not real, they weren't even massive-ridiculous-castle dwellers.

And that was just insult added to injury.

"Oh my god. You take that back," she finally said, more fiercely than she intended.

But even the fierceness didn't make him bend reality back to what it was supposed to be.

"I can't, it's the truth. There are no castles at all. Or even fancy houses. In fact, I know of one of them who lives in an apartment with two other dudes. And the apartment is pretty crappy. Two of them share one bedroom—and not in the cool way, either. In the sad way that makes me want to ask them how come they've been alive for hundreds of years but don't have so much as a bean between them." He sighed and shook his head. Then seemed to consider something, before adding, "Though to be fair, I'm not sure I really need to ask them that. It's pretty obvious, when one of them thinks televisions have tiny people living inside them."

And what could she say to that? Except what was now dawning on her.

"So basically you're telling me that *What We Do in the Shadows* is somehow the closest," she said, and to her astonishment and horror, he just shrugged. He *shrugged*. He even did it with his face—lips pressed inward, chin out.

"I want to say no, but honestly after I devoured the movie and the TV show, and maybe wept because I felt so seen for the first time in over a decade, I spent an entire afternoon frantically googling everybody involved to see if I could unearth any signs of their obvious supernatural secret."

He wept, she thought. And felt yet *another* little pang for him.

Truly it was becoming an epidemic inside her.

"And did you find anything?" she asked.

"Well, no. Though that doesn't mean anything."

"It must. I mean there would be signs. There have to be signs."

"You know there aren't. In fact, you and me used to talk all the time about how disappointing it was that there wasn't so much as a hint of any of this being real," he said. Then looked away, eyes suddenly hazy.

And she knew he was doing what she had been trying not to since he'd turned up on her doorstep. He was thinking about their shared past. About the way they used to whisper together, while tangled in the nest of old clothes and discarded bubblegum wrappers and popcorn crumbs that was her closet. Sometimes sticky with summer heat, more often freezing from the frost that crept in underneath her rickety bedroom windows.

It's so unfair that nothing is fantastical, she remembered saying to him.

And him saying something similar to her, when they'd found that hollowed-out tree in the woods. The one that they'd been sure held something creepy inside, but turned out to contain nothing but bugs and mulch and bits of bark. Still cool for a hideout, but not quite what they had hoped. Not enough to stop him turning to her, in that faded, forever dusty darkness, to tell her: *I was thinking this would be our door to somewhere other than this, but instead it's just rot and ruin.*

Then he looked back at her, and she knew she'd been right. She could see the memory of those times all over him a moment before he spoke. Softly, wistfully. "It was good to have someone to be disappointed with. Someone who got it. By the time all this happened to me, you weren't even living here anymore."

And now she was the one who had to turn away, before he could see how glossy her eyes were no doubt getting. Because he was right: it had been good. But more than that, it reminded her powerfully of all the things they could have had. All the talks about this they could have shared. The turmoil they could have gone through together, as they realized reality was not what it seemed.

But instead, she'd had nothing.

While he'd fumbled through this torment alone.

"Well, it's not my fault that we moved away. And definitely not my fault that you don't have someone who gets it anymore," she said, and hated how sour her voice sounded. But what else could she do? She couldn't just forget it all and go back to how they'd been. Most likely he didn't even want her to.

Though, man, he made it sound otherwise.

"I know," he simply said in this soft, sad way.

And then she found she could look back at him, no problem.

"I bet it's not been so good or so bad anyway. It just seems like it's the way everything is. Only, you know. With more deranged things attacking you, followed by weird sweating and bottom-lip-eating and all your clothes getting annihilated."

"Yeah. It's really more okay than anything else."

"Right. You just go about your business. Like the castle-less vampires."

"I do. Heck, most of the time I wouldn't even know anything was going on."

"You *look* like nothing else is going on right now."

"Well, sure—I mean, apart from the fact that my arm is inside out."

He held it up when he said it. Almost like a joke, she thought.

But then the fabric of the nightdress fell away, and honestly she almost screamed again. She had to grit her teeth to stop it happening, and even so a groan leaked out. Understandably so, because *god in heaven* the look of it.

It was like his elbow was caught in his sleeve.

Only the sleeve was *skin*. It was *flesh*.

And it was surrounded on all sides by bones that weren't supposed to be there. Honestly, she had no idea how she hadn't seen it before, because even under the nightdress it should have been clear. It was the wrong shape, the wrong everything; it was horrendous in ways she couldn't process.

Clearly transformation isn't straightforward, her logical side was saying. But the rest of her was just screaming about the supernatural being real and bodies turning into entirely other things and the fact that he wasn't somehow dead. It should have killed him, the state he was in. He should have been sprawled on the floor.

So it wasn't a surprise when he sagged.

And then did just that.

CHAPTER SIX

There were a lot of things wrong with having your werewolf mortal enemy pass out in your hallway. But top of the list had to be the fact that werewolves should not exist. That to most people, they absolutely didn't. And so there wasn't really much she could do about it. There was no first aid book to quickly skim that told you how best to solve his medical problems.

And she couldn't call 911.

But despite this—and the fact that she'd vowed only five seconds earlier to not get invested in his problems—the urge to fix this was getting hold of her anyway. Something clenched in her chest whenever she glanced at him all spread out on her floor, looking pale and sweat-slicked and sort of crumpled. Not to mention more like her friend than she could remember him being in years.

His face seemed almost soft and sweet—and young, too.

Put some glasses on him, and he'd almost be the boy she'd known.

And that really helped her do what she had to do next. She took some deep breaths and knelt beside his gargantuan body. Then she just reached out to him. She touched him, somewhere incredibly innocuous like his arm. Shakily, gingerly, but she managed. She got to a point where she could push him into the recovery position.

No big deal, she thought.

But it was, because the moment she did it she felt the enormous swell of his biceps, pushing back against her palms. She got the thickness of it, the firmness, the solid weight of his body that was almost too much for her to heave over. And oh god, the heat that rolled off him as he went. It was so lush and intense she would have called it a fever.

If she hadn't known it was something else.

Animals run hot, her brain threw out.

And just as she was busy hating her brain for it, she got a hit of his scent. That sweet bubblegum scent—the one she remembered from when they were kids. Only now it was mingled with something else, something like warm fur or skin made shimmery by the sun, and okay no, no this was too much. This was all too much.

She didn't like it. She had to stop touching him.

It was actually starting to make her feel a bit weird to carry on. Like it sometimes had when they were teenage friends, and she'd accidentally brushed something she hadn't meant to. Like that time when she'd gone to pass him a book from a low shelf at the library, and somehow slid her hand inside those little shorts he had loved. All the way up, right to the highest point of his thigh.

And just as she was thinking this, she glanced at his face.

And saw that his eyes were wide fucking open.

"What the heck are you doing?" he asked, and god the way he sounded when he did. It was like he'd caught her molesting him. Or seen the flush she knew was all over her cheeks and assumed that meant something other than what it did.

Even though it didn't. It fucking *didn't. I'm just not used to big dudes who smell like great sex*, she found herself thinking at him, frantically. Then was incredibly grateful to know that (a) her brain was only saying something so ridiculous because it was very stressed right now, and (b) he could not hear it doing so.

All he got was her words. And she had the perfect ones.

"I was trying to make sure you didn't die."

"By groping my biceps and my butt?"

"Hold on a second, I didn't touch your butt."

He tilted his head to one side. "No, but you were getting pretty close to it."

"I didn't even know I was. Probably because your big, immovable body just barged right into my tiny hands. And before you make any crack about how tiny my hands aren't, remember that I was trying to save your life."

She shoved herself to her feet then. Angrily, and with the intention of stalking away from him. But here was the thing: he got up too. Like he was just fine now—or at least fine enough to continue making her life a misery. And sure enough, here he was, following her into the kitchen, expression all outraged.

"Okay, first of all, I wasn't gonna say anything of the kind. Your hands are cute as heck. I don't even know what you're talking about," he said, all exasperated. Then just as she was processing that weirdness, just as she was thinking, *he thinks my hands are cute,* he burst out with more: "And second, were you seriously trying to save my life? As in, you were actually super worried that I was dying?"

At which point, she wasn't quite sure what to say.

Because he sounded like . . . she didn't know what he sounded like. *Hopeful,* she wanted to say. But she couldn't let herself believe that. He was probably just all mixed up from being mangled, she decided. Then turned her back to him, so she could appear convincingly casual.

"Well, yeah. Anyone would be. You just fainted."

"I didn't faint. I just ran out of energy."

"Oh sorry, I didn't mean to suggest you were anything like the weakling you used to be. Lemme just reassure you that you're still an enormous, macho machine who can crush absolutely anyone or anything with the blink of one eye."

Okay, that was way too far, and now he's gonna bite back, she told herself.

But no, he apparently still didn't feel like it. Instead, he sighed wearily.

"Cassie, that's not what I meant. And that's not what I want to be."

"Okay. Cool. So then tell me exactly what you do want to be, Seth."

"I don't know. I guess whatever made you like me enough to be so tender."

She could hear the shrug in his voice. Like it was no big deal to say what he just had.

Even though it made her spin back around like a cartoon character doing a double take. And she knew why too: because he had meant it *that* way. The good way. The way that suggested he *liked* her being that way with him.

Or at least hadn't been mad about it.

He had maybe just been surprised. Or pleased.

And now he was so pleased that he was willing to . . . what? Be different, so she would do it again? God, it sounded like it. So much so, in fact, that she couldn't bring herself to shrug it off or say something wholly dismissive. She had to go with something half kind, and at least somewhat accepting of who he appeared to be now.

Even if she was scared to do it.

"It wasn't anything in particular that made me be tender. I would have done it anyway. I still want to do it, in fact. I mean, your arm continues to look incredibly gross and horrifying. I feel like something needs to be done. And hopefully before it rots right off your body," she said.

That didn't help, however. He just looked like he'd been electrified.

"Oh my *god*. You think that's an actual possibility?"

"Dude, *you're* the one who's supposed to be telling *me* that."

"Yeah, but this arm thing has never happened to me before, in all the times I've changed. And you were always so good at figuring stuff like that out. Remember that time I came off my bike and thought my leg was gonna fall off?" he asked, and she tried not to, she really did. But it came over her anyway. The raw-meat color it had become. The gritty feel of the asphalt under her hands. Him not wanting to look; her telling him she would for him.

But she couldn't concede the point, she just couldn't. Not when it meant actually talking to him about soft and loving things they'd experienced together. "I didn't do anything about your leg falling off."

"It seemed like you did, to me."

She shook her head. "All I did was hold your hand."

"That wasn't all. You called 911."

"Yeah, and anyone on earth would have done that."

"Would anyone on earth have known it was only broken?"

"I didn't know for sure. I just guessed and happened to be right."

"You happened to be right a lot about things like that."

His gaze was steady now. Fixed on her. Like he was trying to make her see something.

Though she couldn't imagine the *something* was anything good.

So she stepped away. Casually, she thought, like she was just going to the sink. But of course she didn't have anything to do once she got there. And she was pretty sure he'd caught the flicker of emotion that had moved across her face before she'd turned, anyway.

She could almost feel his reaction to it, before it came.

Then it did.

"I guess all that feels like a waste of time to you now, huh," he said, and oh wow the way it hit her. Because, truthfully, she hadn't thought he could understand something like that. Yet, somehow, he had. And now she had to face it.

Even if she couldn't look at him, as she tried.

"Waste of time wouldn't be the way I would put it."

"So how would you then?"

"I don't know. Just the way stuff goes, I guess. Things are good and then they're not. People you love turn out to be not what you thought. Or they get tired of you and leave you behind. Sometimes you're just not enough."

Don't cry, she thought at herself. *Don't you fucking cry.*

But all she could manage was not letting him see it happen. Because, yeah okay, maybe he was a little better than she thought. And true, he was going through a lot now. But he was not good enough or wounded enough to have earned anything like her tears.

He wasn't. He wasn't. He just wasn't safe.

Even though his next words were these: "Cassie, god. Is that what you think happened?"

"That *is* what happened. And it's fine, okay?"

"It isn't fine for you to think you weren't enough."

"Why not? It's obviously true. I was a boring dork, and you wanted something cool. And I don't blame you for that. I don't blame you for grabbing it when you had the chance. I just wish, you know. That you—"

"Hadn't treated you like shit?"

God, the way he just keeps copping to it, her brain hissed at her. As if she didn't know. As if she wasn't feeling it—and so hard now that it was making her want to do some very inadvisable things. Like maybe yelling, *you didn't treat me like shit* and *anyway I forgive you* and then *let's be best friends again.* Even though she definitely didn't want any of that.

And there was no way he did.

He was wanting her help, that was all. So that was what she needed to focus on.

After she'd wiped her eyes, and firmed up her voice.

"You know, we should really get back to important stuff. Like what you need to stop any potential arm rot so you can leave me in something like peace," she said, as she turned back to him to see exactly how convincing she'd been.

And judging by his relieved expression, the answer was: convincing enough.

"I think I just need my medicine."

"You mean the herbal remedy you were searching for last night."

"Yep. That's it. That's exactly what I'm talking about. You got it." He snapped his fingers and gave her some finger guns.

"Right. So then it's the one my grandmother made for you."

"That's totally it. She totally did."

"Because she knew you were a werewolf."

"Well yeah, of course she did. What else were you thinking?"

"Oh, I dunno. That my grandmother wasn't apparently a *witch*," she said—and even managed to do it pretty calmly. But not so calmly that he didn't wince in response. Like it was just hitting him that she hadn't known or understood any of this.

And he was breaking most of it to her really badly.

So of course he tried to calm things down. He put his hands out, like, easy, easy. "Well, she wasn't exactly a witch. She was more like a cobble," he said. Like a total fucking dipshit.

"And you think some weird supernatural term I don't understand is going to make this new piece of information any less shocking? That just makes this whole thing seem even more enormous than it already is! I mean, it has *terminology*."

"Cass, it's not terminology. It's just a description of someone who can sort of half make spells. Like, they can repeat what a real witch made up, and it will kind of work. As in—they cobble together some magic."

"So some real witch did what, exactly? Leave her spell book here?" she asked, one eyebrow raised as sardonically as she could possibly make it. But he just carried on being as exasperated as he already plainly was.

"There is no spell book. Your grandmother just had everything written down in a journal. Like stuff from memory, probably. She was once buddies with Gertrude the Great, and Gertrude the Great told her a thing or two, and there you go."

"Well, can we call this Gertrude the Great?"

"Of course not, she doesn't exist. I made her up for the purposes of this demonstration." He glanced at the ceiling for inspiration. For some sort of way to explain this that made sense. "Look, Cassie. I just need those books she scribbled everything in. You don't even have to give me them. I can simply jot down the recipe and, you know. Try to make it myself."

"So you're a cobble now."

"I'm not anything. I just have to give it a shot."

"Fine," she conceded. "So then tell me what they look like."

"I don't know. They're little notebooks."

"That doesn't really narrow it down, Seth."

"Okay then, these ones were blue. Pale blue. And leather, I think."

She went to say something scornful, like, *well, that could be anything*. But suddenly there was a sound like the wind rushing in her ears, and a million memories were clicking into place, and then she snapped a look at the mess on the kitchen counter next to her.

The mess, and the thing that lay between them.

The thing she snatched up, before she turned on him.

"You mean *this* blue leather-bound journal? As in, the one that probably led to her telling me I should never make anything again because I was terrible at it and would probably kill someone? And that I made *soup* from, *last night*?" she somehow managed to gasp out.

Only he didn't say no. He didn't say of course not. He looked immediately to the pot that was still on the stove. Then he practically leapt to his feet and launched himself at it.

"Oh my god. That's it. That's my stuff," he said.

And oh no, oh no, oh fuck, what had she done? What had she made?

Something nightmarish, her brain screamed at her. Then she didn't even think twice about it. She jammed herself between him and the probable hell soup. "Whoa, what do you think you're doing? That is *not* your stuff. That is most likely a magic bomb."

He peered into the pot. "It doesn't look like a magic bomb. And honestly I don't see how it could be."

"Dude, did you not just hear me? I was seriously bad at doing whatever is in that book. So bad in fact that my Gram said I should never cook or bake again at all. Most likely to make sure I never accidentally cobbled some nightmare spell."

"Maybe she was just worried about food poisoning."

"And you think poisoning someone with magic food is *better*?"

Yes he did, she suspected, if his reaction was anything to go by.

He was still trying to get at the pot. And she imagined that the only reason he wasn't managing was that thing she had noticed the first day he'd come to her door. That hint of stress over the idea of being aggressive with her. Like he needed to be extra careful, and not even so much as touch her or even get in her way, no matter how much he needed to.

Though she supposed that made a lot more sense now.

He was a goddamn werewolf. He probably had the strength of ten men. One flick of his hand could most likely break her bones—so of course he wound up fumbling, and only sort of half grabbing for the pot in her hands. And when she moved it before he could get a hold, he didn't try again. He just stepped aside. Almost politely.

Even though his face was a picture of the purest frustration.

Please, that face said. And that pleading was in his voice, too.

"I'll just put some on my arm," he said, as he held said arm up. To have an effect on her, she thought. Which it did, of course. It made her guts twist and her breath catch in her throat, to a far greater extent than it had before.

Because now you're really *starting to warm to him*, her brain singsonged at her.

And she hated it for doing so. And him, for making her really feel it.

"Oh don't do that," she said. "Don't play on my anxiety about what that looks like."

But he just gazed at her, half irritated and half that other thing, again.

That soft, soft thing, like she'd done something that felt so good. Rubbed a hand through his hair, maybe. Or told him that everything was going to be okay. And after that, she didn't just think about how long it had been since she had cared about him. She thought about how long it had been since anyone—her grandmother aside—had cared about him at all.

His parents never really had. In fact, it was the reason he'd spent so much time at her house when they were kids. Because although her parents didn't much care about her either, they had let her watch and read most of the things she wanted to. And they hadn't punished her forever if they even suspected she'd done anything devil-like. She remembered him once wearing some strong aftershave, and getting grounded for three months for drinking alcohol because of the smell.

It was undeniable that they would never have wanted to look after him now.

And last she'd heard they were in the ground anyway.

So who did that leave? Some buddies, maybe? People like Jason and Tyler? It was at least a little possible that they were still his friends. Though, somehow, she couldn't imagine them giving a shit. Most likely they would find it funny, then cut out on him.

He must have been so lonely, her brain whispered, in this far too sympathetic way.

And that was before he spoke.

"See, I don't think anybody this concerned about someone who fucked up their life could make some poisonous potion. So maybe you should trust me. And trust in yourself. You're better than you think you are, Cassie. You always were," he said. And that was how she wound up letting Seth Brubaker walk away with a Tupperware container full of nonsense.

Oh, and magic that would most likely liquefy him from the inside out.

Then quite possibly destroy the world.

CHAPTER SEVEN

Cassie spent the day googling everything she could about the term he'd used. But all that came up was a ton of stuff about shoes, and streets in England, and baked desserts. There wasn't one thing that she could see about the sort of witches who could half do magic.

Or how you could figure out if you were one.

And that was good, in one way, because it meant that she wasn't about to be unearthed as an unwitting destroyer of worlds. But it was bad, in another, because now everything made even less sense than it had before.

She had a million more questions, and what seemed like no way to answer any of them. There didn't appear to be anything in the house of horrors that really explained things. No secret note saying, *now I shall finally reveal your legacy to you.* No ancient books handing down the secret lore of some supernatural cabal.

All she found were spooky things all over the house, ready to scare her half to death.

Heck, even *non*spooky things made her jump out of her skin now. When the doorbell chimed the next morning, she came extremely close to screaming. And it wasn't until a voice called out, "Hey, I have a delivery here for Cassandra Camberwell" that she managed to open the door.

But even then she kept the chain on.

The deliveryman had to squeeze the parcel through the gap, while she eyed him suspiciously for signs of the supernatural. Which turned out to be a bummer, because the parcel was apparently a fruit basket. And fruit did not take kindly to being crushed between a door and its frame. The bananas were mush; the grapes had been flattened. Her fingers were sticky from the pulp of an orange when she read the card.

Saw you were back in town, so happy to see you. Pretty sure you hated the flowers I sent after everything that happened, so thought I'd try a fruit basket instead, she read, and felt her heart lift and sink all at the same time. Because oh, Nancy was lovely, she was so sweet, it was so nice to know that someone who barely even knew her cared that much.

But it also meant she was definitely going to have to make that call. Even though she was now mired in even wilder stuff than she'd been before. *How would I ever manage to explain any of this to someone that sunny. I don't even know how to explain it to myself*, she thought, as she did her best to rescue the rest of the fruit.

And that was probably why she didn't sigh and roll her eyes the second she saw him through her kitchen window, strolling out from the woods and across the grass. Instead, something weird happened inside her. Her stomach seemed to clench and collapse at the same time; for some inexplicable reason her breath caught in her throat. And she had the strongest urge to do something very inadvisable.

Like race immediately to the door and fling it open. Then yell about seventy different questions at him.

But thankfully, she managed to get hold of herself. She focused on drying her still-wet-from-the-sink hands on her jeans. And straightening her series of misshapen sweaters and cardigans into something resembling an outfit. Then she waited, calmly, for him to knock. Or maybe call out her name with the same sort of impatience she'd seen in him the night before.

Only for some reason, all she got was the clomp of his boots on her porch. Back and forth, back and forth. And it was followed by something even weirder—a rifling, papery sort of sound. Like he was busy going through a bunch of legal documents on her doorstep.

So of course she had to go and prove to herself that he wasn't.

This will have a normal explanation, she thought as she crept to the door.

Then she peered through the peephole, and somehow he was doing something even more deranged than she had imagined. He had a *notepad* in his hands. And he was *scribbling in it,* furiously. He filled an entire page with that thick print of his, as she watched. Pressing down on the page too hard, as usual. Every letter just as cramped together as she remembered.

Then—best of all—she looked at his face in the middle of this note-writing, and caught him doing the thing he had once been so self-conscious about. The thing he'd forced himself out of when he'd made the jump to being cool.

He mouthed the words he wanted to write as he wrote them.

Like he was really struggling to get them just right.

Then he folded the piece of paper and stooped, and next she knew those words were skittering under the front door. They slid to a stop by her right foot, about a second before she heard him clomp his way back off her porch. Like he was just going to leave, she realized. And she couldn't force herself to hesitate.

She snatched up the note, and flung open the door, and called out his name.

And watched him jump almost out of his skin. He actually clutched his chest in shock. "Oh god," he gasped. "I didn't think you'd want to come out and talk to me, after . . . you know. All the breaking into your house and almost biting you into pieces and the whole mangled arm being trapped inside my arm thing."

All of which made her feel better about her choice to stop him. Not to mention even more curious about the piece of paper in her hand.

"So that's why you just left me a note," she said. "To explain all of that."

"Well, no, not exactly. But anyway, you'll see when you read it later."

"*Later*? Dude, I am not waiting for later. I'm looking now."

She unfolded the note, all in a scramble. But he stepped forward before she could actually get to the words. "Oh god, please don't, not in front of me," he said, and she narrowed her eyes in response.

"Because you want to run away before I see the mean things you've put."

"I haven't put anything mean. I just. I wrote it in a rush. It might not be all that. You know, it's kind of like. I mean the thing is—" he tried, then cut himself off in the middle of this nonexplanation when he saw what she was doing. "And you're just going right ahead. Okay great. Awesome. Fantastic."

But what did he expect? She couldn't afford to wait for him to waffle his way out of this. That would just make her a fool who constantly fell for his evil pranks. Plus she wouldn't get any opportunity to yell at him about the probable horrid contents.

And she really wanted to yell at him about them. She wanted to yell so much that when she read the words *Dear Cassie*, she felt her entire body tense up. As if he'd actually written, *Hello You Ridiculously Naive Butthead*. And she didn't unwind as she read on. She didn't relax. Even though the rest was even more astonishing than that first part.

I just wanted to somehow tell you without bothering you that I'm really sorry about the whole arm being inside-out thing. And the almost eating you thing. And the breaking into your house thing. And the making you think I slept with your grandmother thing. Damn, I apparently have a lot of things to apologize for. I haven't even gotten to the high school thing, he had written. Though she went over it so fast she wasn't sure she had read it right. It felt as if she couldn't have, if it was that full of contrition.

Yet a second go told her the same thing.

And then there was more.

Well anyway, I know that I can't make up for any of that, both because there's so much of it but also just because it's all really bad and scary and you're probably traumatized. In fact I know you're traumatized after seeing the way you hold yourself when you even so much as see me. So god knows where you're at now, trauma-wise. But I promise I will not make it any worse anymore. I will stay away so you can find peace and heal and be happy, she read, word by excruciating word. Heart pounding harder and harder with every single one she fully processed. Half of her wanting to laugh at the ridiculous way he'd put things, half of her wanting to cry over how much more true the ridiculousness made it feel.

And even more so when she read the sign-off: *Yours sincerely, your ex-best friend, Seth Brubaker.* Because it was pretty much the exact thing he used to write when they were kids. The ending he'd always given his notes before he passed them to her in class or slipped them underneath the front door or left them for her in secret places. Those strangely formal words, which felt so personal and so warm at the same time.

And still felt like that now.

She knew they did, because she was fucking tearing up. She had to blink a lot to stop it happening—and still only really managed because something else caught her eye. More words, after the sign-off. A postscript, just casually there like no big deal. Only it *was* a big deal, it was a very big deal, it was so big a deal she briefly felt like she was choking on her own breath.

She had to reread the words about ten times before they sank in. Yet still didn't fully know what to say about them once she had. Instead she looked up from the page, slowly. Eyes narrowed. Part of her sure this must be the gag. Most of her knowing it wasn't.

All of her irritated beyond belief that he'd put it like this.

"Seth, did you just seriously end this really nice, otherwise mostly normal-seeming note with an absolutely bonkers thing like *oh shit p.s. I think you might be a super-powerful witch*? Or am I just hallucinating that part?" she asked.

But he didn't even seem to get what the problem was.

He just hit her with this hopeful, reaching sort of expression.

"You think the note is really nice?" he asked.

At which point, her heart started hammering for a different reason. A very supernatural, witch-based reason.

"Well, I did until I got to *this* part."

"But that part isn't meant to be a mean joke."

"Seth, I get that. But what I don't get is you tacking it on the end like it's not extremely vital information that's making me want to pass out. I mean, I spent last night convincing myself I'm not even half a witch, and you're throwing this at me?"

"I didn't mean to throw it. I just wasn't sure how to fit it in with the other, more important stuff," he said, and, oh dear god, he meant it. It was all over his face—that look that said he was puzzling through something, inwardly, instead of trying to convince her of something that wasn't true.

He really thought being sorry was the big deal here. Everything else didn't matter. Or at least, it didn't matter to him. And that was so overwhelming she didn't know how to deal with it.

But thankfully, she had a whole other overwhelming thing to focus on.

"You fit it in by *leading with this*, Seth. You *lead* with witch things. And then you explain why exactly you're thinking something this nuts, so, you know. Maybe I don't end up thinking your brain must be melting. Because I melted it. With the super witch powers you mistakenly think I have," she pointed out. She even mimed some of the melting and the powers, for emphasis.

But all she got in response was: "Okay, so then maybe I'll just write you another note."

And then he *actually* got *out* his *pen* and his *notepad*.

"For fuck's sake, Seth, don't write it down when I'm directly in front of you."

"But you've made it pretty clear that you don't want to talk to me."

"I don't want to talk to you about *ordinary things*. But when what you need to say is about harrowing, incredible supernatural nonsense that might make me accidentally turn the world inside out, then please. For the love of god. Feel free to disregard those instructions. Disregard them *to the maximum degree possible*," she burst out, and oh thank god, thank god, she could see it sinking in.

Though it seemed to take him a long time to come up with an answer. She could practically see him doing conversational algebra in his head.

"Okay, so I should just go hard on this one particular topic," he finally said.

And though she didn't want to mentally bless him, she could feel the blessing happening anyway. It made her give him two thumbs-up as she answered. "You bet. Really swing for the fences. Say seventy thousand words."

"I don't know, Cassie. Seventy thousand fence swings might be a lot for you."

"They won't be. I need to hear them. I want to hear them. Please go for it," she said.

Only then he just started lifting his jacket and his jersey, for some reason.

"Oh thank god, now I can just show you," he said, and when he did she got this little frisson of fear. And it doubled when he added, "I mean seriously, look at this."

Because it sounded as if there was something terrible there.

She almost didn't look. And when she finally forced herself to, she went about it whip quick. One turn of her head, one narrowed eye, and there it was. His torso, all honey-gold and smooth and perfectly normal. Nothing wrong with it at all, it looked like.

Yet somehow, she didn't relax on seeing it. Instead, her body seemed to tense harder. Like it had that time they had gone swimming together as newly minted teenagers. And he had stripped off, like all the other times he'd done it before.

But, weirdly, it hadn't felt like all the other times.

It had felt different, very different. Suddenly she had found herself staring at a lot of things—like how smooth his skin was, and how big his chest looked, and how hairy he was getting. And not just hairy on his upper body, either. But lower down. Close to the waistband of his shorts. That little trail, leading down down down to things she never, ever thought about.

But she had started thinking about them, then.

And she was definitely thinking about them now.

He was a lot thicker and furrier, at this point. And his jeans were very, very low slung. She could almost make out the start of something more, something that made her go all hot and weird and embarrassed. Just like she had that heated summer day.

Only this time it was much, much worse.

Because back then, he had gone all hot and weird and embarrassed too. He had clocked her suddenly much bigger chest, and gone bright red. She remembered him whipping his head away, fast, and then looking at almost anything but her for the rest of the swim.

Like they were in this thing together, somehow.

But of course that wasn't the case now.

She was fully dressed. And even if she hadn't been, he clearly didn't care about whatever her boobs looked like. His eyes almost never left her face. They stayed there no matter what she was doing—and that was good. It was fine by her. She didn't need his approval, his desire, his gawping at her body like he had back then.

But it did make her gawping at him more mortifying.

Never let him know that you like a single thing about him, she told herself, firmly.

Then she put her shoulders back, and lifted her head, and responded. "Yeah, okay, Seth. I get that you have a six-pack now," she said, and rolled her eyes. Though it didn't exactly have the intended effect. He just glanced down at his own stomach with this pleased look on his face.

"You really think I still have a six-pack? I thought I kind of lost it when all this madness made me want to eat everything all the time, and sleep so long it feels like a coma, and also—just generally being this way makes you a lot thicker and burlier, you know?" he said, all affable and blasé about it. While she carried on floundering in this sea of weird feelings.

First there had been that flush and the urge to stare, and now here was another fucking rush of concern. *Your entire body and metabolism and sleep cycle changed*, she wanted to say. But even after she managed to fight that down, nothing good took its place.

"Well, even if it has, it's definitely still there," she blurted out.

And could only thank her lucky stars that he didn't take it like a compliment.

"Right, but I mean, it's less defined."

"Something being less defined is not a bad thing."

"So you like it thicker like this, you like more of a belly."

"What the fuck does it matter, Seth? That's not the point."

She flushed even harder at the end of those words, thoroughly flustered now and not sure how she had somehow made everything worse. Though, thankfully, he still didn't seem to notice. "Right right right, the point is the scar I'm trying to show you," he said.

So now all she had to do was go with this.

"I don't see any scar," she tried with as much confusion as she could muster.

Then almost let out a sigh of relief when he seemed to seize on it. "Exactly. *Exactly*," he said, like a mad scientist gasping that he'd proven his deranged hypothesis. "There used to be a ten-inch groove in my side right here, where things didn't go back together properly. It was so deep I could put my finger in it up to the first joint. For *years*. And now look. It's *gone*."

Then he actually made the gesture with one hand. That magical poof gesture.

All of which made it even easier to stick to the meat of this conversation.

"What, as in you lost it somehow?"

"Lost it? What the heck, *no*."

"Don't say 'What the heck' at me as if what I said is so absurd, Seth. Yesterday you told me vampires exist. I watched your face grow fifty extra bones and a thousand more teeth. Things wandering off your body is not that far-fetched by comparison."

"Okay, and that's fair. But nothing wandered. I drank the soup, and it *healed*."

He said the last word in a breathless, almost hushed tone. Like that mad scientist hadn't just proven something deranged. He had proven something awe-inspiring. Something that was going to make her mind melt right out of her head—if she would only dare to really look.

And it was this, more than anything else, that made her reach forward and lift the jersey he'd just dropped. Just with one finger, just enough so she could see the side he'd pointed to. No big deal, she told herself. She could be cool and scientific about it.

Only it didn't feel scientific, once she was there.

Because the thing was, *he let her do it*. He didn't act weird about it, or wonder aloud what on earth she was doing. He simply watched her expose his body, in this almost curious and kind of eager sort of way. And for some reason, the curiousness and the eagerness made her go even hotter than just seeing him had. Her whole body flushed the second she realized his eyes were on her; suddenly her hand seemed to be shaking.

Even though he was only doing this because of the scar.

He just wanted her to see what was there. Or more accurately, what wasn't there.

Because once she had managed to get herself under control, she could see he had told the truth. There was definitely nothing. No marks, no grooves, no scars. Not even any evidence of what must have initially mauled him into being a werewolf. His skin looked flawless—better than flawless, in fact. It was as if he'd started using some kind of rejuvenating moisturizer, of the kind that made everything dewy and glowy and healthy looking.

Though she still wasn't sure if she should concede.

"Well, maybe you're mistaken," she said.

So of course he hit her with an exasperated look. "How could I possibly be?"

"Maybe the scar was on the other side."

"You think I might have gotten the position of a ten-inch groove on my own body wrong. And then failed to check all the places it could have possibly been." He shook his head. "Man, your opinion of me is really at an all-time low."

Good, think that, she thought. *Believe that I think nothing of you.*

But the problem was, she knew she was only trying to paper over her own weird feelings. About the quarry, about his body, about the way he had looked at her. So she couldn't exactly go with something like that. "It isn't. I just. You know. Maybe all this body horror messed you up."

"Oh, this body horror has *definitely* messed me up. But not enough to get this wrong. There was a hideous half-healed scar right here, and now it's not. And it disappeared about thirty seconds after I took your medicine."

"It wasn't medicine," she protested, as she dropped the jersey and looked up at him. Though staring at his completely earnest face wasn't any easier than staring at his side. He still looked just a little too eager. And, plus, now he was trying to make her face the other elephant in the room.

The magic elephant, which he somehow believed she had made.

"Whatever it was," he said. "It happened."

"Okay but. Maybe it wasn't the soup I created."

"Then what would you suggest did it, exactly?"

"It could have been your werewolf powers kicking in late."

He chuffed out a laugh at that. And shook his head too. Like she was being *that* ridiculous. "It doesn't work that way."

"Well, I don't know, Seth. I just learned about this stuff ten seconds ago."

"And I didn't. So I know what happened. Whatever you make doesn't just work the way your grandmother's soup did. It isn't just a cobble-level thing. It doesn't just lessen the impact of transforming or make me less aggressive. It actually obliterates it. It stops it in its tracks. And then it reverses whatever transforming did to me."

Again, with that surety. That confidence in all the mad things he was saying. It was unshakable, in a way she was starting to find very frustrating. Mainly because she had no way of knowing, as things stood, about how right he could possibly be. He had all the understanding and she had none of it, and that made raising questions incredibly difficult.

But damn it, she had to try.

"Okay, but you can't know that for certain yet. I mean, don't you have to, like, wait for a full moon to see if it has that effect? Because it might come and you might drink the stuff and then still turn," she pointed out.

But all he did was look at her like she was mad.

"The moon isn't what makes me transform. It's usually—" He

stopped midsentence and swallowed thickly. Then his eyes seemed to briefly skitter away from hers. Like it was hard to think about. Though if it was, the difficulty passed pretty quickly. "It's usually other things. Different things for different wolves. Maybe some turn because they get angry. Or sad. Or too happy. Maybe for others it happens because of hormone . . . fluctuations. Something spikes inside them and a kind of countdown starts. And when that happens with me, I can do all my breathing exercises and maybe play solitaire or stick my . . . my head in a freezer to slow it down. But sooner or later it will happen. It was starting to happen again this morning when I woke up . . . in an agitated state. Then I drank that soup, and you know what I feel now?"

"Tell me."

"*Nothing.*"

He leaned forward as he breathed the word.

Which put them very close together, because apparently *she* had been leaning forward too. And she couldn't stop, because now he was explaining exactly what that one word meant. "For the first time in ten years, my whole body feels quiet. It feels completely at peace. It feels normal. Do you know what it's like to get even five minutes of normality? To not have my heart race and pound, and my skin feel like it's burning off my body, and my gums ache until I think my teeth are trying to burst right out of my head? I can't even make out the pain of all the old scars. Because that groove wasn't alone—I had dozens. Look at this."

He turned his back to her, lifting his jersey again as he did. This time, however, it wasn't quite as jarring. She didn't have the urge to avoid looking at the smooth expanse of skin he revealed, right up to the nape of his neck. No, she had the urge to do the opposite. She almost stepped forward to see it more closely.

Even though she didn't need to. He was already making things clear.

"*Four years* my left shoulder blade has been in the wrong place. You'd never know it now. That arm you saw yesterday, I thought I'd be living with that for the rest of my life. Check it out. Gone.

Like it was never there. And then there's what seems to be going on here," he said, in a way that sounded ominous. Though she didn't realize how ominous, until he started unbuttoning his jeans.

And then it was flustered panic time, again.

"Oh my god, I believe you, I believe you, please do not take those off, okay? I'm already at my limit. The sight of your probably enormous werewolf dong will absolutely push me over the edge," she blurted out before she could stop and think about it. And even though that meant she'd accidentally talked about his penis, she couldn't regret it.

Because it *did* make him hesitate.

But then he said this: "Cassie, I was just going to show you my thigh."

And her face immediately went all hot again. "Right. Right. Your thigh. Of course," she squeezed out. Much to his amusement-slash-indignation.

"I mean, what do you take me for?"

"Sorry, I'm just all shaken up."

"I know, but come on. I'd at least warn you before I flashed that huge thing."

He shook his head, still appalled by her terrible assumptions.

Because clearly, he hadn't fully realized what he'd just said. That was okay though—she definitely had. And it meant that her eyes went really big, no matter how much she tried to make them not. She even attempted to turn her face away, before he saw.

But it was too late.

"Shit," he said. "Shouldn't have confirmed that it's huge, should I?"

Because he was ridiculous, utterly ridiculous, he was almost as much of a big goofball as he'd always been. Like a golden retriever if it suddenly became a person, she'd once thought. And that was super nice. But also infuriating.

"Probably would have been best for my mental well-being if you hadn't," she said.

"Sorry. It just sounded like you knew already. You said it so confidently."

"I was *joking*. I was just being *funny*."

He nodded, regretfully. "Yep, I see that now."

"Wish you'd seen a second ago, so I didn't have to have the image lodged forever in my brain. But you know, those are the breaks. One second your head is empty of your mortal enemy's potential penis, the next you have to live with it endlessly unraveling in your head like a Fruit Roll-Up," she sighed, weary and sarcastic enough that she thought this would be the end of the matter.

But oh no. No, no. He kept right on going.

"Well, you know it's not so long that I have to wind it up. Usually I can just kind of keep it down one thigh and then wear long, tight shorts, and it sort of stays in one place and oh my god I need to stop talking."

"You really do. Before I die of this conversation."

He winced. "Sorry, sorry, I just felt like I needed to explain."

"Explain important things, Seth. Like the scars and the soup and you somehow thinking I'm a more powerful witch than my grandmother."

"You *are* more powerful than her. It's not up for debate."

She made a frustrated sound and looked away. Tried to give herself time to come up with fifty reasons why he was wrong. But before she'd even managed to get to one, he cut in. Firmly, like on this he had no doubts, no worries, no sense that he was fumbling things.

"Be honest," he said. "Who wrote those recipes?"

"*She* did. She wrote them all down."

"You don't sound so sure about that."

"Well, I am. In fact I'll get them. You can see her handwriting for yourself," she said, then went to do just that. She turned, but didn't even make it up the porch steps. He had an answer for her, almost immediately. Just loaded in the barrel, ready to fire right at her back.

"Her handwriting might be in those journals, but I'm willing to bet you told her what to put," he called out. Then after a beat, "Go on, tell me that's not true. Tell me that she would scribble away based on some other witch's ideas that she just failed to mention in any form, and you never get this overwhelming feeling that she was doing it ever so slightly wrong. You never stopped her, you never corrected her, you never thought if she just stirred three times instead of four, all would be well."

She tried to scoff. Only the scoff didn't want to come out.

All she managed was a faint breath puffing out of her, as his words sunk in. As her mind went back over those summer days, and the number of times her grandmother had paused while writing, and looked back at her, and said something like, *what do you think, Cassie? What do you think, one spoon, or two?*

And hadn't she always had an answer? Hadn't she always just—

"That's not. That didn't. I didn't," she stuttered out.

But oh, the memories that were rushing in. The way she couldn't fight them, no matter how hard she tried. And of course it was showing. Of course her gaze had turned inward.

"You did. I can see it all over your face," he said.

Though she wasn't yet willing to give in. She couldn't give in, this was bonkers.

"Well, you're not reading me right. Because I am not Gertrude the Great. I didn't come from an ancient bloodline of all-powerful witches, or learn things from terrible arcane texts that no mortal eyes should behold."

"Yeah, and that doesn't make it any less likely that you did this."

"What do you mean? Of course it does, that's all witches are."

"That's all people *think* witches are. But that is not what your grandmother told me. According to her it can happen just as easily to anyone, as it can to someone who got it from their mom or their auntie or their assortment of weird ancestors. And it's not always on purpose either. You don't necessarily have to study great tomes of spellcraft. Sometimes it just happens. Sometimes it's just an instinct, an accident. You want something enough, and it converges with something you're most likely messing up, and that's it. You know how to make magic happen. You feel it, down deep in your bones. You see it, even if you don't know you do or understand how you're doing it. Like making out the image in those magic eye pictures, is the way your grandmother described it to me," he said, all in a rush that should have sounded ridiculous.

But here was the thing: it didn't.

It sounded perfect.

As soon as he said the words "magic eye," she felt something inside her click. Like, *yes, that is exactly it. That was exactly what it felt like when my grandmother said do you think we should add more of this? Do you think we should do that?*

The image just . . . became clear.

But oh that knowledge only made her feel more desperate to deny it.

"I don't believe you. I don't believe any of this," she said, frantically.

While he stayed calm. God, it felt like he got calmer by the second.

"Fine, then I'll prove it to you."

"Oh, what are you going to do? Shake me until spells fall out?"

"No. I'm going to tell you that what I need is a really good night's sleep. So I've decided to make myself something that will put me out like a light. And I think maybe the best way to do that is to start with some milk, and then I'll add some cloves, and some nutmeg, and oh, you know what? I bet if I put it all in the microwave for thirteen minutes and—" he said, all nice and slow and easy. Deliberately nice and slow and easy, she felt, until every word built on this feeling inside her, this terrible feeling that she couldn't stop or shake or do anything about.

And then she just broke.

She had to break. She had to cover her ears and yell.

"Stop stop stop, okay, stop! Oh my god, it's like I have bees under my skin, it's like I want to claw my own face off just listening to you get it all wrong. Sleep is well water under the moonlight, you put well water under moonlight for three nights and then stir in a single seed from a dandelion counterclockwise and oh my god, how do I know this? How is this in my brain? Where did it come from?" she cried out, half wanting to know and half not wanting to know and all of her sure he was going to reply with something completely useless.

And then he did, and it was even worse than she had feared.

"I have no fucking clue. I only know that it is *definitely* in there."

"So then help me get it back out, Seth. I don't want to melt in the rain."

"Witches don't melt in rain. They don't melt in anything."

She put her hands on her hips, fuming for reasons she couldn't even grasp. "Okay then, maybe I'll be the one accidentally doing the melting."

"You won't. Unless you want to, that is."

"And how do you know I can just want to and it will happen?" she asked, sure that she had him there. Only now he was looking at her in this steady, soft way. And his voice, when it came, was soft too.

"Because your understanding of what to do and what not to do is so deep in you that your grandmother told you that you should stop baking and cooking. And without even understanding on a conscious level what she meant, you did. You made no mistakes, you had no accidents, you conjured up precisely nothing," he told her. Then when she offered nothing in reply, when she felt too stupefied to form words, he held her gaze. He said, "Tell me I'm wrong."

And she just didn't know how to argue with that.

All she could come up with was something shaky as fuck.

"You're not wrong. But only because I ate a lot of takeout."

"Come on. I bet you've made at least one sandwich in that time."

"Well, yeah. Of course. But a sandwich was never going to do anything."

"Right. Because I'm willing to bet you made sure it didn't. Like one time you were reaching for something like elderberry jelly, and you stopped with your hand almost on it, and looked down at the ingredients you had already combined, and then for no good reason you could think of, you chose something else instead."

She went to protest again. Her lips parted, her breath hung

at the back of her throat, waiting to push the words out. But the words never arrived. They couldn't, when her mind was too busy going back, again. And this time, it was over every single little thing that exactly fit what he'd just described.

She remembered brands she'd chosen at the grocery store over other brands, for no good reason. Things she'd wanted to add to coffees but hadn't; food other people had made that she'd hesitated to eat. Like she'd had a constant little voice in her head, telling her danger danger danger. Even if it was just about a certain combination of ingredients that she hadn't made.

But that still felt wrong.

And it went deeper than that. There was more than what he'd suggested. Like the times some colleague or semifriend had said they wanted something they couldn't have. And she'd come so close to telling them—just add honey to that cup of tea. Just let it sit outside, when the moon is fat. Just do this and this and this, and everything will be okay.

Then kept her mouth shut, instead. Because she'd promised.

But also because she had been afraid.

Deep down, she'd felt fear about what she could possibly do.

And so she'd limited herself, in the same way she'd limited herself about other, more ordinary things. Going from temp job to temp job because she might fail at something more secure. Never filling out those college applications to study medicine the way she'd always wanted to—because what if she wasn't good enough there either?

All the friendships she'd been afraid to make. Every date she'd avoided going on.

Always afraid of having the rug pulled, the way he'd pulled it.

And now here he somehow was, being the one spreading it all out before her. Bigger than before, better, enormous. Because this wasn't just friendship or a possible career or something she could study. It was way beyond that. It was her entire sense of self being turned on its head.

And she just didn't know how to cope with that.

"Oh my god. Oh my god. I'm going to throw up," she found

herself saying. But when she did—when she had to lean over and rest her hands on her knees and take deep breaths—he kind of came toward her. He held out his hands to her.

He said, "Okay, okay, just tell me what to do. Should I hold back your hair?"

As if it weren't enough on its own that he was being so steadfastly the opposite of everything she'd believed about him for the last ten years. He had to keep compounding it, over and over. He had to keep proving her wrong on that point at every turn.

While also telling her that she was something powerful and incredible.

I could turn you into an ant for what you did, and you don't care. In fact, you're happy about it, she thought. Then had to hold a hand out to stop him, as the swell of affection toward him grew. As it started to make her feel warm again, like his goddamn juicy stomach had. "Fuck no, that will only make it worse. Stay over there, just stay there," she gasped out. Then he did, oh god, he actually listened and stopped in his tracks. And he remained there, a foot from her, while she wrestled that sick feeling back under control.

She had to sit down and put her head between her knees.

Yet when she looked up, he was still there. Face a maze of concern. Every muscle tensed. One hand sort of hovering close to her, like he was waiting to catch her if she slumped into a faint. Even though his hovering hand was the thing most likely to make that happen. She saw it held out and felt even hotter and weirder than she already did.

But this time, she got her feelings under control quick. She made herself focus.

Think about what's actually important here, she told herself. And she did.

"So what do I do now?" she asked. A little bit weak and wavery about it at first. But then firmer. Surer about things. "Do I have to go look for others like me? Do I have to find a coven?"

"I don't think covens really exist anymore. Witches are pretty rare."

"Because of all the witch trials and things like that?"

It has to be, she thought.

But he was already batting his hand at her.

"Oh god no. No human dude could burn a real witch. In fact, real witches spent a lot of time burning those dudes for burning ordinary people. No, no—they just tend to attract certain types, thirsty for their magic. And then said witches end up dead or missing. Or they hide. Plus, often they never even realize what they are. Their magic is so minor they just chalk what happens up to the universe being weird."

"Which means there's no one I can ask the millions of questions I have."

He hesitated then.

She saw it happen—he took a breath as if to say something, before letting whatever it was just hover on the tip of his tongue. Then after a moment, he just went for it. "Well, there might be someone. But I don't know how you'd really feel about him being that person. You know, because he did a really bad thing to you. And then almost ate your face off and accidentally humblebragged about his giant penis," he said. Because he was absolutely ridiculous.

"Yeah, and now he appears to be doing it again."

"I know. Which probably gives you no confidence at all in this suggestion."

"A lot of things give me no confidence. I mean, why would you even want to help me with this? What are you going to get out of it? Because I can't imagine you want to do it just to hang out with me," she said, and laughed as she did so. Of course she did—that idea was preposterous.

And so much so that he laughed too. He laughed *loudly.*

He was animated about it. He even slapped his knee, like a cartoon character.

"Right. Right," he said. "Because it would be super weird if I did. Is what you mean."

"Well yeah. And especially considering how much it would suck for you."

"Oh god, yeah. It totally would. You know because . . . because of the. The . . ."

"The fact you would have to spend endless hours in my company, having tons of long, long talks about what I've become and what you've become and what the world is actually like," she finished for him, when he didn't seem to quite know how to. Then she shook her head, still half laughing. "I mean, can you imagine? We'd probably have to have lunches together and dinners, and I'd have to call you at midnight when I'm melting down. It would be a nightmare for you."

"Wow, yeah, that sure sounds the way a nightmare is."

"Doesn't it though? Just completely awful."

"Uh-huh. Really bad. I do not want that at all."

"Exactly. So then you should probably retract your offer," she said. Lightly, she thought. Though somehow it didn't feel quite as light when it was out. It felt more like she was nudging him. Like she was saying, *okay, so why aren't you taking it back? Why aren't you saying you don't want to help me after all?*

And especially when he did not immediately do it.

In fact, he didn't immediately do anything. He just kind of stared at her. Then he swallowed, very thickly and very visibly. Like something about all of this was making him nervous. It was putting pressure on him, and he wasn't sure how to resolve it. Even though she couldn't fathom what that pressure or resolution might be. It was a fact that doing this would be a bad experience for him. It was totally a fact.

Tell me it's a fact, she thought at him.

And was relieved when he said, after a moment of thought, "Okay. Okay, but what if there was something I wanted in return? I mean, something other than being nice to you. Or getting to do all that stuff together, all that talking and hanging out and sharing-grilled-cheese-sandwiches stuff you just said."

Because yeah, that made sense. Him wanting something made sense.

Even though that last part sounded a little weird.

"I don't think I mentioned grilled cheese," she said, and for just the barest second it seemed like panic flashed across his face. Before he let out a little laugh, and gave her a shrug, and finally responded with something reasonable.

"Oh you didn't? Well, you know. I was just . . . embellishing. Based on what we used to do a lot together. When we spent so much time with each other, talking and having fun and eating good stuff like that," he said—and okay, that all made sense.

But there was still a question that needed answering.

"Great. Then that just leaves what you want in return for helping me."

"Yeah, I was getting to that. If you just give me a second."

"You need a second to come up with a reason you're offering me your help, when you made the offer already? Come on, I don't believe you. You must have something in mind. Like something to do with me being a witch. A spell you need me to do, or something along those lines," she said, rolling her hand in the air like come on, get to the point.

And he did. All in a big burst, like it was a relief to get it out. "Oh god, of course. Of course that's what I could want. A spell—like my soup. You could make me more of the soup that heals my wounds and helps me not to turn so often," he said, and then snapped his fingers.

Like, *yes, I got the answer.*

Even though he must have had the answer all along. He must have known he was only really making the offer for his own gain. It made no sense if he hadn't.

Though now that she was thinking about it, how much sense had she made? Because she hadn't thought of the soup either. She'd just imagined random other magic he might want, instead of the most obvious thing. And she didn't know why.

Or at least, she didn't until she went to answer him. Then had to stop herself, because what she wanted to say was: *Yeah, but I would do that for you anyway. I would do it just because I can't bear the thought of you suffering. And I know that makes me weak and soft and foolish, but I can't help it. All I can do is pretend it's otherwise.*

"Oh yeah. The soup. Right," she said. "That makes total sense."

"It does. Because then all of this is just a perfectly practical deal."

"A deal. Yep. That is exactly what I was thinking."

"No feelings involved. Nobody owing anybody anything."

"Just a straightforward, unemotional, completely reasonable transaction."

He nodded firmly. And she nodded back. *Done and done*, she thought.

Although she had to say, he didn't seem to be in any rush to look away. And for some reason, she didn't seem to be breaking their eye contact either. She was just staring at him and he was staring at her, and it was going on and on in such a weird way that it was a relief when he suddenly said, "So we should probably shake hands then."

Or at least, it was a relief until she realized:

What he'd said required bodily contact.

Way more bodily contact than had already occurred. And worse: there was absolutely no good way to get out of this one. "I think shaking hands is the thing two business partners usually do," she just had to squeeze out. Then she expected him to simply go ahead. To be confident about it in a way she couldn't be.

Only, for some unaccountable reason that didn't seem to be happening.

Instead, he looked like he was psyching himself up for battle.

He bounced on his toes. Clapped his hands together.

"Okay, so I'll just go for it. I'll just reach forward and take hold of you," he said. But still, he didn't. He just looked nervously at her hands. And back up to her face. And back down to her hands. So now it was on her, again, to make this seem normal.

"Yep. Just go right ahead and touch me."

"And then you'll touch me back."

"I definitely will," she said.

But honestly, she wasn't sure what was going to happen when he tried. It felt like she might scream, or slap his hand away, or maybe even run back into the house. All three possibilities were certainly building inside her, when he took a step forward.

Then he reached out his hand.

And somehow he wasn't forceful about it. He didn't do it firmly, the way she had imagined he would. He did it slowly, in stuttering stages. Like he was waiting for all the things she'd thought she might do: the scream, the slap, the run. And it was only when those reactions didn't immediately happen that he touched her. Just with the tips of his fingers, along the soft side of her hand. No pressure, no sense of him pulling her into anything.

As if he was still waiting for permission.

Even though that was silly, wasn't it? It was just a handshake. Nothing weird about that. And she told him so, by turning into his touch. Only a little, to indicate it was fine. But enough that he would know that it was, and go ahead.

Just get it over with, she thought at him.

And he obviously heard her, because he did. He took her hand in his.

Though *took her hand* didn't really cover the way it felt.

It was as if everything beyond her wrist had been swallowed up. She couldn't see one hint of her inside that enormous grip. All she could make out were his knuckles, so thick and heavy-boned that they almost seemed to have worn down the skin around them. And his fingers, big enough that they could fold around hers. And the way the thick, lush hair on his forearm had started to spread over his wrist, and downward to the base of his little finger.

Like the wolf had begun to make a mark on him, even when he looked as human as he currently did. And not just in terms of the hair, or the sheer size of him. There was something else too. Something she didn't notice immediately.

But she definitely started to, after a few seconds of his hand surrounding hers.

Because, oh dear god, the *heat*. The sheer *blaze* that seemed to be coming from inside him.

It was like he had molten lava for blood. She could feel it radiating through his skin and into hers, in a way that seemed to flood through her. It slid through her body and between her bones, until she started to feel thick with it. Ripe with it. All burned up and sort of blurry around the edges.

"Seth," she tried to say, but somehow it came out slurred.

Like she was in a steam room set to high, and someone had locked the door.

Another ten seconds and she was going to pass out from heat exhaustion—and she couldn't let that happen. He'd think she was all affected by bodily contact with him. Like before, only worse. Because this time, he seemed even less affected than he had by anything else. He was still shaking away at her hand, like he hadn't a care in the world.

Though she had to say, the handshake was going on for a long time. And he didn't seem to be saying a lot. He didn't seem to be doing anything. She couldn't even hear him breathing.

So when she went to pull away, she looked up.

But he wasn't looking at her face. He was looking at their hands. He was staring at them, transfixed, like they were the most fascinating things he'd ever seen. And it was only when she tried to pull away that he stopped. His head jerked up, as if he'd been caught spying on something he shouldn't.

Something filthy, she thought.

Even though that was ridiculous.

It was just a handshake. Nothing more, nothing less.

And if he walked away with one hand clenched and the other held spread open like it had just touched fire, like it had been burned by heated blood she didn't actually have—well.

She would tell herself that it didn't mean a single thing.

CHAPTER EIGHT

She knew his exposed body and the conversation and the resulting handshake had affected her too deeply. And not just because a lot of the things he'd said had left her puzzling over them. Or because that contact had been weird and intense enough that she could still feel it for hours afterward. Or because he'd walked away the way he had. No, there was also what happened in the middle of the phone conversation she had later that day with her mom.

Her mom asked, "So how are things going?"

And her first instinct wasn't to say, *well, my mortal enemy is a werewolf*, or *hey, just so you know, Gram was a half witch who never told me I have magical powers*. Or even just a normal update on non-mind-blowing things like: *I found a downstairs toilet under the stairs that Gram was weirdly using as a cupboard*.

Instead, she almost blurted out, *Seth Brubaker made my hand go really hot. Then it looked like I made his hand go really hot*.

As if that mattered. As if it even remotely measured up to anything else that had happened. *You should be asking your mom if she knew anything about this witch business*, her mind scolded her. Though of course she knew why she didn't.

There wasn't a chance in hell her mother had any idea.

And even if she had, Cassie knew her mom wouldn't have believed it. Her mother was the most practical person alive. Both her parents were. Their advice, after the whole high school business, had been to simply become a different person so it would never happen again.

"Things like that never happen to thin, well-dressed people," her dad had said, without looking up from his paper. And that was the reason she'd moved across the country the second she could. It was why she'd relied on Seth for the kind of support her parents should have given her, just as he'd relied on her for the freedom his parents had rarely allowed.

So relaying any of this—including the hand thing—was pointless.

She simply told her mom that she was staying longer than she'd planned, that she was having fun catching up with old friends, that she had sublet her apartment so it didn't matter anyway. Even though she hadn't. She'd just let it go, figuring that she would use the money from the sale of the house to get a new place.

And at this point she wasn't even sure if she wanted to do that.

I think I might have to live here now, she almost said at the end of the conversation with her mother. But of course she couldn't explain why, so what was the point? It seemed better to just end the call and carry on trying to muddle through all of this in whatever way she could.

Which basically meant a lot of not daring to read the little stack of journals she'd gathered and set on the kitchen table. And not sleeping, because now the rocking chair might really be alive. And feeling relieved again when Seth showed up the next day.

Even though she didn't want to be relieved at all. She wanted to be closed off, and guarded, and cautious. But instead, when he said, "So should we go inside and make ourselves comfortable?" she actually almost told him *sure.*

More than that, in fact. She didn't think *twice* about saying sure. It felt like the most natural, casual thing in the world to simply go ahead. Like they were kids again, like they were buddies. Instead of the utterly deranged adult enemies they'd become.

He did that awful thing to you, she told herself.

And then she put the brakes on so hard, he almost crashed into her as she made her way up the porch steps. She heard him screech to a halt behind her, followed by a blurted out, "Whoa, easy there. I almost had you."

And, okay, she knew he meant *I came close to knocking into you*. Yet, somehow, she just couldn't shake the idea that it had a double meaning. *He almost hoodwinked me*, she thought. Then proceeded accordingly.

"You know what? I don't think we should go in the house," she said, as calmly and firmly as she could. Though somehow, it still came out too loud, and sounded sort of panicked. He actually held his hands up on hearing it. And he pretty much jumped back.

"Well, all right," he said. "You tell me where you want to do this."

"Outside. On the porch."

"So the swing then."

He pointed to it—the rickety, old white bench tucked cozily under the roof of the porch to her right. Almost hidden from view, and just the right size for two people to squeeze onto together. Though of course, as soon as she considered all these things about it—how closed in it was, how small—she knew it couldn't be a contender. "There's no way I'm facilitating that much contact with you."

"Oh come on. That's not so much more contact than a handshake."

"What are you talking about? It's loads more. Our arms would touch."

And all that weird, probably one-sided heat would happen again, she mentally added. Then shook it off to concentrate on what he was saying.

"You say that like arms are way worse than hands somehow."

"Because they are. And even if they aren't, well, there are other things that could happen. Loads of things. Really bad things."

"And what? You think I'm going to do those bad things to you?"

"Don't say it like I meant sex, you massive dillhole."

"Dude, I would *never* think you meant sex. In fact I feel pretty sure you see me as utterly null and void in that regard. Just completely smooth below the waist, like a kind of evil Ken doll," he said, and when he did he gestured to this supposedly smooth area. As if to help illustrate this completely reasonable concept.

Even though it wasn't reasonable at all.

It was so astonishing she didn't know what to say about it. She opened her mouth to speak, but nothing came out. Like all possible words had died a death in the back of her throat. And she knew it wasn't just because he had imagined she thought so little of him.

It was because of how he clearly thought of himself.

Somehow, he was able to see himself as unattractive. He could accept that idea, despite being as attractive as he objectively was. Even right now, this early in the morning and days after massive trauma, it was all there. The way the dappled light made his wide-set eyes look so honey-pale and dreamy, how his hair fell across his forehead soft as butter and black as spilled ink.

And he wasn't wearing the leather jacket.

He had a plaid shirt on. A really warm, cozy-looking plaid shirt, of the kind he used to wear.

Bet it feels like fur against your cheek, she found herself musing. Then had to immediately overcompensate, for ever thinking those things about his face and clothes.

"Well, you're right. I *do* think of you like an evil Ken doll," she said.

But he didn't even seem perturbed by her agreement. Like it was just a given to him.

"So then what's the problem?" he asked, in a way that sounded genuinely baffled. So baffled, in fact, that she almost couldn't think of a good-enough answer. It took her a second to work out exactly what her objection to sitting close together was. And when it came it felt more mealymouthed than she would have liked.

"I just don't want to get too cozy," she eked out, and felt relieved when he didn't seem to notice anything was amiss.

"Right. Of course. That makes sense."

"I mean, things are sort of okay between us. But this is still just a deal."

"Yeah, I totally get that. You don't want to be best buds over one touch."

"Exactly. Exactly. So, you know, I will be here on the porch steps," she said, and pointed to them. Then when he nodded, she pointed to where she thought he should reasonably seat himself. "And you go sit over there."

"Sit over where?"

She gestured harder. "Look where I'm showing you."

"I'm looking, but all I see is a bird bath at the very end of the garden."

"Right. Because that's what I mean. You can totally perch on that."

He looked back at her, on the word "perch." And she could tell by his expression that she'd gone too far. It was pure *you can't be serious*. Like he was brewing a snarky comment about it. And sure enough: "So you're wanting to do this via semaphore."

"We're not going to need semaphore over that distance."

"No, you're probably right. I'll just search my pockets for my handy travel megaphone instead," he said, and oh the teasing smile he gave her as he did. It looked like he was sucking on a sour candy.

And it was this that made her almost laugh.

She had to bury it under some semiserious words, quickly.

"You know I can demote you back to mortal enemy any time."

"Oh, you mean I've recently had a promotion? What's my position now?"

"Standard enemy," she said, with a surety she wasn't certain she felt. She had to add more caveats, just to firm it up. "Which is just basically the same thing, except I don't plot your untimely demise in my spare time. Instead, I come up with creative ways to keep you at arm's length."

"Well, you're doing a great job. I am really feeling the length of your arm, no question about that. But just know—I am totally dedicated to this company, and absolutely ready to work ceaselessly for a chance to move up through the ranks."

He saluted on the end of those words. And now her amusement was really fighting against her rigid face muscles. She had to look away, to hide the grin that tried to burst through all her defenses. But of course, he caught it anyway.

"That was really charming, wasn't it," he said.

Like the annoying puppy dog of a man he was.

"It's less charming if you say that it was, Seth."

"Right, right, I'll stop while I'm ahead and just find a not-too-close spot to sit," he said.

Then proceeded to search in the most impossibly goofy and adorable manner she could imagine. He pointed at things and shook his head to himself. Started toward parts of the yard before visibly indicating they would be no good. One hand went to his chin; he ran the other through his hair, puzzled.

In the end, she had to break and find him a goddamn lawn chair. And even after she had, he was super careful about placing it. He waited until she had taken a seat on the porch steps, and gestured that closer was okay. And only then did he set the rickety thing down, and sit.

Or at least, he *tried* to sit.

Because, oh boy, did he struggle to get his enormous self into that tiny seat.

He had to ease himself down, gingerly, as it creaked and groaned. Then he just kind of squeezed himself in, between arms that didn't want to accommodate his meaty thighs. It was like seeing an elephant trying to ride a tricycle. All she could make out around his enormous arms and his enormous shoulders and his juicy butt was the green canvas, bowing under his weight beneath the chair.

And even that was barely visible.

Because his legs were so long they'd sort of formed two massive pillars in front of everything. His knees were practically in the way of his face. She had to tell him to lean back and sit with them spread right out—though of course she regretted it once she had.

Now she had to talk to him while he was all sprawled before her. Like a model, posing for his centerfold spread in a nudie mag. And that was . . . well. That was a lot to deal with three seconds before he demanded she kick her brain into gear.

"All right. So hit me with your questions," he said, while she was still floundering. She had to spend way too much time pretending to search for the notebook and pen she knew she'd stashed in her cardigan pocket, just to reach something like composure.

And even then, she couldn't come out with anything good.

"Honestly I don't even know what I wanted to ask now."

"Head full of penises and awkward hand touching, huh?"

And nudie mags full of men with their shirts riding up, she answered mentally. Then had to somehow reply without seeming the least bit flustered or uncomfortable. "Little bit, yeah. Or even, you know. A lot."

"If it helps, mine is too. I'd forgotten what it was like to talk like this."

"Yeah, I guess it must be hard to have long, weird chats with people when you might accidentally become a man beast at any given moment. Or *they* might become a man beast at any moment."

"Well, kind of," he said, as he wobbled his hand back and forth in the air. "But that wasn't what I meant."

"Okay. So what did you mean then?"

"That only me and you were this way with each other."

It didn't seem to take him anything at all to say the words.

But it took a lot for her to hear them. She felt her stomach lurch into her feet the second they were out. She had to pretend to scribble something in her notepad, just so he wouldn't see the naked shock all over her face. And only when she felt sure that she was calm and normal did she meet his gaze and say what she had immediately wanted to.

"You can't possibly really think that," she tried.

But he just snorted. "I don't see why not."

"Because we were never like this before. When we were kids."

"You can't be serious," he said. Then when he saw she wasn't smiling, or laughing, or anything of the kind, he carried right on. "Cassie, that's *all* we were. Just forever talking at a million miles an hour about the weirdest things, filling each other's heads with nonsense, always cracking each other up."

As soon as he said it, she remembered just that. She saw herself having to use the inside of her T-shirt to wipe away the tears of laughter streaming down her face. Felt what it was like to have him nudge her with his elbow, and point to something weird to snigger over. Heard the sound of his wheezing, braces-smothered laugh in her head.

Then felt so much warmth toward him she couldn't speak.

Because he had known they'd had something special. He knew it, and he acknowledged it. It didn't even bother him to accept it. Or consider that maybe they even still had it now. Even though they'd didn't, they didn't. She would not accept that it was true.

"Yeah, but you aren't cracking me up now," she said, but god it sounded weak. So weak that it took him no effort at all to wave it off. To roll his eyes at her.

"Oh come on. I've seen you force down a laugh about fifty times."

And what then? He was right.

So now she had to face that he was. By being completely ridiculous.

"Okay, but in my defense, I did not know you could see that happening."

"Did you also not know that it was happening to you at the time?"

"No, I did. I just . . . it was just that I—"

"Wanted to pretend a little longer that our connection was nonexistent, or that I found it nonexistent, or at the very least that it's still completely dead in the water? Because you know, if you want I can pretend that too."

She shook her head, frustrated. "I'm not asking you to pretend."

"Then tell me what it is you do want."

"Just call it something more fitting to the place we currently are."

"Okay," he said, and she could see him thinking. Like he was really trying to consider all of this carefully before he answered. "So . . . we have the ability to get along in a reasonable manner."

And that was good. That was great. She could deal with that.

"Yeah, that'll do," she said. "Now carry on telling me supernatural stuff."

"It's kind of hard to when you're still mad."

"I'm not. I'm okay."

"Cassie, we might have been downgraded from connected to barely getting along. But I can still read something that simple when it's all over you. It's as clear as it ever was, just—you know. With an extra sprinkling of witch glow."

He waved a hand around the general shape of her. Though it took her a second to realize why: because he meant that last bit *literally*. And, okay, now she actually was mad. Or at the very least, taken aback. "Oh my god. So I *glow* now? I *actually* glow?" she gasped.

Then she had to watch him try to avoid saying yes.

Even though there was no way out of it now.

"A little, yeah. It's kind of golden. Shifts in and out when you move," he finally said.

Kind of sheepishly, but unavoidable all the same.

"So like I'm surrounded by holographic glitter of some description."

"More like a mist. That sometimes sort of hums."

"And what exactly am I humming? Show tunes?"

He smothered a laugh. "It's not a song. It's just a soft single note."

"Jesus, that sounds like a *dial tone*. I'm an ancient phone, awesome."

"You're not an ancient phone. You're just you, with magic."

"And you're sure about that. You're sure I'm a witch."

She hadn't meant to ask it. She wasn't even sure why she did.

It was too obvious, too undeniable, too clear even to her.

Yet still, when he nodded and said, "I am," she felt every inch of her body bristle and prickle. And for just a second, she thought she could see what he'd described.

That glow, around all the bits of herself that she could see. All the bits she had spent a lot of time learning to love, and about which she now found herself wondering—why had it taken so long? Because when her rounded shoulders and plump cheeks and the curve of her cleavage were touched by that light, they looked unbelievable. Glorious.

No matter what anyone has ever said, you are beautiful, she thought, as she turned this way and that. Then as she did, she heard it. Faint, but still unmistakable: a sound, low and sweet and somehow intense all at the same time. *Like the song at the start of the universe*, she thought, weirdly. And then had to think about something else, quick.

"Do you think my grandmother was sure about what I was too?" she asked, eyes still on her fingers and the faint trails they made in the air. Though she looked up when he answered.

"You know she must have been."

"But she never told you about me."

"No. She just said she understood what I was, and that she would help me."

One of his shoulders lifted. No big deal.

Even though it kind of was. Or at the very least, it was missing a lot of details.

"But why?" she had to know. "How? How did she figure it out?"

"Well, finding me naked in her garden might have been a clue."

"After you were mauled by something, you mean."

He hesitated. Went to answer, visibly, then stopped.

Like he was thinking really hard about what to say. Like doing so was causing him some difficulty. And when he finally spoke, he was strangely halting about it. "No, no it was later. Kind of a while after I first . . . got turned. Because after I did I didn't really know. I didn't realize what had actually been done to me," he said, finally. And then it made sense. There was trauma from whatever had done this, obviously. Maybe even amnesia, if his blank, vaguely disturbed expression was anything to go by. But then it cleared, and he looked back at her. And he added, "I mean, nothing at all really happened to me for a long time. And then boom. My bare ass is in her face."

So instead of pressing him on it, she kept things as light as he'd tried to make them. "You're really not beating those sleeping-with-her allegations, Seth."

"Yeah, as soon as I said it like that, I regretted it." He shook his head ruefully. "I should have gone with the fact that my butt at the time was still 90 percent massively hairy, muscular werewolf."

"Honestly, I don't think that helps you."

"Probably not, no. But it's what happened."

"And then what? She told you all about what you had become?" she asked, and though she tried to stop herself from leaning forward, she couldn't. It was impossible. He had her completely hooked now. Just ravenous for what came next.

"She told me what she knew. The ways you can be turned—sometimes from a bite, sometimes from an ancient curse, sometimes a spell or a potion. Though all of them mean you basically end up the same way. In fact, the only difference is that you can get it reversed if it was magic done *to* you. But I don't think that really applies to me," he said, almost as if he were musing to himself. Then he seemed to refocus back on her. "Everything else is the same for all wolves, though. Heightened emotions make you transform, things don't always go back the way they should, it gives you weird instincts and enhanced reflexes and senses even when you're in human form."

"So, like, you chase sticks now and can hear dog whistles."

He shot her a withering look. "I can hear dog whistles. I do *not* chase sticks."

"You sure? Not even once, almost?"

"Never."

You little liar, she thought, automatically.

Because, yeah, maybe they weren't connected the way they once had been. But she could still read him, just as well as he could read her. She could hear what he really meant when he went too firm on a single word. And she could see it, too, in the way his head shake seemed so sure, but that same surety didn't quite reach his eyes. No—his eyes were all wince and *oh wow, this is not convincing at all*.

So she couldn't resist giving him a little push.

"I don't know. Maybe we should test it. Like you tested me," she said, and stood, searching for the exact thing she needed.

And there it was, in the corner of the porch. Just waiting for her to get it.

"But I didn't test you," he protested. "I just wanted to prove that I was right."

"Okay, so we'll call it that when I grab this fallen branch here."

"No, don't grab the fallen branch, Cassie. Cassie, just. Wait a second," he said, as she stooped to snag it. Then she strolled back to the porch steps, in time to watch him already struggling to resist. His hands were actually squeezing the chair's arms, hard enough that his knuckles had gone white. And the way his eyes were trained on the stick . . .

It was *wild*. It was ridiculous. It was impossible to stop herself.

"Or instead of waiting a second, I could say, ready, boy. Ready. *Fetch*," she said. Then she drew her arm back, and threw the branch as hard as she could. All the way across the garden and into the tree line.

And oh, the sound that came out of him when she did. It was like someone trying to say the word "fuck" around a mouthful of gravel. Somehow he managed to hiss the *f* at the start of it. But by the time he got to the *k* there was almost nothing left. The letter just sort of sputtered out, between incredibly gritted teeth.

And even when he managed to get his reaction mostly under control, he still couldn't say anything normally. He had to squeeze words out, around jaw muscles that seemed to have locked into place. "See," he said. "I totally did not do it."

"Yeah, but how hard are you clenching every muscle in your body right now?"

"I'm not clenching them. This is just me being my normal, non-clenched self."

"Seth, if this was normal people would worry you'd pooped your pants."

"Yeah, well, they wouldn't need to. Because I've just squeezed my butt cheeks together so hard I think they've fused into one smooth globe," he said, because of course he couldn't maintain the lie. He had to let it out, and he did. All in one big relieved and half-laughing breath that had her laughing too.

Though she felt bad afterward.

"Sorry, I shouldn't have made a joke of it," she said.

But he shook his head, waved her off. "No, no. I'm glad you did. It's good to find it funny with someone," he said, in this contented sort of way. Though what he was contented about only raised other questions. Ones that had kind of haunted her for a while now.

Who did he spend his time with?

"So there's no pack that you're a part of, then," she said, and he shook his head.

"There aren't really packs, the way you get in movies and stuff. No alphas, no betas, no omegas. Although you know it usually ends up with, like, werewolves hanging out with other werewolves, that kind of thing."

"But you don't want to do that either."

Again, she saw a hint of hesitation. Then, in a strangely steely voice, "No. No I don't."

"Because you hate what you are?"

"I don't hate what I am. I mean, I hate *some* things about it. The pain of turning, the inability to control it, the weird injuries. The fact that I searched for years for solutions to the pain and the inability to control it and the injuries, and all I had to show for it was getting scammed out of a thousand dollars by a vampire who sold me tomato juice sprinkled with glitter. And, of course, whatever your grandmother could cobble. But, I mean, you have to know that I find the rest of it completely cool and awesome."

"So tell me why no wolf buddies."

He looked away. "The other ones in this area—they're just. They're not . . . good people. They're not good wolves," he said, and seemed to hesitate again before continuing. As if what he had to say was difficult to express, or maybe something she wouldn't understand. "They do . . . mean things. And harass people. Or threaten to harass people."

He had to know, though, how easy it was for her to relate to something like that. "You mean like the Jerk Squad used to do to us," she said to help him. But that just seemed to make it worse. Now he was rubbing the back of his neck. He wouldn't meet her gaze.

"Kind of, yeah."

"So I should definitely avoid local wolves then."

"You won't have to. I made sure they won't ever come near you," he said, suddenly so grave about it that her heart tried to flutter.

Though she held it in check. She reminded herself of other similar promises he had made in the past. *I won't let those jerks hurt you again,* he'd whispered, once, as he applied a Band-Aid to some war wound they had given her. A book they had thrown, she thought it had been.

But whatever it was, it hadn't mattered.

He'd huddled with them and whispered about her barely a year later. Stopped talking when she got close. Carried on when she was far enough away. And things like that? Well, they cut worse than the corner of a Stephen King hardback.

They made her sink into silence.

And when she finally spoke, it wasn't to believe in his solemn vow to look after her.

"Do you still see those jerks?" she asked. Sure that he was going to shrug in response. More happy than she would have liked when he didn't.

"Never. I haven't since a little while after that night I did what I did," he said firmly enough that she could believe him. She could let that remove a weight from her mind. And even more so, when he continued. "All the things I thought they were, all the things I thought they might help me get—it was all just bullshit anyway. I mean currently, my main source of income is selling goblin droppings to weirdos. I live in my dad's old condemned hunting lodge. And I still feel like I have more now than I ever did when I hung out with them."

After which, she kind of had to fight not to thank him.

In fact, it was only the other wild things he had said that saved her.

"Dude, a second ago you told me you were happy being a werewolf. And now you're telling me that being a werewolf means you have to collect poop for a living and live in a place that has horrible dead-animal heads on every wall?" she asked. Convincingly, too, because he didn't even seem to notice how full of hearts her eyes were.

He just gave her a withering sort of look. "Okay, for starters, I took the dead-animal heads down and gave them funerals," he said. So now she was thinking of how much they had wanted to do that as kids. Though it was fine, because he didn't seem to clock that she was doing that, either. "And for seconds, I don't consider the poop thing a career. Being a supernatural being is what I wanted to be when I grew up, and that's what I am. And that is only reinforced by stuff like goblins giving me their weird butt marbles."

And now she *did* know what to say. She leaned forward and practically gasped it.

"Their poop comes out like *marbles*?"

"Swear to god."

"That's incredible."

"It is," he said. Then, pointedly, "*All* of this is. And that's why I'm okay, even if there are downsides like not having much money and living in a monument to my shitty father and sometimes wishing I had someone to be a dork with about it."

Like me, she thought. I'm *the dork*.

And just as she was mentally dismissing that idea, he went and proved it correct. "You know, you're asking me an awful lot about werewolves, and who I am as a person, and not a lot about witches. Or anything else, for that matter. I thought you'd super want to know about other stuff that you can hardly believe is real," he said.

Like he was just dying to get into it all with her.

And that was terrifying. But it was exciting at the same time.

Too exciting to refuse. "Well, you know," she said. "I was getting to it."

"You're scared to find out, aren't you?"

"Last night I slept in the closet so the boogeyman couldn't get me."

He let out a little half laugh. Spread his hands, like, *whoa there*. "Okay, then, you can rest easy. Because there is no boogeyman," he said. Though how reassuring that really was felt debatable at this point.

"Yeah, but there are goblins."

"Yep."

"And ghosts."

"As far as I know, yes."

She raised an eyebrow. "So you've never seen one."

"Apparently you can't see them. They just do stuff."

"And you think that's going to make me feel less terrified about this."

"I did, until the words came out of my mouth. Then I realized I'd just told you invisible dead people make possible unnamed horrors happen around you," he said with a wince.

Which of course only made things worse.

"You didn't use the word 'horrors' before."

"Yeah, but I know that's what you're thinking."

"And am I right to be doing so? Do they, like, thump up your stairs and then throw you around until you're dead? Or pull you into the television? Because I have to tell you, it's not like when *Poltergeist* came out. The TVs were *massive* then. Now they're so small and thin, it's gonna be hell getting me in there. They'll have to run me under a steamroller first."

He went to answer her then. But she could see he didn't know whether to laugh or be serious about it. His face was half amusement, half distress—so she felt it best to reassure him. "It's okay. I was trying to be funny," she said, and was glad she did.

He all but burst out with what he had clearly been holding back.

"All I can see behind my eyes is you being slipped into a television like a letter into a mailbox," he said, voice threaded with amusement. Before composing himself enough to actually answer. "Which they do not really do. They're mostly not violent, I think. They just move furniture around and try to communicate using whatever they can get their hands on."

"So, like, refrigerator magnets and Scrabble tiles."

"We have phones now, Cassie. They can type things."

"Right. Right right right. That makes sense. This all makes sense," she said firmly. While nodding. In a way she knew wasn't convincing in the slightest to him, even before he responded.

"I feel like you're just telling yourself that."

"Because I am. This is all unhinged."

"Yeah, I know. It gets easier though."

"It must. You're so matter of fact about it all."

"Well, when you see your millionth weird thing, it becomes a little less startling," he said, in a way she knew was meant to be reassuring. But honestly, all it did was kick up a hundred more questions.

"Right, but how *do* you see the weird things? Do they, like, just start appearing because you're a werewolf? They sense your werewolfiness and are just all, 'Hey, hello, here I am, the friendly pooping goblin that has been living under your stairs this whole time?'"

"Okay, I just gotta say goblins are not friendly."

"Noted. Good to know," she said, as she jotted that down.

Fast, because he was already on to the next thing.

"But other than that, yeah, you're pretty much right. Once you become a supernatural being or creature, and you accept that's what you are, you will see things humans either won't or can't. And that will either be because certain stuff will now just be visible to you, or other beings and creatures will drop their wards and hiding methods now that they know you're safe."

"So that's why things didn't appear to me before. Because I hadn't accepted it," she said, almost to herself. Though, bless him, he answered anyway.

"Pretty much, yeah. Though I think you were already starting to see, once you were back in this house. You must have been, because usually things don't go the way they did in the basement around humans. It can happen. I can turn—but it's never clear to them what's really going on. I just look sick and maybe stuff gets destroyed and then in the paper the next day someone says I must have hulked out on some new super drug. Or maybe they forget entirely, and blame massive, rabid raccoons," he said, after which she tried not to gape.

"So supernatural events can, like, warp someone's perception?"

"They can warp a human's perception, yeah. Anything else— cobble, witch, being, creature—no."

"And this isn't just because Hollow Brook is on some kind of

Stranger Things upside-down kind of deal, right? Like, it's every-where. All over the world. This whole time everything just living alongside humans and looking like something other than what it is?" she asked, then regretted putting it so ridiculously. She sounded ridiculous, she was sure.

But he just nodded. He *nodded*.

Jesus, she thought. *That is some next-level power.* Though she couldn't focus on that right at this moment. She had to focus on the other issue with all of this. "And now I'm going to get it full in the face. All the time. Constantly."

"Probably. Though you don't have to be scared. Most things aren't going to chase you up the stairs and then try to eat your foot," he said—a little sheepishly, it seemed to her. Like he thought that was the thing that had troubled her. Instead of everything else being the actual culprit.

"Okay. Okay, but could you maybe list the things that might possibly?"

"Well, I guess trolls can be kind of aggressive. But only if you cross the bridges they live under without their permission. They might, like, make you answer a riddle if they catch you. Oh, and I know gargoyles don't really like witches. I think at one point there was some kind of feud between them—but even that you don't really have to worry about. They mostly make themselves stone ornaments on buildings and then stay like that for centuries. They aren't likely to be around Hollow Brook," he explained, slow enough that she could scribble the main points down.

Might need to learn the answers to some riddles, she wrote. Then she jotted down the thing about gargoyles, with an instruc-tion to stay away from old, fancy buildings. In fact, she went fur-ther. She started noting down other questions she wanted to ask, and things she wanted to google, and had almost filled a page and started on a new one when she realized. . . .

He had gone quiet. Very quiet. Like in the middle of his ram-bling, he'd run up against something he thought it might be a bad idea to say. So she cocked an eyebrow at him. "Anything else?" she asked. And he quite obviously squirmed in response.

"Um, not that I can think of."

"Okay, but you're totally lying."

"Honestly, I'm not. That's truly it."

"If I get murdered by whatever it is, you're gonna really regret saying that."

That got him. She could see it did the second she said "murder." He sort of went all stiff, like he was thinking about such a thing happening. Before he finally shook his head, as if he'd reassured himself it wouldn't. Then went to reassure her about it, too. "Demons don't murder anyone. They just maybe try to drag you to hell," he said.

Only there was absolutely nothing reassuring about that *at all*.

"Yeah, but that's massively worse. You see that this is worse, right?"

"I do, but in my defense they almost never come to this plane of reality."

"Seth, I don't care how often they visit. I care that hell is apparently *real*."

"Well, yeah, of course it is. I mean, I don't think it's like in religious fables with the pits of fire and the red devil-looking things pricking your butt with pitchforks. But you know. It does exist in some form," he said. And had the nerve to do it in this scoffing, why on earth are you so shocked about it kind of way. As if *she* were being the weird one here.

When obviously it was him.

Did he not know it was him?

"Right," she said. "And you get what that means."

"Yes, sure, absolutely I do."

"But you're still calm about that."

"Well, why wouldn't I be?" he said, laughing.

As if he genuinely did not get it. He didn't know.

So she leaned forward. And made her voice firm and low. And spelled it out.

"Because this isn't just like some little vague idea of an afterlife, where maybe you move furniture around after you die. This means there is genuinely something beyond this plane of existence. That there is some sort of being or beings that created the universe, and they have a place, a good place, probably full of whatever the opposite of those demons you just mentioned are. And that we go to either there or the other one, or maybe something in between, when we die. All of which is dependent on whether or not we're assholes," she said, as clearly and simply and kindly as she could.

Then she watched his expression slide from breezy and half listening, to something that could only be described as horror. His eyes went so wide she could see the white all the way around the irises; his lips parted as if to say something, but no sound came out. And even though she could see he kind of wanted to stop staring at her, he didn't seem able to do it. Like he'd been frozen in place.

Which only meant one thing, of course.

"You've never actually thought about that at all, have you?" she said.

And to his credit, he managed to answer her. "No, but now to make up for it I'm super thinking about it a *lot*."

"Do you need *me* to hold *your* hair back this time?"

"It's more like—just don't let me land on my face if I pass out."

Funny, she thought. Only then she noticed: it seemed like he was actually going to do it. He appeared to be slowly curling over and sliding forward, in a way that made her jump up off the porch steps. "Okay. Okay, I can do that. I'll get you some cushions to fall into," she said, and started in the direction of the front door. But he stopped her. He held up a hand.

"No, don't leave me, don't leave me. I think it's already happening."

"Well, just breathe. Breathe and think about other things."

She mimed taking big breaths.

Took a step closer to him, in as comforting a way as she could.

It didn't help, however. Now he had his head in his hands.

"I can't," he moaned. "My brain is full of my own doom."

"No doom is going to happen."

"Of course it is. I'm a *jerk*."

"Come on, you're not a jerk, Seth."

"Oh my god, you think I'm so much of one you're lying about

thinking I am to make me feel better about the probability that I'm going to spend eternity having my butt pricked by devils," he said, and oh she wanted to laugh at that. She even suspected he was trying to be funny.

The thing was though: she also knew he meant it.

He really did think he was that horrible. Specifically, he thought he was that horrible because of what he'd done to *her*. And that kind of made it a lot less amusing, a lot more gut wrenching. She took a couple of more steps forward and almost reached for him— even though he'd stopped sliding out of the chair.

And she definitely had to come up with better reassurances.

"But you just said that devils didn't prick butts," she tried.

To absolutely no effect at all.

"Yeah, because I was trying to make *you* feel better. But I don't know how to make myself feel better. Myself doesn't listen to reason. It just wants to panic about being endlessly tormented by imps, for being horrible to my best friend," he said through his fingers.

So she tried again. Harder.

"I don't think imps are really going to happen over a high school prank."

"Don't downplay it. That's not going to make me not go to hell."

"Okay then, maybe I forgive you. Now you won't."

"Of course I still will—because we both know the forgiveness you just offered isn't the least bit real. It can't possibly be real, considering I haven't done one single damn thing to earn it."

He dropped his hands. And that was bad, because it meant he was staring directly at her now. He could see everything she was doing, and oh boy oh boy everything she was doing felt like *way* too much. She couldn't seem to breathe normally; she was pretty sure she'd started trembling.

And not just because he'd so casually accepted the concept of earning it.

No. It was because all she wanted to do was tell him he already had.

That it was enough to know he wanted to. To know he believed that his contrition alone didn't just grant it.

And the effort it took to not say any of that was *intense*. It felt like trying to hold back a truck with one hand. She was sweating within seconds, head swimming with all the reasons she should go ahead. But also all the reasons it would be a terrible idea. *The moment you let him in, he can hurt you again*, her mind whispered.

Which was true, she knew it was true.

But god, it tasted so bitter. And in the end, she had to say *something*.

"Maybe it's not me you have to earn it from. Maybe whatever is out there has to decide, and you know what? I'm willing to bet that they think you're doing okay. That you're doing a good job. You're trying, and I have to believe in a higher being or beings that is okay with trying," she said, wincing a little when her words got too close to her own feelings. But glad anyway that she'd done it. She'd told him he was doing good things in some sort of stitched-together way. Then got to tell him this too: "And not just for you. For me too. Because I know that I can't always do the right thing, exactly. Not even if I want to."

Though of course he couldn't quite get what she meant by the last part.

"You always do the right thing, Cassie," he said, soft as anything.

While she died a little inside.

"No I don't. Sometimes I just. I can't."

"But I bet you have your reasons."

"Maybe. And if I don't, well. Guess we're sitting next to each other in hell."

She laughed. Because she was joking, obviously. But when she looked at him, he wasn't rolling his eyes at the gag. Instead, his expression was all warmth and surprise and delight.

"That is weirdly the most comforting thing you've said so far," he said.

And oh, the *way* that made her *feel*. It lingered in her, all the way up to the moment when he had to go. Then once he had— once she'd shut the front door on his retreating back—she leaned against it, and said aloud the thing his happiness had made her want to say.

"God-like entity, if you are indeed out there please know that no matter what I say to him, I truly forgive Seth Stanley Brubaker. So whatever you do to me for keeping that fact from him, you shouldn't do it to him. I accept his sorry, wholeheartedly, and in that way spare him whatever hell there might be."

CHAPTER NINE

She didn't expect him to show up every day. But he did. At the same time each morning too. Like they had penciled it into planners neither of them actually owned. *Every morning at nine thirty, meet up with standard enemy to have an enormous existential crisis,* she thought.

Even though she wasn't sure he was her standard enemy anymore.

Or that what they were having was an existential crisis.

It felt more like being with the friend you longed to have back, sharing things you never believed could be possible. Though of course, that was overwhelming in its own way. Sometimes something he'd said would hit her, while she was in the middle of doing something mundane like mopping the floor. And it would feel as if her heart had snapped to a stop. Twice she had to clutch her chest to make sure it was still going.

But even after she was reassured, the sensation of everything being so heart-stopping wouldn't fade. Of course it wouldn't. The veil between worlds was really starting to peel back for her now—and oh, she could see why Seth didn't mind the downsides of any of it.

Why would he, when it was this awe-inspiring to behold?

She looked in the mirror in the morning, and somehow nothing about her was the same. One second she was as ordinary as could be. Then the next that glow he'd talked about would suddenly reveal itself in a faint shimmer of gold.

And that wasn't the only amazing sight.

There was also what she saw when she went outside in her socks to grab the paper. The low hang of a delicious fall mist—at first a soft gray, like always. Then suddenly it was shot through with other colors. Wild colors that never existed in the human world. There were slivers of deep blue, and streaks of purple, all swirling and seething and intertwining. *Beautiful*, it seemed to her, in a way that made her heart feel like it was bursting out of her chest.

And it did it even harder when she came back inside, and spoke into the empty air of the house. "Gram," she said. "Why didn't you tell me?" Then of course expected no answer at all.

But she got one. She got one. She saw the keys on her laptop being depressed all on their own just as she stepped toward it, open on the kitchen table, ready for her to send that email to Nancy to thank her for the fruit basket. And after a second of holding her breath, there it was. Her beloved Gram's words.

I was afraid for you, my darling.

Just one sentence, nothing further—as if that was all she could manage from whatever place lay beyond—but it was enough. It was everything. It was more than Cassie could have ever dreamed. The people you loved didn't simply *end*.

There was something more.

There was *loads* more. And all real in ways she could never in a million years have imagined. It seemed too fantastical to believe it. But even if she could have doubted, Seth was there to reinforce it all. She came out onto the front porch, the next morning, to find the paper, and found him already parking his butt in the lawn chair. And once she had settled onto the step, notebook in hand, he just launched right in.

"Okay, so the first thing you need to know about fairies is that they are super gross," he said, and she just couldn't help it. She snorted with incredulous laughter.

"No fucking way," she said. "Fairies are fancy."

But knew from his raised eyebrow that she was wrong.

"So you now believe there is a god of some kind, and that there are apartment-living vampires, and trolls under bridges who make you answer their riddles three, but fairies who fart on each other are where you draw the line," he said.

And yeah, there was no way around that.

"I didn't say I drew the line. I just—"

"You just what? Need proof? Okay. Get your jacket."

"No, honestly I don't need to see anything. You don't have to show me."

"But I want to show you. I think I *should* show you. I think being shown all this stuff is what you need right now," he said, and as he did he stood, as if to show how firmly he was resolved. Which probably would have worked better if the lawn chair hadn't gone with him.

He had to spend the next few seconds wrestling his wedged butt out of it.

While she made absolutely zero effort not to laugh.

"You know, you can hardly blame me for being slightly incredulous about any of this when I am currently watching a supposed werewolf being felled by garden furniture," she said—much to his obvious irritation. He tossed the chair aside and gave her a fuming sort of look, hands on his hips.

"Don't say 'supposed.' You've *seen* me."

"Yeah, but what I've seen is somewhat overridden by . . . this."

She waved her hand at everything. Much to his disgruntlement.

"You're such a liar," he said. "I know for a stone-cold fact that *this* only makes it more believable to you. That it only makes it feel more like reality. Because it's like you always said: in the movies everything is always cool. But real life? Real life is a *mess*."

So now of course she was trailing in his wake again. Stunned that he'd remembered, trapped by his logic. And unable to argue when he added, "Now are we going? I have more messy stuff to blow your mind with."

She simply grabbed her denim jacket, like he'd suggested, and found some fucking walking boots, because apparently he thought she needed them, and then followed him across her garden, in the direction of the woods.

Even though the woods now seemed a lot scarier than they had once seemed.

No no no, I'm not quite ready for whatever is in there, she thought.

But by that point it was too late. She couldn't back out now. She'd acted like she was barely rattled by any of it, instead of wildly vacillating between fear and awe. In fact, by the time they made it to the tree line, her heart was practically beating in her face. When he disappeared between two old oaks, she came incredibly close to telling him to stop. *I changed my mind. I don't need to see any further evidence that the world has cracked right open and spilled its sloppy supernatural guts,* she imagined herself saying. Yet somehow, instead, her feet kept walking one in front of the other. She followed him, right into it all.

And was immediately assailed by how mundane it had seemed, before.

And what it was like now.

Every tree looked about fifty feet taller and wider and more ancient than she remembered; the snap and crackle of the undergrowth beneath her feet felt much louder than it once had. And the shadows were definitely darker. Darker, and deeper, and hungrier. They seemed to seethe around her, in a way that almost looked normal when she stared at them directly.

But the second she turned away, she could sense them reaching out. She could feel them watching her, in this strangely familiar manner. Like they were just waiting for her to drop her guard, somehow, so they could get her.

And the worst part was, she couldn't even say for sure that her impression wasn't real.

There was now every possibility in the world that it was.

It made her almost stop, about half a mile in, and call out to Seth's plaid-shirt-clad back, *is there such a thing as a shadow creature?* Then only hesitated because she realized that he did not seem perturbed in the slightest. He just strolled along like nothing was going on. So probably nothing was. It was just that her mind had broken, a little bit.

And for very understandable reasons that just kept coming.

"Oh shit, I forgot that the bridge is out," he called back to her abruptly, as she emerged from the trees into the clearing where he stood. And then she saw the cliff edge—which lay about three feet beyond him—and below it the gorge and river, and on either side the battered remnants of the decades-old footbridge.

Like something out of Indiana fucking Jones.

"What do you mean, you *forgot*? When was the last time you were here?" she hissed, and to his credit he appeared to consider her question.

"I think it was, like, last Wednesday. Or maybe Tuesday. Wait, let me think."

"You don't have to think about what day it was; that's not the important part."

"Then what is?"

She flung a hand at it. "How you got across it, Seth. How you got across."

"Well, you know. I kind of. Just maybe sort of . . . jump."

She'd known it was coming. Of course she had—there was no other possible explanation for his blasé attitude toward the missing bridge. Yet still, that one word knocked the breath out of her. She found herself looking over the huge chasm in a wondering sort of way. Then up at him, with one eyebrow so far raised it felt like it had lifted off her forehead.

Though, naturally, he did not accept her incredulity.

"Don't look at me like that. I told you my reflexes are different now."

"Yeah, and I thought you meant you can catch a cup when I knock it off the table. I didn't think you meant that you are now Superman, and can apparently leap tall buildings in a single bound."

He gave her a withering look. "Okay, this is *hardly* leaping tall buildings."

"No, honestly it's better. That has gotta be a hundred feet wide."

"Gimme a break, it's not a *hundred*," he scoffed. But then she could see him eyeing it, and the scoff buckled into something that looked a lot more like the clenched-teeth emoji. "Give or take. Hardly anything."

"You're really thinking now about how nuts it is that you can do this, right?"

"Look, it just sounds different when somebody else freaks out about it."

"I'm not freaked out."

"You will be when I make my next suggestion," he said, and all she could think about was *The Incredibles*. *The Incredibles*, when Mr. Incredible hurls Mrs. Incredible hundreds of feet up into the air so she can catch their baby.

"I swear to god, Seth, if you say you want to throw me across."

"No, god no, I'm not going to *throw* you."

"Well, thank fuck for that."

"Yeah. I mean, I'm just gonna *carry* you."

He said it like a kindergarten teacher telling their class that they were super going to enjoy playing on the swings today. All bright and eager and peppy, she thought. Even though he had to know his idea was completely deranged.

And if he didn't, well. She was going to tell him.

"Oh fuck off. Fuck you. Fuck all of this. I'm out," she blew out.

She stormed back toward the trees, intent on doing just that.

But then he called after her. He called after her.

"See, I knew you were going to react like that," he said, and with just enough exasperation that she had no choice. She had to whirl around on him and throw her hands up. He was acting like *she* was being the unreasonable one.

"Of course I am. You just said you wanted to somehow lift me into your arms and then leap over a canyon. When, to be honest, even the idea of you doing it *without* someone my size clinging to you is, at best, preposterous," she snapped.

And waited for him to snap back.

Only somehow, it wasn't happening. He was just staring at her with this odd expression on his face. This kind of grave, tense sort of look that made no sense to her at all. And what he finally said didn't make it much clearer.

"Don't say 'someone my size' like that."

"Why in god's name not?"

"Because it makes me want to fight you in your own defense," he said. Fiercely too, like it really mattered to him. It really made sense—even though it didn't. He was being ridiculous.

"There's nothing to defend me about. It's not a crime to be fat. Despite how much you seemed to enjoy trying to make me think it was," she said. Though as soon as the words were out, she wanted to take them back. Because, okay, they were true. They were fair enough.

But oh god, his reaction on hearing them.

He jerked like she'd slapped him. Then his face just *dropped*. Every bit of animation went out of it; all the light seemed to leave his eyes. And it took him a long, long time to say anything. Like it was a real struggle to put how he felt into words.

"Is that why you think I did what I did? Because I enjoyed the idea of making you feel horrible about yourself? Cassie, that was not the reason. There *was* no reason. I told you, it was just an accident. It was all one big accident."

"Yeah, but you've never really explained how this supposed accident could have happened."

"Because I don't have a good explanation, Cass. I just have a bunch of excuses, like—I honestly thought you would do a great job icing that cake for the talent show. I wasn't just trying to prank you. I didn't even know it was supposed to be a prank, to be honest. Jason just bugged me into repeating words *he* was saying, into a microphone I didn't know was there, that was all. But of course none of that makes what I did okay. So it didn't seem like there was any point in telling you," he said, all in a tumbling rush. As if he thought the words were too silly to linger on.

Even though they weren't, at all.

They almost made her scream *why didn't you just say these things to me?*

But then she saw his face—the rueful look all over it. The way he was nodding to himself. And she knew he had the answer before it came. "But *now* I see the point," he said. "I get it, in a way I just didn't before. In a way I couldn't before, because the idea of you meaning that little to me is so impossible a concept that I had no clue it could ever be a thing that you believed."

She fell silent then.

She had to—there were no words left in her, after that. All she could do was stand there, watching him be all sheepish and ashamed and baffled by something lovely and heartbreaking. *He doesn't even understand that it is*, she thought, and felt her heart lurch in her chest. Tears stung her eyes; all she wanted to do was tell him what his words meant to her.

But luckily, she didn't have to. Because then he added, "So, you know, I get it if you don't trust me to do this—" And before he could go on, she cut in.

"I trust you to do this. I trust you, Seth," she said.

Then watched as his eyes drifted slowly closed. As he turned his head up to the sun, like he'd been in the dark so long he'd forgotten what it was like to feel light on his face.

And only after he'd drunk his fill of it did he walk over to her. Slowly, like she might startle and run away. Gaze always on hers even as he bent, and slid a hand behind her legs, and another around her back, and then just scooped her up. Right into his arms, so fast and so sure it kicked a little sound out of her. She had to grab him around his shoulders, fingers digging in—and tight enough that it felt like an apology was needed.

"Sorry," she said, as she went to pull back.

But he stopped her before she could.

"No, hold on," he told her. "Hold on tight."

Then he backed up, right to the tree line.

And he ran. Oh god, he *ran*. He went so fast that he turned the world around them into a blurry tunnel of green and white and blue and brown. Like they were in a car, she thought. Like they were on a train, watching the landscape streak past.

He has to be hitting seventy, she thought mindlessly.

So of course she knew what the jump was going to be like. She knew, she knew, she could sense it coming—and doubly so when he tensed and crouched. All she could think of was an enormous wild animal, roiling with muscle and sinew, ready to pounce.

Yet even so, she wasn't prepared for the punch of it.

The way the momentum flattened her against his chest, hard

enough that it hurt. How she wanted to scream and couldn't because all the oxygen in her had been knocked right out. And oh god, when she managed to open her eyes. When she glanced down, and saw the sheer amount of empty air they were briefly suspended over. The swirl of that river beneath them, so suddenly small.

It was impossible. It was unimaginable.

And then he hit the ground on the other side, and somehow things only got more mind-blowing. Because it didn't send them both careening into the trees, or cause a big jarring jolt to go through her body. Instead, he seemed to control the whole thing, utterly. He stayed on his feet, and sort of slid. She looked down and saw his sneakers forming two deep furrows in the dirt. And as he did all of this, he just put a hand to the back of her head. He laid his arm diagonally across her back, like a seatbelt. To absorb all the impact, she realized.

And it worked.

She felt almost nothing.

Apart from a great rush of awe, of course. Oh god, she had never felt so much awe in her life. Because holy fuck, he was really something that incredible. He could really do those things. He had supernatural powers, and they were amazing and beautiful, and oh she just couldn't stop herself from saying so, she just couldn't. Not after that.

It all came tumbling out, as he set her down on her feet.

"You are *truly* a magical thing," she gushed.

But here was the strangest part—she didn't even regret it.

Even though she'd sounded so breathless, even though her hands were somehow still on his chest as she spoke, even though she knew she was looking at him with wildly marveling eyes and a dizzy grin plastered over her face, she didn't. And after a moment, she processed why:

Because he had made it all right to.

Because he'd said those things and undone one of the barriers between them. And now he was looking down at her upturned face, the same way he'd looked up at the sky when she'd said she trusted him. All faintly disbelieving relief and surprised happiness.

Like he couldn't believe she would be so open and warm toward him.

And that just made her want to be more so. To be sweeter. To take his face in her hands and say that everything was okay now. So she did. She clasped him there like a long-lost friend, finally seeing someone after years apart. Not bothered about it, not worried, no fear of anything going wrong. Then she watched, delighted, as his expression mirrored hers. It lifted into something like awe, too. As if she had done something just as magical, somehow.

But it only lasted a second.

Then for some reason, it started to melt. It slid down, from sheer bliss to something else. Something that could only be described as panic. And it panicked her, for a moment. She almost pulled away, embarrassed.

But then he jerked back.

He groaned. He clutched his stomach.

And she knew. She knew.

"Oh my god, are you turning?" she gasped out.

Much to his distress. "I don't know. I don't know what's happening," he said. Like he didn't want to accept it, either. But was being forced to, anyway.

"What do you mean you don't know what's happening?"

"This feels new. It feels weird. I can't explain it."

Oh fuck, she thought. *The soup. The soup has done this.*

"I told you that you shouldn't drink anything I made," she groaned.

But he just shook his head in a vigorous, jittery sort of way. Like he could shake the wolf out of him, alongside the denial. Though, of course, it didn't have any effect at all. When he finally managed to answer her, she could see the razor edge of those teeth, glinting beneath the curve of his upper lip.

"I can feel your magic fighting it. But whatever this is, it's *strong.* It feels like it's burning me up from the inside out. Like some kind of fever," he gasped out, in between all the pacing and heavy breathing and her own futile attempts to calm him down.

"Then maybe do the things you said. The meditation-type stuff."

"I'm trying, I'm trying, I'm trying. It's going too fast."

"So look at me. Watch my hand."

She held it up as she spoke. Then she did something she remembered from TikTok: close your hand into a fist as you breathe in, slowly unfurl it as you breathe out. Only she forgot the instructions, and he couldn't concentrate anyway, and oh god she was about to get eaten in the woods by a werewolf.

"No no, that's making it worse. It's getting worse. It's getting really intense. Oh no, oh wow, that is so much heat. I think I just need to, like. Take my clothes off," he said. And it was funny, the way he did it. It was hilarious—like watching someone stoned out of their mind come up with an idea that only they thought was smart.

But the problem was: it was also him stripping off.

When she had barely been able to cope with his bare body, in the best of circumstances.

And that really put a dampener on her urge to laugh. "No no no, don't do that. Don't do that. I can just fan you," she found herself babbling as he attempted to get out of his shirt by pulling at the buttons with his teeth. But of course fanning him with her hands wasn't going to help him. And not just because it was incredibly silly.

Oh no—there was also the fact that it put her extremely close to him.

Her. A juicy whole person. Who he had almost eaten the last time.

"*Cassie, stay where you are,*" he snarled the second she got close. Those teeth flashing, eyes suddenly stark, bones pressed against his skin even more brutally than they had before. Then he skittered away from her, half on all fours and half upright. Like he was almost mostly animal.

Though, thankfully, he was still human enough to search his pockets. And he found what he was looking for: a bottle full of the stuff. Her medicine, she knew.

Only his hands were shaking too badly to unscrew the cap.

He kept trying and failing to get a grip. And then he got a grip, finally, and misjudged the pressure. The bottle somehow flew out of his hands, so close to the edge of the cliff it almost went over. He had to scramble to get it back, and even after he managed he still couldn't do it.

And now it was making him angry. It was making him frustrated, in a way that definitely wasn't helping the state he was in. As she watched, his plaid shirt—drawn taught over his hunched back—seemed to ripple right down the center. Like something was pushing against it from the inside, to the point of popping the seams.

So she took a deep bracing breath, and stepped closer. One tentative foot after the other, until finally she was next to him. Then she crouched, close enough that he definitely registered her presence. He grasped what she was doing, through the haze of whatever this was. And he tried to scrabble away from her immediately.

But he was too frantic, and too clumsy. He barely managed an inch.

She didn't even have to reach to take the bottle from him, and unscrew the cap, and offer it back. And doing it wasn't scary either—not even when he snarled and snatched it off her. Because, true, she saw those rows of extra teeth. Yes, the sound was deeper and more guttural than any human could have managed.

But he didn't do anything except drink, deeply.

And as he did, she got to see a million things she'd been too afraid to take in that night in the basement. Like the way his face had been completely reshaped. How those heavier bones turned his cheeks from sharp to something bulkier and more brutal.

Something that should have been ugly, really.

But somehow it wasn't ugly at all.

And the eyes were even less ugly than that. They flicked to her as he drank. Watchful, she thought. Like the beast inside him believed that she might steal the bottle back. Like it was guarding its prize. And oh, it was something to see. The flicker of light in them, dancing over the water-pale color. The black of his lashes and his brows, against that nothingness.

He was beautiful like this, she realized.

Even as her heart tried to shy away from that idea.

You've got to be a little bit afraid, and not just of the wolf, that wounded part of her tried to say. But even as it did, she was reaching forward. Because she'd seen something underneath his suddenly shaggier hair, and for just that one moment it overrode every bit of sense in her.

She had to look.

And when she did, there it was: the curve of his ear, now a sharp little point. *Like a Vulcan,* she thought, and couldn't help letting out a little sound of delight. Plus she knew she was grinning goofily. She couldn't seem to budge it from her face.

But it was fine, it was fine. Because he didn't seem to care.

Instead he turned his head into the fingertips that were still touching his hair. The way an animal did when it wanted to be stroked. And sure enough, the moment she pushed her hand into that thick fur, he rubbed into it. He made a sound, low down in his throat. A warm rumble, of the kind anyone would have called a purr.

Though god, it was amazing to know it was.

And so much so that it was almost a disappointment, after that, to see the wolf start to dissolve. Those bulky bones seemed to ripple, strangely, before they slowly sank back to something like normal size. Color bloomed in his eyes, like ink in water; those ears cracked and snapped and returned to a smooth curve.

Then last of all, he came back too.

He looked at her, half smiling through shuddery breaths. And so of course she saw the one thing that hadn't disappeared yet. Those teeth, those sharp and numerous teeth, still hanging on long past all the rest of the incredible changes.

Because they're stubborn, her mind suggested, and the strangest feeling followed. A kind of burr under her skin. A prickle, intense enough that she knew it wasn't anything ordinary. And sure enough, there were suddenly words in her mouth that she hadn't even known she wanted to say. But did say anyway. "Rub some on your gums," she instructed him.

Then in answer he reached up and gingerly touched his still

sharp teeth. Like he hadn't realized they were there until she suggested they were. "Starting to sense how to do this stuff, huh?" he
said with a kind of weary but amused knowing.

And though part of her wanted to say, "What do you mean?" or
deny what he was suggesting, she couldn't. He was right, and she
knew it. The prickly feeling had always been in some witchy corner
of her soul, telling her what to do. Telling her what was wrong and
how to fix it.

More than that, in fact. It made her shrug. "I already think I
know how to make the potion stronger," she said, and wasn't surprised when he went with what she was trying to discuss. Because
being recently wolfed didn't really matter to him.

This did. "Honestly, I don't think the strength of it is the whole
problem."

"Yeah, I don't either."

"So you can sense that, too."

She considered. Looked inward, searching for something that
would say what was true. And sure enough, there was the prickle
again. Quietly working away in the background of her mind.
Pushing some thoughts forward, others back.

Until finally the answer coalesced, the same way answers did
for things she knew well.

"I can feel that whatever happened might need something else
to make it better. It seems, I dunno. Keen-edged, like hunger or
something close to hunger. Kind of like you're missing a nutrient
out of your diet. An important one that you really need," she said,
then had to laugh. "Oh god, I sound nuts."

"You sound amazing. Like an honest-to-god witch."

"Well, you knew I was one. You're the one that believed."

"It's one thing to believe it, and another to see it start to happen."

"And yet you thought I was being so annoying with my incredulity."

She gave him a look, and he had the decency to nod his head
like *yeah, okay, okay, I get it*. And in between doing what she'd
suggested—rubbing the potion on his gums—he asked, "You still
want to go see, then? Wash some of that incredulity away?"

Though it surprised her how much she wanted to.

The way excitement sprang up in her, where trepidation had been.

"Only if you're okay," she said. But he didn't even hesitate.

"I am. It's gone. Heck, you probably *know* it's gone."

She paused, and thought. Did that inward look again.

Then sure enough: "Fuck. I do. Wow, I really do. This is so weird."

Which got a laugh out of him. A carefree laugh, of the sort that confirmed she was right. This was the way things were now. Witch senses. Sudden werewolves. And the thing he said as he stood and helped her up.

"And it's about to get weirder. Come on, let's go find a fairy orgy."

CHAPTER TEN

She didn't know what to expect when they finally got to the supposed site of fairy shenanigans. But it wasn't Seth telling her that they had to crawl across the ground from that point on. "They don't like humans or any being or creature that's humanlike," he said before she could ask. Then just as she was about to wonder aloud if they were the former or the latter, and whether that felt weird to him, he came out with something even more alarming.

"Okay, you see that shimmer? When we go through it, hold your breath."

He pointed, and sure enough she saw something in the air suspended between two trees. A kind of curtain, it looked like. Or a veil. Only not as obvious as those things would be. When she turned her head just slightly, it seemed to disappear. Then she turned her head back again, and there it was. A gauzy glitter, painted on nothingness. Unsettling, but sort of lovely.

"What is that?" she whispered. Then had no idea why she was already keeping quiet. It just felt like a hushed sort of moment, she supposed. And anyway, he whispered back.

"It's how they hide."

"So they actually use something."

"They kind of have to. I mean, people would trample them."

She pictured it when he said it. A bunch of hikers, unwittingly stamping on a twee little fairy village. Though if what he had said was true, the village probably wasn't that twee. Or even a village. It was something else. Something she had a lot of questions about.

"But the veil means people can't trample them somehow?"

"It makes people swerve around them."

"And it does something different to us."

The nonhumans, she thought. And this time her inward shiver was less pronounced. Like it was starting to sink in. It was starting to be a thing she could accept.

In part, she thought, because of Seth's eminently matter-of-fact and kind of goofy way of describing things. "Yeah. We see it," he said. "We can go through it. But if we breathe it in, it will absolutely wreck us. It will just make you feel like the most drunk you've ever been in your life. You won't even be able to stand up straight or remember what you did."

Though of course she knew why he was describing it that way.

She felt it immediately, and not with her witch senses. With her Seth senses.

"And did someone tell you that before you ever tried going through, or did you find out the hard way?" she asked, one eyebrow raised. And in response he grimaced and hung his head.

"Yeah, I found that one out the hard way."

"Woke up hungover and missing one shoe, huh."

"Only because the fairies stole it. Some of them *live* in it now," he said, almost marveling.

It was okay though. She understood why the marveling was happening.

"Holy crap, you weren't kidding about them being menaces."

"Oh, you don't even know the half it. Sometimes they get inside your walls."

"You mean like . . . you mean like *The Borrowers*?"

"Yeah, but if *The Borrowers* ate your cat," he said. Then before she could dig deeper into that little nightmare, he added, "Now stay low." And just started crawling forward. As if she were going to be able to follow him, with the concept of cat-eating bug-sized people in her head.

"Seth, wait," she hissed after him. But he was already halfway through the veil and still going. And once he was through she would be out here, in the woods, amongst the shadow people.

So she shuffled forward, reluctantly, through the mossy undergrowth. Clothes snagging on twigs and brambles, dirt getting just about everywhere, breath held before she even reached the shimmering thing. Then she got to it and realized:

It wasn't just the fairies making her nervous.

It was this curtain of colors. The one that she could now feel buzzing and humming faintly against her face, her hands. That she could feel buzzing and humming *inside her body*—as if some part of *it* resonated in some part of *her*.

Someone like me made this, she found herself thinking.

And ultimately it was this idea that made her plunge forward.

Quickly, so she didn't have time to think about it too much.

Though she kept her eyes closed as she did. And she didn't open them, even after making it through. She just lay there on what felt like a bed of yet more twigs and dirt, taking tiny sips of probably alcoholic air. Looking at nothing, taking in nothing, not even sure if Seth was with her still.

Until she felt his hand on her shoulder.

His breath against the side of her face. A hushed whisper: *Hey, you can look now.* So she did. She let her eyes open a tiny bit. Just enough, she felt, to only see the smallest part of whatever horrors they were perpetrating.

And saw instead what seemed like the whole universe.

Just there, laid out in miniature, in a bowl of ivy and brambles.

Clear as day, thanks to the glow cast over the whole scene. Then she realized with a jolt: it wasn't just a glow. It was their *moon.* They had made an actual moon, somehow, in a sky as vast to them as hers was to her. Then somehow, they had dotted that sky with stars. Every single one a different color, and of a sort she could never have imagined. Even after what Seth had said, even after everything she'd thought, pastels were the thing that came to mind.

But this wasn't pastels. It was like the veil. It was almost holographic.

She thought of kaleidoscopes, of mirror balls. And even more so when her eyes adjusted enough that she could see them.

Because they weren't easy to glimpse. They were fast—just flickers of movement at first. And so small she honestly mistook them for motes of dust. But then one of them flitted directly into the beam of that great light, and turned just so, and oh *god* it stole her breath. It stole her words. She wanted to say something to Seth—to grab him and say "Oh my goodness oh my goodness."

But she couldn't. It was too much.

It was a whole tiny person.

She could see it had a perfectly formed, pretty little face, skin a deep brown, leaves woven between locks of curled hair. Clothes made out of bark, tiny hands and tiny feet, and when she squinted, oh yes, there it was. A set of wings, fine as gossamer, iridescent as oil in water, and fluttering so fast she could hardly make them out. She had to wait until one landed on what looked like an upturned can of beans, before it really became clear.

Then of course it was the can of beans that had her attention.

The way they'd carved windows into it. And used cobwebs instead of glass.

Two of them emerged from a door made out of a bottle cap, as she watched.

And there was more, there was more. There were streets lined with pencil cases, and makeup palettes turned into hot tubs. Old Barbie cars full of seething little bodies of all shapes and size; bottles filled with fairies licking the obviously intoxicating insides.

And all of it, always, surrounded by magic.

Suffused with it, in a way she could feel even more strongly than she had with the veil.

This didn't just hum inside her. It *sang*, down deep in her bones. She saw one of them—naked and plump and pink and streaked with mud—hurl a bomb of stuff that sparkled when it exploded, right in the face of the fairy no doubt responsible for the filthy state it was in. And when it did, two things happened:

Said fairy immediately turned into a tiny frog.

And Cassie felt her entire body vibrate.

A great burst of words went through her head: *I can do that, I can transmogrify, I just need caterpillar cocoons and the reflection of starlight in a puddle and walnut shells, lots of walnut shells crushed into a fine powder.*

And oh god, it was just. It was so overwhelming.

It was everything she'd ever hoped was waiting for her, just beyond the reach of reality. Which was probably why, when Seth turned to her, he said, "See, I told you they were a completely awful, terrible nightma—Oh my *god*, are you *crying*?"

And she couldn't say anything about it.

He was absolutely right. Tears rolled down her cheeks.

"Of course I'm crying. It's all so beautiful."

"Cassie, one of them is eating its own toenails."

"Honestly, stuff like that only makes it more amazing. It makes it more real. They are real beings, they really exist, even though they're tiny and they have wings and they light their world with a moon they made up," she said, and wanted to say more too. But she had to stop for a moment, because she was getting choked up. And when she finally managed to continue, she could only ask, "I mean, can't you see how wondrous this is? How amazing? How beautiful?"

Then felt incredibly silly about it.

Because he didn't answer right away. He was silent for quite a while. And then he gave her a single, solitary, sad-sounding *yes*— but when she turned to look at him, he wasn't even looking at this amazing, beautiful thing. He was looking at her. He was staring at her, only her.

Much to her exasperation. "You're not even paying attention to them," she chided.

And in response he sort of jerked. He seemed flustered. Like he'd been caught red-handed cheating on a test and couldn't think of a good way out of it. He just looked at the fairy world spread before them—as if to make up for not listening or not seeing what she saw.

Though all it did was make her feel strangely awkward.

And the awkwardness increased when she stared out at the scene in front of them, and realized what was going on a few inches from their faces. A bunch of fairies, romping away together in a big heap of tangled limbs. Everything all messy and sticky and greedy, in a way that *should* have been funny. It *should* have been ridiculous.

But instead, she found herself thinking of that time they had watched *Dracula* together.

Sometime after the thing at the quarry, she thought it must have been, because she remembered she hadn't wanted to wear a big T-shirt and nothing else, like usual. She had gotten under the comforter in her closet with full pajamas on. And he hadn't even taken off his jeans.

Though it hadn't mattered.

Everything had still felt so incredibly naked. As if every accidental touch dissolved the clothes between them. His forearm brushed against hers under the comforter, and she had thought of the thick hair he had there now, the muscles burgeoning farther up. And when their thighs had accidentally kissed, he'd muttered a word under his breath.

Shush, she'd wanted to believe it was. *So soft*, she knew it had been.

Because it had made her blush. It had made her go over and over it in her head, wondering if he'd meant it in the good way. If he liked how plush she was, in a manner she had struggled to imagine anyone doing, at the time.

In fact, she still struggled now when it came to Seth. She looked back at that heated moment through a kind of fog. All of it blurred by memories, of him hanging out with those jackasses. Of things he said he hadn't meant to say, but still had anyway.

And it made it hard to see. To understand what had happened, as that little closet grew hotter and hotter, and the film grew more and more seductive, until finally they sat side by side, their eyes locked to the screen, both of them breathing too quick and sweating too much.

Silent, she remembered.

Until finally he'd said, in a strangled whisper, "I don't think we should watch anymore. It's making me want to . . . you know." And of course, she'd pretended she hadn't known what *you know* meant. But she had, and she knew even harder here, now, looking back on it through adult eyes.

If I'd said go ahead, what would we have done, she found herself thinking. Then even more intensely: *What would we do now, in the same position?* Because it felt like they were—she couldn't deny it. They were trying not to watch something ridiculously steamy, while sitting far too close together.

Just like they had then.

In fact, this was worse, because they weren't even sitting. They were lying down. And neither of them had thought a thing about where they'd put their limbs, after they'd messily crawled through the veil. Which meant their thighs weren't just accidentally touching. They were practically tangled with each other. She could feel the heavy weight of one of his over hers. His hips against what felt like her waist.

And then lastly, oh lastly.

His hand was on her back.

She could feel it, as burning hot now as it had seemed cool and insignificant before. It was searing through her sweater. In a second it was going to leave a brand, in the exact shape of his too firmly pressing palm.

Then that palm abruptly slid down, and god, god.

He wasn't going to actually do that, was he? He wasn't going to touch her *there*?

He hates me there, she told herself. Only, telling herself that wasn't working as well as it always had in the past. How could it, when he'd said what he'd said just before he'd carried her over the gorge? *He told you he didn't mean the insult*, her brain rambled. *He told you he was just repeating what Jason said.*

And even though that likely meant nothing at all, even though it didn't mean he found her butt suddenly sexy, she held her breath. As if she actually wanted him to. As if she liked the idea of him liking it. As if she had just been waiting around all this time, mooning over the idea of the Great Seth Brubaker being all gone over her ass.

Which was not the case, at all.

Yet somehow, it didn't feel like terror or disgust over him doing it, either. It was some jumbled, messy thing in between. Thick with heat, but sharp with fear and confusion. And each of those feelings seemed to feed on the other, until she could hardly stand it any longer. She thought she might go mad, she might do something completely terrible, if this lasted one second more.

So it was really a relief when reality brought her back to her senses.

Or not *reality*, exactly.

More like a screech, of a sort her human ears had never heard before—tiny and thin, yet somehow painfully shrill at the same time. And when it came, his hand snapped away from her lower back. Like it had never been there. Like she'd just imagined it all, the same way she'd probably imagined it all back then, too, while watching *Dracula* in her closet.

Things just aren't like that between us, she told herself.

And that put her mind straight.

Which was good, because that shriek? It meant that they had been spotted. One of them had seen, and now it was shrieking its little lungs out. It was shouting so loud, in fact, she could actually make out the words after a second. *Big ones, big ones are here, big ones have invaded*, it cried in a weird language that she could somehow understand, anyway.

Then in response, a bunch of them immediately swarmed up to where this little snitch sat, on the tip of a leaf. Most of them clearly furious, some of them already carrying tiny weapons, others wearing bits and bobs as armor. Like they had a little defense force, she thought, and tried not to marvel over it all.

Because right now, she really needed her wits about her.

Seth was already getting up. And he was dragging her with him.

"Okay, we have to run," he said. "We have to run this instant."

Then suddenly they were barreling through the undergrowth in what felt like the wrong direction, with a fairy army hot on their heels. And it *was* hot and it *was* heels. She could really hear the fairies now, loud and clear. *I claim their butt cheeks for my next batch of bottom soup*, one of them yelled. *Get his shoes*, another cried. Then ridiculously, inexplicably: *Dave needs a new house.*

So of course all she could think was: *One of them is called* Dave?

As she tried to avoid crashing into a tree.

In fact, she only managed because Seth grabbed her. He got hold of her arm and hauled her left, just as she tried to go right. And when she almost stumbled into a hole covered with rotten wood, he did something even wilder. He somehow grabbed her around the waist, a millisecond before she went in, and lifted her over it.

All in one smooth motion.

Like he didn't just have feet that were on wheels.

Every part of him was. Right down to his senses.

"Duck," he said, and she did, narrowly avoiding a branch that would have whacked her in the face. Then just before they reached the veil, he called out a warning. But it was okay, it was fine, because that sense warned her first. She felt it ring through her, loud as a gunshot.

Then she held her breath. She plunged through.

She made it to the other side, and safety.

And was surprised to find it was actually safety, too. The fairy armed forces hadn't come through. It was just them, breathing hard, half terrified, half laughing. His hands on his knees, hers on her hips. Everything as it had been before.

Yet not the least bit the same at all.

Oh, she knew it wasn't the same. She could feel it clearly in everything they did, from that point on. It was in the easy way they walked back to the gorge together, and jumped over. And in the look on his face, when she told him she'd make more potion for him. And how, as she walked up the steps to her house, he briefly caught her hand and clasped it.

Like it was nothing now, to touch her.

Then just as she was feeling overwhelmed by *that* gesture, he spoke. He said, "Oh wait, I almost forgot. I got this for you." And he took a book from his back pocket. A guide of some sort: *Taking Your First Steps into Accidental Witchery.*

Nothing, really, on the surface.

But underneath, she knew what it meant.

She felt it immediately, keenly: the deal didn't matter to him.

He didn't care if he was no longer the only source of help to her, and so might possibly lose what she did for him. All that mattered was that he had something she needed—and oh that thought made her heart ache. It made her almost burst with the need to say, *I would do the same thing for you*.

But by the time she looked up, he had gone.

CHAPTER ELEVEN

She knew exactly what she was going to do the second she got in the house: use everything she had so far learned, and this book, to work out how to prepare awesome potions. And then make Seth an extra-strength, super-long-lasting potion that communicated to him exactly what his gift of the book had communicated to her. That told him she would do what would help him, even if it meant she got nothing from him ever again.

I won't let you think that's all this means to me, she thought.

Then started in on the book right there, while standing in the hallway with her jacket still on and mud and twigs in her hair.

She examined the cover first—which was just as bonkers as the title suggested. The background was a sickly cream color, with a swirling pink title at the top, and the strangest-looking illustration in the middle. A smiling moon, hugging a fabulously overdone purple flower, above a name—Dr. Annie Taylor Watts—that felt strangely but powerfully familiar.

Though if she was being honest, everything about the cover gave her that same feeling.

But it was only when she opened the book that she realized why. Because there was a tasteful black-and-white photo on the inside flap. And in it, Dr. Watts seemed to be wearing an enormous pair of glasses, and a turtleneck, and a big, floppy wig of the sort Cassie remembered from so many sick days and summers spent watching daytime TV.

She looks like Sally Jessy Raphael, she thought.

Then knew what the book reminded her of:

A self-help book from 1987 about exploring your inner self.

She'd seen a million of them on her mother's nightstand over the years. And this one would have fit right in. It had the right look, the right author, and if the contents page was anything to go by, the same tone and style and way of describing things.

She spotted chapter headings like "Accessing Your Inner Witch" and "Maximizing Spell Potential" and "Maintaining Healthy Magic Boundaries."

And when she flipped to page one, there was more of the same.

"When your magical inner being first manifests, you may find dealing with this blossoming a little difficult," Watts had written, and all Cassie could think about was the textbook people had been given in school, to inform them about their first periods. She wanted to race to the end of that chapter—"So You Think You Have Become a Witch"—and make sure that she wasn't about to start bleeding out of another orifice once a month.

Which thankfully didn't seem to be the case.

But apparently, according to Watts, there were other symptoms of being a witch. "The main indicators of your possible emergence," she had written, "are as follows." And below that appeared an actual list. An incredible, ridiculous, nightmarish list that included things like:

* Excessive night sweats.
* Urge to wear hats massively increased.
* Chances of cats adopting you very high.
* People stop liking you.
* People like you to a disturbing degree.
* You may only want to eat potatoes.

No real explanation was given for why any of this might happen, however. And, okay, Cassie could guess the reason for some of them. They were practically witch clichés that Watts most likely just thought would sound right.

But then there was the thing about potatoes. Why on earth would she only want potatoes?

And that wasn't even the weirdest one. The last on the list read simply, "Trolls." Which left Cassie wondering what these trolls might be about to do. Did witches attract them? Was she likely to wake up one morning and find a great swarm of them scaling the front wall of the house? Or was she now mortal enemies with troll kind?

She didn't know. And Watts didn't say.

But she *did* say that the best way to avoid causing too much destruction was, of course, to try exercise: "A brisk constitutional, taken twice daily, has been known to decrease the instances of accidental melting of household appliances and unfortunate family members threefold," Watts had written. As if the disintegration of your mom was just a slight aberration in an otherwise completely normal existence. And if you felt like it wasn't, well.

Walking would really help with that.

Yet, somehow, Cassie still couldn't stop reading.

She sat on the stairs, devouring every word. And at least some of the words were as useful as she had imagined when Seth first handed the book to her. There was stuff in there about how to gather moonlight (coat the inside of a lidded Tupperware container with witch saliva, then poke a hole in the top and cover the hole with plastic wrap), how to keep spiders from your house forever (stash goblin whiskers beneath the floorboards), how to obtain goblin whiskers (leave a tomato out on a silver plate on the fourth of any month).

Plus at the end of the book was a straightforward glossary, which plainly explained what certain terms meant. "Knack," for example, was used to describe what exactly manifested a witch's powers. And apparently it could be done in all sorts of strange ways.

Baking and cooking were of course familiar to Cassie. But other possibilities ranged all the way from writing or painting or dancing, to weird things like data processing and wall building and wearing things. You put your shoes on just a little bit wrongly and there it was. You were a shoe witch. Forever searching for just the right sandal to hang on one of your ears, in order to make time turn backward or make night into day.

All of which, according to Watts, were absolutely feasible.

"Anything is possible," read the final sentence of one chapter.

Though Cassie couldn't really be sure if that was just yet more self-help, can-do-attitude speak, or an actual fact. All she knew for sure was how she felt when she read the book:

Both disturbed and thrilled at the same time.

And even more so when she read something similar to what Seth had said: "Your spells or potions or curses will be at their strongest when your Knack and your desire and your instincts all converge. If one fights the other, the magic will not be as strong or as accurate as you might wish it to be. Therefore, it's very important to not fret if conventional wisdom tells you that what you are creating is wrong. Feelings, a tingle inside, a strong sense of self—all will better inform you which is the correct path to take," she read, and her heart pounded harder and harder as she did.

Because a tingle was exactly what she had been feeling.

Plus, she knew for a fact that desire was making it stronger. Even as she devoured the book, she could feel that need to make the potion for Seth. And that need was sharpening every idea and instinct in her head. It made them crystal clear and almost bright—until she stood, and went to the kitchen, and started rifling through her grandmother's recipe journals again.

Then when she found the recipe for Feel Better Soup, she grabbed a blank journal. And she opened it to the first page, smoothed it out on her knee, and started writing. No rational thinking about it, no troubled doubts allowed in, just whatever came to mind. "Extra-Strength Soup," she wrote at the top, under-lining it firmly.

But god it was a shock, when everything just flowed.

The soup needed fewer garlic bulbs. But more chili. And beans had been a substitute for something stranger. Something that her mind hadn't let her imagine. Something like a supernat-ural caterpillar, she felt, then flicked to the "Creature" heading in the glossary.

And there it was:

"Hogarth," she read. "Often found in fairy hollows, commonly used by such creatures as a method of transportation. Skins may be obtained by leaving out a thimble of honey next to any tree of a good nature." Then all she had to do was find a thimble in her Gram's sewing kit, and grab an old, sticky jar of Goodwin's, and head outside. And she did, without even thinking about things like *It's pitch-dark outside by now,* or *A second ago you were afraid of shadows.*

All that mattered was seeing if her insect-attraction method worked.

Even though it *was* actually scary outside.

She had the strangest feeling when she stepped out the door— like in the woods with Seth, when she'd thought something was watching her. Only this time, that feeling wasn't just familiar. She knew *why* she had it. She remembered how she and Seth had stopped using the stairs by the science wing in high school, where it was too easy for the Jerks to see them coming, but impossible for them to know the Jerks were there.

Ambush Alley, Seth had called it.

And that was what it had felt like earlier that day in the woods.

And what it felt like now. It made her stop and scan all around the house, straining her eyes to see if she could make out one of those assholes. Even though it wasn't going to be any of them, of course it wasn't. They were probably off having football careers, or busy fucking up Wall Street. They hadn't stayed around to live in what they had always thought of as a loser town.

So she took a bracing breath. And plunged across the dew-dipped grass.

Only to discover that she'd been so rushed and so distracted that she hadn't put on shoes. She was just in her goddamn socks. By the time she got to the tree line she was soaked all the way up to her ankles, and so cold her teeth were chattering. She could hear them going and going, as she assessed the trees for something as seemingly daft as a good-natured one.

Does it give you a hearty hello, the rational part of her brain tried to sneer, as she stood there in her soggy socks, shivering, staring dumbly at the four or five live oaks that stood between her garden and the woods beyond. Then just as she was starting to think her rational side had a point in mocking her, one of the trees groaned. It *groaned*.

And it seemed . . .

To almost . . .

Lean toward her. Like it really was greeting her somehow.

Then, even wilder, she felt something in her head. A sort of voice, a kind of word, something that seemed like speech but wasn't, and had to be translated somehow before she could understand it. *Same as you did automatically with the fairies*, she thought.

And she knew all at once what she was hearing: the tree's name.

A big, blank space of weird symbols, it sounded like, and the closest human-language approximation she could get was *Ivor*. So she said it aloud, in greeting, and watched the tree shimmy its remaining leaves in response. Before it reached a branch down, pointing to where she should put the thimble full of honey.

All of which was overwhelming enough.

But then she did it, and the creature actually appeared. And oh, she didn't even know what to think of it. What to do with the sight of a caterpillar, with a fairy riding on its back. The former barely the size of a thumb, crawling slowly over tree roots and other rubble. The latter urging it on, proud and pleased as punch about it.

And very visibly one of the same fairies from earlier.

"Sorry about the intrusion," she managed to squeak out, once she had gotten hold of her senses. But the fairy didn't seem to care. It said something like *well, if we knew you were going to bring honey for our horses, we wouldn't have chased you*. Then it made the Hogarth drop something that looked very much like the skin she needed, and the fairy attached the thimble to the Hogarth's saddle, and both of them disappeared.

Leaving Cassie completely buzzed about two things:

Fairy forgiveness, and the Hogarth skin she held in her hands.

Plus a third thing that made a little less sense. *It had a tiny saddle*, her brain kept gasping, for some unaccountable reason. But by the time she returned to the kitchen, it was cooperating again. It told her to grind the surprisingly substantial shells using a pestle and mortar, before she'd even taken off her soaked socks.

Though she barely noticed her wet feet anyway.

She was too busy building up a sweat, creating what looked like a bowl full of sparkly, incredibly thick peanut butter. And then she lit the ancient burner under her Gram's big old pot, and dumped in the stuff, and poured in some water.

And not from the tap.

From the barrel outside.

Because before, she'd been afraid that rainwater in a potion might poison someone.

But now she knew it wouldn't. It wouldn't hurt anyone, and it definitely wouldn't hurt Seth. *Nothing can*, she thought absently, as the brew began to bubble and the kitchen filled with a too-thick, strange-smelling steam.

Like smoke, but less acrid.

Spicy, she wanted to call it. But that wasn't it either. In truth, it was more a feeling than a smell. *Like lying under a blanket on the couch as Gram brings me ginger ale.* And just as she had this thought, she tossed in five whole garlic bulbs all at once. And got the exact reaction she'd expected. In fact, she jumped back the instant she did it, and sure enough: the pot rattled. It shook.

Then it let out an almighty *POP*. As if she had stuffed several balloons in there.

Funny, she thought. But amusement wasn't what she felt. No, what she felt was satisfaction, unmistakably satisfaction. And it was so strong, she didn't really know what to do with it all. It filled her body all the way up, until it simply had to overflow.

So it wasn't a surprise when tears spilled down her cheeks. When she had to sit down. When she had to think over all the fears she had ever had, and all the ways they were no longer true.

"I think I'm okay to do this now, Gram," she said to the spirit that was sometimes there, and sometimes not. And in reply that spirit brushed a hand over her hair, gentle but unmistakable.

I think you are too.

CHAPTER TWELVE

She didn't want to go into town while in the middle of an enormous burst of personal growth, and acceptance of her hidden skills, and the new awareness that there were racing snails and talking trees and ghostly grandmothers around. But the simple truth was: she didn't have half the things she needed to make the other potions she wanted to. She didn't even have the right kind of container for the salve the Extra-Strength Soup had turned into.

It needs a small jar with a screw-top lid, that little witch voice inside her said.

And it wasn't just that she wanted to listen to the voice.

She was starting to *like* that voice. So instead of doing anything sensible, like sleeping for three days, she grabbed her jacket, and remembered her shoes, and wheeled her bike down off the porch. Then sped off into the misty, slightly pink-tinged early morning, in a much more sprightly manner than she had any right to.

This is going to hit me hard later, she thought as she weaved around the puddles that pocked the lane into town. Though as soon as she did, her head filled with a dozen more ingredients she needed to make the perfect Stay Awake Draught. She even thought a Sleep Substitute type of thing might be possible—something that didn't just keep you going, but replenished the body as if it had in fact slept. And had to brake because of it, in the middle of the golden-leaf-littered road, and get out her journal, and scribble feverishly for twenty minutes.

By the time she arrived in town, it was practically a normal time to be there. Signs adorned with Halloween decorations and promises of pumpkin spice were being set out. Awnings were being unfurled, bright in the light drizzle that fell. And smells weaved their way down the street.

All of it the same as it had been before.

Except for one difference.

One shocking difference, that nearly made her careen into the nearest mailbox. She had to brake so hard she almost went over the handlebars. Then couldn't do anything but sit there on her bike seat, eyes as big as moons, mouth hanging open.

Because there, across the street, was a supernatural creature of some kind.

Not even of *some* kind—it was completely recognizable to her. It had the legs of a human, clad in what looked like a pair of jeans. But above the waist it was a bull. A great big bull, with a snout and enormous curling horns and everything. A Minotaur, she knew. Just standing in front of the movie theatre, examining one of the posters.

Like that was normal. Like it was considering going to see the latest Marvel movie.

How on earth do people not see something that enormous, she wondered.

Though size didn't really seem to be the issue. There were two other normal-sized beings down the street—one with a set of leathery wings, and the other without a face. But nobody reacted like that was the case. She saw the old dude who ran the hat store lift a hand in greeting, to the one with a blank swirl instead of an expression. Then Blank Swirl lifted a hand back.

And Blank Swirl was not alone in being acknowledged. There was what looked like a goblin—green-faced, vaguely moist—carrying a donut and a coffee in its hands. Which meant that somebody at the donut place must have served it. Somebody must have taken whatever weird money it offered, then handed over a strawberry glazed.

Though why this was the fact that unglued her mind she had no idea. It felt more like the whole idea of a goblin having a morning latte should've been the thing to do it. Or the hand wave between

Blank Swirl and the hat-store owner. Or even the very existence of Minotaurs.

Hell, *especially* the very existence of Minotaurs.

Because Seth had definitely not said anything about them. And she didn't remember seeing them mentioned in the guidebook either. She pulled it out of the bike basket, propped it up on the handlebars, and flipped to the glossary to make sure. Then was startled to see them listed. As if she'd just missed them there.

Even though she knew for a fact she hadn't.

She would have absolutely noticed this listing in the book—mostly because it opened up a whole other avenue in her head. Now, suddenly, she had to add *mythological* beings alongside the more traditionally *supernatural* sorts of things and the whole *religious* aspect.

So what exactly did this mean?

If the book didn't describe everything, did that suggest it didn't always know? Did it show the same things to everyone who read it? Or did certain things only exist inside its pages if it realized you believed in them? *Like in that weird movie Seth found on Netflix about the Vikings,* she thought, *when one of them doesn't think Valhalla is real, and so it isn't to him.*

Though of course she couldn't be sure.

Until she glanced down at the book again. And there it was, right by her thumb at the bottom of the glossary page. "Yep, you're absolutely correct, that is exactly how it works."

At which point, she almost threw the damn thing. She had to fight just to slap it closed and stuff it back in the basket. And she wobbled as she set off. In fact, she wobbled all the way past the library. She saw Tabitha inside, frowning with concern as she zigzagged by, but couldn't do anything about it. Her leg muscles didn't seem to have the power anymore to make the bike run smoothly. Or in a straight line.

So it wasn't a surprise when she almost ran into someone.

She just wished the someone hadn't been Mr. Hannigan.

Because the thing was, Mr. Hannigan was the sort of person who grabbed your handlebars when you veered too close to him.

Or even when you didn't. She remembered him doing it a dozen times to her and Seth when they'd rode on the same one together. Her in the saddle, Seth up front. Hannigan always ready to tell them that they were a disgrace, riding in such a manner.

And he did the same now.

"Cassandra Camberwell, still a nasty little beast, I see," he hissed as he slapped a hand down too close to hers on the left handlebar. And so firmly and forcefully that she came close to flying off the thing. The back wheel almost lifted off the road; the front wheel screeched and skewed a little to the left.

She had to hang on for dear life.

Then automatically tried to get away.

She twisted the handlebars and backpedaled. But of course, if he was strong enough to stop a bike in its tracks like that, then he was strong enough to stop her from riding away. And he did. He held her fast. He watched her squirm like a worm on a hook.

And when she looked up at him again, something else was there.

The writhing ghost of a smile, concealed beneath that tombstone face. Like he was enjoying watching her struggle. "Oh *now* you're in a hurry," he said, then he leaned close, so close she could see strands of yellow saliva oozing between his enormous teeth. "Well, perhaps you should have thought of that before you meandered around, mouth open like a fish, almost running into your betters."

Did he say 'betters?' her mind popped out.

But he had released the handlebars, so it was hard to answer that question. She was too busy focusing on getting away from him, before he did something worse. Though naturally he did something worse anyway. "You go about your business in a seemly fashion, Cassandra Camberwell," he bellowed after her, as she swerved across the street, and careened around a car, and finally somehow found herself in front of Nancy's bookstore.

Accidentally, she assumed.

Although once she was in front of that pumpkin-and cobweb-and-book-filled window, she didn't think it had been an accident.

She thought maybe her brain had automatically searched for a safe haven. For a place where words like "seemly" and "betters" had no effect.

And it had found this place.

And it had been right to.

The second she was inside she felt like her normal adult self again. But not just because she was surrounded by shelves stuffed with books, and lighting that reminded her of reading by candlelight in a fat little armchair. No—there was also Nancy, who looked up from the counter tucked into the corner, the moment she wheeled in.

And instead of (very reasonably) saying *bikes go outside*, she squealed. And launched herself at Cassie. "I knew you'd come," she said as she hugged Cassie so tight her ears popped. Then once the hugging was through, "I even had a feeling just now that it would be today."

Which, taken on its own, meant nothing.

But given everything else that had happened over the last week, felt slightly suspicious.

I'm giving out witch signals now, Cassie thought. And rather than telling herself that this was silly, she found herself glancing back over her shoulder, out the store's window. To the place where Hannigan had stood, but now no longer was.

Go about your business in a seemly fashion, she went over in her head again.

Then itched to get out her new book and look up "seemly."

"Unwitchlike," she imagined it saying, before she shook herself, and turned back to Nancy. Bright-as-a-button Nancy, peering at her curiously through those little round glasses of hers. Like she knew something had happened. Like it was possible that Cassie wasn't the only one with witch senses and signals.

And that idea only grew as she watched Nancy fly into action.

There was something familiar about it—the flurry of activity. The way she bustled around, brewing coffee in a big old brass machine behind the counter. Then stopping when she remembered she hadn't asked if Cassie actually wanted one. Before flying back to stir and pour and forget where she'd put the milk, once Cassie said she'd love one.

And all the while she chattered away, in the same absentminded yet somehow completely focused manner. *So how has your life out there in the big city been?* was one question. *Is Seattle as cool as it seems?* was another. Then just as Cassie tried to swallow a mouthful of a frankly delicious latte, Nancy said, "You look fabulous, by the way, like you're glowing."

And when it did the coffee almost came back up.

She coughed and spluttered and shot a long, suspicious look at Nancy. But Nancy's back was turned, intent as she was on finishing the pouring of her own coffee. And by the time Nancy took a seat opposite Cassie, there was no way to tell if Nancy had really seen anything.

All Cassie had to go on was that one word: glowing.

Which could have meant that Nancy was just being nice about her skin care routine. Or kind about how happy Cassie seemed. But she couldn't deny it might have meant something more. And *especially* when the books right next to her were doing that very thing. She could see them all out of the corner of her eye, just blazing away brightly. Glowing, just like she did.

Plus most of them written by an author she now knew well.

Annie Taylor Watts.

Creator of possibly sentient guidebooks.

Just right there an inch from them both.

So of course she had to say *something*. It felt like Nancy had introduced Cassie to her boyfriend, and her boyfriend had turned out to very visibly be Slenderman. She couldn't just ignore weirdness like that, any more than she had been able to ignore Hannigan's hand on her bike.

But the thing was—she simply didn't know how to go about it. She couldn't just segue from the weather in Seattle to a topic like that. It felt too jarring, too almost rude. As if she were breaching some supernatural etiquette, of the sort that she didn't understand. Apparently, you were supposed to do something like a courtly bow. Or maybe you had to perform the secret handshake.

And until you did, people pretended to be oblivious.

After all, Nancy wasn't saying anything about it.

She was now on to the food in some city Cassie no longer cared about. Seattle had great sushi it seemed. But it was so far from Maine, and she hated flying, and, oh by the way, had Cassie heard? This great new eatery had opened up on the outskirts of tow—and oh god, oh no, she just couldn't hold it in any longer.

"I see you've got some supernatural books there," Cassie blurted out.

And knew it was a mistake, immediately.

Partly because it sounded absolutely ridiculous, once she heard it aloud.

But mostly because of what it did to Nancy's face.

Her whole expression simply dropped, the moment Cassie spoke. Like someone had cut the strings that held up every muscle. More than that, in fact. The light seemed to disappear from her eyes, too. And she didn't answer the question Cassie had asked. She just kept staring, silently, blankly, in a way that made Cassie think of what Seth had said, and which the book had elaborated on: *humans can't see supernatural things.*

And here was the proof, right in the slightly creepy flesh. Nancy, unable to even accept the presence of certain books on her own bookstore shelf. Dead to the world, until Cassie changed the subject.

"So how have you been, Nance?" she asked, more cheerily than she had ever asked anything in her life. And to her relief, Nancy immediately snapped back to normal. All the animation rushed back into her face; the flat look disappeared from her eyes.

And she answered as if continuing a perfectly normal conversation. "Probably not as good as you clearly have been, you sly thing. Come on, tell me honestly. Have you been rekindling any old flames since you got back in town?" she asked.

Then she dropped a wink, in a way that made Cassie's stomach lurch.

Seth is not an old flame. That isn't a thing, she had the strongest urge to say.

Despite the fact that Nancy hadn't mentioned Seth at all. And why would she? To her, Seth was still the guy who had humiliated her in front of the whole school. They were enemies, as far as Nancy knew. She didn't know about the deal. The apologies. The fact that they'd grown so close that things were getting kind of weird.

And anyway, why was she even focusing on this?

Nancy had turned into a robot version of herself, right before Cassie's eyes. Cassie had a book in her bike basket that could grow words while you weren't looking. Hannigan thought she was unseemly. Minotaurs were looking up the movie times for *Dr. Weird and the Way of Whatever the Fuck* down the street.

It had been a hell of a morning. And a yesterday. And a week before that.

Yet, *this* was the thing she was flustered over? It seemed absurd—even as she felt the answer to it pressing against the panicking part of her. *You're not used to the idea of Seth like that, but you* are *getting used to the supernatural stuff,* a voice inside her wanted to say. And though she tried to bat it away, she knew it was right. She could feel it slowly settling over her. A kind of calm, and an understanding that what had happened to Nancy was nothing to worry about. It was normal. It was natural. Like breathing.

Whereas everything with Seth?

Well, that wasn't. It felt reckless and raw. Too full of seventy different weird emotions.

And it made her want to steer clear. To change the subject. "Oh gosh, not at all. I guess I'm just enjoying being back in town," she tried. Then for good measure, she added, "Especially when lovely people send me fruit baskets."

Which seemed to please Nancy.

Her dimples deepened; those bright eyes sparked.

And thank god, the topic was now something else entirely.

"I'm so glad you liked it. I wasn't really sure if that was the right thing, you know. In fact, I almost sent donuts, or muffins, or books. But I wondered what the first two might imply, and the third one—well, I couldn't remember if you even liked to read all that much. I know it was always you and Seth and movies," Nancy said, all in a way Cassie recalled very well. That sweet overspill of honesty, the chirping, chattering manner that had often overwhelmed her in high school.

She'd be pondering at least three different subjects Nancy had raised, while Nancy was off on the next one. Or worse: looking at Cassie sadly, because it seemed that Cassie didn't want to respond. Even though she did. She always had.

It was the reason she made herself respond now.

"Oh no, I do like books. In fact, I was thinking of buying some while I'm here," she said, and didn't think twice about it. There wasn't even a twinge of *you don't have much money to spare.* Because the second she had the afterthought, the little witchy voice in the back of her head responded, *you never have to worry about that again.*

And she knew it was telling the truth.

She could already feel the outlines of several money-making potions taking shape in her mind. And okay, some of them were risky and difficult. They might draw attention. But if she was careful, as she suspected Gram had been with her weird coins and such, they would keep her fed.

Not to mention in reading material.

"Well, you have to let me recommend some stuff. I just got a selection of these old creepy ghost stories, and a bunch of vampire-type things. You like horror, right? I think I might have the perfect book, actually," Nancy babbled away, and then she was off again, bustling around her store, gathering this volume and that—though never going near that glowing shelf, Cassie noticed.

So Cassie went to it herself.

Once Nancy was in the back, rummaging around and calling out questions, she looked over the shelf feverishly. And confirmed that its contents were almost all guidebooks. *Healing Your Inner Horbeast,* she saw, sat alongside something called *Goblin Etiquette.* Then another one about growing magical vegetables. But it was the last book on the shelf that really caught her eye. *Werewolfery for Beginners,* she read, and snatched it up.

She didn't get any further, however. Nancy came charging back to her in a great flurry of dropped books and fluttering pages and curly hair—god, the girl had so much curly hair. Cassie often thought her own dark waves were a bushy, messy disaster. But she had nothing on Nancy. Nancy was an explosion in a hair factory.

Yet somehow, it only made her prettier.

She practically glowed herself, as she busily used brown paper and twine to wrap the books Cassie said yes to. And said glow only disappeared when she got to the werewolf guide. The one Cassie had slipped onto the stack, hoping Nancy's blank look wouldn't come back.

But it did.

Her whole face changed. Even though *she didn't actually stop what she was doing.* She still rang it up, still wrapped it with the others, still accepted money and said thank you. Then it was done, and she was Nancy again. Nancy, who said *stop by again soon,* and waved cheerily as Cassie left.

As if it were that easy to slip into and out of worlds, that you couldn't even see.

CHAPTER THIRTEEN

Cassie pedaled back home, bags hanging off both arms and crammed into the bike basket. Every one of them so full of ingredients she couldn't quite remember what she had—until she started unloading them on the kitchen table. And even then she didn't take much of an inventory. She couldn't, because seeing all the spices and herbs and vegetables and grains immediately set her brain on fire.

Like they had at the market. Like they had *before* she'd gone to the market.

Only it was so much stronger now. She barely had to think before she began yanking out pans and pots and setting all the burners going. High heat for some, less for others—and yet more, she knew, could go in her Gram's old microwave. Because as it turned out, things like cauldrons and campfires weren't necessary.

The right temperature and the right ingredients and the right sitting time were what mattered. Alongside a few other things, like stirring direction, and the temperament you had when making whatever it was. If you were too angry for a calming potion, it might spoil. Too calm for a rage inducer and you could get milk.

And if you balked in the middle of the process because your rational brain said it was wrong, well. She learned the hard way what that meant. She tried not to add vinegar to a very sweet-seeming recipe for restoring energy—something she sorely needed, considering she hadn't had much sleep for the past goodness knows how long—and the pot it was in didn't just pop. It groaned, and creaked. Then rumbled, ominously.

Before finally letting out such an almighty bang the whole

house seemed to shudder. Plates rattled in the cupboards; something somewhere smashed. *Cassandra,* she was sure she heard her grandmother say in disapproval. Then all she could hear was a deep ringing, and all she could smell was burning, and everything was suddenly hidden by a huge plume of smoke.

And once she had wafted it away, there it was.

A great black mark on the wall behind the burner the potion had been on, and nothing else. Like she'd broken some covenant, and so winked the whole thing out of existence. And it was scary. Terrifying, in fact, to think of the forces she was meddling with.

But in a way that seemed different from most things in her experience. Usually when she messed something up, it felt as if all her own instincts were at fault. She was fundamentally a fuckup, somehow. She had made a mess. However, there was simply no way to believe that here. It wasn't the core of her that had gotten this wrong.

It was her rational, practical part.

The part that sounded like her parents.

You have to trust yourself, your true, clumsy, silly self, her brain whispered. And though her heart thumped too hard to hear it, she suspected it was right. All she had to do was listen, all she had to do was believe. She could be more, she knew she could.

Then she set about making money, with that in mind.

She used salt when sense told her to use sugar, warmed up things that she was sure would curdle, stopped stirring even as the stuff she had boiled started to catch. And when that was done, she sat, and she waited. Half of her sure it was going to work. Half of her sure it wasn't. All of her scared as she stood, and went back to the pot.

But there it was.

The liquid had boiled away, leaving ten weird coins at the bottom of the pan. Copper, she knew, without checking. And she knew a lot of other things too. Like the fact that this money was worth precisely one hundred dollars, to someone who looked like a man, but wasn't, living two towns over. And that this man would buy a kind of potent cleaner from her, too, if she could actually manage to make it.

Which she absolutely knew she could.

She was this person now.

She was a witch. And this witch could do anything.

Including make a better potion for Seth. Oh, she definitely knew how to make a better potion for Seth. The sense of it just shimmered through her, so brilliant now she didn't hesitate. She scribbled in her new notebook, until she had three full pages of notes. Then she stuck her pencil behind her ear, and started chopping, stirring, fermenting. She boiled, bubbled and baked. Crushed things up, and remade them. Got her hands dirty, made them clean again with other potions.

And got so lost in it, she didn't even hear someone come in.

She actually screamed the moment she turned and saw Seth standing there.

It was okay though—because he screamed too. He even put both hands over his mouth.

Though judging by the way his eyes were roaming all over everything, she suspected it wasn't just the sound she'd made that did it.

It was also the absolute state the kitchen was in.

Because now that she saw it through someone else's eyes, she could process that it looked like a bomb site. You had to actually wade through discarded containers and peelings and spills to get to anything. There were scorch marks on almost every surface and wall. A permanent fug hung in the air, like the room had developed its own weather system; she might have slightly turned one of the chairs into a giant toadstool without knowing exactly how she'd done it.

Oh, and the microwave was now almost certainly partly alive. Its timer no longer showed numbers, but words. Some of which might have been "feed" and "me." And then when you did feed it, the door would suddenly fly open, and disgorge an almighty belch.

So, you know. It felt like she should possibly try to explain, somehow.

"Okay, I get that the mess in here is a lot," she started. But before she could continue, she took in his expression. She grasped what he was staring at. And realized it wasn't just the kitchen he was startled and then flabbergasted by.

It was *her*. It was how *she* looked.

Because apparently she was a bomb site, too.

The blast that had winked the pot out of existence had blown half her hair straight upward. And it was exactly half, too, in a way that seemed impossible—but obviously wasn't in this brave new witchy world. No, in this world she carved a better part into her hair than any hairdresser had ever managed, just by exploding something.

Which was kind of cool, in a way.

But the soot, on the other hand? Well, that was definitely less so.

She picked up a pan that was still miraculously clean and looked at herself in its bottom, and saw that she had somehow managed to put a giant handprint across her face. It made her look like she had been mugged by a monstrous child.

And that wasn't even the weirdest thing. No, the weirdest thing was definitely the fact that all her clothes were somehow inside out. Even though she'd not so much as touched a button on her high-waisted jeans or a sleeve of her sloppy sweater. It had just happened, all on its own, in the middle of all this chaos.

So it was no wonder that Seth only managed a few words when he could finally speak.

"*Cassie*," he gasped. "You . . . you're so . . . you're just . . ." Then before she could rush in and stop whatever was coming after those ellipses, he reached out a hand. He let it drift through the air, to about an inch away from her cheek.

And she saw what he was talking about.

Her glow moved with his fingers. It trailed after them in sparkly tendrils. And he followed those tendrils, with eyes like dinner plates and his lips all parted and his chest heaving. As if what he saw was so shocking that it put him through an aerobic workout inside.

It took him forever to gather himself. "I guess that book really helped, huh?" he said finally, and oh the urge to reply *it did, but so did you* was extremely strong. She had to bite it back. To think of her purpose here: to show him that he didn't have to give her anything. That he could go if he wanted to, and that would be okay, and he wouldn't lose anything.

"It did. In fact, it helped me make this for you," she said, and held it out for him.

But he just looked puzzled.

"Some magic Vaseline?"

"It's not magic Vaseline. Or maybe it kind of is, because I guess it helps werewolf injuries. You just smear it on, and it'll activate superfast and very strongly. And you only need a tiny little bit too, so that one jar should last you forever."

"And by forever, you mean—"

"Six months, maybe."

He took the jar, turned it over in his hands. "Wow. That is a long time," he said, in a voice that sounded just a little something. Relieved, maybe? She couldn't be sure. But it was close enough that she could go with her plan.

"Yeah. So, you know. You don't have to help me, if you don't want."

Only now he was looking at her weirdly.

Half frowning, half amused.

"Why on earth would I not want to?"

"I don't know. Maybe we have a fight and we hate each other."

The frown deepened. "So you think that's going to happen. You can feel that it might."

"What? No. God, no. I just wanted to show you that you don't have to worry if we do. That you have something now that will keep you okay, always. That I would want to keep you okay, even if things went bad," she said, then couldn't help hesitating. Because there was more to say, but she wasn't sure if it was a good idea to say it. Until she looked up at him, and saw that his expression was just so suddenly full of earnest emotion. So touched and surprised. Really, he deserved to hear. "In fact, you know, I kind of wanted to say that before. When we made the deal. But I don't know, I felt embarrassed. And like it was too big a thing to promise someone who might . . . hurt me again. Or at least to promise it out loud."

"But you promised it in your heart."

"Yeah, I guess. Yes. That's what I did."

"Do you want to know what I felt in mine?"

"I think I know. I think that's why you gave me the book," she said, with just a hint too much pain. Then she braced for whatever his reaction was going to be. Agreement, maybe. A few words that suggested he did actually want rid of her. And just as she was starting to never want to be rid of him, too.

But all she actually got was this startled look. A softening of his gaze.

And then a sigh, and he started speaking. Oh god, he started saying a lot of things.

"Cassie, I almost didn't give it to you," he began, which was enough on its own to tell her where this was going. Yet still, he had more for her. He had so much. "But not because I was worried you'd never make me another potion. You have to know that I knew you would anyway. That I know you well enough to already guess everything you just told me. No, no, it was the idea of losing you that made me want to never hand it over. It was the idea of not having a chance to get my friend back. And the only way I managed to ignore that terror was because you being the person you should be means more to me than my own misery. I'd give up anything, anything at all, even something I want that much, if it returns to you what I took."

She went to speak, once he was done.

But she couldn't get anything to come out.

Chance to get my friend back stole all her words from her.

Then the word *took* removed any breath she had left to say them, anyway.

And both of those things seemed to take a million years to come back. She had to really fight against a thousand conflicting feelings to find her voice, and even when she finally managed, it just sounded so small. So threaded through with tears she didn't want to shed.

"You didn't want to make a deal, then," she said, as one of them spilled down her cheek. He didn't seem to care, however. He watched her swipe it away with eyes so full of wounded warmth it almost made them worth it.

"Not even remotely," he said, in a voice as hoarse as hers.

"All you wanted was to be friends and to help me."

"That is exactly, one million percent the case, yes."

He nodded firmly. He didn't have to, though.

For the first time in years, she believed him. She knew she did, because the urge to hold back was gone. "Then I guess I should probably tell you that I want that too. That I think I've wanted it for a while but just couldn't say it. Like when we talked about me for-giving you so you wouldn't go to hell, and I didn't know how to tell you I already had. And that time you suggested you come in the house and I almost said sure come in, just because that sounded nice. And other things, things you said that made me cry and feel happy, and I forced it all down. But now I don't want to force it down," she babbled, as his expression got warmer, and warmer, and more struck by what she was saying, until finally, god, finally, the way his gaze reached for her.

She was amazed he managed to push out words, to say:

"What do you want to do then?"

Instead of just doing what he clearly wanted.

So she did it for him. She stepped forward, and slid her arms around his waist.

And she hugged her friend, hard.

CHAPTER FOURTEEN

One of the best things about being friends again was definitely all the stuff Cassie got to tell Seth. About Nancy and the shelf she couldn't see, and the creatures that were suddenly visible, and the tiny Hogarth with its saddle. Plus there was all that weirdness with Hannigan, and the feeling she'd had that he somehow knew. "I think it might just be that sweater and the way it keeps revealing your scandalously nude shoulder," Seth said.

And then she got to laugh about it, instead of feeling anxious.

Heck, she didn't even feel anxious about Seth noticing it. Because even when she caught him looking a second time, she knew it didn't mean anything. Like at the quarry, and in the closet, and when they had seen the fairies doing all of those sweaty things.

It was just how their friendship was. Sometimes they got a little mixed up.

But they always went right back to being normal again. Like right now—they just went right back to cleaning. She wiped down counters with a lemony, super-powerful cleaning potion she'd created; he scrubbed soot off the walls. Then they both tackled the pots, and the pans, and the *definitely* sentient microwave.

Its readout now said, *What am I?*

Plus it got mad when Seth tried to clean it.

Put your hand in me again and I will boil it, the digital letters spelled out. And it didn't seem to make a bit of difference when they unplugged it. They had to hold it open with a broom, and squirt cleaning potion inside using a spray bottle. Twice it tried to snap the wooden handle in two. Once, it almost succeeded.

Before it finally gave in. It let them finish.

And then it had the nerve to say it felt much better.

All of which was much more fun to deal with together.

Everything was more fun to deal with together. And so much so that she had to tell him about the potion she wanted to try, once the kitchen was pretty much done. She just saw him holding up an almost-clean pan, wearing an apron she didn't remember him grabbing, face all grubby and a grin as big as the world, and there it was. The almost inescapable urge to go ahead.

"Okay, so don't freak out when I explain this," she started.

But of course he immediately did just that.

He stopped dead in the middle of trying to scrub the last stains from a pan that now had an extra handle that hadn't been there before. And his eyebrows were already at alarmed. "If you say your television is also alive I'm definitely going to. Just FYI," he said, and really she couldn't blame him. It had started making disturbing noises about half an hour ago.

But she stuck to the matter at hand.

"Great, because that isn't it. And so absolutely nothing else can be an issue."

"Wait, no, I didn't say that. I didn't agree to that. That's not how it works."

"Okay, but I'm gonna pretend it does, and expect your calm reaction to me saying that I may have an idea for a potion that could make me fly. And that I need your help with it, because I'm afraid I will go up and then not be able to come back down," she said. Quickly, so he didn't have a chance to look at her with incredulity.

Like he absolutely did anyway.

"You sound like a billionaire who's about to be exploded in a spaceship he poorly designed," he said, in this exasperated way she really wanted to argue with. But before she could, he seemed to consider. And then he laughed and shook his head. "Except you have no money, I definitely want to be involved, and I have total faith in your ability to pull off something so deranged-sounding."

Much to her absolute delight and surprise.

She almost bounced on her toes, before reining it in.

Better to seem reasonable about this, and not like a toddler on a sugar high.

"Wow," she said. "That is a lot more support for this scheme than I expected."

"Well, you know. That's what friends do. They help their friends."

"Even though helping your friend in this case might kill us both?"

"We're not gonna be killed. Mainly because we can't be, but still."

He shrugged one shoulder and turned back to the pots and the sink.

And she almost returned to her job too—arranging her growing collection of potion jars in the pantry. Then she realized what he'd said, and stepped back out again. "Did you just say we can't be? About being killed?"

"Well, you know. I mean *technically* we can. Someone could chop off my head, or make a spell or a potion that turns me inside out, or maybe cut out my heart with a silver knife. So really it's more like . . . we are super hard to kill," he said, and so matter-of-factly, too. Even though there were several problems with his statement.

"Yeah, but that's just werewolves. You could kill me with any knife."

"Only if you didn't have a potion protecting you, for some reason."

"So you're saying there's a potion I could create that makes me unkillable?

"Cassie, the potion you've just used to clean the kitchen could probably do it," he said, then gestured at the spray bottle full of the stuff on the kitchen counter. The one she'd labeled Make Nice, because that was what it had felt like to her when she'd come up with it. She'd even heard it in her head, like a commercial jingle for a solution that gets your oven sparkling. Use it twice to make things nice.

So what he was going on about she didn't know.

"Be serious," she snorted. "I just made a kind of soap."

"You cannot possibly really think that."

"Well, why wouldn't I? Look at my gleaming counters."

She spread her hands to illustrate. But he just rolled his eyes.

"Yeah, they are most likely gleaming because this place was covered in germs and it destroyed them to protect you. Or maybe one of the ingredients was laundry detergent, I don't know. Either way, a protection spell is definitely what this is," he said.

And this time, her brain responded with way less of a "no." It started ringing that witch bell like whoa. But still, she couldn't quite let him have it. "Okay, I am going to need to know where that 'definitely' is coming from," she said with as much skepticism as she could still muster. And again, all she got was that maddening casualness.

"Before I slapped some of this extra-strength stuff on, I felt myself start to turn, a little bit. I got the jitters, I was sweating. And then suddenly the water coming out of the faucet was scalding hot. Like it wanted to hurt me to stop me. Check it out," he said, as he held his hand up. But it didn't look that burned to her. And even if it had, what did that prove?

"That might not mean anything. Maybe the water heater is set too high."

"Well, there's only one way to find out, isn't there? Let's see if the cleaning potion will try to subdue or neutralize any other threats. Grab that spray, put it on yourself, and I'll try to jab you with this broom."

He picked up said broom. And even though she wasn't quite sure what he was planning to do, she trusted him enough to grab the bottle and squirt some of the potion into her hands. Then when he pointed, she slicked it over that bare shoulder.

Too messily, she knew.

His expression was a peach when she finally finished rubbing. Just completely bemused, in a way she had to snap him out of. She had to click her fingers in front of his face, and tell him, "Hey, at least it's done," just to get him to refocus on what they were doing. But to his credit, he didn't make any snarky remarks about her clumsiness.

He just attempted to poke her in the shoulder with the handle end of the broom. Gently, she thought. Though gently didn't seem to matter. The instant the handle got within a foot of her, the whole thing jerked away. As if someone other than him had grabbed it. Then that someone seemed to yank it back, away from her.

And somehow smashed it *directly* into his *face*.

Like right into it, hard enough to make a cracking sound. It made his whole head snap back. He actually stumbled a little—it was that brutal and violent. And when he finally managed to right himself and look at her, oh dear *god* in *heaven*. His mouth looked like a car wreck. All she could see was blood.

Then he spat into his hand to clear it and—fuck.

There was a tooth. She had knocked his tooth out with a potion she thought erased stains.

"Okay, you could have told me it was going to bludgeon you," she gasped out as she tried to grab paper towels, and excavate some ice, and find a spell called Teeth Restorer, all at the same time.

But he just laughed. He laughed. His mouth was a bloody mess, and he was laughing. "I didn't need to," he said, as he dropped the tooth in the trash. "It hasn't hurt me."

"Seth, you just had an incisor in your hand."

"Yeah, and it'll grow back in about five minutes. Because like I just told you—even my heart can do that, after it's been stabbed. Heck, I'm not even sure if decapitation is a real killer. I think it's entirely possible that my head will just sprout another body. While my body sprouts another head."

She tried not to look aghast. But failed horribly, obviously. Her face felt like a rigid rictus of disgust. "And you're telling me that horror story now, while I'm still trying to process the last horror story you told me? Do I have to worry that there might end up being two of me if someone attempts a beheading?" she asked. Yet somehow all she got in return was an eye roll.

"Nobody is going to attempt a beheading."

"That's not what I am concerned about, Seth."

"Then what is?"

He looked genuinely curious, she thought.

And right as it was dawning at her that none of her concerns really mattered.

"I have no idea," she said. "Now that I'm calming down, being sort of invincible seems like something I am supposed to be really pleased about. And also should have understood. Because seriously, I don't know why I didn't grasp this. Or what made me miss it when I was updating this potion."

You still can't really believe your own power, her witch brain informed her. And that sounded right. Or at least more right than what he said a second later. "Maybe it's like me not wanting to think about hell."

"Hell is a lot more horrible than being sort of indestructible."

"Possibly so, but it takes a similar amount of shifting things around in your head." He set down the pan he'd picked up. Folded his arms. "Suddenly you don't have to worry quite as much about getting your brains bashed in. Or having to have an operation for your bashed-in brains. Or needing to somehow pay for the bashed-in-brains operation. You just smother yourself in that potion, and if someone aims the brain-bashing hammer at you, they knock out all their own teeth."

"It does sound pretty goddamn mind-melting when you say it that way."

"Gets even more so when you process that you, like me, won't ever age."

"Fuck you. There's no potion that'll stop that," she said, half laughing. Even though she knew she was already mostly believing him. In fact, more than already mostly believing. The confirmation was there, in the back of her mind, tingling away. She felt it before he replied.

"You already know there is."

"Okay, fine. But I'm not going to drink it."

"Oh, I think you will, eventually."

"How do you figure that?"

"Because you'll realize how many movies you won't get to see once you're gone." He gave her a smug look, on the end of his sentence. He had a right to, though. He was so bang on that she couldn't stop herself from groaning in despair. And of course he understood what that groan meant. "Yeah, I figured that out because I, too, was weirded out at the thought of never aging. Until I realized *The Conjuring 37* could be but a month away, when I'm on my ninety-year-old death bed."

"You motherfucker, you understand just how to get me."

"Of course I do. I know you. And I'm gonna use that for this, especially."

"Why this especially? What the hell does it matter if I live forever?"

"Well, it matters because I want you to be around. I mean, I don't want to just drift for all eternity without you," he said. Then he snorted, like that was just obvious. Or not a big deal at all. In fact, it was so little of one that he didn't even wait for her reaction.

He turned his back. Grabbed a saucepan to check on his newly regrown incisor.

And finally he clapped his hands together. "Now, are we going flying, or what?" he asked. As if he wasn't even thinking about their shared immortality anymore. He was on to the next thing. While she stood there, still stranded in the land of *oh my god, he wants to be with me always.*

Worse than that, really, because all she wanted to do was say the same thing to him.

Five minutes too late, and too heartfelt to stand.

So instead, she nodded. "Sure," she said.

And that was the end of that.

CHAPTER FIFTEEN

She didn't explain what she was planning on doing.

She just grabbed what she needed, and followed Seth out into the now dark garden. Then when he turned at the sound of her footsteps on the front porch, and raised his eyebrows in anticipation, she dragged it out from behind her back.

And got the reaction she'd been expecting.

"You want to do this on a *Hoover*?" he gasped, in a voice that sounded torn between excitement and incredulity. But she could see the excitement winning out, even before she started laying out her carefully considered reasoning.

"Well, you know, a broom is so thin."

"That is true."

"And I'm so clumsy."

"You're not that bad."

She gave him a *look*. "Oh come on, you know I am."

"I do, but I'm trying to pretend otherwise to be supportive."

"Okay, well, you can stop. You're being supportive enough, I promise."

"Thank *god*, because all I can see behind my eyes is you plummeting to the ground from so far up that it somehow tests the limits of that lemon potion. I'm honestly about thirty seconds away from desperately begging you to ride me instead," he said, all in a rush. Then he saw her taken aback expression, and seemed to realize what that sounded like, and hurried to explain. "And you know, by 'ride me' I mean because I'm large, and I have lots of things you could hold on to while you did it."

Though it hardly seemed to explain anything at all.

It just made her eyebrows climb higher. And his face get even redder.

"Not that you would want to hold on while you rode me," he tried again, then almost immediately and visibly cursed himself. And she could understand why, because, oh dear god, what was happening? What was going on? How was he saying something even worse than the original thing? *Stop*, she wanted to tell him. But he didn't, somehow he *didn't*. "That's not what I was trying to say. I just wanted you to use me in whatever way would work best for you."

And okay then she *had* to cut in.

He gave her no choice at all. "Seth, what the fuck are you *doing*?"

"I don't know. It's just coming out of me."

"So put it back in again. Like, superfast."

She rolled her hands to illustrate. Which just seemed to make him more panicked.

"I'm trying, I'm trying. I swear to god I am. And some kind of god actually exists to me at this point, so you know that I must be telling the truth."

"I know that you're being extremely weird right now."

"Okay, but not so weird that you're going to stop being my friend all over again, right?" he said, despairingly. And then with even more despondency in his voice: "Because if I've blown it already over innuendos I definitely did not mean to say, I might lose my mind just a little bit."

"You haven't blown it, and you don't have to lose your mind. Just, you know. Calm down."

"I will. I totally will," he insisted. But he still looked flushed. He still looked jittery. As if the whole thing had unsettled him far more than it really should have. And when she went to hand him the rope to tie around her middle, he didn't seem to want to do it.

He just stared at it in his hands. Then stared at her waist. Then back at his hands again. And all in a way that made her want to shake him, and say, *I am never going to get the wrong impression here. I barely even got the wrong impression over your hand almost*

on my butt while we accidentally watched a live sex show. That was
all nothing, so why would I ever think anything more about this?

But of course she couldn't.

That would only draw attention to the weirdness.

So instead she laughed and nudged his arm and said, "Come on."

Then watched him visibly swallow, and reach toward her, in
the slowest and most agonized way she could imagine. As if she
had said she believed his sexual innuendoes, and now he was terrified of making the situation worse. Of making her moony-eyed,
over his big hands on her body.

Instead of how she actually felt: like stone, like a rock, like a
completely immovable mountain. She didn't care that he slipped
the rope around her, so gently. Or that she felt his fingers brush her
skin, where her sweater rode up at the back. And it didn't matter
to her that every breath he took seemed all hot against the nape of
her neck.

Not to mention shaky.

Man, it was really shaky.

He sounded like he'd recently run up a hill. He *looked* like he'd
recently run up a hill. She could see perspiration gleaming on the
curve of his throat, out of the corner of her eye. But still she didn't
react. She didn't do anything but stand there, frozen, until he finally, finally pulled away.

And if she let out her own breath in one long almost-gasp when
he did, well. That didn't mean anything. Nothing meant anything.
It was fine, everything was fine. Nothing to see here, she thought,
as she turned to face him.

Or at least, she tried to turn to face him.

But he suddenly appeared to be at a different angle.

A very low angle. *Did you just step into a hole*, she almost said.

Then she saw the startled look on his face. And the way he
was scrambling for the trailing end of the rope. And realized
what was going on, about a second before he gasped out, "Holy
shit, it's happening."

Because it was. She looked down and saw that her feet were
no longer touching the grass. She floated a foot above it—and she

was still climbing, slowly but surely. Another ten seconds and she was going to be beyond his grasp.

Though there was nothing she could do about it.

She'd been so wrapped up in the idea of Seth holding her in place, and pulling her back down, that she hadn't really thought about how she would steer this thing. She had just wanted to try, and now she was going to actually end up so high that death somehow happened. Possibly by her getting beyond the point where oxygen existed.

"Seth," she yelled, as she did the only thing she could think of. She tried to point the handle of the Hoover down. Only somehow, she didn't quite get the angle right. The whole thing veered violently to the left. It sent her skimming six feet above the grass, fast enough that it made a bubble of giddy joy rise through her.

Though terror soon took over.

She seemed to be headed for the trees.

And Seth definitely did not have hold of the rope. She could hear him behind her, scrabbling for it. Trying to pounce and snag it, and completely missing. *Yeah, like now is the time for you to lose that supernatural grace and skill and speed*, she thought at him. But knew even as she did that it wasn't fair at all. He'd just spent the last hour going through emotional upheaval, inadvertent sexual innuendo, and trying to touch someone without giving them the wrong idea.

Of course he was suddenly clumsy.

She would have been clumsy too, if she weren't already the clumsiest person alive.

She tried to turn back and just somehow ended up climbing higher. And steeply too—to the point where she had to really hang on. She had to get an arm around the Hoover's handle and squeeze the bag tightly between her thighs.

But even so, she came close to sliding off.

She was only saved by the broad base that housed the brush, which acted as a kind of safety seat for her butt to land on. It allowed her a second to scrabble her way back up toward the handle, hand over hand. And once there she hooked her feet together, so nothing could jolt her free.

While the Hoover sent her higher and higher.

Seth now looked incredibly far away.

All she could make out was the white of his face, and his frantically waving hands. Before a wave of vertigo made her look away again. *Focus on flying,* she told herself, frantically. But that just made her think of the impossibility of what she was doing. The fact she was actually soaring through the air on an electric appliance, at a speed that turned her hair into a streamer.

Soon, she would be in the sky.

She'd be able to brush the tops of the trees with her hand.

She even thought she might dare to, once she was there. But just as she thought of something that strange and wonderful, just as she started to see things in a more positive light, something bad seemed to happen. She felt a jolt go all the way through her, violent enough that she almost lurched off the Hoover. And it took almost everything she had to haul herself back on. She heaved so hard her muscles screamed at her. Bones got bent into positions they didn't want to be in.

Then somewhere in the middle of all of this, she tried to look back and figure out what was going on.

And that was when the Hoover seemed to jackknife. It swung toward the nearest tree, in a way that spelled out exactly what had happened. The rope had caught on a branch. It had gotten snagged—and, oh that was bad, it was very bad. It made her brace, and press her face into the backs of her hands, and try to make her body as small as she could.

But she still felt every twig and leaf and bit of bark bashing into her.

Something jabbed her in the stomach. Suddenly there was a leaf in her mouth, bitter and wet and choking. And though she tried to grab hold of something, she couldn't, she just couldn't, it was all going too fast. There wasn't even time to breathe or think. She just had to close her eyes, and hope something kept her from plummeting.

Because the Hoover sure wasn't going to do it.

She lost it, somewhere amid the maelstrom. Heard it crashing through the tree below her, loud enough that it made Seth make a terrified sound. Then there was a crunch, and she felt something rough against her cheek, and suddenly everything was quiet. Everything was still.

She had come to rest on a kind of hammock of branches.

She was all right. She was all right.

Or as all right as anyone could be, while jammed in a tree about thirty feet above the ground. With absolutely no way to get down.

Yeah, you didn't think of that when you were getting all high on being almost impervious to harm, her brain sneered. And sure, it was being a jackass. But it was also completely correct. She couldn't even see the Hoover anymore—which meant it was most likely too far away to retrieve. It might have even hit the ground by that point.

Can you see it and possibly send it back up like an elevator, she wanted to yell at Seth.

But then Seth bellowed, "Cassie, do not move. I'm coming to get you."

And to her surprise, she found she didn't doubt him. She didn't even worry that he might do it badly and fall. She just peered through the leaves, fully expecting to see him grabbing branches and hauling himself up.

But somehow, he still did more than she had imagined.

He climbed the *trunk*.

And he used his claws to do it. As if he could summon them up at will—which, honestly, until that point, she'd had no idea was even possible. She'd thought he needed something to spike it, and yet here he was shredding bark to get to her. And not just with his hands either. His feet were bare, and in very much the same state.

It was like watching a jungle cat scale its way up to her.

Several times she almost moved to get a better look, before realizing what that would mean for her. *You try, and you will test what plunging to the ground is going to do*, her mind hissed. Then she forced herself to stay still and wait.

Not that she had to do so for long. Ten seconds later, there was

Seth's face, peering at her from between the branches. And he wasn't furious or mocking. He just looked incredibly stressed.

"I seriously thought you were going to end up on the fucking moon," he said, between frantic breaths. "And that was not a fun thing to experience. I mean, sure, the potion will protect you. But how would I get you down from outside earth's atmosphere, huh? Answer me that."

But he didn't wait for her to try.

He just reached forward. He got a hand around her waist. And then he pulled her, carefully but firmly, into the circle of his arms. He cradled her, gently enough that it gave her weird goose bumps, everywhere he was touching her body. Between her shoulder blades, against her upper arm, just a little at the nape of her neck, where it still felt sensitive from that lick of his warm breath.

Breath that she could feel now, against her cheek. Too quick, too harsh, she thought. But before she could process that, he gruffed words in her ear. "Hold on," he said. Then he simply jumped. He whole ass jumped. No sliding down the tree. No climbing. Just straight down, so abrupt and so fast it felt like she almost ate her own stomach. She tried to scream and couldn't, because her lungs were in her face.

She honestly thought she might die.

But of course she didn't, because there was that hand on the back of her head again. The sense of him absorbing any impact, of him cradling her through it.

And cradling her afterward, too.

Because he didn't let go right away. He just held her like that, one arm around her waist, one hand in her hair. Her body firm against his side, her legs still tangled around one of his. Plus he was staring at her so intently, with so much fierceness in his face— honestly, she thought he was going to fume at her. She prepared to hear him say, *that was so reckless. What were you thinking?*

But instead, she got this: "You really flew, god, you really did."

And spoken so softly, so breathlessly, too.

While his gaze stroked her upturned face like a warm, soft hand.

So it only seemed natural to want to say something back. Something as heartfelt as she'd longed to say before, back at the house, when he'd said that thing about eternity so casually. *I did it because I can do anything when you're with me*, she thought, and came so close to just letting it out. She could almost taste it on the tip of her tongue. Almost saw his reaction to it, already dawning.

But a millisecond before she could do it, there was a sound from the garden.

One she could barely hear, but knew was bad.

She knew it, because Seth *immediately* whipped his head toward it.

Then he growled. He growled *loudly*. She saw his throat vibrate; he bared his suddenly sharpening teeth. He even took a step in the direction of whatever had his hackles up, seemingly and suddenly insensible of anything but that. She had to pull him back, just to get some answers.

Though he gave her none. He just told her to stay where she was.

As if she was ever going to be able to do that. The second he set her down and disappeared between the trees, she followed. And she only stopped when she saw that he wasn't going any farther. He was just past the tree line, at the very edge of her garden. Sort of frozen, like he had seen something terrible. Then she stepped forward, she went to say something, and she saw it too.

And now she was frozen, just like him.

Because good god, it was *them*.

It was them. It was them. The stars of her every high school nightmare. The three members of the Jerk Squad, right there on the grass. Bold as brass and twice as terrible, in a way that almost made her run back into the woods. She had to remind herself that running was ridiculous, considering where they were. This was *her* yard. Outside *her* house.

If anything, *they* should be the ones fleeing.

But of course they weren't, and would probably never feel any urge to. Why would they, when they had quite clearly been planning this for some time? Because she knew now that they had. It was them she'd felt watching her. Watching the house. Watching her and Seth's every move.

So they had to know she was no threat.

And even if they weren't entirely sure—well, what did it matter?

They were just as strapping and sure of themselves as she remembered. Just as powerful, just as intimidating. Every one of them over six feet tall, bulging with muscle, and full to the brim with that lazy, careless cruelty she remembered so well. She even thought of it all now:

Letting a door slap closed in her face, then calling it an accident.

Tripping her, but blaming it on her clumsiness.

Then the taste of blood at the back of her throat. The memory of Seth's face as he held a bag of frozen peas to her swollen lip. *I'll stop them one day,* he had said over that. But of course that day had never come. Him being buddies with them hadn't changed much of anything. And now here they were, again, even worse than they'd been before.

Much, much worse.

Because the thing was, they weren't just jerks anymore. She knew they weren't, immediately and completely. The same way you know it's electricity shocking you when you stick your fingers into a socket. It was just there, blazing through her, burning everything away as it went. That knowledge, that understanding:

They were werewolves.

Somehow, they were absolutely and totally werewolves.

Even though not one of them had any physical signs. In fact, they looked almost exactly as they had in high school. Jason stood in front, blond and blue-eyed and all bully-boy energy. That fucking letterman jacket still on his back, like he'd just arrived from central casting for the villain role in an eighties high school movie. Like he'd peaked in that role, and never moved past it.

And it was the same with the two flanking him, Jordan and Tyler. The former too red-haired and pasty-skinned to ever be considered as attractive as the others. The latter with that dough-faced, small-eyed, buzz-cut look the girls had gone wild over, in a way she had never understood.

Hell, she'd never understood why *anyone* went wild over any of them.

They looked like jackals to her.

And even more so now, with that animal energy radiating off them. It made her prickle in places she couldn't name. She wanted to spray them all with the lemon potion, and watch them smack their own faces instead of hers.

Though really, it was Seth she was most concerned for.

Because it seemed that he was their focus. "Well, hey there, buddy, long time no see," Jay said. And the others tittered, until a look from Jay made them fall silent. As if some kind of alpha hierarchy did exist among wolves.

But just for these assholes, obviously.

These are the ones Seth was talking about when he said the only other werewolves around here are not good people, she thought, and knew she was right. It was obvious even before he replied. She could feel him urging her to move behind him, so skillfully and subtly she barely knew it was happening. Until his body blocked her view of them.

And he sounded mad as hell when he answered.

"I'm not your buddy," he said. "So get the fuck out of here."

But in answer they only sniggered and hooted.

Then just as abruptly fell silent, in a way that had always creeped her out. Like they didn't really understand what laughter was, and only did it to imitate real human behavior. Just before they did something so soulless, you sort of doubted they were.

And god, she didn't want to know how soulless they could be, now that they had fangs and superhuman strength and who knows what else. She didn't want to look at Jay's suddenly blank, flat-eyed expression, or hear him sneer, "Ooohhh, big talk now that you've got your little girlfriend with you." While knowing that he could probably bite her arm off.

It was too unsettling. And not just because of the horrifying mixture of that coldness, and the high school gibe, and the idea of them being able to do something incredibly brutal. No—there was also how it affected Seth. Immediately, like they'd hit a button marked sore spot.

"Just shut the fuck up. She's not my girlfriend," he said, so fiercely it almost stung her.

Who cares if they think I am, she wanted to say to him. *We both know it will never be a thing.* But of course she couldn't. Because doing so would have felt like admitting that she thought it might have been. It gave those three power over her.

And they already had enough as it was.

"Yeah, so you always said. But it's all these years later and here you two are, thick as thieves. Practically hugging each other in front of us. Flirting in the woods. Being concerned about what the big bad wolves might do to you," Jason said.

While Seth stood like stone.

For a second, she thought he wasn't even going to respond. But then he did, he did. "We're not hugging, and we weren't flirting, and if you try to do anything to her I might have to slap your goddamn faces off your smug little skulls," he snarled.

Which, if she was being honest, made even her look at him.

So there was no surprise that his statement got a strong reaction from the Jerks. Jason's face twisted into an even uglier expression than he'd worn before, all deep furrows above his usually perfect nose, lip curled high enough that she could see how sharp his teeth were. And the other two could barely contain themselves. Tyler actually started barking and snarling; Jordan lunged forward.

Only Jason's raised hand stopped them. Though even then, Jordan tried to protest.

"Can we get them now? I want to eat her, I'm hungry," he whined, and two things happened when he did. She thought automatically, blankly, *Oh, we are in even more trouble than I initially thought.* And Seth *snarled.* He snarled and jerked forward in almost the exact way Jordan had done.

Like a dog on a leash, she thought.

Only in Seth's case, the leash was her.

She put a hand out and grabbed his arm, instinctively. Then

was pretty shocked when he didn't yank away. He obeyed her, even though she could feel the wolf inside him, buzzing just beneath his skin. She could sense it pushing against the potion on him, and the potion on her. A little more pressure, and she would be holding on to something decidedly more beast-like.

Though she wasn't entirely sure if that would be a bad thing, given what they were facing. Because although Jay said, "Okay, cool your jets, nobody is eating anyone," she didn't think he was telling the truth. And sure enough the whiny twosome had things to add.

"But, boss, you promised."

"You said I could have her right thigh."

"We were told we would feast tonight."

Much to Jay's equally deadly sounding exasperation.

"Yeah, and that was before I was sure about what she is," he said. Then he leaned to the side. He peered around Seth, right at her. "And now I am sure, and it's a lot tastier than lunch, isn't it, Cassie? Come on, don't be shy. Come out from behind your boyfriend and show us what you are."

But oh, she didn't want to deal with whatever that meant. So she tried going with what Seth had. Something ordinary. Something that made sense. "He's not my boyfriend," she said, and in answer, Jason chuckled mirthlessly.

"And that's not the point."

"I don't care what your point is."

"Sure you do. That's why you're hiding behind him. That's why he's trying to hide you. Trying to keep you away from us. Trying to keep you all to himself, just like he did with your grandmother. Because he's a greedy fuck."

Oh Jesus, she thought. *Is that why Seth wanted to know how Gram died? Because he wondered if these chucklefucks did it?* Then felt extremely thankful that it had been indisputably natural causes. Because if it hadn't?

She felt pretty sure she would have let go of Seth's arm.

And god only knew what would happen then. The things that were happening now were bad enough. "He doesn't eat me, if that's what you're implying," she blurted out, and couldn't even pretend that nobody had noticed the innuendo. She actually felt Seth go all hot, in a way she knew must be embarrassment. She knew, and couldn't help fretting about it. Because what if he decided he didn't like the way she was making him feel? What if he thought, again, that her friendship wasn't as valuable and cool as theirs? Hell, maybe one of them was even his maker. Maybe he had to obey them somehow.

Which felt wrong as soon as she thought it.

But it still compounded the other issues. It still made her think, *then I'll be on my own.*

And this time, it would be against four werewolves. One of whom was still talking in a manipulative, sly sort of way. "Maybe he does, maybe he doesn't. Either way, he enjoys keeping that magic in you all to himself. Hasn't so much as said a word to any-one in the community about a brand new witch in our midst."

And now the other two were gasping.

And after a second they echoed that one word—*witch witch witch.* They said it over and over, in a way that sounded like leaves rustling.

"That's not what she is," Seth tried to say. But it was useless. It was pointless.

"You fucking liar. I can smell it from here," Jason said. And the others agreed.

"I can see it, I can see it now—look, she's shiny."

"Oh my god, she is, she's got all that stuff on her."

Jordan pointed, clearly pleased with himself for seeing.

At which point she couldn't help it. *She* lunged forward.

"Yeah, and if you come anywhere near us I'll get that stuff on you. Because I can do it, you know. I can throw spell bombs and turn you all into frogs. And then guess what? It's frog-fucking-soup time," she said, and was gratified to see the two dipshits look at each other worriedly.

Though Jay didn't seem worried at all.

"She's a baby. She probably can't even turn herself into any-thing yet, never mind us," he said. Then he seemed to consider. He seemed to narrow his eyes, before adding, "Though I know one thing she can do, if her boyfriend is any indication. Yeah, if he's running this hot and not even turning, she can make something that keeps it at bay. Something that heals stuff right."

And oh, that was bad, that was real bad. Yeah, that was going to be worse than the whole eating thing, and she knew it. She could see it in the way the other two reacted—like they'd been struck by lightning. Tyler actually gasped; Jordan seemed to freeze for a second.

And then the latter just couldn't seem to contain himself.

He lunged forward again. And this time he did it so violently, and so haphazardly, he actually made it past the calming hand Jay put up. He got all the way to about a foot in front of Seth—close enough that it made a sound kick out of her. It made her step forward, as a million ways to stop him tore through her head.

Yank Seth away, her mind screamed.

Hit him with something, it demanded.

Let him hit you so he hits himself, it suggested.

But before she could even try to do any of those things—before Jordan got even an inch closer to her—Seth lifted his hand. He drew it back, fast enough that everything else seemed to go into slow motion.

And then he just fucking *belted* him one. Oh, he hit him so hard she felt it impact *her*. That meaty thudding sound went right through her body, heavy as anything.

And the blow didn't just knock Jordan off his feet.

It sent him flying across the garden. Farther than she could have imagined. Farther than any smack should have done. So far, in fact, that when she finally dared to peer around Seth, she couldn't see Jordan at all. He'd barreled into the woods behind her grandmother's begonias, like a fucking cannonball.

And now the only thing she could make out was the tunnel he had cut, through the trees.

That fat, velvety darkness, the hint of leaves stirring.

Then after what felt like a long, tense silence, he showed himself again.

Only he wasn't exactly Jordan anymore.

He was a pair of eyes between the branches, bright and pale as the moon. Then more came, more terrifying than that. She glimpsed gray fur, slick and sickly looking. Shoulders so muscular they'd worn said fur to nothing, a set of teeth like knives. And all of it was followed by a growl, so low and heavy it took things from a ten on the terror scale to a ninety-seven.

It made her want to scream. To say to Seth that they should go.

But the thing was, she couldn't do anything. She couldn't move.

Not even when Seth tried to surreptitiously urge her in a certain direction.

Toward the house, she thought it was. Toward the door she didn't even have to unlock. They'd left it open in their rush to try flying, and now it was just right there, easy as anything.

Though he had to know: there was no way she was going without him.

Jordan had him flanked on one side, Tyler was trying to flank him on the other. And Jason was stalking forward, under the guise of trying to calm things down. "Easy there, big boy," he said. "We're not looking for trouble. We just want her for a little while, that's all. Just long enough to get what we need, spell-wise. And then you can have her back, good as new."

But of course, Seth was having none of it.

"There'll be no back."

"Oh, how do you figure that?"

"Because there isn't about to be a going."

"I think there will be. Three of us. And you all leashed."

"I'm not leashed when it comes to something like this."

"And what might this be, exactly?" Jay asked, and cocked his head.

Like it was all just a big game to him. A high school prank, the same as before. Only this time, nobody laughed. Nothing humiliated her. Instead, everything seemed to go very still and quiet.

Then Seth spoke, into the darkness and the silence.

"Defending the person I belong to. And who belongs to me."

And just as she looked at him, startled and full of questions, he turned, and took hold of her by the front of her sweater, and hauled her up off her feet. All in one motion, and so quickly the Jerks didn't have time to do a thing. *She* didn't have time to do a thing. She dangled there for a millisecond, his name still in the back of her throat.

Then he wound his arm back, and *threw her.*

He *hurled* her, the way you might a set of keys to someone waiting with an outstretched hand. Only there was no hand waiting. There was nothing, just the porch and the house and oh god she was going to crash through a window. She was going to smash into a fence post.

Why the fuck did he do this, her brain yelled.

About a second before she hit the porch, so softly and perfectly it felt as if the floorboards kissed her butt. She practically skimmed over them, straight through the door and into the hallway beyond. Like she was on an ice rink, executing the kind of glide that shouldn't have been possible. *Olympic skaters would have missed that move*, she thought.

But then, he was better than any Olympic skater ever would be.

He was better than any athlete to ever exist.

He was a wolf.

And that had never been clearer than it was now, as she came to a graceful stop by the stairs, and looked up. And there he was, framed by the open door. Caught in the porch lights perfectly, in a way that made him glow.

It made him, as monstrous as he was, beautiful.

Though she suspected he would have been anyway. His fur was the color of night dissolving into day—black and gray and everything in between. And he was enormous, truly immense, bigger than she'd ever pictured. He filled the whole of that bright rectangle, a riot of muscle and sinew and fangs and claws. All of it terrifying, utterly terrifying.

Yet somehow, so awe inspiring she couldn't do anything but stare.

As if nothing else was happening. As if time had stopped. All the fighting and snarling and violence hung suspended, just long enough for her to live in that glimpse of him. She got to glory in it, feel it down to her bones, know that she would never forget it.

Before one of the others struck him, and they tumbled into the darkness.

And all the horror restarted, like someone pressing play on a movie. She heard snarls, and something breaking. The bird bath, she suspected. Or maybe someone's bones. Then just as she started to get to her feet, there was another sound.

A strange clicking, beneath the roar of rage. Like nails on wood, she thought.

About a second before she saw one of the wolves, stalking up the porch steps.

Sickly, and meaner looking than Seth had been. A wolf as ugly on the outside as it was on the inside, seizing its chance to slink into the house, while everyone else was distracted. Slowly, so slowly she had to think it was afraid of her.

And all she could think about that was:

Well, if you are, I'm gonna make sure I prove you right.

She made two fists, like she'd seen that fairy do. As if she was going to hurl magic right at the thing. And when it hesitated, when it growled, she started to ease herself up again. Cautiously, with her eyes always on the beast. Hands always out, ready to strike with spells she didn't have. Breath held, every bit of her willing herself to get to where she needed to be:

On her feet, so she could run.

And the second she managed, she did.

She went straight for the kitchen, faster than she'd ever done anything in her life.

Yet still, she felt something snag the sleeve of her sweater. She got a gust of hot, fetid breath against the nape of her neck, and thought that it had her. That it was going to get some part of her that wasn't covered in potion. And even if it didn't—this move had been a mistake.

It wasn't going to work.

She had to grab something. Hit it with a chair, anything.

And she went to—she got hold of the back of the nearest

one. But when she turned, chair only partly in her hands, and screamed, and went to smash the creature with it, she saw it was already cringing away. As if something had frightened it.

Then she heard the sound.

The one it had obviously heard before her, building in the background. Like metal grinding against metal, and wood shoving against wood. And just as she thought, ridiculously, inexplicably, *that is the noise a kitchen cabinet makes when it tries to uproot itself and lunge at something,* it happened. The cupboard next to the sink tore itself free, and *flew* at the wolf behind her.

She felt the wood graze her cheek. Utensils spilled out as it went, showering her right foot with spoons and forks and knives. But the spoons and forks and knives didn't stay there. No, they jumped up, and flung themselves at the beast too.

And oh, they did it *hard*. They broke skin.

It looked like a porcupine, within seconds. Forks jutted up from its thighs; knives now covered its arms. And it wasn't just the sharp items, either. What looked like a plastic spatula was lodged in one of its legs. As if things like blunt edges and the laws of physics no longer mattered.

Nothing mattered, except repelling whatever was attacking her.

Which was probably why the microwave flung itself at the beast next. She heard it beep wildly as it went by, and almost tried to stop it. *Not you, you're alive,* she thought wildly. But the thing was, the whole kitchen currently appeared to be. It moved and reacted and breathed all around her, in a great whirlwind of activity. Like a living hurricane.

Only somehow it was one that never touched her.

She didn't so much as get a splinter in her cheek.

While the wolf howled and writhed and tried to attack anything that came at it. It snapped a chair into splinters in one bite; it swiped at utensils with its huge paws. But of course by the time it did anything, something else was already hitting it from another angle. She saw a jar smack into its back, as it finished destroying a cupboard.

And when it did, it exploded. Liquid came boiling and frothing out, all over its fur.

Clear, at first.

But then suddenly it seemed to turn pink, and red, and finally it hit her. Whatever had been in the container was acting on the wolf like frigging *acid*. It was blistering skin, and melting fur into a gelatinous goo. In fact, for one harrowing moment, she thought she glimpsed bone. She thought she glimpsed *skull*.

Then the beast shrieked, and fled.

Leaving Cassie leaning against the skewed kitchen table, sucking in all the breaths she hadn't been able to for the last half hour. She gulped air by the great, shuddering lungful, every inch of her shaking like she never had in her life. She lifted a hand in front of her face, and it quivered so much that it made her think of Jell-O. In a cement mixer. Set to high.

And she couldn't think rationally. Her mind was a great, roaring noise, full of mangled werewolves, and kitchen utensils like arrows, and the microwave—god, the microwave had taken a bullet for her. *It does love me after all*, she found herself thinking, then for some ungodly reason choked up. And she fully broke down when she heard it beep, forlornly, from somewhere in the hall. In fact, she almost went to it.

And then it struck her:

Seth.

Fucking Seth.

Holy shit, Seth was out there with those monsters, while she stood here blubbering over a kitchen appliance. But it was okay, it was good, because she knew what to do now. She'd seen what hurt them, and the spray bottle was right there, intact, as if it had been waiting for her to grab it.

Like a spare bullet, she thought, and snatched it up.

Then she did what she knew had made the beast's flesh melt. She poured some of the extra-strength werewolf potion into the bottle, and shook it up. Because that was the secret, she was certain. That was what had acted like an acid. It had knocked the

Make Nice formula up from a protection potion, to an outright Werewolf Killer.

And now she was going to kill some fucking werewolves with it.

She didn't even think twice about it. She ran to the front door, and flung herself out of the house. Took the porch steps in one go, and practically flew across the grass to the first enemy she could find. Jordan, she thought it was, because he was barely in the fight that was taking place between Seth and Jay. He was just on the sidelines, snapping ineffectually.

Plus, the moment the spray hit him, he *howled*.

He practically shrieked, like the little coward he was—and immediately turned tail.

Which left Jay. Jay, who in wolf form was almost as big as Seth. Pale-furred, like his hair, and as grisly looking as the other two. Tiny, beady little eyes, paws all knuckle, bones in places no bones should be. There was a great muddle of them, over the curve of his back. More making impossible spine-like ridges, down the backs of both hind legs. And oh, his face was grotesque.

Ninety percent teeth.

He looked like a shark, she thought, that had somehow gained the ability to walk on land.

But it didn't matter. Nothing mattered, the second she thought of those fangs sinking into Seth. Seth, who had done everything in his power to protect her. Seth, who had looked at her like that, as he held her in his arms. Seth who had said *return what I took*, as if it wasn't anything at all.

Even though it was the whole world. It was her best friend, come back to her.

And so she didn't just step forward and spray the thing attacking him.

She unscrewed the top of the bottle, and smashed it into the first part of the wolf she could reach. She turned the bottle into a hand grenade, without caring what it might do. *If he dies, he dies*, she thought wildly, as flesh boiled to bone beneath her hands. As the beast shrieked and writhed and struggled to get away from her, before it had nothing left to get away from her with.

Most of its hind leg was gone now.

It had to stumble on the remaining three to make it to the tree line. Then it disappeared into the undergrowth, as the others had done. Like it was just as much of a coward as them, when facing a real threat. A serious threat.

Because that's what I am, she thought as she looked down at her bloody hands in the ringing silence and stillness that followed. *I am powerful enough to threaten the boys who once held me against my locker with one hand while smacking Seth across the face with the other.*

And she really wanted to marvel over that, for a while.

But she couldn't, because the second there was real silence she heard the pained sounds. Desperate ones, of the sort that made her heart clench, in the same way it had all those years ago. Although this time, it wasn't over a bloodied nose or a broken finger or a bruised rib.

It wasn't any injury at all.

It was her friend doing his best to turn back. To go back to being a person, now that the danger was past. Despite how much the effort seemed to be hurting him. God, she could see how much it was hurting him.

"Seth, it's okay. It's okay. Stay like that. I'm not afraid," she said as she stepped toward the humped shape he was making on the grass. But he didn't listen. He kept on fighting it. He gritted half-human teeth, saliva foaming between them as he strained. Eyes closed tight, as everything ripped. As some muscles shrank and others remained, as bones cracked and popped like fireworks, as fur seemed to shrink or shed or simply melt away.

So she went to crouch next to him, like she had at the gorge.

To put a gentling hand on him, and soothe him out of the state he was in.

But before she could, he scrabbled away. He squeezed out words.

"No," he gasped. "No, stay where you are."

And his voice held such a note of desperation that she didn't know how to disobey. She just stood there, helpless, as he slowly and agonizingly became something like a man again, and shakily got to his feet. Though even after he had, he didn't seem to want her to come near him.

She took a step, and he held up a hand.

Shook his head, when she suggested that she get him some clothes.

"You can't leave like that," she tried to half laugh—because he was barely wearing a stitch. He had on the collar of his shirt and one leg of his jeans. And that pants leg was not covering a lot. She had to keep her eyes well above his waist, to spare his blushes.

But he didn't seem to care.

In fact, if anything, he seemed more afraid of her getting close to him than he had before. He almost stumbled back when she so much as reached a hand out to him. *Like he's ashamed of something*, she thought. And the flush all over his face seemed to confirm. As did the way he sounded when he spoke.

"Just protect yourself, protect the house. I'll be back soon," he said, as wavery as wind through reeds. Then before she could protest—before she could say, *But what about you, what if they try to get you again?*—he turned his back to her. He aimed for the woods.

And he was gone.

CHAPTER SIXTEEN

Cassie didn't mean to sleep once she was safe inside the tornado-wracked kitchen. But somehow in the middle of hugging the microwave—which informed her that it would be speaking to its lawyer about being spell-pressed into werewolf fights—she managed to sit on the floor, and slump against the refrigerator.

And that was it. She went out like a dropped anvil.

She didn't even stir over the sink collapsing. Or when the microwave somehow maneuvered her body, until she was curled up on a heap of dish towels and pot holders and aprons. It even managed to drape a tablecloth over her, by roping in the help of the refrigerator. Like a bizarre version of *Cinderella*, with kitchen appliances instead of birds.

And so, when she finally did wake, there was no crick in her neck. There were no aching bones. In fact, she felt more rested than she had in ages. Like she had slept all night.

Then she checked her phone, and realized.

She had.

She'd been asleep for *hours*.

It was well into the morning. Scarily well into the morning.

Because apparently, Seth had not returned. He hadn't messaged, he hadn't called. There was no sign of him anywhere. And that meant one of two things: either he was sound asleep too, as peaceful and happy as a clam. Or he had been captured, and was being tortured by the werewolf super bullies from hell.

And she had to know which.

So even though her kitchen was a bomb site, and everything

was really bad, and there was still goddamn werewolf blood under her fingernails, the first thing she did was make an Are They Okay potion. She threw it together, in the only intact pot she could find, so impatient about it that she burned herself twice. Then once it was finally, finally done, she poured some on the hallway mirror, to see what it revealed.

Though it still wasn't exactly clear. All it did was give her the sight of Seth, grabbing a tree and trying to haul himself forward. Like he was straining against something, somehow. Like some instinct was making him act weird. Before that same instinct forced him back, back, to what was definitely his dad's old hunting lodge.

And that was good, in one way.

It meant he wasn't dead. And that the Jerks didn't have him.

But at the same time, something bad was very obviously going on. Something that meant flying to him as soon as she could. So she made sure the microwave was all right and back in its place on the countertop. And she whipped up a general tidying potion to sort some of the wreckage that was her house. And finally, for good measure, she set a protection spell around everything. Just a quick Repel You If You Come Near type of thing, that probably wouldn't hold.

But it was enough.

Then she grabbed some werewolf killer, just in case, and the still slightly busted but usable Hoover, and she went for it. She tried to fly, across her yard. At first with one foot still sort of on the ground, kind of propelling her forward and keeping her anchored—like a kid on a skateboard. But then with more confidence.

She picked up a bit of speed. Wobbled, but managed to right it.

Went a little high again, and somehow got it under control.

And suddenly she just felt it, instinctively. It came over her in a great wave—how to sort of pull to make it slow, and tilt to make it go in the direction she wanted to. What to do when it wasn't going fast enough, so the speed increased.

You had to kind of urge it with both feet.

Like the Hoover was some kind of very oddly shaped horse.

And when she got that, and acted accordingly, the whole thing simply surged forward. It darted between the trees, fast enough that she came fairly close to crashing. An oak was suddenly in her face, and she had to bank hard to the right. But even that seemed to come easier.

Everything was suddenly easier.

She wove between branches, and swooped over fallen logs.

Went higher on purpose, just to see if she could. Then she plunged back down, so steeply it almost made her feel sick. Suddenly, her stomach was in her throat. She went to scream and couldn't, because every bit of air in her was abruptly somewhere else. Though she wasn't entirely sure that was a bad thing.

It felt pretty incredible.

She found herself laughing over it giddily.

But it was when she reached the hunting lodge that the truly astonishing thing happened.

She saw the building looming up from between the trees. And instead of carefully coming to a stop, she swooped down. She made a staggeringly steep arc, all the way across the scrubby yard in front of the place. And while the Hoover was still in motion, she simply climbed off.

Only "climbed off" was probably the wrong way to put it.

It was more like she sprang off in a graceful leap, like she floated, like for once *hers* were the feet that had wheels. She didn't even stop when she touched the ground. She strode toward the house, Seth's name on her lips.

But before she could get there, his voice stopped her.

"I can't come out right now," he said.

And that was good, because it meant he was alive.

But it was also bad, because why the hell did he need to stay inside?

"Seth, if you're injured so much that you don't want me to see, you really should," she tried. Yet still, he didn't emerge. There was the sound of shuffling, and maybe sighing, and then finally he answered.

"I'm not that injured. In fact, I'm totally fine. So you can go now."

So you can go now? she thought, incredulously. Then had to insist.

"Think I'm gonna need a little more proof-of-life type stuff there, buddy."

"Honestly, I'm alive. And I'm gonna stay alive."

"That sounds exactly like the kind of thing someone who *isn't* going to stay alive would say."

Silence then. A long, long silence.

So long in fact that she started to feel more than nervous.

She almost walked right up and burst right in. But just as she was about to, the door abruptly swung open. And Seth stepped out, looking surprisingly not dead in the slightest. There were no wounds anywhere, no signs that any body part was falling off. He just seemed kind of sweaty and panicked. Jittery—like something had happened that he didn't like.

Though she couldn't help wondering what that something might be. Or why he hadn't checked on her the way she was checking on him. He didn't even seem that concerned about her being here, despite how dangerous they both knew the woods might be right now.

All of which was odd behavior, for a friend.

But maybe *less* odd if he didn't feel as friendly anymore. If maybe something had happened to embarrass him—like, say, his old, cool buddies sneering at the idea that she was his girlfriend. And him blurting out that thing about belonging.

God, even she couldn't believe he'd said that thing about belonging.

He probably meant to say something less romantic-sounding, and is now mortified and certain you're going to take it the wrong way, she thought, and oh this all fit just a little bit too well. It immediately made her think of that time in high school when she'd realized that Seth had moved on from her. She had run right up to him to gush about the latest episode of *Hannibal*, and he'd looked at her so awkwardly. He'd fumbled his words, as those three assholes had laughed.

And that was what this was like.

In fact, it was so much like it she couldn't help but blurt words out.

"Look, you should just say if they made you change your mind about being friends again. Because I'm not going to wait around for your hints and weird responses to my questions this time. I won't keep coming over and checking out how you are, while you do nothing, and then look at me like I've grown three heads," she said.

And sure, it made her heart feel like it was throwing up to do it.

But it got something out of him besides this weird awkwardness. He took a step forward, expression suddenly a little more desperate. And he sounded it, too, when he spoke.

"Cassie, that's not how I'm looking at you, that's not—I did try to check on you—I wanted to come to—" he stuttered. But before he could finish any sentence that made sense, he seemed to jerk. Like he'd been slapped. And for some reason, he stumbled backward through the door.

Then he tried to *close* it.

All he left was an inch-wide gap to peer through.

"Okay, you know what? I gotta go. I'm sorry they mortified you with all that girlfriend talk. Maybe you'll grow up one day and get over them teasing you out of liking me. And until then, look at me as your local pharmacist. I dispense your medicine, that's it," she told him, more calmly than she really felt.

Because inside, everything was screaming.

It felt like tears were bashing on the insides of her eyes. She had to turn before he saw.

But oh god, he was opening the door back up. He was calling after her. "Cassie, come on, you can't possibly believe I would listen to those guys. I mean, they tried to kill you. They tried to kill me," he said, and okay he had a point there.

Though maybe less of one when she put it in the context of past events.

"Maybe that was just a ruse. Part of a new prank."

"Oh my god, it wasn't a prank. I swear, I didn't even know they were in town. We haven't spoken in years, I told you," he protested, and as he did she heard him crossing the porch. She heard him trying to come to her. So before he could do it she whirled around, ready to yell at him to stay where he was.

But she didn't have to.

He got within thirty feet of her and just *dropped*. He went right to his knees, clutching his guts. Like at the gorge—only worse somehow. Way more intense. Like he was straining against something, or straining toward something, or some other action that she couldn't quite name.

He looks hungry, she thought.

And to her shock, she got that witch tingle. The one that told her she was correct.

Even though that seemed bonkers. Because why wouldn't he be allowed food? Was he injured in some way she couldn't see or sense? It was possible, she supposed—and enough that she found herself taking a step forward. She reached out a hand, thinking she would help him back into the dingy old lodge behind him.

But that just seemed to make things worse.

He jerked back, eyes wide, the moment she moved toward him.

And he clutched himself again. Like being near her turned his stomach.

"Oh holy fuck, don't come any closer. In fact, move farther away," he stumbled out, as he tried to wave her back with his free hand. And when he did, another portion of her fear and disappointment slid away.

Though it left a lot of questions behind.

"Okay, I am going to need you to tell me why you want me farther away," she said, and knew right down to her bones that he was going to prevaricate. She could almost see him straining to come up with something that wasn't quite the whole truth.

But maybe seemed close enough that she would back down.

"It's not because I hate you somehow, I swear."

"Yeah, I can see that. However, I still need you to explain."

"But it might go away soon, and then I won't really have to."

"You will always have to. Because look what happens when you don't—I fling myself through the woods, beside myself at the

thought that you're hurt. Or worse: I start imagining you've abandoned me forever, again."

That got him, she could tell.

His face twisted in agony the moment she said "beside myself,"
and then again when she said "hurt," and even more so when she
said "abandoned me forever." Oh, he could hardly stand it when
he heard that last one. He had to really fight to keep himself from
saying whatever this obviously embarrassing truth was.

And in the end he just couldn't win. He couldn't hold it in. "For
god's sake, Cass, it's none of those things. I would never abandon
you again. It's just that getting fucking horny makes me turn, all
right?" he burst out, all in a half-growled rush. Like he was saying
the worst thing the world had ever known. Like he had commit-
ted some harrowing crime. He even made a mortified moaning
noise as soon as the words escaped. Then he pressed the heels of
his hands into his eyes, like he couldn't stand to see her expression.

Even though she kind of had no idea what the problem was.

All she felt was confusion, the second she grasped what he had
said.

Because, actually, hadn't he almost told her that before? He'd
said emotions and hormones did it. This was only one step further.
And even if it wasn't, well. It didn't seem like a big deal. "That
doesn't seem like something you needed to keep from me," she
said. But his response was just a mirthless-sounding laugh.

Then he dropped his hands, so she could see exactly the extent
of his despair.

"Yeah, well, just wait until you hear what's making the horniness happen."

"So it's something so disturbing I will scream?"

He sighed, in a bone-weary way. "Probably, yeah."

"What do you mean, probably?"

"I mean definitely," he said. "In a friendship-ruining way."

And okay, *now* she was worried. *Now* she was starting to think
she couldn't handle it. Like maybe it was something so repulsive
nobody on earth could accept it. Even though the options for a repulsive thing were pretty limited with Seth. She remembered him

vomiting in the aisle during the five-fifteen showing of *The Last House on the Left*. And he'd never even made it all the way through *The Hills Have Eyes*.

Because he loved being scared by horror movies; he truly loved it. But he hated watching stuff like that happen to women. *I'm in it to watch them fuck baddies up,* he had once said to her.

So what did that leave, really? What disgusting thing could it be?

Something incredibly weird, she thought. And to her horror, a possibility came to her.

"Oh god. If you tell me you need to stop coming around because you are super into frog-fucking, and all the ones that hang out under my porch are making you mad with lust, I will just lose it. I will not be okay with it," she said.

And her only consolation was the way he rolled his eyes.

"Honestly, I don't even know how your mind went there first."

"Because you acted like the thing that makes you horny is the worst thing ever."

"Yeah, and I meant in an emotional way. Not in a go-to-prison way."

"You're not going to go to prison for making love to a frog, Seth."

He let out an indignant sound. Threw up his hands. "Don't say it like this is actually a thing I want to do."

"So then just tell me what is making you lose it enough to stop seeing me."

"*You* are. *You* are what is making me lose it."

She could see as soon as he'd said it that he hadn't meant to. That he'd just gotten lost in the argument, and frustrated enough that he hadn't been able to help blurting out the words.

But she couldn't comfort him about it.

She was too busy trying to swim through a sea of *What The Fuck*.

And when she finally reached some kind of shore, it wasn't a good one. It was a suspicious one. A very suspicious one. "Oh, I get it. This is a joke, right?" she said.

Much to his irritation. "What sort of joke could it possibly be?"

"The one where those jerks pop out and start laughing the second I believe this ridiculousness. Even though I swear to god I never will. And even if I somehow could, you know full well that I would *not* be into it. That I'd die before I started mooning over you," she said—and hated that it felt like a lie.

But loved that she'd managed to say it anyway.

And loved even more that his expression said he believed it.

"Okay, for starters, the idea of you mooning over me is so ridiculous I want to laugh my ass off. In fact, I *would* be laughing my ass off, if I didn't have to be extremely serious when I say: absolutely none of this is a joke. None of it. This is just the truth. Everything I'm telling you is just the very humiliating truth."

She folded her arms across her chest. "Even though it's absurd."

"Yes, it is absurd. But then so is being a fucking werewolf."

"Being a werewolf is not enough to explain this, and you know it."

He went to protest then. She saw him do it. She saw him wind up whatever he wanted to fire back with. But he stopped, and he blew out a breath, and kind of shook his head. And she knew what he was thinking:

Fine, you have a point there.

Though the realization didn't exactly hold him for long. He seemed to consider for a second, and then she saw his eyes gleam. And she knew he'd come up with another way to make this madness work.

"Okay, so what about if I have other mitigating circumstances," he tried.

And she couldn't help going with him on that, just a little bit.

"What kind of mitigating circumstances, exactly?"

"Well, you know. I haven't had sex in a while."

"A few years of no fucking is not going to cover this, Seth."

"Yeah, but I don't exactly mean a few years. I mean more than that."

"Well, how many are we talking here?"

He rubbed the back of his neck awkwardly. And the expression on his face was pure reluctance and embarrassment, she knew it was. But it didn't make his eventual answer any easier to swallow. "All of them," he said.

As if that could ever possibly make sense, instead of being so ridiculous she almost didn't get it at first.

She started to ask him what he meant—and then it hit her.

And oh god, he just could not be serious.

"There is absolutely *no way* you are telling me you're a virgin," she said. But here was the real kick in the pants—he didn't even take it back. He saw how hilarious and impossible she found it, and stayed the course. He doubled down.

"Is it really that hard to believe, considering what I am?" he asked.

Even though that did not work as an explanation, on any level at all.

"Yeah, what you are *now*. But you weren't a werewolf in high school. When you were fucking homecoming king and captain of the swim team and half the school had a crush on you. I once saw a girl try to hit you in the face with her boob. One of your fan club called me at work five years after I moved away to ask me if I would ask you to marry her. You were a god to those people."

Okay, hot shot, get out of that one, she thought at him.

Then watched him have the nerve to actually try.

"That might be true, but I was still a dork inside."

"What, so much of one that you didn't bone Missy Taylor after prom?"

"I didn't even want to take Missy Taylor to prom. Never mind bone her," he said, and his voice went convincingly high and strained and indignant when he did.

But there was still a problem.

"Well, you know what? Even if you didn't, and never have with anyone, this still makes no sense at all. Because doinking someone isn't the only way to alleviate intense werewolf horniness. I mean— just jerk off, like everybody else," she said, in as withering a tone as she could muster. She even demonstrated at the end with a lewd gesture. Like what she was saying was the most self-evident thing in the world.

Then she saw his expression.

The way his eyes slid upward, away from hers. How he flushed a brilliant red—like her mocking him had really hit him in his embarrassment bone. Even though (a) she had only done it because the very idea was obvious proof of his lies, and (b) oh dear god, it meant he wasn't lying. It meant he wasn't lying.

And now she had to put her hands on her knees to absorb the impact of that.

"Ohhhhhh my god, you're saying you can't do that either. You're saying that you cannot masturbate. That you have not masturbated in eight years. Eight whole enormous years. Almost an entire decade without so much as a hand on yourself," she said, between the calming breaths she was trying to take.

While he just made things even worse and more undeniable.

"Well, I mean, I have had a hand on myself. Just, you know. Not fully."

"I don't think the extent is really the issue I'm having with this, Seth."

"So tell me what the issues are," he asked, desperately.

But all she could come up with was: "That it *should* help. If being horny makes you wolf out, that is the cure." Even though she knew it wasn't going to fly. She knew he was going to have a terrible, terrible answer. And sure enough, he was already shaking his head.

"Oh yeah, you would think so, right?" he said, in such a falsely cheery way her heart dropped. And it dropped harder when he continued. "Ha ha, no. No, that is not how it works at all. If I get riled up, it happens. If I try to relieve being riled up by being with someone or being with myself or being with any number of appliances I might have made out of ice packs and sandpaper, it happens. There are no circumstances where it doesn't. Except living like a member of the Jedi Order."

Oh god, he's a space monk, she thought. Even though she knew the truth was somehow worse. "To be honest, I think the Jedi Order gets more than ice and sandpaper," she admitted reluctantly. But not as reluctantly as he conceded.

"Yeah, I do too. I was just trying to make myself feel more cool."

"You deserve to, considering you've almost reduced your dick to sawdust before today. I mean, good god, is that a real thing you tried? Or were you just exaggerating to make my eyes go enormous?"

He seemed to hesitate. She saw his tongue touch his upper teeth.

Before finally, "First, tell me which answer sounds understandable."

Because he was ridiculous, oh god, he was the most ridiculous man to ever live.

"Okay, so now, see—all of this is making everything sound so understandable that I have to wonder why on earth you didn't just tell me. Because I would have totally grasped 'Being a werewolf means that having sexual feelings of any kind makes me turn into a beast, and so therefore I have repressed all my urges to the point where literally anything can make me deranged,'" she pointed out.

And he had the decency to look sheepish. "Yeah, but when *you* say it, it sounds reasonable."

"Well, what way were you thinking of saying it that didn't?"

He shrugged. "I don't know. Every scenario I ran in my head just wound up with me saying terrible, friendship-ruining stuff. Like how strongly I was affected when you rubbed your hands all over my chest, and called me amazing. Even though, I swear, I didn't intend to feel that way. I didn't even fully know it was happening—that this was the thing causing it all—until after the fight. But then I looked back, and I realized," he said, and now a lot of things were becoming startlingly clear. In fact, one of them made her roll her eyes at herself, it was that obvious.

"So *that's* why you had that spike, at the gorge."

"Oh yeah, for sure."

"And it probably explains the weirdness when we watched the fairies."

"I was super glad when they suddenly started trying to kill us."

"Then when I rubbed potion on my shoulder . . ."

He snapped his fingers. Pointed at her. "Definitely also a top contender for reducing me to a drooling mess."

"And the fight, when there was all that grabbing of me—"

"It wasn't just the grabbing. Though I'm loathe to say what else it was," he said, embarrassed enough again that he looked at his feet. It was okay though. He didn't have to explain. She already knew enough to fill in the answer for him.

"The protectiveness. The possessiveness," she said, and he shot such a look her way.

It was practically a gasp in the form of a facial expression.

"Damn, how did you guess that?" he asked.

Then she just couldn't resist. All her emotions had been running so high and hot for way too many hours. She had to break it with a joke. "Oh well, I read about it in *National Geographic*."

And of course he gave her his biggest goofball look. All big earnest eyes and excitement.

"Holy shit, no way. I can't believe it said that in there," he said.

Like the adorable little dipshit he was.

"Because it didn't, doofus. I got it from every movie, TV show, romance novel, and piece of fan fiction ever. Like with most of this stuff, no human scientific journal on earth has ever gotten it right. But *Fated to Be His Sexy Mate* sure did," she said—and his amused reaction was how she knew they were really back to being friends. Because this weirdness was a thing, and they'd had this blip. But he could still laugh at her teasing him, over being a fool.

Then bat it back at her.

"Right right right. And where can I get a copy of this, again?"

"I would tell you, but I'm afraid it might make you rampage through the bookstore. And as much as I like you, I'm not willing to sacrifice said store for you."

"All I heard was you still like me. Even after I confessed all of that," he said—and he did it just as lightly as everything else he had just told her. Like that was nothing, too. Even though the words sunk through her like warm syrup the second he spoke them. She almost clutched at her heart. And it took everything she had to focus on the problem at hand, in reply.

To not gush all over him, like a soppy fool.

"Of *course* I do. Literally the only thing you did wrong here was not tell me—but even that, I understand. Because, to be honest, if something made me horny for you completely against my own will, I'd be mortified at the thought of telling you too. In fact, the very idea is making me cringe, just thinking about it. So, you know, don't worry. I get it," she said. Then when he still looked a little tense, she added something more. "And you know what? We're gonna fix it."

Though she didn't realize how possible that actually was, until the words were out. Because the second they were, she got that tingle. She got that urge to start boiling and brewing and baking. To figure things out, in a way that gave her more satisfaction than anything in her life ever had.

And it was good that it did, too.

Because oh, his *reaction*.

The look of pure warmth and openness and gratitude all over his face. The way he stepped forward, like he wanted to wrap her in a hug. And the thing he did, when he realized he couldn't.

He made a heart with his hands. And pointed right at her, to make sure she knew who that heart was for.

Because sure, he could have said it with words.

But she could tell that tears would have made them unclear.

CHAPTER SEVENTEEN

She knew things wouldn't change much between them, after that. Because of course whatever lust he was feeling toward her wasn't real. It was just a weird werewolf thing, triggered by events he barely understood. Like a gushing comment, or too much contact after too little, or violent assholes making him be all protective. Or her scent, which was most likely loaded with all kinds of hormones and pheromones and other chemicals his body appreciated.

And she could simply avoid every one of those things.

The assholes weren't going to be coming back any time soon to trigger protectiveness on Seth's part. *They're afraid of you,* he told her simply, when she asked. *You made them shift their whole territory twenty miles away. I checked them out a few days ago and they ran when they caught my scent.*

So that was that. Or, at least, it was for now.

And as for the other triggers, well. She could easily stop herself from gushing over him, or touching him unexpectedly. Neither of those were things she had done intentionally, or liked doing. Which only left her scent—and there were definitely ways to mask it.

A simple blocking potion, used like soap and shampoo, saw to that.

By the time he came over next, she felt pretty sure she smelled like nothing to him. In fact, she knew she did, because after she'd called for him to come in, he just stood tensely in the archway that led into the kitchen. Breath held, shoulders hunched, one hand raised. Like he was just there for a quick hello. A reassurance, she thought, that he hadn't abandoned her.

And that felt pretty awesome, she had to say.

But even more awesome when she saw the realization dawn all over his face.

His expression went from strained panic, to a kind of soft confusion, to something so full of relief it made her heart lift. And he let himself come into the kitchen. Tentatively, while taking slow breaths. But he did it. He got all the way to the kitchen table. Tried sitting down, just to see how it went.

And when he managed, oh the laugh that broke out of him. "Fuck, that is so smart. A scent blocker. Why didn't I think of that?" he asked, then seemed perfectly content to be across from her. As if everything else—her face, her body, her personality—meant precisely nothing to him, attraction-wise. And that was good. It was fine.

It was great, in fact. It meant they had a stopgap now.

A way to spend time together—both as friends, and as a team to work on his problem.

Because if she was being honest, she already knew she was going to need his help. This potion—to break the connection between horniness and turning, or to stop him from feeling desires he didn't want—felt complicated, in a way the other potions hadn't. In fact, every time she tried to think about it, her mind seemed to slide sideways, or circle it nervously, or give her answers she didn't understand.

You need to satisfy the requirements, it kept telling her.

And all of this made her really glad for his presence. And not just because it meant he could offer solutions or suggestions, or give her clippings of his hair and his fur and other bananas stuff like that. No, there was also something else. Something he had often done back when they were kids, and now just started up again like it was nothing.

He organized the study area.

She had spilled the contents of her old pencil case over the table; he neatly lined up all the pens and pencils and erasers and highlighters. Then he grabbed the two guides whose pages she'd been dog-earing, and replaced the folded corners with little Post-it labels. Ones that he scribbled on, and cross-referenced, in a note-pad she didn't remember having.

She saw him jot down ingredients and how to obtain them—like fairyroot, which involved burying an item owned by a fairy beneath a patch of moss, and frostweed, which could be found growing over anything dead beneath a frozen lake. Then he added questions to terms that weren't quite clear. Need to find out what molloch is, he wrote, on a tag he applied next to the circled and mysteriously definitionless word.

And finally, he tidied the file she'd opened on her laptop.

Instead of *hiw to hekp an horny wwrwolf*, in a terrible font, it became: How to Help a Hungry Werewolf, in his favorite one, Book Antiqua.

Because she had always been the sloppy ideas girl, and he had always been the tidy idea polisher, and apparently nothing had changed. They just fell back into their old patterns, like it was nothing. Like horny awkwardness wasn't even a thing.

In fact, by day three she was starting to think it possibly wasn't.

That maybe he had gotten worked up over nothing.

It's not just that he isn't actually attracted to you that's keeping him calm, her mind suggested. *But the fact that lots of simple, boring exposure to the way you are is actively killing whatever pheromones and danger and touching briefly created.*

And okay, that sounded a little extreme. But a lot of things did seem to bear it out.

Like the day before, when their hands had accidentally brushed as she passed him a spoonful of potion to try. The contact had sent a jolt all the way up her arm. It had made her drop the spoon. But he had just mused about the taste of the sample. *Sort of reminds me of root beer,* he had said. Nice, but does nothing at all.

And then there was that morning. When she'd leaned over him without thinking to look at something he'd pointed to on the laptop screen. *She* had immediately registered the mistake. *She* had felt every inch of that sliver of space between them, like a crackling forcefield she shouldn't cross.

But he hadn't. He'd just smiled at her blandly.

Like it was all nothing to him, in a way she should have felt relieved about. She *was* relieved about it. There was no other way to feel, if she was being honest about it. Things were exactly as they had always seemed. They were exactly as they were supposed to be, in every single possible way. Because even though he had shown her he wasn't an ass about how she was, he was still the kind of man who dated Prom Queens.

And that was fine by her. She no longer felt like she had to be Kayleigh Mathers or Jessica Yates, to be attractive. She didn't base her self-esteem on whether the Great Seth Brubaker deemed her acceptable to date.

It simply made sense, when he didn't react to certain things about her.

Like when the top button on her jersey popped open, as she stood, revealing most of her cleavage. And he didn't even glance at it. His eyes were firmly on her face when she said, "I think we should grab some dinner, you coming?"

Then they just flicked back to the laptop screen.

"Yeah, I'll catch up. Just give me five minutes," he said. As if by that point he was so disinterested, he wasn't even concerned about her walking alone in the near dark.

First day we did this he wanted to get breakfast together, just in case those assholes did dare try something, she thought, as she tugged on her jacket, and pulled on her sneakers. But he still wasn't looking up. It was like his eyes had been magnetized to the screen. She was starting to wonder if someone with boobs he did want to look at was on there.

Then just as she went for the door, she heard a sound.

A kind of long, keening whine that seemed to get louder and louder and louder. Until finally, blessedly, it broke. And suddenly, there was Seth, barking out words. "Okay, stop. I can't stand it, just stop. Please. Don't go out without me," he said desperately. Like it was some kind of unbearable agony not to.

Though when she turned, he was still sitting at the table.

And he didn't do anything to rectify that, as she stood there waiting.

"All right. So are you going to get up, or . . ."

"I can't just yet. Gimme a minute."

"But why? Are you in pain?"

He winced, which suggested he was. Though he didn't exactly explain. "Something like that," he said without looking at her. And that meant dragging it out of him, before he wound up dying of some other terrible thing he wasn't telling her about.

"So then let me help you. Let me fix it."

"No, you can't fix this. It'll go away. I just need to concentrate."

"On what? Wishing the agony would leave? I have pain potions."

She stepped to the potion shelf, and started gathering ones she could imagine him needing. Ache Healer seemed like a safe bet, she thought. And Muscle Relaxer was probably going to be of use. But just as she was getting to the pouring-into-a-spoon step, he stopped her.

"That's not gonna help," he said.

And she knew, as soon as he did, that she was not going to want to know what would. Though like a fool, she went ahead and asked anyway. "Give me one reason why not," she demanded, all cockily. Hands on hips, and everything.

Then got this in return: "Because I am pretty sure that the magic equivalent of aspirin does nothing for giant erections that I have been desperately trying to keep my buddy from beholding with her poor innocent eyes, for what feels like a week."

And oh god he was not kidding.

He was really not.

She could see that he wasn't, because he stood as he said it. And *man*, there was a lot to see. Too much, if she was being honest. She almost proved him right on that "poor innocent eyes" comment, by covering them. Before she managed to get hold of herself, and react sensibly.

"So what you are saying is you have just been sitting there with an erection for the last three days. Without even thinking that this might be worth mentioning to me at any point during that unhinged amount of time," she said, as calmly as she could. While he quite clearly panicked, for no good reason she could think of.

"If I mention it, I have to explain why it happened," he said.

"Well, you managed before."

"Before, I had good-sounding reasons."

She gave him a look. "And now the reasons are all really bad?"

"Well, they're definitely getting worse, let's put it that way."

"Maybe you should let me be the judge of what's worse."

He flopped back into his chair. Sighed, heavily. "I can't. If I do, you'll try to do something about it. Which was totally fine when it was just you blocking your scent, or not grabbing me, or not saying sort of hot things to me. All those things were not fundamental changes to who you are. But this is. This would be. You would do things differently to make it easier for me to cope. You would feel self-conscious. And I just don't want you to. The very idea is gross to me."

"So it's something like—you saw my bra strap."

"Cassie, I have barely looked below your chin the whole time we've been doing this."

He said it so casually that for a second she couldn't respond. Her brain just ran slap-bang into a wall of *that means he's deliberately avoiding looking at things down there. As if those things down there might trigger some kind of horny response.*

And that was . . . well, it was a lot to process, for someone who'd spent the last few days thinking nothing like that could be affecting him. Who had spent the last *decade* thinking it could never. He had pressed the idea into her so firmly she didn't know how to think anything else.

So it left her panicking a little. And searching for ways to laugh it off. "Maybe if you did it would help, considering the overalls I'm wearing," she said, but wow, the withering look he gave her. The snort he let out, before he spoke.

"You mean the ones I know are so tight I can see every one of your soft, delicious curves underneath them, and also so threadbare it would take almost nothing to tear them off? Those overalls? Yeah, they're a real buzzkill."

Soft, she thought. *Delicious*, she thought.

Then seemed to hear sirens blaring at the back of her head.

She had to ask for clarification just to keep herself sane.

"Seth, I'm going to need you to explain this more."

"But it doesn't matter what explanation I give you. How respectful I want to be of you, how careful of our friendship, how much I attempt to push these feelings down or tell myself they're not real. All that matters is what my body is telling me."

"And what is your body telling you here, exactly?"

"That you look fucking hot in tight clothes," he said, like someone had whacked him on the back, and forced a cough out of him. Only the cough was just the truth, of a kind he definitely didn't want to say. He had to put his face in his hands after he had. He groaned the rest of his words through his fingers. "I can't believe I just confessed that to you."

And god, she came so close to saying, *I like that you did.*

In fact, the only thing that stopped her was the other things he said. That it wasn't real, that he wanted to push it down, that it was all just something inside him, warping his usual perspective. All of those things ran through her head, and then reassurances came out of her, instead.

"You should be glad you confessed," she said. "Because now I can tell you it's not a big deal."

"It will be when you choose a gigantic fucking sack to wear tomorrow."

"Somehow I don't think a sack would put you off, if these don't."

He let his hands drop. Most likely because the embarrassment was fading, as the argument took over. "Of course it would. I mean it would drown you," he said in an almost exasperated voice. But then he made the mistake of continuing. "Nothing would be visible. Everything would be hidden, and secret, underneath all that material. You'd only ever be able to see the smallest hint of something sweet, and so soft, and—ohhhh okay, right, yeah, I see what you mean. I might be grasping the issue now."

And she laughed to see and hear it happen. The way he'd started out making sense.

Then somehow talked himself into drooling over her imaginary sack dress.

"Yeah, because the issue is any clothes would do," she said, and knew she was right.

Even if he wouldn't yet concede entirely.

"Maybe. But there are other things. More specific things."

"So tell me them. We already managed to explain one, in a way other than you being super into me or just behaving like a massive creep. I bet we can manage to do whatever else there is, too. So come on. Stop repressing it. Get it off your chest."

He raised an eyebrow. "So is this your professional witchy advice, Dr. Camberwell?" he asked. And okay yeah, he was joking. But at the same time, she kind of didn't think he was. His gaze didn't quite hit amused; his smile was teasing, but not a smirk.

Like maybe part of him really was starting to see her that way:

As someone two seconds away from getting their medical degree in witchery.

And weirdly? That kind of felt right. She found herself thinking of what they were doing as treating him, as treating a patient, as treating a supernatural patient, and felt a strange little thrill. Like the kind of feeling she imagined other people got, when they realized what they wanted to do with their lives. Or simply remembered dreams they'd once had, come back to them in a slightly different form. *Maybe that was why some part of me wanted to be a doctor or a nurse*, she thought. And that felt so satisfying she could feel a smile trying to spread over her face.

Though she didn't let him change the subject entirely. "Honestly? Maybe," she replied. "I've got the strongest urge to write this down."

And got an eye roll for it. "Great. So my shameful lusting will be preserved forever."

"It's not shameful to lust. It's shameful to foist it on other people when other people haven't asked. To act on it in ways that you are definitely not doing. I mean, you just hid your erection from me for three days, Seth. You've been a complete gentleman, despite the extreme pressure you're under. So you know what? Go ahead. Hit me with your best shot."

That got him, she thought. She even knew exactly what word had done it—gentleman. She said it, and his eyes flashed all bright and hopeful. Like maybe, just maybe, he was getting through this in a decent manner. And if he shared it with her, maybe that decency would become a permanent fixture. A part of his foundation. Something immutable and steadying.

"If I tell you this stuff, will you swear to not change who you are? Or think I want to be thinking this?" he asked. And in response, she held up the Vulcan salute. Like they used to do when they were kids, and a promise was being made.

"You have my solemn and most heartfelt vow that I shall never. On the name of our lord and savior Wes Craven. Amen," she said, then got a laugh for her troubles.

Though when she looked back, the amusement was gone.

And in its place was something hesitant. But determined.

"All right. All right. If you think it will be okay, I'll tell you. I can do this. I just have to, you know. Do it real quick. Like ripping off a Band-Aid," he started. Then he closed his eyes, and took a breath, and let it just burst out of him. "Every time you figure something out, you make this really incredibly super-excited noise."

And after he had, he seemed to brace. As if he was just waiting for her disgusted reaction.

Even though she had absolutely no idea what he was talking about.

"You mean the one where I sound like a chipmunk?"

"You don't sound like a chipmunk to me."

"So tell me what I do sound like, then."

"Close to coming."

As soon as it was out, she could see he hadn't meant to put it quite like that.

He winced on that last word. Then mouthed the word "sorry."

But unfortunately, the word "sorry" didn't help her. Because now she had to pretend that she wasn't reeling. *You just heard Seth*

*say "coming." He said "coming," as in an orgasm, as in me making
that noise makes that happen,* her brain babbled, before she could
stop it, and force it back into being an adult. *Adults discuss things
like their sex lives,* she told herself.

Then made her voice as dry as she could.

"That is very cool to say, Seth, but you're drunk on werewolf
hormones."

"Werewolf hormones are making me super feel it and say it.
They're not making things that are false and ridiculous suddenly
true and reasonable. That little breathy noise is sexy. Most of your
excitement is sexy. You always get all flushed, and you bite that
plump, soft, lower lip of yours, and then you—" he started to say,
then seemed to realize *what* he was saying, and hauled himself
back.

Even though he didn't need to.

They were grown-ups. This was fine. It was fine.

She was going to prove it was fine.

"Then I what?" she asked, nonchalantly.

But he was definitely losing his nerve. He shook his head.

Looked at his fingers, and the eraser they were busy fiddling
with.

"No, Cass. I don't want to go over this part."

"Oh come on. You've said all the rest."

"Yeah, but the next part is really graphic. And I already feel like
I'm talking dirty to you."

Because you are, she thought at him, automatically, unbidden.
Even though that wasn't true in the slightest. He'd barely said anything, for starters. And even if he had, well. This was just helping
him through stuff.

It was almost a science project. A doctor's appointment. A way
to test how far he could go while under the extra-strength Feel
Better, and the scent blocker, and the threat of the Make Nice.
They're probably mingling in the air to hold him in, she thought,
and that sounded plausible.

Or at least plausible enough to let him go on.

"All you did was mention my squeaking. I think you're safe

to continue without veering into the land of saying filthy things to me," she said—which seemed to work. He hesitated again, but eventually, eventually, he managed to digest that concept enough to confess a little more.

"You suck your pencil when you're thinking," he said, too loud and too fast.

Though the words were still pretty tame in her opinion.

Not to mention nonsensical.

"It can't be that. You hated when I used to do it."

"I hated it because you never knew where the pencil had come from," he sighed. "Not because it was super horrible to look at or anything. I mean, I didn't get turned on over it, of course I didn't. That totally never happened. But it wasn't unpleasant. And now it's really super not unpleasant, in about twenty ways."

"Name one way, I dare you."

"Your lips look all pouty when you do it."

"My lips are not pouty," she snorted.

But all that did was get him almost rolling his eyes at her.

"Come on, Cass. They are—and even if they weren't, it wouldn't matter. They would still look good doing something like that. Because the thing is, you do it really slowly, and you slide it really far in, and sometimes I can see your tongue curling around it as you do in this really slick, dirty-looking way, and ohhhh god what am I saying?" he asked, so despairingly that he ended his sentence by putting his face in his hands.

And then she had to somehow hide that she wanted to put her face in hers.

"Nothing that I can't handle," she said. But that didn't seem to help him.

"Don't say that, it makes me want to go further," he groaned through his fingers. And okay, at that point she couldn't help being a little shocked. Or sounding somewhat breathless.

"There's *further* than me giving a blowjob to a writing implement?"

"Well, maybe not when you put it like that."

"I'm only saying what you said."

He gave her an indignant look. "All I did was describe it."

"Describing is worse."

"Then I'll stop. I should stop."

"It doesn't sound like you want to anymore."

What the fuck did you say that for, her mind wanted to know. Because she had to admit, it didn't seem like she was merely running a test anymore. It didn't sound like her professional opinion on the matter. It seemed like she was urging him on, for her own reasons. Like she *wanted* to hear him talk like this. Like she was *enjoying* something about it.

Even though she wasn't, she truly wasn't. She simply couldn't help encouraging him, every time it seemed as if he wanted to go further. And especially when there was no reason he shouldn't. Her kitchen was a safe place. She had no objections. If he felt like it, why not?

And she could tell he definitely did.

He dropped his hands from his face when she said those last words. And now he was holding her gaze, steadily. Almost dazedly. As if he were slowly falling into a dream.

Though she didn't think it was an ordinary one.

She thought it might be the kind that made you wake up to wet sheets.

In fact, she knew it was, because his gaze now looked even heavier than it had before. And when he spoke again, his voice sounded like it had been dipped in warm syrup. "Because I don't want to stop. I want to tell you all about what you looked like earlier, when you were eating. What it did to me, to see the gloss of that sauce all over your lips. How it felt, watching it spill over your fingers, and down, down, down. And though I tried not to think about where it went, I knew anyway. I knew it made a long, slick trail over the swell of your gorgeous breasts. And all I could think about when it did was how good it would be to lick it off you, nice and slow," he said.

At which point, she felt that maybe things were careening *slightly* out of control.

And not just because he'd said words she could never have imagined Seth saying to her—about her breasts, and about licking them, and about doing it slowly. No, there was also the fact that she found herself leaning forward when he did.

And worse: he was leaning forward too.

He was so close now that she could see the flecks of deep brown in those caramel eyes. She could smell the tang of strawberry from the bubblegum he apparently still liked, on his breath. Could feel the heat rolling off him, and sliding all over her.

Then suddenly there it was, on the tip of her tongue.

"And after that?" she asked.

Like it didn't matter if things were getting out of control.

All that mattered was sleepwalking right into this with him.

"That depends on what you might do if I did," he said, and now she didn't even think twice about it. She answered, too quick and too breathless.

"So if I moaned, and arched into your mouth," she said.

Then got his eyes stuttering closed as a reward.

"Ohhhh god, you're not serious."

"Why wouldn't I be, when we're talking about someone licking me?"

"Just 'someone' then. Just anyone. Just the idea of it is making you think you would," he said, because apparently even in the midst of horny hypnosis, he was thinking the same thoughts she was. He was feeling out the boundaries, and wondering whether they were crossing them. Trying to see where she stood, so he didn't go beyond it.

But the problem was: she didn't know anymore.

All she knew was how much she wanted to go with it.

"Well, it's not really me that's making you hot, right? You're just stuffed full of werewolf hormones and sex-starved and so desperate to come, oh god you must be *aching* to come. I bet anyone could do almost anything, and you would cream your jeans," she said, and this time his eyes didn't just stutter closed. They rolled closed, helplessly. Like someone passing out from near indescribable levels of pleasure.

And right on the end of that, he murmured words under his breath.

As if he didn't want her to hear them.

But kind of did, at the same time.

"Just you talking like that is enough," he said.

After which, she simply had to keep going. "So maybe I should say more."

"Honestly I'm a second away from begging you to."

"You don't have to beg. I *want* you to feel good," she said. And the second she got his reaction—the second he looked at her with heated desperation—more words spilled out of her in a great tumble. "I want you to moan, and buck, and get so hard that you just can't take it anymore. You can't do anything, except stroke yourself, right here in front of me. And then just when you're about to burst, just when you tell me, *oh Cassie I'm gonna come,* I'll unbutton my top for you. And you can do it all over every single thing you wanted to lick with that dirty little tongue."

Though, god, she didn't expect the reaction she got.

Somehow she had imagined they were still in the shallow end of whatever this was, barely doing anything at all. Yet he just seemed to lose it, the second she finished speaking. Like all of this was some kind of trigger. Pull it, and every last bit of his sense was blown away. He could no longer sit still, or stay calm, or not make many sounds.

He groaned, loud and long and guttural.

And then he said things. Impossible things. Incredible things, like *oh you dirty girl.* Then just as she was reeling over that, she realized what all of this meant. She grasped it, in a great rush of heat and shock.

He was coming.

He was actually coming, without so much as a hand on himself. And so hard, too. God, she had never seen any man come the way he did. She'd never seen any man shudder like that, violently enough that it rocked the table. Or arch their back as he did—in one long, sinuous roll that left him sprawled against the chair.

It was incredible.

Too incredible, if she was being honest about it. Because even though she tried to stay calm, she knew she wasn't at all. She could feel how flushed she was. She could see her hands shaking. And even though neither of those things meant much on their own, she knew the sound she made did. Because it wasn't surprise, or amusement, or encouragement.

It was excitement, plain and simple.

It had excited her to think of him like that.

And there was no undoing that now.

CHAPTER EIGHTEEN

She didn't know what to do in the aftermath of whatever that was. It felt like she should apologize, for pushing him so far, and feeling things she was pretty sure she shouldn't have felt. Only somehow, he got there first.

"Oh my god, Cassie, I am so sorry. I cannot believe I just did all that in front of you," he fumbled out. Then he shoved his chair back so hard it shrieked on the linoleum. And before she could stop him, he staggered almost drunkenly out of the kitchen.

He's gonna wolf out when he crosses that threshold, she thought, panicked.

But he didn't. He just disappeared into the bathroom by the stairs. She heard the lock on the door snap shut. Followed by silence.

And more silence.

And so much more silence after this, she started to think he might have done something worse than wolf out. *He could have died of shame*, she thought. After all, that was what he'd said, wasn't it? That his lust was shameful? Then he'd released a lot of lust, courtesy of her potty mouth, and so now here they were.

With him probably trying to escape out the bathroom window.

And her unable to decide how to fix the situation. Or, if she was being honest, to get up from the chair to even attempt fixing it. Because seriously, it was at least half an hour later, and she still felt dazed. She still felt hot, and sort of wobbly. Like everything she'd seen and heard had affected her, to a far greater degree than she'd let herself believe.

You were supposed to be helping, not getting hot for him, she chided herself. Though really, when you broke it down, was getting hot for *him* what had happened? *Anyone* would probably have gotten into this state under those circumstances.

And especially if they'd had the sex life she'd endured.

It had been years since she'd done anything with anyone.

Plus none of the people she'd been with had ever done what Seth had a moment ago.

They had never moved like that, with such complete abandon. Never said those words as heatedly as he had. And they'd definitely never made those sounds.

Usually she got little more than a faint grunt. Or even no grunt at all.

So even though she couldn't quite excuse herself, she sort of felt that this level of heat was to be expected. And if it continued when she finally stood, and went to the bathroom door, and knocked and asked him if he was okay . . . well, that was understandable too.

Because, sure, it was awkward to do it. It should have brought an end to any sexy feelings. But you really had to take into account the ratio of hot events to embarrassing ones. So far hotness was 99 percent of the last hour. Embarrassing events were thirty seconds.

Less than thirty seconds, really, because he answered right away.

"Yeah, totally good, no problems here," he said, in a voice that sounded a little ragged and strained, but otherwise okay. So it made sense that the heat did not appear to be going away. Or even increased a little, when he added, "Do you by any chance have a pair of pants that might fit me? I seem to have made an absolutely ridiculous amount of mess here."

Though little was probably an understatement.

In truth, it went through her like lightning. She almost had to bite back a moan.

But it was fine, it was fine. She had just made the mistake of picturing what he was suggesting, that was all. She'd thought about his come, all thick and slippery and copious, completely coating the insides of his thighs. Then getting all over his hands as he tried to tug down his jeans, and—

"I think I might have a pair of sweatpants, hold on," she burst out, and dashed to grab them before her own thoughts could go any further. Before she could cross any more of those lines than she already had.

Only when she came back downstairs, he was out of the bathroom.

Just there, leaned against the frame, with nothing but a towel on.

And that was kind of a lot on top of everything else.

She had to look away without seeming like she was looking away—like at the quarry, like in the closet, like all the times when things had seemed too naked and too weird and on the verge of something unhinged. Only now, they really *were* in the aftermath of a sexual event. Now they really had crossed some kind of line. And on top of this, she was currently trying to hand him some clothes. So it wasn't exactly easy to seem casual.

She couldn't even manage to avoid seeing his body.

She caught at least three glimpses of a nipple, amid the fumbling. Then somehow, she ended up dropping the shirt she had grabbed for him. And when she stooped to snag it, oh the things she accidentally saw, courtesy of the split in the too-small towel.

Shadowy things. Heavy-looking things. Things that immediately made her face heat up.

Worse: she started sweating. Like her whole body had caught a fever.

And the only thing that saved her was him getting completely the wrong idea. "Oh jeez, you're completely mortified. I've mortified you. By being a giant pervert who you're never gonna want to speak to again in case I accidentally do whatever that was when you do," he rushed out, in a voice so broken and full of remorse she had to do something about it.

She'd *wanted* him to do it.

And okay, not for weird, sexy reasons. But still.

"You're not a pervert, Seth. Everything you did was fine."

"You can't really think that. It was awful. It's still awful. I just flashed you."

"No, you didn't. I shouldn't have looked in that direction."

"Don't blame yourself for my dick being right there."

He pointed in the direction of where *right there* was.

But of course she didn't look. No matter how tempted she was.

"It's right there because all my grandmother's towels are the size of postage stamps. I'm surprised you even managed to close it around you at all, never mind doing it in a way that doesn't leave a gaping triangle," she said instead. And was pleased with the amount of exasperation she got into her voice. Then she turned around, and he rustled the clothes on, and everything was fine.

Very oddly silent, but fine.

She even asked if she could turn back around.

And got this from him, when she did:

"It's gonna sound weird if I say no, right?"

"Maybe it won't if you explain why I shouldn't."

"Okay," he tried. "So, uh. These sweatpants are a little bit tight on me."

"They can't be that tight. My butt could eat your butt for breakfast."

She heard him make an annoyed sound. "Don't say that like it's a bad thing. Or use the words 'eat' and 'your butt' in the same sentence. Or tell me that I must be wrong, because, hoo boy, I am not, and not because of any ass-based reasons."

Don't ask him what he means by that middle bit, she told herself.

And thankfully succeeded.

"Then what are the reasons based on?"

"Let's just say these sweatpants are riding super high."

"Well, I am quite a bit shorter than you are, Seth."

"It's not really my height that's the problem."

"So what—" she started to say. But couldn't finish, because it had clicked in her head. And now her face was even hotter than before. She wasn't sure how she managed to get words out. Or make them jokey. But she did. "So basically you've got a bulge the size of a bus."

"Honestly, 'bus' is probably understating it."

"Jesus *Christ*, dude."

"I know, I know, somehow I'm being disgusting again."

"No you're not. That wasn't why I exclaimed."

"Then why did you?"

Fuck, she thought. *Now I've got to explain.*

Even though she was barely sure how to explain it to herself. Everything just felt so muddled and confused and heated—in a way that *should* have been resolving itself now that nothing sexual was happening. Now that this was just Seth, partly nude.

But somehow resolution was not happening.

If anything, she felt significantly hotter.

And her voice shook when she finally managed to force some words out.

"Because it's astonishing. Not because it's bad. Nothing you've done is bad, okay? I encouraged you to keep talking. I knew what was happening, or what could happen—because seriously, how could it not? It's been years. The only surprise is you didn't do what you did the second we started that conversation," she said, and heard him let out a relieved-sounding sigh.

"Yeah, I had a few close calls somewhere in the middle."

"And that's all right with me. All right to do, all right to tell me. In fact, if anything it's me that should have behaved better. I shouldn't have pushed or been so—" she went to say. But thankfully he cut her off, before she could finish.

"Cass, I don't care what you were like. You could have done anything, absolutely anything. I wouldn't have been bothered. All that matters to me is that you're okay with everything that happened."

So that is that, she thought. "I am," she said, and to prove it, she turned and faced him.

Eyes firmly above his waist, of course.

But she did it. And just in time to see his face flood with warmth and gratitude. "I can't tell you what that means to me," he said.

"What everything you did means to me, honestly. Because I know it might be weird to thank you for what just happened, but god, I've wanted to say it for the last half hour. It was actually about five minutes of cleanup, then twenty-five trying to think of a way to apologize and be overwhelmingly grateful, all at the same time."

"You have nothing to be grateful for. I barely did anything."

"Cass, you created magic that made this possible. And then you didn't even think about your own feelings toward me. All you thought about was helping me, even if that meant being embarrassed and uncomfortable. And that is just so . . . so . . . oh god, Cass, I would hug you if you were into getting hugs from me," he said, in so heartfelt a way she knew she couldn't lie.

There was no way to tell him, *no, I'm not. Please never put your arms around me.*

Even though the very idea of being hugged by him made her body prickle and heat, and her brain immediately go over all the things that might press against her. His bare chest. His nude biceps. That goddamn bus between his legs. Hell, maybe it would be all three at the same time.

But she had to force out the truth anyway.

"I am into it, Seth. We're friends now. And friends do things like that."

"So even after that disaster, I've been upgraded from standard enemy?"

"You've probably been upgraded because of it, if I'm being honest."

He shook his head. "That is ridiculous. There's no way."

"I don't see why not. It told me you were telling the truth, and it showed a lot of trust in me, and then it led to us having this heartfelt conversation. Apparently, in part, about your enormous package," she said—mostly to see if she could break the tension that seemed to be building inside her.

Though she was surprised when it worked.

He laughed. She laughed. Everything was cool.

And in a second, she thought, *he will be gone.* He was going to leave as usual, armed with Werewolf Killer, and other protection potions, and lots of promises on his lips to text her the second he got back to his home-slash-shack. And she would finally be able to relax. She was already relaxing, in fact.

Then he leaned forward, and did what he told her he would do.

What he *could* do, now that the combination of the protection potions and the scent blocker and the Feel Better and his first orgasm in eight years was providing a moment of calm.

He put his arms around her. Awkwardly, but it didn't seem to matter.

Because the second he did it, she didn't just get a wave of that syrupy heat.

She felt more pleasure than she'd ever known, from any touch at all.

CHAPTER NINETEEN

Cassie decided the best thing to do was sleep on it.

But the problem was—sleeping on it was not exactly easy.

She felt as if every horny atom in her usually pretty quiet body had been shaken up. Her entire being was a bottle of Pepsi, that had been dropped on the floor. And she had no way to safely unscrew the cap. Every time she thought *just stop being ridiculous and fuck yourself out of this*, her mind immediately followed it up with an image of Seth.

Like she'd filled out a masturbation-fantasy order form.

And been supplied the exact opposite of what she ever wanted to want.

Just give me some Carmy Berzatto for a few seconds, she begged her brain. But her brain wasn't listening. And it continued to not listen no matter what she did. She tried sexy pictures, sexy books, sexy fan fiction. Nothing shook Seth's face out of her head.

Seth, who was now her friend. Maybe even her *good* friend.

And good friends could not think like this.

Good friends had to answer the door to each other, while being a normal, calm, non-horny mess. But somehow, she didn't think she was going to manage that. It took so much effort just to get dressed without getting flustered. And even after she heard him let himself in, she couldn't immediately go down. She had to take deep breaths and tell herself that she would feel fine when she saw him, just to make it to the top of the stairs.

Then she made it, she finally made it.

And she took one look at him.

And somehow her feelings actually *increased*.

Even though he looked more ordinary than she'd hoped. Heck, he looked *worse* than the ordinary she'd hoped for. No jeans, no boots, no leather jacket. Instead, he was wearing a plaid shirt. And the kind of boring pants and footwear he used to love: brown cords with a cuff, and a pair of old Converse high-tops.

Plus his hair had not been styled, in the least. It was shaggy, and soft, and kind of fell over his forehead, instead of swooping up to the sky. Yet somehow it still made the thing happen. That hot rush, that syrupy sensation, that buckling in her legs.

And now it seemed even keener. Sharper.

Almost like greed, in some inexplicable way she didn't know how to fight. She couldn't tell herself, *No, you really don't want to eat that poison cake.* Her body didn't register the *no*. It didn't accept that the cake was poison. It just acted, without her permission.

It made her reach forward.

And put.

Her hand.

Directly into that soft hair.

Much to his astonishment. His eyes went enormous; he tried to step back and failed. Then finally he blurted out her name, in a strained, nearly outraged tone.

And that pretty much snapped her out of it. She drew her hand back whip-quick. Fumbled out an excuse. "You had something in your hair," she said—and thankfully, it seemed to work. He lost the panicked look, and calmed down enough to follow her into the kitchen. And once there she felt a little more stable. Now they could get to work. She could show him her ideas for new potions.

Then she turned, and realized that he wasn't into idea-showing right now.

He had brought some goddamn breakfast.

Lots of breakfast, apparently, from what looked like the Spinning Top Diner off Main Street. She watched him lay out folds of omelet, oozing cheese, onto plates. Then biscuits wrapped in paper, rich gravy in a carton, mounds of browned-into-a-crispy-mass hash browns, deliriously spiced pumpkin muffins, coffees that he described as bonfire flavored. And finally, just as she thought he was done: pancakes so soaked in blueberry compote that they came apart when he tried to lift them out of their foil container.

"We can just eat them right out of there, I guess," he said.

But she wasn't listening. She couldn't listen.

The thing was happening again—and this time she had almost no clue why.

Because there was no shock of something sexual here. Or even him looking kind of nice. He was just laying out breakfast. That he had brought specially for her. That he had carefully selected because he knew they were her favorite foods. And without so much as a thought about things she'd always assumed he must have cared about.

Like bullshit about fat girls and calories.

Plus there was the cost. What had this fucking cost?

He barely made any money. This was way too much to spend.

Though it felt no better to her when he explained. "I did a favor for the owner, and so she did a favor for me, so I could do one for you. To say sorry and thank you again," he said, as she stood there staring at him. Every bit of her sure that she should just be pleasantly pleased, maybe. Or possibly just intent on paying him back.

But somehow instead, she was burning up.

And she had the strongest urge to do another mad thing—like touch him a second time. Because, really, wouldn't it be fine to do that? Hadn't he hugged her the night before? That had been okay, so she couldn't see why not. She could just slip a hand around his waist, and maybe squeeze him a little bit. Get closer to that heat, radiating off him. That gorgeous heat, that amazing heat, like being close to a bonfire, a lovely bonfire, oh, wouldn't it be okay to just bur—

"Cassie, for the love of *god.*"

She knew what she had done the instant she heard his voice. That strained tone, the words he'd used—he sounded exactly like the day before. And sure enough, it was all over his face when she finally looked. That flush, deep enough to show even through his thick stubble. The heaviness of his eyelids, the heated desperation in his gaze.

And of course he was looking right at her hand.

The one she had thought was hovering in the air, an inch from him. But was actually on his body. It was right on him. And not even anywhere near his waist, either. Fuck no—somehow she'd placed it on his stomach. Low down on his stomach. Really low down.

God, she was almost at his belt.

"Sorry," she gasped, and snapped her hand away. But she could tell it was already too late. He was shivering all over, gaze heavy. And there was that hint of sharp teeth beneath the curve of his lip. Kept in check, she thought, by the potions. But still a terrible pain to him.

Just like it had been yesterday.

Only without the same recourse.

After all, she couldn't simply *suggest* dirty talk. It had been bad enough when they'd simply stumbled into it. No—she needed another option. Something simpler, and more practical. Like maybe the potion she'd made, in the middle of the night. Half-asleep, but determined to have multiple reasonable ways around whatever was going on.

Though it didn't feel as reasonable, once she had the tin of it in her hands.

Because now she had to explain what it was, and god, that felt way more awkward than she had imagined it being. She started to say, and fumbled it. Tried again, and trailed off. Then finally, she just tried to make her words sound as cheery as possible.

"Okay. Okay. I can see I have completely messed you up. But don't worry. Because I made this for you. So you can—you know. See to things," she said, as she held the tin out. But he just looked confused. And even hornier. And that meant more godforsaken words. "Because I kind of thought, oh maybe if stuff like yesterday happens again, I could just leave you in the kitchen and probably you can safely get down to business. But then what if the kitchen isn't available? What if you're somewhere else? What if you'd rather be more comfortable, in, like, a shower or a bed or even on a couch? Or you're still nervous, and want to be locked up? Well, this will help you consider all of that."

She smiled brightly, relieved that she had gotten through it without being explicit.

Mission accomplished, she thought.

Only for him to just go ahead and fucking say it anyway. "Cassie, are you seriously telling me you've made some kind of magic lube?" he said as he took the tin from her hand. And okay, yeah, she definitely had. But did he really have to spell it out?

She'd been so careful. Now the word was out there, fucking her up.

Her whole body tingled the moment he said it. Then somehow, it was all she could think about. What the potion was for. What he could do with it. How good it would feel. He even seemed to agree on that last part. He all but gasped his gratitude.

Then he disappeared into the bathroom, so quick and thrilled about it that it really should have been a relief. His problem was dealt with, he'd asked no questions about her touching him, and now he was far away from her. She could breathe. Calm herself down.

Everything was going to be okay.

But then she heard it.

A metal-on-metal sound, that had to be his belt being unbuckled. Hastily, like he just couldn't wait long enough to do it at a normal speed. She'd put a hand on him, and talked about magical lube. And now he was so beside himself she wasn't even sure if he had done much beyond that. If he'd actually taken the time to get his pants all the way off.

Because a second later he made the most ungodly sound.

A deep, guttural groan, so thick with desperation and relief and shock that she was able to clearly picture the probable sequence of events. He had slicked his hand, or maybe both hands. Then he had just stroked, over his no-doubt bursting cock. And apparently the pleasure had been so intense and so long-awaited, that he had made this sound.

The one seemed to grab her and *squeeze.*

For a second she couldn't breathe. Or think rationally.

It took her a good minute to comprehend that she needed to put on some loud music, right now. But before she could, she got another groan. Lots of groans, all as intense as the first. She heard him panting, and gasping, and choking out a long *ooohhh* of pleasure.

And underneath it all, there was something else now, too: the slick slide of skin on skin. Sometimes slow and easy, like he was trying to savor it. Other times devolving into something more frantic, something more desperate, something that made his breathing high and tight.

And then, oh fuck, *fuck*, there were words.

"God, yeah baby, that feels so good," he gasped out.

Like he was in there doing someone. Or someone was on her knees, sucking him off, and he had his hand in her hair. He had it right there, encouraging her to take more of his big, heavy cock, until finally he could hardly stand it. Whatever this imaginary person was doing, it was too much. He had to let it out. "Fuck, baby, you're gonna make me do it," he groaned.

And just as Cassie tried to use that image to calm herself down—just as she thought of all the girls that make-believe person might be, and all the ways that meant she should stop, that she should not listen, that she was intruding—his voice dropped. It went low, almost too low to hear.

But not so low she could have ever missed it.

"Cassie," he gasped. "Cassie, oh god, Cassie, make me come, oh yeah my sweet girl, make me come, just like that."

Because, it seemed, it was only her he was thinking of.

Only her name he spoke, like a prayer. Like a promise.

And just for that moment, she could almost believe it.

CHAPTER TWENTY

She knew she needed to do two things, before he came over.

One was to concoct some kind of anti-horny potion, for herself. The other was to find a way to get her hands on that one ingredient neither of the guidebooks was willing to describe. Because she felt pretty sure by now that it was key to cracking the *make a werewolf stop feeling horny for me* potion. The idea buzzed in her head whenever she made yet another failed attempt to create such a blend.

So she did what needed to be done.

Even though doing it was fucking *hell*.

She felt like a mass of quivering, overheated Jell-O as she biked into town. And not just because of the now-constant thrum of weird arousal. There was also just plain old embarrassment, trying to destroy her peace of mind. All she could think about was listening to him, like someone obsessed with him, and then doing the very dirty thing she had done a little later on, in an even more obsessed way than that.

And the memory made her face flame about every thirty seconds.

So of course Nancy was going to notice. But she plunged into the bookstore, regardless. *If she asks, I'll tell her I recently rode my bike up Mount Doom*, she said to herself firmly. And she believed it would work, too. It sounded perfectly reasonable.

Until she got inside, and saw who was with Nancy.

Right there, leaning on the counter. Marley Maples. Marley Maples, dressed extra awesomely. Boxy little leather jacket, red distressed skirt, blue tights, chunky-heeled boots. And that sharp little smile just to underline her probable intent: *one wrong word, one hint that you're doing anything as ludicrous as wanting to fuck the guy who called you a fat ass, and I'll put you in the paper.*

She could even imagine the headline—"Woman Last Seen in High School Being Weird Is Hot for Her Former Enemy." And came very close to running back out the door at the thought. In fact, it was only imagining another headline that stopped her: "Town Weirdo Dashes Away to Perv Some More over Local Man."

Because true, that sounded bananas. But so were all of Marley's articles.

And worse: they were smart. They were very smart. *Marley* was smart.

Her black eyes glittered as she took Cassie in.

"Good to see you again, Cass," she said, cool as anything.

While Cassie did her best to avoid saying a single self-incriminating word. She smiled and nodded and walked over to the shelf, heart hammering for two reasons, now: the thought of Marley guessing about Seth, and the idea that Marley would somehow know about the supernatural guidebooks she wanted to grab.

Despite suspecting that Marley probably wouldn't.

And sure enough, when Cassie turned around with the book she'd selected—*Weird Terms and Wonderful Definitions*—both Marley and Nancy had that blank look about them. Neither seemed to register what she held in her hands.

Though was it Cassie's imagination, or did Nancy's gaze seem to linger on the book? Like a witch's might. Or maybe a cobble's. And after a second, a frown even slid between Nancy's soft brown eyebrows. Like she was trying to identify someone through a thick fog. "You okay, Nance?" Cassie found herself saying.

But Nancy answered as though Cassie had been asking about something else altogether. "Oh well, you know. Things are kind of tough at the minute," she said, in a way that tugged at Cassie more strongly than she could have imagined, for someone she still didn't know that well.

But before Cassie could ask what she meant, Marley swooped in. "Better than you're doing, huh, Cass?" she said. "What with that dipshit hanging around you all the time. My sources say he stops by your place every morning. So, you know, just gimme the word and I'll write something scathing about him, until he leaves you alone."

All of which should have felt nice. It kind of put Cassie in the clear, on the question of *can they see how horny I am for him?* But unfortunately, Cassie kind of suspected that Marley was really saying something else. Like she was maybe wanting Cassie to know that she knew. Or trying to make Cassie feel like she was being watched by whoever these sources were. Or possibly she just wanted to press Cassie until she broke.

And sure enough, a second later, here it was.

"Unless he's not bothering you at all," Marley said.

Then she raised one already pretty arched eyebrow.

While Nancy looked back and forth between them, visibly uncomfortable. "Here's your purchase, Cass," she squeaked as she handed Cassie a carefully wrapped parcel. Because, bless her, she clearly wanted to get Cassie out of this, as much as Cassie wanted to be out of it.

And now all she needed to do was say a quick "Gotta run," and she was free.

She was out the door, and down the street, as fast as her bike would take her.

SHE CRACKED THE book as soon as she got through her front door. Stood in the hallway, flipping the pages, until she found a clue about the mysterious molloch. But it took cross-referencing the book's mention with a site she found online—one that seemed to stutter in and out and randomly showed her some very weird things—to get the answer she needed.

Then it was just a matter of waiting for Seth to show up.

Though he took his sweet time doing it. It was around four in the afternoon by the time he clomped up the porch steps. Much later than whatever Marley's spies had told her. Late enough, in fact, that Cassie was starting to worry.

But as soon as she laid eyes on him, she could see there was nothing to worry about.

Or maybe everything to worry about, depending on your point of view.

Because he looked like someone who had been recently fucked. And so thoroughly that he appeared to be half asleep while standing up. His gaze was lazy, satisfied. His movements kind of lax—like someone had oiled all his joints. And he let out the most contented sigh as he swung into one of the kitchen chairs. Like he had turned into the opposite of everything he'd been for the last week. For *more* than the last week, if she was being honest.

God, seeing him in this state made her realize just how fucked up he had been before.

How skittish, how jerky and jittery.

So it was heartening to see.

But at the same time, *fuck*. She wished she'd managed to make that anti-horny potion for herself. Something really strong, to take away the urge to ask him questions she probably did not want to know the answers to. Questions that, truthfully, she already knew the answers to, anyway. *He's like this because he probably spent all night and all day coming his brains out*, she thought, before she could stop herself.

And all she could do after that was plunge into a different topic, to give herself some kind of fighting chance. "Okay, so I think I've figured out what molloch is for this cure. Dragon scale. Which I am very much hoping is just a fancy supernatural weed, and does not require me to don a suit of armor and find myself a lance," she said, as firmly and funnily as she could.

And if her voice shook as she did?

Well, that was fine. He didn't seem to notice.

"You're totally right, it doesn't," he said.

"Oh thank god."

"You might need a flame-retardant suit, however."

God, the teasing way he said it. That skewed smile, the light in his eyes.

Then just as she was about to lose it a little bit: "I'm kidding, I'm kidding. I know where we can get some essence of dragon scale. Kind of a trek, and the office it's in might be locked, but it won't be a big deal to get around."

"You mean you've just put me through brief terror for nothing."

He spread his hands. "What can I say? I like seeing your eyes go wide."

"Your eyes are gonna go wide when I get you back for this."

"Go ahead and get me back. In fact, I want you to do it. Really hard."

"Oh yeah?"

Oh no, her brain cried. But too late, too late. Now they were doing something that felt way too much like flirting. Like they had at the kitchen table—only worse, so much worse, because that hadn't been intentional. And they hadn't really made it personal. But here he was saying *you* and she was saying *you* and . . .

Was he standing up?

Was he *coming* toward *her*?

"Seth, we really need to concentrate on getting this stuff," she said, in a voice that sounded far too much like a breathless gasp. Honestly, it was a miracle he listened, and stopped, and let her continue. "So just tell me where we need to go."

And after that he finally seemed able to focus.

Sort of. She could tell he had to avoid looking at her to do it. "We need to figure out how we're going to get there first. Because obviously we need to go together, and neither of us has a working car."

"We don't need cars. I have the Hoover."

"Right. And how am I gonna get there on that?"

"Well, it will still fly when you're riding it too."

"Cassie, the problem isn't how much weight or non-witchiness the magic can take. The problem is that I will have to be jammed right up against your butt in order for us to both safely fit. And as things stand, I can barely cope with *saying* that I'll have to be jammed right up against your butt in order for us to both safely fit," he said, and although her brain started babbling about him being into that, and what it would feel like, and whether they'd accidentally rub against each other whenever she turned too hard, she managed to keep it together.

"So, then, you just ride in front," she said.

And got some incredulous eyebrows for it. "I'm honestly worried that you think that will be any better."

"I don't see why. Then it'll just be *me* jammed up against *your* butt and—oh *no*, oh *wow*, you like that. You're saying you like that. Oh god, okay that's. . . . Yeah, that's a lot of information I shouldn't have uncovered."

She had to fully turn away from him, then.

Her back to him, hands on the rim of the kitchen sink, for support. And even that didn't help. Her legs had just gone, they had completely gone, it was almost impossible to stay upright. The only way she managed was by counting sheep in her head—like she was trying to sleep—instead of thinking for even one second about what he had meant.

Because even one second was too much.

She got a mental glimpse of him arching his back, and—

"Okay, we really need to go," she burst out frantically.

But he wasn't even paying attention. "If it helps at all, this talk isn't affecting me too badly. I think the potion you gave me is really helping to even out that instant jump from one to seven thousand, on the horny scale," he said, all cheerful.

While she tried her best not to die.

"Yeah, well, probably best to hurry anyway."

"You're right. So let's hear some other ideas."

"The other ideas depend on something pretty weird."

"Like what?"

He raised an eyebrow. But this one wasn't incredulous. It was worried.

And it was right to be too.

Because the answer was this:

"On you still having that rusted-out old Chevy in your yard."

CHAPTER TWENTY-ONE

Cassie felt a little better once they were outside. The cool evening air helped. As did the need for vigilance. Because she had kind of thought the Jerks were no longer a concern, considering how fast they'd run and how far Seth said they had gone. And how powerful she knew she could be. But when they got to the edge of the woods, there it was. A little present from them, torn apart and shoved on a stake.

Like a warning.

"They know they can't hurt us, so they're being gross assholes instead," Seth said, when he saw it. Though she could tell by his tone that it was a little more than that. So she stayed on guard, and he stayed on guard, and they got to his place in one piece.

Then it was just a matter of coating that dilapidated old car with flying potion.

Or so it seemed to her. But as she started in on it, Seth definitely had some concerns. "You know, there's a hole in the floor on the driver's side," he said as he peered in through the grimy window. Though from what she could see, it really wasn't that bad.

As long as she kept her feet on the pedals, she'd probably not even notice it.

The family of raccoons living in the back seat, however, would be a little harder to ignore. As would the roof that peeled up just a little bit when Seth tested it. And the door on the passenger side that didn't completely close.

"You're just gonna have to make sure your seatbelt is fastened," she said as he shooed the critters away. But unfortunately the seatbelt didn't seem to be working either. It came away in her hands when she gave it an experimental tug, and then it just disintegrated into plasticky crumbles. She was forced to add, "Or make sure you hold on super tight."

But Seth wasn't listening.

He was too busy trying to wrestle a raccoon off his face. A big, pale-gray one, with a super-fat little butt, and a high-pitched chitter that sounded like words. That really, *really* sounded like words. In fact, it sounded so much like words that for a moment she simply stood there, unable to believe her ears.

"Holy crap, I can understand what it's saying," she said, in a hushed whisper.

Because dear god, she could. It was telling Seth off, quite clearly.

Bad hoo man, it squeaked, as it grabbed tufts of his hair in its tiny fists, and used them like a ladder. It clambered over his head, until most of its butt was in his face. Then it settled there, like it had found a particularly nice perch. And whenever Seth tried to protest, it fought him off. It slapped him, with those tiny, weirdly human hands.

While she watched, with what felt like love hearts for eyes.

In fact she knew they were, because Seth did not seem impressed.

"Cassie, no. No. Not a raccoon. Or at least not *this* raccoon," he huffed out around a mouthful of fur. And just as she started to ask him what he meant, she remembered something from the guidebook. *Witches gain a familiar when the familiar speaks to them.*

Though she couldn't quite credit it.

Or at least not until the raccoon chittered to her, while trying to squirm away from Seth's big hands. *My one, help me*, it said. As in, *You are my witch, and so you should do this for me.* And it was the damnedest thing, because she found she actually wanted to. More than anything, she wanted to. "I don't think I have a choice. I think he's chosen me," she said, wonderingly.

Much to Seth's disgruntlement.

"But he's trying to eat my face."

"He isn't. He's just mad that you heaved him out of bed."

"So he wanted a nap, and I'm his terrible father forcing him awake?" he asked, as he attempted to wrestle the thing away from his eyeballs. And she went to say something funny in return. She almost laughed.

But then she realized:

The raccoon had stopped struggling.

Now it was just looking at her. Eyes bright black stars, little face suddenly so much more than it had been before. It seemed almost human to her now. Like it had become a little person, full of its own feelings and thoughts and ideas about things.

And what it thought, right now, was about her and Seth.

This one yours? it chittered.

Because clearly, it already saw her as some kind of mother figure. And now it wanted to know if she claimed Seth, so that he could be its father figure. It wanted to know if Seth was telling the truth, she thought, then didn't know what to say. Of course she didn't. A fucking raccoon was attempting to get her to define her relationship with a man she was trying not to be horny for, while they stood together in a scrappy yard, in front of a Chevy she was going to fly.

It was kind of a ridiculous situation to be in.

She almost wanted to say *get off my back, raccoon.*

But then she'd have to explain to Seth what the raccoon was asking, and she couldn't. She couldn't let Seth know what any of this was about. She just had to nod, instead. And to her surprise, it worked. The second she did, that ball of fur and those tiny fingers started to climb down. It got to his shoulder, and then his chest, and then, and then, oh lord in heaven, then . . .

It held out one little hand to her.

And wow, tonight was really being a lot.

She didn't know how to cope with the sight of that. Or with the way it felt when the raccoon clambered into her arms, and pushed his face into her hair, and whispered that his name was Pod. It was just all very overwhelming, to the point where she couldn't help tearing up a little bit.

It was all right, though. Because when she began to explain herself to Seth—to describe the feeling of finding a familiar, of finding a raccoon familiar who could actually talk to her, like all her childhood dreams of being in some fantasy novel about a found family—she discovered she didn't have to.

He was fucking tearing up too.

"Look, I'm just very emotional at the moment, okay?" he said. "There's too much happening at once. I had my first ten orgasms in almost a decade last night, and now my buddy who I can't stop wanting to bone has a talking raccoon. Like something out of a movie, made by Amblin Entertainment."

Then he tried to pretend he wasn't wiping his eyes with his shirt.

She didn't know why he was embarrassed, however. She'd seen him cry a million times—usually over movies with plots just like this. And even if she hadn't, well. It wasn't unpleasant to see. In truth, it was very, *very* not unpleasant. As in *tingly* not unpleasant. *Sexy* not unpleasant.

Oh god, now I suddenly want to fuck him because he can access his emotions and express them in a heartfelt way, she groaned to herself.

As soon as she did, however, she had to wonder if that "suddenly" was accurate.

If there had never been a time before now when she'd enjoyed that about him in a more than friendly way. And though she told herself no—though she told herself that it was only weird like that between them when there was nakedness, or sexy stuff going on around them—the idea lingered and lingered.

She saw him as he had been, clutching his chest at the end of *28 Days Later,* upturned face all agony and longing for things to be okay. The way he whispered, "Run, run," through the darkness to a woman onscreen who couldn't hear him. Then later on, he would always text her.

I'm still not okay after that. Are you okay after that?

And she would reply no.

But now she suspected she had meant yes.

Yes, yes I am, because you are with me. Because you feel the same way I do. Because we are the same and you're never afraid to say so.

It was just that she hadn't been able to say such sentimental words, to someone who probably would have gushed back, if he'd felt the same. Hell, he probably would have gushed first. He wore his heart on his sleeve, why wouldn't he have said if he did? So clearly he could never have felt it. *Obviously* he had never felt it. It absolutely had to be that he'd never felt it.

You know, it might not only be werewolf hormones that are making him act like this, her mind suddenly blurted out. And such terror gripped her when it did, she got in the car while Seth was still trying to determine if it was safe.

He tried to stop her, with dire warnings about the rear suspension.

Though after a second, he followed her anyway. He climbed into the passenger seat, and Pod scampered over her shoulder to the back, and now all that was left was doing this thing. "Okay, you ready? Here we go. Turning the engine on," she said, as she reached for the key that still somehow sat in the ignition.

And of course got a snort of near derision from Seth. "But there's no engine to turn on. I don't see why you need to do that. It should just go—" he started to say. But he got no further than that. The car cut him off the moment she turned the key. And not with an ordinary engine sound, either. Oh no, this was something else. This was a ground-shaking roar, of the sort you might hear coming out of an enormous dinosaur.

Seth actually jumped, and squeezed her leg.

She was so stunned she couldn't even react to the squeeze.

And it wasn't just the engine noise that stunned her. It was a great kaleidoscope of about five thousand wild things happening, all at once. The entire dashboard lit up in colors no dashboard would ever have been allowed to display. Purples and neon greens and bright blues washed over their faces, as brilliant as a goddamn disco.

With the soundtrack to match.

The ancient tape deck actually fired up, alongside the rest of the car. It made that weird reversing sound she remembered from her mom's old stereo, then suddenly the entire interior was full of incredibly loud music. *Recognizable* music. "Take on Me," she thought it was, as those weird horns piped the central tune. And sure enough, a second later, Morten Harket was singing the words.

Hell, *Seth* was singing them.

"I'll be coming for your love, okay," he belted out—and so exuberantly, so full of astonished laughter, that it was infectious. She found herself laughing and singing too, as she pressed her foot down on the gas.

And then they were in the sky.

Her, and Seth, and their newly adopted raccoon son.

In their flying eighties disco of a car.

CHAPTER TWENTY-TWO

She kind of believed that Seth was messing with her when he pointed out a place to land. Because as far as she could see, there wasn't any building in sight. Just a great, grassy hill, like a giant's knee, surrounded at its base by trees. Though she listened anyway, and began to urge the car down. She pressed on the brakes, and the thing started drifting toward the crest of the hill.

But that didn't get the response from Seth she expected.

"No god, not in the middle," he gasped, and grabbed the wheel to steer her toward the trees. And it was only once they were safely on the ground, nestled between two oak trees, that he sighed with relief, and tried to explain. "Sorry, I should have been clearer. The house isn't actually here."

"Well, then, why are we landing? And what did you panic for?"

"Because I meant that you just can't see it."

"So you're saying it's invisible."

He made a *not really* face as she turned off the engine. "Kind of. It's more like it exists somewhere else, but it can be accessed from our world. So that's what we all call it: the House That Isn't Here. Supernatural creatures and beings use it as a kind of meeting place. Sometimes they might live here for a time. A few have offices here, storage rooms, that kind of thing," he said, at which point Cassie thought two things: *you really should have told me about the interdimensional building before I plunged us into total spooky darkness,* and *oh my god are we going in there to steal from Cthulhu?*

"So the stuff we're going to get *belongs* to someone?"

"It does. But don't worry. We can write an IOU."

"That sounds dubious in the extreme," she said.

And Pod seemed to agree from the back seat. *No go, no go,* she heard him say. Seth had to hiss at him to shush—and he did. But only after she reached back and held his little hand. And after he'd called Seth an *ugly beefhead*.

Which made her have to smother a giggle, as Seth sighed heavily and tried to continue. "I promise it's not. An offer like that from a witch is worth a lot."

"Yeah, I can imagine it is if they're gonna ask me to make them a death ray."

"They're not gonna ask that. It's up to you to decide what you give in return."

"That seems like a weird system. I could give them a fart in a jar."

"Are you going to, though?" He glanced at her through the darkness. She knew he did, because his eyes gleamed just a little more than usual. They looked like mirrors catching light that wasn't actually there; like glass at the bottom of a deep lake. *Beautiful,* she thought, and promptly forgot what she was supposed to be saying.

She had to fumble her way back to it, through a sudden wave of that syrupy feeling. But she got there, she got there. She felt the answer to what he'd asked, sure as anything: *no, what I give in return will instinctively be commensurate.*

"Okay, good point," she said. Then, after a beat: "So I guess if there isn't going to be a problem, we should just do this."

"Yup. Nothing to do now but get out of the car and go in there."

"Right. Cool. After you, then."

She got another look. But this one was less *beautiful wolf* and more *little shit.*

"Scared to go first, huh?" he said, with just a hint of laughter in his voice. Because of course he knew what all the stalling was about. Of course he did.

"Well, if I do, I might bang into a mailbox from another dimension."

"You won't. You'll feel the presence of the house before that happens."

"That's not reassuring, Seth."

"It doesn't need to be if I'm leading," he said.

Then he just got out of the car and strode across the frost-tipped grass, fast enough that she started to fear he would get too far ahead. That she wouldn't be able to see how he'd dissolved through some magic wall, and she'd end up trapped out here in the dark. *He'll notice I'm not with him just as an interdimensional beast grabs his face, and all I'll be able to do is hear his screams for help across the void*, she thought, as she told Pod to stay, and scrambled after Seth.

She stumbled over the grass, calling his name. Then felt very silly when she got to where he stood, and he lifted a hand and knocked on the air, and a door swung open. Just like that. One second there was nothing but the slope downward and the forest beyond; the next there was a rectangle of a very particular sort of light.

A golden, glowing, slightly flickering light, that made her think of gas lamps.

And that was exactly what lay beyond the now-visible threshold of the door. A row of them, mounted on the walls of a cozy-looking but mind-bendingly long hall. *The door at the end of that hall should lead off the edge of the hill*, she thought, half marveling, half terrified.

While Seth just strolled right in.

She watched him wipe his high-top sneakers on the mat, inside the door. The one that said WELCOME, and looked worn—like something an old lady might put down. And the rest of the decor had a similar vibe. The carpet was patterned with curling roses; the wallpaper had stripes below the chair rail, and a floral motif above.

Then further down she could see pictures, between each door.

Portraits, of what looked like the ancestors of a person she hoped didn't exist.

"Are you sure no one owns this place?" she asked, as she tip-toed far enough in to examine one of them. A painting of a woman in Edwardian clothes, expression stern, one hand on the shoulder of a small, wan-looking child.

But Seth didn't seem concerned.

He made his way down the hall, answering her over his shoulder.

"Some think it belonged to a person once. A witch who got lost, or who lost her own home. But even if that's the case, she's gone now. She has to be, because there'd be at least some wards left here if she were alive."

"But there's nothing?"

"Not a thing."

Still, Cassie couldn't help wondering. About who that witch was, and if she had died a good death or a bad one. *This is serious business*, she thought, as she turned to see where Seth had gotten to. And found him very unseriously trying to spring the lock of the tenth door down the hall.

He was using a frigging Blockbuster card.

She didn't even know how he still had one.

"So I guess now I know that goblin poop isn't your only source of income," she said as she strolled up to him. And he didn't even have the decency to look shamefaced. He look positively gleeful. He actually had his tongue in his cheek.

"Cassie, I hope you're not implying I regularly steal from rich pricks. Because I will have you know, I am a moral and upstanding citizen, and would never. In fact, I barely even know how to do such things," he said, and on that last word he shoved the card upward.

Then there was a snap, and the door popped open. Just like that.

Much to her absolute delight. Too much delight, really. It made her want to blurt out *god that was sexy*. And she only caught herself by keeping up the disapproving charade.

"Wow, that is some *wild* beginner's luck."

"I know, right? So weird and fortunate of me."

"Sure hope you're being as weird and fortunate to the ex-mayor."

"Oh you mean the guy who embezzled six million dollars and escaped prison? I mean, I did hear that his seventy-inch flat-screen went missing, and is now next to the mattress on the floor of my, quote unquote, *bedroom*. But I'm sure that's just a coincidence."

"Definitely a coincidence," she said solemnly. "Fingers crossed another one happens soon so you can have a bed. Because otherwise, I'm gonna have to do something about that. In fact, ever since I saw that death trap you live in, I've been thinking I might have to do a lot of somethings about that. I mean, do you even have electricity to run the TV?"

"I do not. But sometimes ghosts show me *The Great British Baking Show.*"

"Yeah, I'm not sure you should be watching that."

"Me neither. Paul Hollywood is scary enough without his eyeballs melting."

She exclaimed with delight. "That's *exactly* how I feel about him."

"Of course it is. I could have told you that."

"Because we're practically the same person?"

"At this point it's undeniable."

"Unquestionable."

"Beautiful."

That doesn't fit the other two words we used, she wanted to tell him. But she couldn't, because he'd said it all low and breathless-sounding. And he was standing very close all of a sudden. He was almost leaning, one hand high on the doorframe into the room they should have been going into, the other sort of hovering in the air between them. Like it wanted to do something.

But didn't quite dare.

Go on, dare, she thought.

So naturally had to change the subject, instead.

"Anyway, we should probably—" she started to say. Then was grateful when he picked up the thread. He gave her about ten *rights* and turned to the room beyond, which was fortunately just as distracting as the rest of the place.

More so, really.

In the hall it was just pictures and gas lamps. In this room there were wall-to-wall and ceiling-to-floor shelves, absolutely filled with a complete assortment of the weird and the wonderful. There were jars stuffed with eyes that still seemed alive, sat alongside perpetually frothing cauldrons. Stuffed animals of species she had no hope of recognizing, with eyes that seemed to watch you no matter where you stood.

She spotted vials that were only empty from one angle, plants bursting out of their pots to attack light fixtures, a row of tins with labels that bore phrases like *void tea*. Spice racks filled with substances other than spices; husks and veils of cobwebs and ropes of hair on hooks.

And all of it so fascinating and idea-charging that she could have spent a week examining everything. But just as she was about to ask Seth if she might possibly do so, she turned from the jar she was peering into, and saw his face.

His frozen, stricken face.

Then before she could form a single question, he took hold of her. He put his hands on both her arms, and started moving her in the direction of god only knew what. *The nearest wall so he can fuck me against it*, she thought, automatically, ridiculously.

Though of course it didn't *feel* ridiculous.

It felt like the heat between them had been building again all this time, and now it was at some kind of delirious crescendo. She almost blurted out, *oh yes please, thank god*, and only managed not to because she grasped what he was urging her toward. Not the wall. Or the desk he had to maneuver her around.

No—it was the big wardrobe behind the desk.

The one that did not seem very big at all once he'd stuffed her inside, and followed her in.

In fact, the whole scenario sort of felt like a reverse Narnia. The enormous, exciting, fantastical world was out there. Whereas *this* was just a cupboard. A boring empty cupboard with about as much space inside as your average coffin. In fact, it was so small he had to sort of lift and position her over one of his bent legs, just to be able to close the door.

Though why he would choose to do such a nightmarish thing was still largely unclear. All she knew at that moment was that his thigh was jammed between hers, and his hand was still on her waist, and that the only light around them was a thin sliver from the room beyond, illuminating only the most utterly terrible parts of him.

Like the gleam of one wolfish eye, and the slash of his meaty jaw, and the curve of his collarbone , and the slant of thick muscle just below, and and and—

"Seth, I have to get out of here right now," she blurted out.

But instead of listening, he just seemed to go rigid.

Then for some ungodly reason, he put a hand over her mouth.

Though the reason *why* he did it didn't really matter. Even when she heard voices from down the hall, loud and brash—and obviously belonging to the Jerk Squad—she couldn't really care. Every bit of her focus was on only one thing, now:

That his hand was so big it spanned the whole lower half of her face.

All she could feel were his thick fingers, pressing into her lips, her cheeks, her chin. She could barely breathe because of it. And even when he let up enough for her to, things didn't get any better. Because now she could feel where his other hand was.

It had her by the nape of her neck.

Fingers under her hair, in her hair, almost tangled in it.

As if he was about to do something more than encourage her silence, it seemed like.

And he knew it. She could see it in his eyes, the moment he glanced away from the sliver of light, and back to her. There it was—that deep understanding of how much he was touching her. And how little he could stand it.

It was the reason he jerked away, despite the risk of noise.

Then he actually wiped his hands on his shirt. Like he could get the feel of her off him by doing so. Even though that was ridiculous, this was all ridiculous, *why* had he done this? They had the means to fuck those assholes up, he knew they did—and if he had somehow forgotten, well, she was going to tell him so. She raised her fists. Mimed fighting them. Tapped the spray bottle she always kept at her hip now.

But he shook his head sharply. Looked frustrated.

More, he mouthed. And though it took her a second, she got what he meant.

It wasn't just the original three Jerks. They had others with them. At least five others, if the hand Seth held up was any indication. And now she could make out their raised voices more clearly, and they weren't saying anything good.

"Look, Hannigan isn't gonna help us. He's too busy with his crusade against that fucking librarian. So this is our best option. And it'll work too, I know it will. Once we have it, we can get that fat witch," she heard Jason say, and immediately had so many questions she almost blurted them out. It took a lot of restraint to limit her reaction to whipping a look at Seth, and mouthing *what do they want?* and *what will the thing they want do?* and *fuck fuck fuck*.

Though of course he couldn't answer her. The Jerks were very close now.

So close, in fact, she had to wonder why they couldn't smell Seth. All she could imagine was that the blocker masking her was also masking him, or that the magic lube was maybe stepping in, because *god* he was a riot of different scents, to her. She could make out strawberry bubblegum, and the airy sweetness of whatever soap or shampoo or deodorant he used, and then underneath it— something heated. Something familiar.

Perspiration, she thought it was—because his skin was lightly sheened with it.

She could see it gleaming in the darkness.

But part of her knew that was wrong. It was a heavier, sultrier scent. Like a stronger, more obvious version of what she'd smelled in her closet that time. Like the kind of thing that filled a room, after you'd spent five hours fucking the living daylights out of someone.

Even if she didn't want to admit that this was the case.

She tried to shrug it off. To focus on the problem at hand.

But it was very difficult to when he felt so boiling hot against her. When that heat seemed to be sliding into her and drowning out all other thoughts. When the curve of his throat was right there, and it was glossy with sweat, and if she just leaned forward and stuck out her tongue—

"*Cassie*," he hissed.

Too loudly, she knew.

The sound froze them both in place, eyes locked. His searching hers with a kind of agonized confusion, hers no doubt hazy with whatever fucking delirium she seemed to be descending into. And then they just had to wait in that position. To see if anyone had heard, to see if anything would happen.

Even though waiting was impossible.

All she wanted to do was move. She wanted to squirm against his thigh.

Though honestly, she didn't realize she was actually doing it, until his eyes suddenly widened. He seemed to stiffen, and his leg tried to shift downward to get away from her, and when neither of those things worked he shot a hand out and grabbed her hip. He forced her to keep still.

Despite how much worse that definitely was. A low moan wrenched itself out of her, the second he did it. And so of course the first thing he said when they heard the Jerks' voices start to fade wasn't *wow, that was close* or *hey, so I guess we should worry more about being killed by those fuckers* or even *let's go figure out what they were looking for.*

No. They were: "Oh my fucking *god*, are you turned on right now?"

Which was fair, given what she was doing. But she had to at least try denying it.

"No, of course not," she snorted. Very unconvincingly.

"Cassie, you just tried to fuck my leg."

"Oh come on. I wasn't trying to fuck it."

"You're still doing it now. I can feel you squirming."

He was right. No matter how much she tried to keep herself still, she found it almost impossible to. That thick muscle of his had spread her thighs too effectively; it had given her too solid and warm a thing to make contact with. It seemed almost unnatural not to ease the ache between her legs by using it.

Even if using it was really bad. And not something she could accept.

"Maybe I'm just uncomfortable with your big thigh right there."

"And did that big uncomfortable thigh also make you this fucking wet?"

She tried to snort dismissively to that question too. But this one was harder.

Because god, it shocked her that he could tell. That he knew.

And grasping that he did made her denials clumsy.

"You can't possibly know something like that," she said.

Which of course only confirmed he was right.

Not that he needed confirmation.

"Of course I can. Cassie, I can hear it every time you move."

"Well, maybe you're just not listening right. Maybe it's something else."

"There isn't anything else that sounds like something slick sliding over a swollen, flushed little pussy. And even if there were, it wouldn't matter. Because I can feel it, too, oh god I can *feel* how wet you are. Fuck, how are you *this* wet?"

He said "pussy," he said "flushed, swollen little pussy," her brain screamed.

Though she didn't know why that was the thing it was focusing on. Why the words made her want to moan and rut against him all over again, as if there were nothing shameful about it. Because after all, there were far more important and potentially lust-killing matters to deal with.

Like the fact that she was. Oh god, she was so preposterously wet she'd somehow made a mess of her panties, and her jeans, and then made a mess of *his* jeans. The whole space between them was a mess, in a way that seemed completely impossible.

Or at the very least utterly embarrassing.

Yet somehow, embarrassment wasn't what she felt.

It was another surge of arousal. And one that took a lot to bite back. She had to count to ten before she could talk. "It must be just the friction," she said. But of course he wasn't having it.

"We barely moved, Cassie."

"Okay, so maybe the situation did it."

"We were just trapped in a wardrobe by murderous werewolves, who are apparently on the hunt for something that makes them immune to Werewolf Killer, or makes you vulnerable to their attacks, or dissolves your protection spells. And that is very easily the least sexy situation I can think of," he said—which should really have shoved her attention firmly back to the danger they were in. But the only thing she could think of were denials. And almost none of them felt like denials anymore.

They felt like explanations. Reasons. *Excuses.*

"Okay. Okay, but you're very hot and close."

"We've been hot and close before."

"Yeah and—you—we—the thing is—" she tried.

But she knew what she had given away before he even replied.

"Oh my god, this isn't the only time that has happened," he said, and he just sounded so wasted by the idea. Like it had detonated a bomb between his ears.

Even though he had to understand.

Wasn't it just a bit understandable?

"It isn't the only time—but honestly, I'm so sorry about it. And I really didn't mean to feel like this, over it all. I think it's just that I'm not used to really graphically sexual stuff happening. I mean, god, I get horny over a fade-to-black scene in a book," she protested. Then tried to see what his expression was in response, through the darkness.

Did it reveal belief in what she was saying? Or something else?

But she couldn't make out a thing. And now the silence was spinning out.

It wasn't even a comfort when she heard the front door open and close and knew the Jerks had left the building. She was too busy waiting for his answer. In fact, by the time she got it, she was holding her breath. *I just can't accept your sorrys and your excuses,* she imagined.

Instead, he answered quietly.

"So you swear that's all it is."

"Of course."

"There's nothing else that did it."

"Look, if you're trying to get me to say I'm superhot for your sexy body—" she started to say, but his frustrated sound cut her off.

"Cassie, I would never think that. I would never believe that. I know you never will be. However, what I do *not* know is exactly how unhinged my werewolf pheromones appear to be making you. Because quite clearly, that is what is happening to you, to an almost nightmarish degree."

She fell silent. She had to, because all her mortification died away, like it had never existed. It just couldn't survive after he said *I know you never will be.* And it burned up entirely based on his other words. The ones that knocked the breath out of her. The ones she couldn't believe.

But struggled to refute somehow, anyway.

"But I'm not a werewolf. It shouldn't work that way," she tried to protest.

Though god, when she did. The sheer sense of wrongness that went through her.

She knew, almost immediately, that he was correct. She knew it so well that she wondered how she had missed it before. *Of course* it was something beyond the physical. Of course it was. What else could it have been, when she was getting so wet that even denim couldn't hold up to it? It was blatantly obvious.

And he seemed to think so, too.

"Honestly, I didn't think it did. But I should have known. Sometimes I could hear your heart hammering so hard, and you looked so flushed, and you smelled so rea—" he started to say.

But it was all right, he didn't have to finish. She knew the last word he had skipped was "ready." She knew, because it made her shiver. It made her want to say, *because I am.* And then she was glad he started talking about something else, before she could.

"Plus there was all the shit I kept getting the urge to do. All the stuff that I should have guessed was just me trying to make myself a better mate to you. As if some part of me knew that you being my mate was possible." He let out a frustrated sigh. Like he was talking about something simple and practical with an easy fix, and not something that had caused him to use the word "mate." But he didn't even stop there. "You obviously prefer the person I was, the person I still am inside, so the wolf kept pushing me to show you that more overtly. Like, you know. A fancy bird showing off the right feathers."

And oh god the doors that were blown off in her head, on hearing that.

She could immediately see exactly what he meant.

She could feel the way his actions had affected her. She could even name them.

"So the shirts and the hair and the breakfast," she said, too breathlessly. Like she was solving a puzzle—and apparently she had it exactly right. He was already nodding.

"More than that, honestly. I would have probably done those things anyway, but there was other stuff. Weirder stuff, that I kind of pushed down. Like wearing my glasses even though I don't need them anymore. Or wanting to bring you little gifts that I would never usually get you, like bottles of vitamins and weird crap you can make a nest out of. God, I should have guessed when it was a fucking nest," he groaned.

And yeah, he had a point.

But really, had she been any better?

She'd never been this horny in her life, and she hadn't guessed the reason for it. She'd just thought it was due to old feelings and weird happenings and him being all filthy and thirsty for her. But clearly it wasn't. Thank god it wasn't, it wasn't. She wasn't taking advantage of things he didn't really feel, or giving in to her own secret desires.

It was just weird werewolf mating urges.

And he was feeling the same. That was why he was trying to make her want him.

And none of it was their fault, no way, not in the least. "Look, even if you were doing those things because of werewolf hormone bullshit, you couldn't have understood that it would actually infect me. And even if it has, well. I mean it's not like this is going to kill us," she insisted.

Then she tried to laugh, she really did.

But she felt him tense up, and somehow knew that he was wincing and, oh Jesus Christ, was that the witch tingle happening? "Oh my *god* you're saying it might actually kill us. You're actually saying that. You're telling me that if we don't get out of this extreme deranged horniness for each other, we will kick the bucket. Like some sort of weird *Star Trek*ian-fuck-or-die-fated-mates-type situation," she said, and got absolutely zero nopes in response. Not one single no.

He just fucking *welp-ed.*

"That's about the size of it, yeah," he said, as her mind tried to race right off the edge of some terrible cliff.

"Okay. Okay cool. Cool cool cool. That's fine."

"That doesn't sound like you think it's fine."

"Even if it isn't, maybe I can fix it."

"You don't seem too sure about that."

"Because my brain is currently being addled by werewolf-sex nonsense, Seth. As soon as we're out of this wardrobe it will go away—or I can help it go away somehow—and I will feel much more certain about things. So make sure the guys are really gone, and open this thing up."

She nudged him toward the door—even though touching him at all felt like being briefly electrocuted. But it was worth it, because he immediately moved to do what she had suggested. He listened, and then he pressed his hand against the door. Firmly, in a way that should have opened it.

But for some reason, he had to do it again.

And again, harder.

Really hard. Scarily hard.

"Seth, please tell me this thing is not fucking jammed shut."

"I want to, but I can't. Because it seriously is."

"But you have werewolf strength. Just use that."

"I am trying. Doesn't it look like I'm trying?"

"It looks like you're sweating and straining and all the muscles in your arms are really standing out, oh they are really visible and they are so thick and good, and oh my god this is unbearable, this is the most mortifying thing ever, oh I have no idea how you stand it," she said, before she even knew any of that was in her to say.

The words simply burst out of her, as if them naming what was happening had dropped the guardrails she'd put up. She no longer had to worry that he might disapprove of her behavior, or that she was taking advantage of his hormonal state, or that she was actually into him. Her only motivator was supernatural werewolf magic.

So why bother pretending? Hell, she wasn't even sure if she *could* pretend at this point.

And nor could he, it seemed. She could feel him shaking. She heard him groan when she said "thick" and "good." Then just to round things off, he said, "Well, currently I manage by masturbating seventeen times in a row." So it really seemed that now was the terrible-but-unfathomably-hot-honesty portion of the proceedings.

"Wait, you said you did it *ten*. You said ten was enough to make you okay."

"Yeah, and I rounded down so you wouldn't be scared."

"And you think *now* I will be *less so*? Seth, I need to get off so badly I can feel it in my fucking teeth. I think these hormones might be boiling my brain. And right at this moment I'm in a situation where I can't even do it once. Never mind dozens of times," she said—both because all of it was true, but also because it was something to do instead of murdering him.

But unfortunately for them both, what he said next made her want to murder him even more. "Just rub yourself against me like you were doing before," he said. As if that were a real and normal possibility.

"I am not going to consciously use your innocent thigh to get myself off."

"My thigh isn't innocent. In fact, all it currently wants to do is jam itself against your pussy, and the only thing that is stopping that from happening is me using every bit of strength I have left to hold it in place."

She looked down. She couldn't help it.

But god, she regretted doing so. Now she could make out his thigh muscle, trembling with effort, through the denim of his jeans. She could see his hands on himself. Both hands, on his leg, actually forcing it to stay down. Then after a long, agonizing second of this, he smacked one of said hands against the wall of the wardrobe, above her head. Like he needed to steady himself. Or force some other part of himself to stay away from her.

He wants to grind himself against me, she thought blankly.

Then got an urge to do just that for him, strong enough that she almost couldn't fight it. The idea simply gripped her and wouldn't let go. And worse—it seemed for a second that there was no argument against it. He wanted to, and she wanted to, so why not, her body wanted to know.

And it was only remembering who they were—and what that would look like in practice—that forced her to talk sense. "That still doesn't suggest I should. Or can. I mean, you'll *see* me," she said. But all he did was sigh in response.

"If being seen is what you're worried about, then stop. My eyes are already closed. They've been closed for the last ten minutes. In fact, I'm not sure I am ever going to be able to open them again."

"Why the fuck not?"

"Because looking at you before was bad. But looking at you while you are this fucking horny is actual hell. It almost makes me wish I didn't have werewolf night vision, just so I don't have to see your hazy-with-lust gaze, and your flushed cheeks, and the tongue you keep using to lick your pouty, parted lips."

"Oh god, I can't possibly look that bad," she groaned.

But he offered her no consolation. He just made a despairing sound. "You look worse. But I don't want to describe the other things."

"Maybe you should. I might be able to stop doing whatever they are."

"Cassie, you can't stop your nipples straining through a fucking sweater."

"I can hold the fabric out. Like this."

She demonstrated with her hands.

So of course he looked. Why wouldn't he? She was supposed to be showing him something less revealing. Something safer, for him to look at. She really didn't mean to give him an unobstructed view, directly down her top.

"Ohhhh my god. Oh my god, you're not wearing a bra. You don't even have a bra on. How do you not have a bra on? *Why* do you not have a bra on?" he asked, as he whipped his face away, and screwed his eyes tight shut again.

While she scrambled to cover up. And give him some kind of answer.

"I don't know. Wearing one feels really uncomfortable now."

"Fuck. Fuck, do *not* tell me why. In fact, say nothing else."

"It's not that bad. Everything just feels kind of super sensitive."

There, she thought. *That will clear everything up in a nice, innocent way.*

But she should have known it wouldn't even before he let out an agonized groan.

"So you can't stand tight material brushing over those hard little nipples. You just want something gentle on them, something soft, maybe something slick and teasing that makes you—oh *fuck*, I told you not to tell me," he said, reasonably enough at first. But as his sentences ran on, he sounded more and more panicked and breathless until finally here they were, in hell.

In a terrible, terrible hell that she somehow didn't even want to escape from.

"Yeah, I really shouldn't have. Now all I can think about is what slick and teasing thing you mean. Like, are you talking about your mouth? Are you talking about licking and sucking? Is that what you are suggesting by that?" she asked, and now she sounded just as breathless and eager as he did.

Much to his frustration. "Of course I am. There's nothing else it could be."

"I can think of some other things."

"No you can't."

"Sure I can. You could suck your fingers and use those. Or have me suck them, and do it that way. Or you could make me do it to myself, you know, while you watched. Or possibly get your cock out, and then you know. Just rub the slick tip all over my tits, all over my hard—"

She wasn't surprised when he interrupted her.

But it was a surprise how he went about it. Oh yeah, that was a shock all right. Because he didn't do it with words. He did it with his hand on her hip, firm enough that it kicked a sound of shock out of her. Then another one, when that hand didn't just stay where it was.

It seemed to move, in this really insistent, particular sort of way. It urged her back and then forward, back and then forward, until finally it was clear. He was trying to get her to work herself against him, quite obviously.

And of course she knew why.

He wanted her to get off, before she said anything worse. He needed there to be an end to this—to her talking dirty and looking the way she did and being so close to him. It was driving him mad, she could see it was, even through the darkness. She could make out the cords in his neck standing out, where the light hit them. And a hint of his clenched teeth.

And that wasn't just his nails digging into her.

It was claws. She could tell it was claws.

She could hear threads of denim popping as they pierced the fabric of her jeans.

And, yeah, that should have been scary. It should have thrown cold water over everything. But somehow it just seemed to make everything hotter. Now all she could think about was how desperate he had to be. How much effort it must have been taking to hold himself in check.

Yet he didn't even pull her closer.

He didn't force her against his groin. Or grope her ass or her thigh.

Even though she could tell he wanted to do both. She could tell he wanted to do more. She could feel the tension in his arms and his grip, whenever he came close to anything like it. He slid one hand over her waist just to make things more comfortable, and somehow slipped a little way up her top. He grazed bare skin over her side.

And it made him gasp and go all still.

And she knew what he was thinking about.

Her bare breasts, only a few inches away. How easy it would be to push upward, underneath her sweater, and cup and squeeze and fondle. Because of course she wouldn't say no. She couldn't imagine, in the state she was in, that she would ever be able to say no to anything. He could have probably yanked her jeans down and had her up against the wall of the wardrobe, no problem at all.

And he was quite clearly struggling with the knowledge that this was the case.

So she did it for him. She pushed herself against him, until his hand simply slid up. And she didn't regret it, once his palm made contact with the smooth curve of her breast. She couldn't—the contact was just too glorious, too intense. It seemed to sizzle over her skin. It set up an echo of pleasure between her legs.

A thick, heavy echo, that forced a sob from her lips.

But that was all right, because the second he felt that softness, the instant he heard and felt her reaction, he reacted in almost the same way. He stiffened, and let out a hoarse sound. Followed by words, all in a tumble. "Oh god, Cassie, you're so fucking hot, you feel so fucking good, oh man, I can't resist when you're this gorgeous and eager."

Then after he had, something more seemed to break.

And he let his hand close over the swell of her breast. He let himself grope her, he let himself fondle her. He let his palm slide so sweetly over her aching nipple. Just for a second, one delicious, soft second—but that second was enough.

It turned that wave of heat between her legs into an avalanche.

An intense and impossible avalanche, of a sort she recognized completely. She felt it pulse through her, in this thick, heavy way. Felt her clit swell, felt her pussy ache and clench around nothing, felt how wet it made her. And she knew, she knew. She knew she was coming. He had made her come, just by passing his palm over one stiff little nipple.

And not even in some small, weak way.

She shuddered over it. Said his name over it.

Made noises that should have made her ashamed.

But they didn't, because he did the same. He let out a guttural, near-rattling moan of pleasure, from between his clenched teeth. Almost a grunt of pain, it sounded like—though she knew it wasn't. He was just coming and coming and coming, hard enough that it hurt.

And she knew, beyond a shadow of a doubt, that it was her that had made him.

CHAPTER TWENTY-THREE

Cassie thought maybe she would feel calm by the time they returned to her house. After all, she'd had that almighty orgasm. And there was a lot to deal with.

There was the dragon scale they had located, that needed adding to the dehornification brew. And now that they had learned that the Jerks were still very much a threat, she definitely wanted to do something about that. She even knew the potion she wanted to brew—something called Forget Me, that would definitely ensure the Jerks couldn't find them. Or even remember where they lived.

If she did it right.

Which took some doing.

And then there was Pod, who continued fighting with Seth about everything.

She had to listen to them squabbling on the front porch, as she put the finishing touches on her potions. Because obviously, Pod wanted to come inside. In fact, Pod seemed to think he was *owed* the privilege of coming inside. That inside was *his,* now that he was her familiar.

And although Seth couldn't understand a word Pod was saying, he got the gist.

And he was skeptical, to say the least.

"You're basically vermin," he shouted as he tried to shoo Pod off the porch. But despite the fact that Seth had a broom and Pod was just a raccoon, Seth clearly did not win the battle. A moment later there was a lot of crashing, and running, and gasping. And then Seth groaned, "Oh god, at least use something other than my shoe to make your nest." Even though there should have been no way for Pod to grab his shoe.

But sure enough, when Cassie turned around from the stove, Seth was wearing just one. While Pod scampered into the cupboard under the stairs with his prize clutched in his tiny hands.

So really, given all the chaos, it should have been easy to avoid feeling the least bit horny.

Yet somehow, she felt as heated as she had in the wardrobe.

In fact, she felt worse. Like she had cracked a door to let one thing through, and now it could not be closed. It was being jammed opened by a million lusty thoughts, and they were all spilling out at once. They were taking her over. She actually found herself stopping the moment she saw him standing there, in the archway between the kitchen and the hall, just to moon over how sweaty he looked. How much his chest was heaving with exertion. How flushed his cheeks were.

And she now fully understood why he kept his eyes above her chin.

Because as he bent over to pick up the broom he'd dropped, her gaze accidentally landed on his butt. And the sight actually made her mouth go dry. She had to take a drink. To force herself to look away. And even after she had, she still couldn't stop thinking about it. About how round and plump it had looked. How tightly his jeans had clung to it. What it would feel like if she slid her hand over that gorgeous curve.

She even found herself justifying it. *Well he touched yours*, she thought feverishly. And had to practically yell at herself that this was not a fair thing to say. He had been as much of a gentleman about ass-touching as anyone could possibly be.

But she was not wanting to be a gentleman to him. Oh no, not at all.

She wanted to stuff her fucking hand down the back of his jeans.

Or maybe down the front of his jeans.

Or just take his jeans off, yeah, just—

"You know you're totally free to go see to yourself, right?"

She snapped a look to him. As if looking was going to prove that he hadn't actually said that. Or that he'd meant something other than what she thought he meant. But he appeared just as teasing as she'd imagined. He practically had his tongue in his cheek.

And it left her blushing. Then turning away from him so he couldn't see the blush.

"I don't need to go to 'see to myself,'" she said, and knew she sounded way too defensive about it. She had to add something more just to claw back some dignity. "And even if I did, I've got things to do. I don't have time for sexy feelings that I have under control anyway."

"It doesn't look like you have them under control."

"Well then, you're not looking right. Or you don't know what control is."

"I know it's not ogling my ass the second I bend over. Which, just so you know—I'm not complaining about. In fact, if you want to do it again, please feel free any time you like. I could even do it a little sexier for you. Maybe go slower, or take something off. Or oh, oh, how about run my hand over it, like this?" he asked, and honestly her first instinct was to be mad at him for mocking her.

But then he did the thing.

He turned and sort of brushed his palm over that juicy curve, and she realized. He was *serious*. He was actually trying to encourage her to look, and to like looking. As if looking were a good thing. And not absolutely terrible and completely off limits. *Five minutes and we might have a cure for this*, she thought, and then did her best to rein him in before anything got worse.

"Seth, do not run your hand over your ass, for the love of god."

"Why not? I don't mind if you want to get off over my butt."

"Yes, but *I* do. It feels weird to think about you while I do that."

"And I totally get that. It feels weird to me, too, to consider you in ways that do not go well with every cherished value I have. Usually I do my best to stop myself before I can't look you in the eye the next day," he said, and when he did she thought of him calling out her name. How broken it had sounded. Like he didn't want to give in, but for one second had.

"You don't have to hold back, I don't mind," she rushed out.

That got such a look of triumph from him.

Apparently he'd set a trap, and she'd run right into it.

"Oh, so there's a thing where if you get permission, it's okay?" he said. "As in, I can just say to you now that you're good to go. That it is totally fine by me for you to think about me in any kind of permutation you want?" *No*, she thought at him, sullenly. But of course her body was already saying yes, before he even continued. "Because it is, you know. You could imagine yourself pinning me down and riding my face, and I'd be fine with it. In fact, that sounds superhot, and like something you should think about more in excessive detail. Go on, picture my tongue fucking your pussy. Picture me groaning deeply as you come all over my face. Picture me coming when you do it. Because you know what? I definitely would."

And after he had she wanted to be furious with him, she did. She even started to say, *You can't just keep talking dirty to me like that. I am going out of my mind.* Then she saw that he still looked triumphant—like he was winning some battle. And the words died on her lips.

"Fuck," she said. "You're just saying filthy things to get me to go do myself."

"Of course I am. Honestly you'll feel *much* better once you do."

"Yeah, but you'll hear me. With your super werewolf hearing."

He held up the Vulcan salute. "I *swear* I won't listen."

"Even though I listened to you?"

"You didn't really intend to. I'm just super loud."

"Yeah, but I am too. Or at least, I am when I'm on my own."

She saw his gaze flash bright. But he kept it together.

He kept things focused on his apparent mission.

"Then I'll wear headphones. And go outside to do what I need to do."

"Fuck—so *you're* gonna do it too?"

"Dude, I'm almost doing it *now*."

She made the mistake of glancing down. Probably because his expression seemed so calm and even. And his voice was so steady.

It didn't seem possible that there was anything major going on down there, no matter what he was trying to claim.

But oh dear god, was she wrong about that.

She'd never seen anything like it in her life. It looked as if he had a fist shoved down the front of his jeans. As if he were about to split the seams. And oh, the *mess*. It was even worse than the one she'd made of herself, back in the wardrobe. She would have thought he'd already come, if he hadn't just said he was merely close.

And that was way hotter than it had any right to be.

She felt as if she should have been disturbed. Instead, all she could think about was getting on her knees for him, immediately. Then taking him in, and licking and sucking and tasting him until he spilled over her tongue, in a way she knew she was *way* too greedy for.

This was far beyond a normal, sexy urge.

It was unholy, it was impossible, insurmountable.

Understandable given what's going on, her witch brain added.

And this made enough sense to give in to. "Okay, can you just go outside now?" she stumbled out. Because honestly, she didn't think she could make it to the bathroom. The need to get off was so keen-edged, so intense, that she could barely wait until Seth had gone out. She didn't even hear the door close, before she shoved her hand down the front of her jeans.

And it took almost nothing. Just the sound of him groaning, loudly, from somewhere outside. While she slid two fingers over her clit, and stroked, once. Just once, and there it was.

A rolling wave of pleasure, even thicker and sweeter than what she'd felt against his thigh. Oh god yeah—this one, this one made her fly. It made her shudder and hold on to the edge of the kitchen table, and partway through she knew she said his name. She heard herself call it out, like it was *his* hands on her. Him working her through the best orgasm of her life. Him doing all the things her mind was full of, now that this sex magic had given her permission to fill it up. Now that he'd given her permission to do so.

It's okay, she reassured herself, *it's okay*.

Then she thought of him coming in her mouth. And in her pussy. And all over her.

And just as she felt the first twinge of shame, she heard him from outside. Saying how much he loved it when he heard her feeling the same.

CHAPTER TWENTY-FOUR

She knew he was embarrassed about what she had done. Because after she'd managed to see sense enough to actually make the potion, and they had awkwardly taken it, he told her he was going to go check if the spell that kept the Jerks from finding them was working okay.

Even though both of them knew it was. They had seen the trio through the kitchen window an hour after she'd sprayed Forget Me all over, mystified as to why they suddenly couldn't find the house. Even when the house was right in front of them.

So it was obvious this was just an excuse to get away. But she didn't know what to do about it. The only thing that occurred to her was to apologize. *Sorry that I really loudly and enthusiastically got off while thinking about you*, she imagined herself writing in a card. But where she could buy such a card she had no idea. She felt pretty sure that Hallmark didn't have an "I Didn't Mean to Enjoy the Thought of You Coming on My Tits" line. And even if they did, she couldn't imagine that the gesture would make things better.

Doubly so, when she realized midway through a conversation with Nancy, that something was off. "I just wanted to come over and apologize for the other day," Nancy said, as Cassie ushered her into the kitchen. Then she added, "You know, about all that stuff Marley was saying concerning you and Seth."

And as soon as Cassie heard his name, there it was: a heavy pulse starting up between her legs. Like she had a second heart down there, and those four letters had jolted it back into action. Now it was hammering away again, and there was nothing Cassie could do about it.

She just had to sit across from her new friend, trying not to let on that she was aroused over the very man she was trying to say meant nothing to her.

"I was just helping him out with something," Cassie explained, and tried not to let it show on her face that the help in question was letting him jerk off on her front porch. And she felt she did so admirably, too.

Nancy nodded and sipped her tea.

From a mug that had grown hands, which Nancy couldn't see.

It's very strange watching someone who can't register magic, the microwave said over Nancy's shoulder. And Cassie had to agree. Because it was all around her, and Nancy didn't seem aware of a single thing. She couldn't even see Pod—as if the mere idea of a raccoon sipping tea was far too much for reality to withstand.

And that was cool.

But it was also sad, somehow. It was another secret Cassie had to keep, from someone so kind and sweet. When even the first secret was too tough for her to really manage. "I promise, Seth and I are barely even friends," she said, and just as Nancy was giving her a relieved look—like all that mattered to her was that Seth couldn't do her any damage—Seth burst into the kitchen.

And oh god, he couldn't have looked less like her friend if he'd tried.

His chest was heaving, his eyes were flashing, he was for some inexplicable reason windswept. There was a tear in his shirt, big enough that you could see his chest through it. And the first thing he did when he appeared in the archway was gasp her name. As if he'd just stormed off the cover of a romance novel titled *Claiming the Woman Who Just Said We Were Only Friends*.

And Nancy clearly agreed.

She actually dribbled a bit of tea down her chin.

Cassie handed her a napkin, while trying to tell Seth to calm down with her eyes. *If only we could understand all this nonsense as well as we can everything else about each other*, she thought, as he looked back and forth between the two women, utterly confused.

Though he seemed to get it enough to avoid blurting out that the potion hadn't worked.

Because clearly, obviously, this was the case.

She went from one to eighty million on the horniness scale the moment she laid eyes on him. And he seemed to be in exactly the same state. He had to grab a book from the table and hold it in front of his groin, so Nancy didn't get an eyeful.

While Cassie did her best to come up with a plausible explanation for all of this.

"He's been working on the roof," she found herself saying.

Then almost collapsed with relief when Seth followed her lead.

"Oh yeah, the roof. It needed fixing. So I fixed it. For my friend here," he said. Very convincingly too, Cassie thought. In fact, she could see on Nancy's face that it had worked. She didn't seem skeptical in the least.

But unfortunately, Seth didn't seem to think so.

Because he clearly decided that something else needed to be done. A little extra underlining of the idea that they were just good buds. And so he put his arm around her shoulders. Just lightly. Barely touching her, really. In fact, she wasn't even sure if any contact was made. It felt more like the air between them just sort of brushed her.

But it made no difference.

It still hit her like lightning anyway. She came within a hair's breadth of screaming. The only thing that stopped her was the fact that her teeth seemed to be welded together. And she had no idea how she kept from falling out of her chair. Maybe Seth's hand, squeezing her shoulder?

Though that seemed impossible.

He was in a worst state than she was. She could feel him shuddering all over. He couldn't even speak when Nancy said, "Well, I'd better get going." All he could manage was to hold a hand up in a stunted sort of wave—and even that looked bad.

It shook like someone had started an earthquake inside his body.

And there was nothing they could do about any of it. They just had to ride it out, until Nancy disappeared down the lane back to town. But even after she was gone, there was no real respite. Because now they were in the aftermath of whatever the fuck all that was.

"Oh my god, I think putting an arm around you made me come," Seth blurted out, the second they were in the clear. As if that would really help the situation. Instead of making it insurmountably worse. Now all she could think about was whether it actually had, and what that looked like, and if she could make it happen again.

Just slip your *hand around* his *waist*, some devil voice inside her said.

But she fought it. She managed to wrench herself away from him.

"Talk about something else," she gasped, as she stumbled to the other side of the table.

Yet, all he could come up with was this: "You'll be pleased to know that we are perfectly safe, and there's no sign of current danger."

Which was garbage, it was terrible, why on earth would he think she'd be pleased by that? She wanted danger, right now. She wanted to be scared. She even found herself grasping at any hint of it. "But how did you get that torn shirt?" she asked, desperately. "Why were you all breathless when you burst in here?"

Though she knew the answer wasn't going to be good.

She could see it in the frustrated, confused expression he gave her, before he spoke.

"Because I had to stumble here in some kind of frantic, lust-filled stupor. A tree got in my way and my body tried to walk through it. Somewhere around the middle of the woods I lost a shoe, and couldn't make myself go back for it. Seriously, it's no wonder your friend forgot how to drink," he said. Then even worse: "What is going *on*, Cass? You said that the dragon scale would make the potion work, but it clearly hasn't. It's barely made a dent. I don't know what we're going to do."

But it was fine, it was fine, because as soon as his words came out, the answer popped into her head. The exact and only solution. As if it had been inside her all along—which she kind of suspected it had. She'd been hearing the words "Fulfill the requirements" rattling around in her messy witch brain for days.

She just hadn't let herself face what they meant.

She wasn't even sure if she could face it now.

For one wild second, she actually considered not telling him.

But not telling him wouldn't have worked. He took one look at the maze of terror and excitement and horror and arousal all over her face, and guessed. "Oh *god*, Cass, if you tell me we actually have to fuck, I might lose my mind. I mean, it was bad enough doing all the things we've done so we *don't* accidentally end up frantically fucking each other's brains out. And now you're saying we somehow must?" he groaned. And to make matters worse, both Pod and the microwave seemed to agree with him on this. Pod called him a bad beast and tried to attack him with a teacup; the microwave declared that it would explode if they dared do such a thing.

They had to go in the pantry to talk.

Not that either of them really wanted to. The tiny shelved room immediately became seven thousand degrees hotter than it had been, the light in there refused to work, and the only words they had to say to each other were hopeless. Practical, but hopeless. "Okay, look. Don't panic, okay? I'm going to think of a way out of this that doesn't involve me having to take your virginity," she said.

But in response he just looked at her like she'd grown three heads.

"You think *virginity* is the thing I have a problem with here? Cass, virginity isn't even really a thing. It's just a made-up concept from weirdo ancient times, to better sell child brides to disgusting old perverts," he said.

Rightly, she had to say. Even if it really made no difference in their situation.

"Okay, so call it something else. Like you having to experience something for the very first time with someone you don't love and only find hot because of rampant werewolfism," she pointed out. Yet somehow, he still tried to protest.

"But I do lo—I mean, I do very much feel—I do care very much about you," he stumbled out, face flushing harder and harder as he did, in a way she understood only too well. Clearly he wanted to draw a line between friendship feelings, and romantic feelings. And werewolf sex feelings. "You mean a lot to me, is what I'm saying. So that's not a concern, for me. That would never stop me from being completely willing to do this."

Then just as she was thinking that he had done a pretty good job there, on the *this is fine for two friends to do* front, he added one last thing on the end. "What *would* stop me, however, is that you might not be really willing to do this."

And now *she* was the one who had to step between the bombs. She had to walk the *I am willing, even if I am pretty sure it's not something I really want and/or feel romantically* tightrope. Even though she was barely sure where she stood on that tightrope herself.

Some of the hot fantasies she'd indulged in over the last few days had just been him, cradling her in his arms. And her, telling him how good that felt. And that didn't seem normal for the aloof practical supernatural doctor she was trying to be. Or even for a person being slowly sex poisoned by magical werewolf nonsense.

But she had to believe it was. She had to push through.

On the other side was freedom. Freedom, from desperately wanting to fuck a friend she really shouldn't want. "Of course I'm willing," she said, and was really proud of how casual she sounded. Because she didn't *feel* casual.

And Seth replying: "Yeah, but only because you think we have no choice" did *not* make things any easier. It just made her think of the day before, and the permission question. About how careful he was to only do what she was okay with. How *easy* that made it all.

And how much hotter, too.

So now she had to somehow agree to this next step in a calm, rational manner. While feeling so suddenly horny and irrational about it that she could've wept. *It's okay, it's just werewolf sex nonsense. It's not real, it's just something you both need and are all right with giving to each other,* she kept telling herself. And after a good long moment of panic, the pep talk did seem to sink in.

She felt that she knew how to navigate the situation without fucking anything up. "We *do* have no choice. However, I can still say I am totally okay with doing it anyway. That the idea is not repulsive or horrifying to me. I mean, it might be if it involved doing something gross or arduous with a horrible stranger I hate. But the thing is, none of that is the case. I enjoy doing the kind of things we have to do. And you are a good guy, and I like you. So maybe we should just think of this as you know . . . casual sex. Or scratching an itch. Or any other kind of fun activity we might do together. Like, say, really weird, intense tennis," she tried.

And thank god, thank god, she could tell it had worked. He didn't seem suspicious that she secretly loved the circumstances they were in. Or secretly loved him. Plus the whole problem did seem more normal when she put it like that.

In fact, she *felt* more normal, hearing it in those terms.

Doubly so, when he laughed.

"We have never played tennis in our *lives*," he said.

Then somehow, she found herself laughing too.

"Okay, then, how about calling it Mario Kart?" she suggested.

"So you're going to start swearing and lobbing shells at my head."

"Actually, I was thinking I would make fun of you when you accidentally get stuck in a corner and can't get out," she said, the memory so clear and so brightly ordinary in her head that she could feel herself relaxing.

Now she just had to make sure he was relaxed too.

Though she could see that she was already well on her way to achieving this.

Because he held up an angry finger. "That happened one time. One," he said, so hilariously that they both broke all over again. He shook his head, half laughing. And she let out a giggle. At which point, she knew they were going to do this. That they *could* do it, no matter the potentially ruinous consequences.

All that was left was to figure out the terms and conditions.

The ones that made him stop looking at her, before he started laying them out. "Okay, so this is happening," he said. Then after a second of slightly pained consideration, he went ahead. "But before it does, you should probably know some stuff. Stuff you might not like as much as hitting me with squid ink, so I end up driving my Kart into a pit of quicksand. In fact, it's possible you might hate it."

"Why would I hate something that means nothing? That's just fun?"

"Because . . . I don't know," he said, clearly frustrated. "It's not really like the sort of joyful tennis hookups you're probably having with actual, normal, super-sexy, cool, ideal-man type human beings. It's kind of a lot to deal with."

"I get it, Seth. You have a big one."

"Yeah. And it's really not as fun as porn makes it out to be."

"It'll be fine. You're not going to split me in two."

"Maybe. Maybe not. But even if I don't, there are other things to contend with. Like the fact that I . . . well." He paused. Swallowed, thickly. Before stumbling on. "I kind of . . . make a lot of mess. Like, way, way more than you're probably used to. And it won't just be—you know. Kind of getting a little bit on you. It'll be going *inside* you."

"Yeah, and I'm sure we can find condoms made of concrete to cover that issue."

"Cassie, I don't think condoms are something we're going to be able to use," he said, slowly and patiently. And as soon as he did, she felt everything inside her sink to her socked feet.

Because he was right. Of course he was right. There was no other way it could be—there had to be actual contact for this to work. There couldn't be any barriers between her body and his body and his stuff and her stuff. Though she tried to stay calm about that, on the surface.

"Okay, but like. That's only one small part of it," she said.

"It doesn't seem like a small part of it. It seems like it made your face drop three feet."

"My face is fine. This is just how it looks when I'm trying to think."

"And what exactly are you trying to think of?"

Whether I can do this without going too far or being weird, she thought. But went with something as businesslike as he thought she was.

"Mostly, how to do this without having your giant hairy babies. Or giving each other any sort of STI. Plus, you know. I've never had sex without using one before, with anyone. So it's kind of something I need a second to process."

"That just seems like a reason to not do it."

"I think I can fix the first one with a potion, though. Probably even the second one, too."

"Yeah, but neither of those are what I'm having an issue with. I know you'll solve the first, and the second isn't a thing. My werewolf body could kill the bubonic plague. I once got attacked by a rabid fox and biting me cured *it*," he sighed. Then before she could widen her eyes over that revelation, he plunged on to the real issue. "No, it's the third one that makes it worse. I don't want to do something you've never even experienced with a person you actually want to experience it with."

She didn't know why that was his focus, however.

They'd already gone over that in great detail.

"Seth, you just told me virginity doesn't matter."

"That was different."

"Oh, because I'm a woman."

"No. God, *no*. Because of what you said," he said, clearly stressed by the suggestion. He was pacing now. Agitated. He had to take a few breaths before he explained. "You just told me that you felt it was only okay with you to be someone's first experience of something if they really lo—if they really liked you. And I know you like me more now, but you definitely do not like me that much.

Not *enjoying some new experience* much. Not even as much as I like you."

"And how exactly do you figure that?"

"Because I hurt you. You didn't hurt me."

"I kind of think we might be past that now, bud. As in *you are my best friend again* past it. Unless you don't think we are, of course. In which case, you know, just pretend I never said that."

She flushed. Got flustered, waved her hands.

Wished she could take back that one word: "best."

Because the thing was, when you claimed that someone was your friend, there were escape clauses in it. You could laugh and say you only meant in a casual way. A *sort of* way. A way that could apply to a million people. But when you said "best," you meant something more. You meant they were your number one. And that you hoped you were theirs.

And that was a lot.

It was so much that she almost took it back. The take-back was on the tip of her tongue, just ready to go. Then somehow he slipped in, before she could. "To be honest, I was thinking of having it tattooed over my heart," he said, voice all threaded through with laughter.

Like it was nothing at all.

When actually, it was almost too much for her to take.

She looked up and saw him still shaking his head, bemused. And she simply couldn't stop herself. She just shoved a hug right into him, without thinking. Face pressed to his chest, body glued to his, hands all over his back. Every part of her solely focused on showing him what those words had meant to her.

Instead of thinking for a second what this much contact would do. Because a minute ago, she had barely been able to tolerate his arm draped over her shoulder. She was still buzzing from things he had done yesterday, for god's sake.

It was obviously going to be way too much.

But even she wasn't prepared for just *how* much.

Suddenly, not one of their concerns mattered. The only thing that did was rubbing wherever her hands were touching, over and over. And then trying to get him to rub her right back, until it made him groan desperately.

"We shouldn't," he said.

But he did it anyway.

He slid his hands all over her, from her shoulders to her waist. And then, after a moment's hesitation, all the way down to her ass. Like he had in the wardrobe—only more fervently this time. As if each instance of them touching pushed things a little further, and so now he couldn't be satisfied with just grabbing. He needed to grope, greedily, in a way that left her in no doubt about what he was thinking.

He loves what he's feeling, her mind informed her, firmly.

And it kind of demolished all the Caution Danger Here signs she had up.

Suddenly, she found herself pushing into those big hands, into that hungry touch. And of course the second she did he seemed to go rigid. Every muscle went so taut, they almost quivered with it. Like someone had plucked some weird string inside him. Then a groan broke out of him, and he almost sank into her. He rolled his whole body against hers, all slow and deliciously familiar. Like someone starting to rut, she thought.

And couldn't help rutting back.

She urged herself into the rock of his hips, and pushed her chest into his, and rubbed and rubbed until that was all they were doing. Right there, in the pantry. Both of them barely sensible of anything, except how good it felt.

And of what she wanted to do next.

Fuck me, I want him to fuck me, she thought mindlessly. Then didn't think twice about shoving her jeans down. Or about bending over the flour bags piled behind them, so he could just do it. Oh god, she wanted him to do it. "I want you inside me," she gasped, so certain he was going to that she could almost feel it. His hands on her hips, that big cock pressing against her. Working in, until she did something unhinged, like beg him for more.

So it was a shock, when he stopped.

And went very still and silent, for what felt like an age. She almost looked back at him, to see what was going on. But he silenced those words before they could come, with his own.

"Actually," he said. "I just remembered, I left the gas on."

And then he fled, before she could say what they both knew:

His house didn't have any gas to turn off.

CHAPTER TWENTY-FIVE

She wasn't bothered by what had happened. In fact, if she was being honest, him panicking made far more sense than him getting excited over her ever had. Clearly, werewolf hormones and weird mating bonds could only give him a certain level of lust for her. They could make him want to touch, to squeeze, to test things out.

But when it came to the crunch, when it came to actually doing more than rubbing against each other or talking dirty, he hit a wall he just couldn't get over. Because, sure, he hadn't meant to insult her body back in high school. He didn't like the idea of hurting her. And sometimes it had seemed as if he wanted more to take place between them.

But that didn't add up to delight at the sight of her naked body.

And that was fine, it was okay. She didn't need that from him. The only thing she needed was knowing he respected her, and never wanted to hurt her, and liked her as a person. All of which were there, regardless of anything else. She could see they were, the second he returned, the next day. He came into the kitchen, hands stuffed deep into his pockets, expression caught somewhere between pained and embarrassed.

And it was obvious he wanted to explain.

Even though she prayed he wouldn't.

Just say nothing, she thought at him. But no such luck.

"Cassie, about yesterday," he started to say.

So she held up a hand, before he could go any further.

"It's okay. I get it," she said. "When the time came, you just didn't want to. Which is perfectly understandable, all things considered. It doesn't hurt my feelings. We're just going to have to be more practi-cal. Like maybe do it in a really dark room, with tons of clothes on."

She was proud of how businesslike she sounded.

Because that was how it had to be. Almost like a transaction.

Yeah, a transaction was what he needed. Even if he just looked more freaked out by the idea than he had about actually fucking her. His eyebrows practically sailed over his forehead. He went to speak, and the words seemed to gag him. Then finally, finally he managed to squeeze something out. "What the heck do you mean, Cass? That sounds even *worse*."

After which, it took her a second to reply.

She had to wait until her own confusion died down, before she could.

"Well, I don't see how, I mean, if you're struggling with the idea of doing me to the point where you flee, that seems like the best option. To make it just about the act, and not about who you're with."

"But that wasn't the problem at all."

"Then what was?"

He hesitated. "I don't know."

"You can't *I don't know* your way out of this, Seth. This is slowly killing us. I'm starting to not be able to sleep or think or eat. And I know it's the same for you. You actually look like you're losing weight."

"Because I am. All I can think about is devouring your—" He stopped himself. Swallowed, thickly. Like he was thinking about the word he wanted to use, anyway. Then he started again. "All I can think about is doing certain things."

"So then help me help you get those things done."

"I can't. I don't know how to explain, exactly."

"Start by knowing it's okay to tell me what I did wrong." There, she thought. Now he could make it as plain as possible. Then she could better navigate whatever the problem was. But he just looked shocked, then frustrated beyond belief.

"Cass, you didn't do *anything* wrong. It just wasn't what I had imagined it was going to be," he burst out, and as soon as he did she could tell he hadn't meant to. Or at least, that he hadn't meant to put it quite like that. Because he seemed to freeze, and his cheeks went from zero to bright red, and then he was fumbling. He was reaching for a way to make his words sound a little less like whatever they currently did. "And by that I mean, you know. Since this all started . . . Since this started I have sometimes thought about how it might go down. And it was never like that in any of my thoughts. It was never so . . . mechanical."

Then he seemed to look at her in this tense, expectant way. Like he was waiting for some emotional blow that she had no idea how to land. Or even wanted to land. Because if that was all, what was the big deal? That sounded fine, that sounded cool, and most importantly: that sounded like something she could fix.

Easily. Quickly.

All they needed was an action plan. A good, practical action plan, laid down on paper, with bullet points and everything. All of which sounded so good, she went ahead. She grabbed a notepad from the kitchen table, and a pencil, and gave him her best *We can do this* expression.

"Okay. So hit me with all the ways you want this to be," she said, sure this would work.

Though it still kind of shocked her when all the tension immediately went out of him.

He even gave her a half smile. And she could tell the words were coming, before they did.

"Well, you know. Not in a kitchen, for starters," he blew out, and even more tension went out of him when he did. Partly, she suspected, for her reaction.

She immediately scribbled his words down.

"Got it," she said, as she did. "No to the kitchen."

Then suddenly this was just a thing. He shared. She made it seem normal.

"And there wasn't a sentient microwave and a talking raccoon so close by."

"Honestly, I was thinking the same thing. It was very weird that they were right in the next room, and you are completely correct to raise that as a concern. Zero creatures from a movie made by Amblin Entertainment while we do this."

She nodded, as she added that to the list.

Despite the chitter of protest from Pod, who was currently rummaging through the pantry for the cookies she'd hidden. And the readout from the microwave, very disturbingly informing them both that this wasn't fair, because it was kind of getting into the idea of them boning, now.

Just focus on this conversation, she told herself.

Which wasn't hard, because Seth was certainly starting to warm to the topic.

"And the lighting. I don't want it to be dark, okay? But maybe less bright."

"So you want, like, a lamp or something?"

"Or you know. Candles could be good."

She scribbled it down. "Candles, okay."

"And maybe we could also have some music on."

"We can do music," she said. "What kind were you thinking of?"

"You know. Like a playlist. Of the sort most people make when they do this."

"Seth, I have no idea what other werewolves listen to when they bone."

"I wasn't talking about werewolves. I was talking about ordinary people being—you know. Intimate. And the kinds of music they might listen to. Like, to set the mood. To make things seem sexy."

She stopped scribbling and looked up from her notepad.

Because the candles thing—well, that had almost made her wonder about what exactly he was suggesting. But sexy mood music on top of that? Yeah, that definitely took what he was saying from *make things less sterile* to something else entirely. Something that made her want to laugh.

Much to his exasperation.

He took one look at the trembling near-grin she was trying to suppress, and didn't just roll his eyes. He rolled his whole body.

"See, this is why I didn't say anything. I knew you'd find it weird," he said. So now she had to somehow explain that her amusement wasn't mockery.

Without letting on what had actually caused it:

An absolute cavalcade of purest joy, of the kind she could hardly contain. God, she almost wanted to burst with it, for a moment. To tell him something inadvisable, like how much that did her heart good to hear. But then she remembered she wasn't supposed to be doing good in the heart department. She was supposed to be problem-solving.

And reined herself back in.

"I'm not finding it weird, Seth. I just wasn't expecting this."

"Well, you should have. You know I like things to be a certain way."

"So this is like creating a nice study environment, but for fucking."

She gave him a single incredulous eyebrow. But he just snapped his fingers. "Yeah. Yeah. Let's say that. Let's put it that way," he said. And okay, that was a little bit more practical than she'd expected. But that was good. It helped her maintain an air of professionalism about this.

Less glee. More straightforward questions.

"Okay, so what else would help?" she asked, briskly, and almost wavered over the delighted grin he gave her. It lit up his whole face. She came close to leaning forward and licking it, and was only saved by him speaking.

"Well, I mean, we had almost all our clothes on."

"So that was a *bad* thing to you. You actually *want* me completely nude."

"Maybe not completely. I mean, I can see your tortured expression at the very idea."

He pointed at her face as he said it—as if she didn't know what was there. It was fine though, because her expression was already turning into something better. Something that felt like relief, at his acknowledgment. And it deepened, when he added, "But you know, I thought possibly we could be a little *less* dressed. Like we could be dressed in something that's more the kind of thing people wear when they have sex."

Because oh, she knew what he meant.

And it made her words come out a little breathless.

"I feel like this is a roundabout way of saying sexy lingerie."

"It doesn't have to be lingerie. Or sexy. Just whatever is most you."

"Most me would be that nightdress you saw me in, in the basement," she said, sort of laughing. Only somehow his eyes went bright and big the moment she said the word. And the weirdly thrilling realization sank in. "Which you are apparently into. You are into that. Despite the fact that it makes me look like an old lady."

"It doesn't make you look like an old lady. It makes you look like—"

"Like what? Someone more middle-aged, maybe?"

"I was trying not to say Nancy from *Nightmare on Elm Street*, but since you keep insulting yourself, you've forced my hand. So you better not say anything else about it. In fact, just pretend I didn't tell you."

She immediately went to laugh and ask him what the problem with that was. After all, it was a nice thing. It was a cute little compliment, no big deal. But then her brain made the connection, and oh. Oh. Oh no, she didn't know how to react then.

All she could do was stare, head full of how he had once thought of Nancy. He had spent almost a whole summer obsessed with her. Watched the movie over and over, talked endlessly about how lovely she was, how cool she was. Hell, she even remembered him drawing her, in his algebra notebook. Then tearing out the page, to keep in his wallet.

She had been his number one final girl.

His favorite, unquestionably.

And now he had said that she looked like, or was like that, in a way that would be easy to read too much into. So obviously, he had tried to head that off at the pass. He was still trying now, in fact. He was looking at her like come on, just get what I'm saying.

And though it took her a second, she did.

She shook off that weird feeling she got, when the memory of those drawings and that love first struck, and shrugged. "I don't have to pretend. I know you don't mean anything by it. I know you don't mean anything by any of this. You've just been addled by supernatural sex nonsense, and so should therefore feel free to say whatever you want about how hot I look in a nightdress," she said.

She even managed to look mischievous on the end.

Like this was all a big joke. A goof.

"Kind of liked hearing it, huh?" he asked, and so she kept that joke going. She held two fingers a tiny bit apart.

"Little bit."

"I don't blame you. I'd like it too, if you told me what I look hot wearing."

"Well good, because I was thinking of suggesting those sweat-pants of mine."

"You mean the ones that are three feet too short?"

"The three-feet-too-short thing is what made them sexy," she said, and she could see a response on the tip of his tongue. A question, she thought.

But then he clocked her awkward blush—the one that gave away that she hadn't meant to confess her attraction so plainly—and she knew he realized what she'd meant. His expression slid from puzzled, to that heavy-lidded, lusty gaze she was starting to find very familiar. And if she was being honest, enjoying way too much.

Doubly so when it came with a side of low, soft words.

"So you liked that, then. You liked seeing what I got," he said.

And this time she didn't even wonder if she should be honest. Honesty just came out of her. *Desire* came out of her. Like it was winning the game of what's okay to do, in her head. "I think I came within an inch of running my hand over it."

"Want to try sliding your hand over it now?"

"If you want me to," she said, and for a second she really thought he was going to say yes. He took a step toward her, until he was close enough that she could feel the heat rolling off his body. She could smell him—all summer skin and winter furs.

But then he stopped and took a few calming breaths. He forced out some frustrated-sounding words. "I do. Oh god I really do. But see—this is the other issue. Everything is just way too fast. It goes from zero to seven thousand, every time, and I don't know. I think maybe we should try a five hundred first. Or maybe even an eighty-seven," he said. Which was annoying, given how close she had come to racing headlong into this, without as many worries. And how hungry his words had made her feel, for something she was so close to getting. A little more, and her almighty ache would end, it would be over with, she wouldn't have to tremble through it another second.

But the problem was, his idea also made sense.

"Okay, so what do you consider an eighty-seven? Third base?"

"Maybe not quite third base."

"So you're thinking more like heavy petting."

"Honestly, even that is a little bit more than I was going for."

"But I don't even know what there is before that, screwing-around-wise." She spread her hands, palms up, and let out a short, frustrated laugh.

And in response he looked sheepish. He ran a hand over the back of his neck. Then he glanced away, as if searching for the right words to explain himself. "Maybe what I'm thinking of is not like screwing around enough, then. Possibly it's too nice and soft and like we're a real couple. Even though I swear, I totally get that we're not. I'm not trying to make it more real. I just thought this one step we could take might make it all a little easier."

And she knew, as soon as he said it, what he meant.

It sank in, slow and sweet as syrup, through her body.

"Seth, is the thing making out?" she asked, and oh, the way the sheepishness all over his face deepened. He actually toed the floor with his Converse-clad foot, and wouldn't meet her gaze, when he answered.

"Kind of, a little bit, yeah," he said.

Because he was a fool. A total fool. Who apparently had no idea how adorable he was. Or how much that made her heart race, against all her better judgment. In fact, she had to give herself a second, before she replied. Because otherwise, she knew her words were going to come out all breathless. When what she wanted was deadpan.

"And you honestly thought I wouldn't want that," she said.

And thank goodness her poker face seemed to have worked. He winced, instead of wondering why she was suddenly even hornier, over something as ridiculous as being asked for a kiss.

"Well, how would I know otherwise? You've not told me anything about what you might like," he sighed. But then he had more to say, and oh no, oh no. "Which to be honest, kind of sucks even more than the speed and the clothes and the weird lighting. Because you know the thing is, it feels like almost everything we have done or are going to do is for me. You talk dirty until I come, or you make me magic lube so I can come, or you spread your legs and I climb on and fuck you. And there's nothing in that for you at all. Which seems super unfair to me."

Because ohhhh, that was hot. Way hotter than it should have been.

So now she had to somehow force herself to be neutral.

Instead of telling him the twelve things she wanted him to do to her, right now. "And what did you have in mind, to make it fair?" she asked, in a voice that shook just a little. And got *this*, for her efforts:

"I don't know. Maybe kissing you on more than just your mouth."

Then he held her gaze, so steadily and so pointedly that there no longer seemed to be much point in holding back. "So maybe my throat."

"Oh yeah, that sounds good."

"And after that a little lower."

"By lower, do you mean, like, unlacing the front of that nightdress?"

Yes, oh yes please, she thought. But managed to be more nonchalant, in reply. "Been thinking about that, huh? About that bow right over my breasts."

"It just looked like it would hardly take anything at all to untie."

"Yeah. You barely have to pull, and the material just parts."

"And then I could just slip my hand inside."

She almost moaned to hear him say it. Yet somehow kept it in.

"If you want to," she said, almost like a shrug in word form. Though of course, he didn't take it that way. Instead, he made a very un-casual sound. A desperate groan, of the sort that made her melt. And his eyes roamed almost feverishly, over everything she had just said he could touch.

"I do. I want to stroke you, softly," he said, voice so low and hoarse she could hardly hear it. She had to lean forward, she had to strain for it. And when she did, the hand he had clenched at his side lifted. His fingers unfurled. Like imagining it was so powerful, it almost felt like he was already in the middle of doing exactly that. He could see the parted fabric, and her arching into a touch he wasn't actually giving.

All of which she only wanted to encourage.

"That sounds really good. You can do that."

"And then I could follow it by kissing you wherever I've touched."

"Oh that's even better. Go on. What next?"

You know what's next, her brain informed her. She couldn't feel embarrassed by it, however. She was too busy devouring every word she knew he was going to say, notepad forgotten, everything forgotten, just every part of her open to wherever he was going to escalate this to. And oh, he did escalate it. He leaned down, his heaving breaths all warm against her face, her lips. One inch away from kissing her, as he answered.

"I do it until you're squirming. Until you're begging me to make you come."

"And you would, wouldn't you."

"Of course I would."

"You'd do that to me."

"It's all I want."

"Tell me how, then," she said, and he broke. His words came tumbling out in a great rush.

"By burying my face between your legs—the way I've been dying to for days, for weeks. God, do you have any idea how desperate I've been to do that? How wild it makes me to catch the scent of your slick pussy? Knowing what a mess you've made of yourself, and what a mess you'd make of me if I just licked and sucked and kissed you there?" he said.

Then just as she thought he was going to do just that, just as she was sure he was actually going to cross that line, he groaned, "Oh, we're starting out at seven thousand again."

And somehow she had to force herself back. To return to the sensible person she'd almost been a moment ago. To call what they were doing setting up a study area, or booting up the Nintendo console, or making it all just basic and straightforward.

"I'll go sort everything out," she said.

While inside she still burned from everything he hadn't meant to say.

CHAPTER TWENTY-SIX

She thought she'd feel calmer after getting everything sorted.

But if anything, she only felt more flustered and feverish and frantic. And she kind of suspected why, too. Because she hadn't been able to find any candles, or choose the right kind of music. So she'd settled on laying a scrap of blue material over the lamp, and leaving a movie with a sexy soundtrack on in the background.

And she only realized afterward that she had shot right past basic and boring, and directly into way too romantic. In fact, it was the exact situation they would have probably found themselves in as teenagers. The room now looked like the hollowed-out tree they used to hide in; the movie in question was one they'd watched a thousand times. She was even wearing the kind of nightdress she used to when they had sleepovers.

The only thing missing was Seth in a jersey and pajama bottoms.

Like the kind of thing he was wearing when he came into the bedroom.

"I wasn't sure if you wanted to see my bare chest or not," he said, which really should have made her say, *no this is totally perfect*. But her mouth had gone so dry at the sight of him like that—somehow boyish-looking, dorky-looking, yet unutterably sexy at the same time—that the words just wouldn't come out. All she could do was stare.

It was okay though. He seemed to be staring too. She watched him take in the soft, bluish light, and the flickering of the TV, and then her, seated on the side of the bed. And by the time he was done, his eyes were enormous. *I should have gone with the longer nightdress*, she thought, as his eyes trailed up, over her almost-bare legs. Then lingered where the material ended, too high up on her slightly parted thighs.

The ones she'd meant to close before he came in.

But somehow hadn't gotten around to it. And now it was too late. She'd broken him.

It seemed to take him forever to walk over to her. And when he finally did, he didn't touch her or kiss her or even lean over her. He sat next to her on the bed, in a way that should have felt as awkward as they were supposed to feel. But instead, it just seemed to deepen that strange sense of familiarity and realness.

He would have done just that back then, she thought. And was not prepared for how tense that made things. She could feel it crackling in the air between their almost-touching arms.

Twice she came close to telling him that this had been a bad idea, that they should go back to doing things in a mechanical way, or maybe just a frantic way, or anything, just anything, besides whatever this was. But she knew why she stopped short both times. The first, because she made the mistake of looking at him as the words rose in her throat. And the second, because of what he said before she could get them out.

"Is it okay if I kiss you now?" he asked.

Then suddenly she was nodding. As if this were a sexy question, when of course it wasn't. She didn't know why it made her heart race. Why it made her want to arch up to him. Especially when he leaned down so slowly and tentatively.

You're supposed to want him to just get it over with, she told herself. But it didn't seem to make any difference. Her body still reacted like he had licked between her legs, when his lips brushed hers. Softly, so softly, to the point where she could almost believe it wasn't contact at all.

But it must have been.

Because it made her ache even more deeply than she already was.

She felt that one point of contact like a brand, like something burning.

By the time he pulled back, she was shaking all over, and so desperate for more she almost grabbed him. But she was glad that she managed to resist, because resisting meant she got to see his face—all full of wonder and surprise—over that one little chaste kiss. Before it slowly slid into something else, something heated and eager and oh god when he licked his upper lip, when he made that soft curve glisten in a way she knew would feel slicker and hotter against her . . .

She almost moaned before he even made contact.

And then he did, and she simply couldn't hold it in. She let out a sound.

Though all that seemed to do was spur him on. He pushed his lips against hers more firmly, almost hungrily, one hand suddenly in her hair. And just as she was thinking it was a lot for her to take, she felt it. The hot, wet flicker of his tongue over hers. Teasing first, barely there, but when she couldn't contain another sound of pleasure and shock, he did it again. He stroked into her, in a way that didn't feel tentative.

It felt like being fucked, and so much so she moaned heatedly into his mouth. Which of course only made him bolder. Now he was pushing against her, his mouth rocking over hers, every move the hottest, slickest thing she could imagine. By the time they broke apart, they were breathless, trembling, beyond any kind of coherent speech.

But they didn't need it.

He put a hand on her waist, and she knew exactly what he intended.

Second base, she thought, and it was ridiculous, it was silly, it was so back-seat-of-his-dad's-ancient-Chevy-during-high-school. But the thing was, they'd never gotten that far back then. Neither of them had ever done anything like that, not with anyone. This was just an echo of all the nights they'd never had.

And the realization made her wilder than she had ordered herself to be. It made her scramble to untie the ribbon at the neckline of the nightdress, and once she'd halfway managed, she took his hand. She urged it underneath that almost-parted material.

Then thrilled right to the roots of her hair, when he did the rest.

He pushed in, eagerly. And oh god, his reaction when he felt what he found, when he cupped her bare breast, gently. His whole face seemed to go slack; his eyes stuttered closed like he couldn't stand to watch on top of touching. And he made such a sound—guttural, almost a growl. Then again, when she arched into that gloriously tender caress.

In fact he did more than that.

He tightened his grip. And oh it was good. *Wow* it was good. She wanted to do nothing but tell him how good it was. To gasp, *oh yes please, more, yes, touch me just like that.* But it was as if he heard her anyway, because she didn't have to say a thing.

He just caught the tight tip of her breast between his finger and thumb, then bent his head. And licked. He licked. Just once, just lightly, like he was testing it out. But it was enough to make her buck and say his name and oh god she thought maybe, oh no maybe oh god definitely—

She was going to come.

She was actually going to come—and over so *little*, again. And okay sure, this wasn't all her. It was something else, something that made her greedy and lust-choked and always half a breath away from losing it when he did almost anything at all.

But even so, that seemed way more into this than she was probably supposed to be. He'd taken longer to come while actually touching his cock, and he was a full-blown werewolf who hadn't been able to put so much as a finger on himself for the last decade. It was understandable for him. It would not be understandable for her, a near-enough human who had masturbated merrily at least a few times a week for that same length of time.

But it was happening all the same.

She could feel it unfurling low down in her belly, and swelling through her clit, intense enough that it took pretty much everything she had to stop herself from making a completely disgusting sound, or shoving herself against him. She sank her teeth into her tongue hard enough to hurt. Grabbed handfuls of the bedsheets to keep herself where she was.

And still it wasn't enough.

Because she could feel the other thing she'd done.

She'd made a slick mess. And it was definitely noticeable. She could hear it when she moved. Hell, she could see it, glistening between her bare thighs. And she knew the moment he saw it, too. He seemed to stiffen all over; a low sound of near confusion came out of him. But just as she was about to explain, he seemed to sink toward her.

Like the sight dragged him too deeply into this to ever get back out.

And once he was there, he couldn't stop himself leaning over to taste what she'd just done. First with a long, slow lick over one glistening inner thigh. Then another over the other, more frantic than the first. And finally he let out a low, desperate groan and just did exactly what he'd said he'd wanted to.

He buried his face between her legs.

Though the word "buried" really didn't do it justice. It didn't cover the way he wrapped his arms around her legs. How he cupped and spread her thighs so he could get as close as he clearly wanted to be. And not one word of what he had said told her how it would feel when he rubbed himself against her.

How the burr of his stubble almost stung, almost hurt. But also seemed to intensify every spark of pleasurable sensation. She got the rough drag of it, right over her clit, and felt that swollen little bud pulse. She felt it ache. She felt that bliss spiral through her, until she knew she was making a mess of him. She knew, but couldn't care.

Because it only made him work harder.

He rubbed his face into all that slickness, like an animal seeking heat. And he didn't just lick as he did. He licked *into* her. Over and over again, until it started to feel like something she didn't want to put a name to. Like it was too much to put a name to it.

But her mind supplied it anyway, in a hot, uncheckable rush.

It's like he's fucking you with his tongue, it said. And it was, it really was, and not just in a normal way, either. Because that firm, slick thing felt wolfish—too long, and thick, and rough. And yeah, that shouldn't have been good in the same way everything else was. It shouldn't have given her the same surge of pleasure as all the more normal things.

But it did anyway.

She came again just thinking about it. Harder than before, fiercer than before, god it was enough to make her scream into her gritted teeth. And loud enough that he must have heard it. He must have *felt* it. Because she knew, when it happened, that she tightened around that intrusion. And it was obvious that she made a slick mess as she did. She could make it out herself—that come spilling from her clenching cunt, and all over his face.

Yet for some ungodly reason, he didn't stop.

In fact, he went *further*. He doubled down. He replaced his tongue with his fingers, and slid them in slowly, steadily, as he eased that incredible tongue right over her clit. Then he just worked her like that, until she knew she was going to do it again. Hell, she wasn't even sure if the last orgasm had fully died away. It felt like it was still ebbing and flowing through her, when the next one started to bloom.

And it was wonderful, it was incredible.

But way too much for her to take at the same time. If things kept going like this she was liable to say a thousand filthy and way too grateful things. So she grabbed a fistful of his jersey. She tugged at him desperately. She told him. "Just do it, okay? It's enough, just do me."

And thank god, thank god, he did as she asked.

He was too far gone to not. His face was slack with lust, by that point, tongue constantly curling up to lick at the slick mess she'd left around his mouth, body a shuddering mess. And so much so that he could barely be considerate about it. His hands immediately went to the waistband of his sweatpants, all overeager to shove them down.

Then he was there, and oh *god*.

She'd expected it to feel less than his mouth, his hands. But somehow it didn't. Somehow, when he rubbed the tip of his cock through her folds, when he teased her entrance in a way that said *careful* but sang *barely restraining himself,* she almost pushed him away, it was that intense. And she knew it wasn't just the physical sensation of that big, thick thing almost pushing inside her. She could feel it wasn't. There was something more there now. Something far beyond the usual.

Her witch senses told her so.

Her witch senses enlightened her: *you're connected,* they said.

That intense sensation? It was how her soft, wet heat felt to him.

Like being scalded with pleasure. Like being swamped by it, to the point where she could hardly believe he was taking the time. He held himself above her on one shaking arm, the other hand on his cock as he worked her open, every move so slow it almost didn't feel like consideration at all. It felt like he was trying to draw out the sensation. Like he wanted to tease himself.

But also maybe like he wanted to tease her.

And it worked. By minute three she barely cared that he was big enough to split her in two. All that mattered was turning that maddening *almost* into *actually*—and she was right to let herself feel it, too. Because she was so ready when he finally went farther that it took almost nothing at all. Her body just gave, so easily it was a pleasure all its own.

And holy fuck, the look on his face when he felt it too. She saw him mouth something that might have been *God help me.* His eyes practically rolled closed. And when they opened again, there was nothing but awe in them. Like he couldn't believe *this* was how sex with her felt.

But, of course, she knew it wasn't really about her.

It was the act itself. It was the sensation of something so good and new and satisfying to every urge running through him. To the wolf, who was definitely making himself known now. She could see his teeth. And when she put a hand on his back, there were ridges there, along the length of his spine.

But it was like with his tongue and his too-big cock.

Exciting somehow. Sweeter somehow. It shoved the pleasure up a notch.

Even though it was already at seven million. She was close to

coming again, and he hadn't even moved yet. He was just holding there, trying to contain himself. Or work up to actually doing
something without savaging her.

Go ahead, she almost said to him. And only didn't because he
broke first.

"I'm sorry, I'm sorry, I have to," he groaned. As if he had anything to be sorry for. As if him moving didn't push her even further
into the sense-obliterating state she was already in. She had to press
her face into the side of his neck, just to stop herself from screaming,
or grunting, or saying his name. Or worse—god she wanted to do
worse. She wanted to say to him that nothing on earth had ever felt
like this to her. That he made her feel so good, that *he* was so good.
Oh god, Seth, nobody has ever made me feel like you do, she thought,
and only kept the words inside by the skin of her teeth.

But unfortunately, he didn't return the favor.

Of course he didn't—he'd already told her that he was a talker.
Hell, she'd actually heard him being one. Yet still, somehow, it was
a shock to the system when he gasped in her ear, "Oh fuck, your
cunt feels amazing." And partly that shock was because of the way
he said it. The way it just burst out of him, full of earnest and un-
controllable desperation.

But mostly it was just the fact that Seth had said that word.

Her big, dorky himbo Seth just coming out with *cunt*, right in
the middle of a fuck she could already hardly cope with. And he
didn't even stop there.

"You're so hot, so slick, you take me so good, baby," he groaned
while she was still trying to recover from his first declaration.
Then he went and added on the end: "Tell me how to make it good
for you." As if it wasn't. As if she were not already trying to stop
herself from singing his praises and grabbing his ass and rutting
against him like a maniac.

"Just keep doing what you're doing. Just keep doing that," she
managed to force out, around the seventy other filthy things she
actually wanted to say. Only he didn't stop. He just kept on whis-
pering in her ear, like some kind of unbearable sex demon she
couldn't shake.

"But I can go slower, I can work you like this, get my hand on you here—" he started to say, and she had to cut him off. Because he was doing exactly as he'd described. He was grabbing her butt and calling it *juicy,* and angling her body just so, and oh oh, no no no.

No, she couldn't take that without losing her last shred of control.

"Oh god, don't, don't. Just do it like you were at first. Please just stay like that."

"But I can feel you shaking when I hit it there. I can hear your heart speeding up and ohhhh you're getting so slick and tight, oh that's really, that's way too good, fuck that's gonna make me come, hold on lemme just stop for a second."

"But I don't want you to stop. I want you to do it. I need you to."

"You *need* me to?" he asked, so desperately she almost didn't keep pushing him. And then he curled his tongue over one sharp incisor, and gave her a heated, feverish look like he wanted to eat her, and she simply couldn't let this go on any longer.

"Yeah," she moaned. "Fill my pussy."

And that was almost all it took. He made an ungodly sound the moment she said it, and just sort of seemed to move without even meaning to. His hips rolled unsteadily. Then before she could catch her breath, he sped up. He did it fast, he did it hard, over and over until it felt like more than sex. It felt like a beast rutting over her, urgently.

All of which really messed up her *make him come before I do something ridiculous* plans. Because it felt as if she were going to do the ridiculous thing anyway. He kept hitting some delicious place inside her, and every time he did it shoved a glut of sensation through her belly and her clit and her cunt.

And then he was doing it, he was coming, she knew he was coming. She could hear it in his hot, guttural groans, and the way he said her name. She could feel it in the shudder that went through him, and the pulse and swell of that thick cock, and the echo of his pleasure, ringing right through her.

And finally there was the worst part.

Or the very best part, depending on your point of view.

Because she could feel it. She could actually feel that slick liquid filling her. It had a sensation all its own. A strange, intense sort of bliss, that shimmered through her every time it touched some part of her body. And it was this, she knew, that took things even higher. Because she didn't just come when it happened. She didn't just feel the pleasure of an ordinary orgasm.

She was unable to breathe because of it, unable to think or speak or do anything at all. She could only lie there beneath him, as he pushed her through wave after wave of body-obliterating sensation. And even after he was done, he didn't stop.

"Just tell me if you want me to," he said.

But she couldn't form words. All she could do was nod, and then he just kept going. Over and over, until she was pretty sure her body was constantly coming. Everything was one long, glorious, completely agonizing climax. And not just for her—she suspected it was that way for him, too. That he was trapped in this state of almost continuous orgasm.

Though she knew when more than that happened.

Because he choked out words. "Oh fuck, I think this is gonna be even more intense, oh man, I don't think I can take it," he said. Then just seemed to go over so hard that he drew lines through the mattress with his claws. She heard fabric rip, watched fluff spiral into the air on either side of her. Felt his groan like a living thing, running through him.

And there wasn't even a word for what that did to her. She clenched so hard around him that he made a shocked sound. Then he looked at her face, almost pained with pleasure. But she couldn't say *sorry*. She couldn't tell him, *I don't mean to like it this much, I don't want to be this hot for it, this greedy.*

Because as soon as he saw her intensely pleasured expression, he pulled away.

And then that thick, hot, sensation-stoking come was spilling over her. It was coating her flushed, slick folds, and the sensitive entrance to her cunt, and her swollen clit. She felt it sliding between the cheeks of her ass like molten lava, triggering a million new feelings as it went.

And oh, it was just too much, it was too much.

But god, it was not enough, at the same time.

When he was done, when he slumped against her, and held her, and said into her hair that she was the sweetest thing, she didn't think, *thank god that's over,* the way she wanted to. She wasn't glad to be back over the line she had promised she wouldn't cross.

She was simply sad to know that the sex cure had worked.

And that she would now never have anything this lovely, ever again.

CHAPTER TWENTY-SEVEN

It was easy to confirm it definitely had worked, in the aftermath. Mostly because he was actually able to leave the house. And once he was gone, he didn't immediately come back. Instead, he texted her a picture of himself in his ramshackle home, with a thumbs-up.

Though she would have known it anyway, even without the evidence.

Everything felt much clearer. Less fraught than it had seemed as she'd laid beneath him. She could think straight enough to accomplish tasks she hadn't been able to while in the middle of a sex fog. Like shop for groceries, and replenish the potions that kept the Jerks away, and make sure Nancy was not too traumatized by what she'd seen the other day.

Then just for good measure, she went to the Halloween decoration–festooned library. Because she could now fully process what she'd heard the Jerks say at the House. And she didn't like the idea that Hannigan was causing Tabitha problems. Or trying to ban books.

So it seemed like a good idea to offer her support.

"You just tell me what you need," she told Tabby. Then once she'd arranged to come and join her in the monthly yell-a-thon that was the town hall meeting, she went on her away. After maybe a *little* bit of potion sprinkling. Just a touch, to possibly make certain people want to avoid the library, for reasons they couldn't quite explain.

And all of this—everything she managed to do—proved beyond a shadow of a doubt that she was all herself again. The weird werewolf sex nonsense was a thing of the past.

There was just one problem:

Thinking about what had happened during the werewolf sex nonsense was very much not.

In fact, the memories hit her every five minutes or so. She'd be stirring a pot or talking to her mom about the weather or doing laundry—which now involved simply sprinkling a potion on her clothes and finding them clean and folded in a random drawer sometime later—and there it would be. The memory of some naked part of his body. Or the memory of what that naked part of his body had done to her. What Seth, her friend-slash-enemy-slash-friend-again had done to her.

It was disconcerting. It left her flushed and flummoxed. She found herself blushing when she was around him, even when they were just working on ways to guard against spell reversals, or making plans to help people without feeling like they were warping anybody's brains. Their hands would brush as they both reached for the same book, and her mind would leap to other times they'd touched like that. It would stall her out, like a broken car.

And it wasn't just her who noticed this was happening.

Pod noticed too. *Get room*, he said, after the thirteenth time they'd danced around each other awkwardly in the kitchen. Then of course Seth wanted to know what he'd chittered at her, and she didn't know what to say, and oh it was just so weird and uncomfortable and impossible.

And even more so after she finally cracked the potion that would fix all the rest of his horny issues for good. Because for some inexplicable reason, she decided the best course of action was flying over to his place, at something like ten past midnight, to give it to him.

He actually came to the door in his pajamas.

Though, of course it wasn't *his* pajamas that were the issue.

"Cassie, what on earth are you doing here in the middle of the night? And why the heck are you in your underwear?" he asked as he took her in. And, okay, fair enough. This particular sleep set was more like shorts and a little camisole-type of thing. But it wasn't *that* revealing. You couldn't actually see anything.

"Okay, it's hardly the middle of the night. And this isn't underwear," she snorted. But as soon as she did, she realized that neither of those two things was the point. The exact time she showed up and the type of clothing she wore didn't matter. What mattered is that those things felt extremely weird, now that they were standing so close to each other.

So weird, in fact, that she really wished she hadn't done this.

Because yeah, it had seemed reasonable back at home, in her kitchen, with the newly minted potion right in front of her, all ready to go. But right now, it did not seem reasonable at all. It seemed like something else. Something that made him look at her so oddly, she simply had to force out an explanation.

"Plus, you know. You've been waiting for this potion for a decade," she said, and to her relief he practically slapped his thigh with dawning understanding and amusement. *Oh, of course*, his expression seemed to say—which put her firmly in the clear.

Or so she thought. Until he added almost casually, laughing, "Wow, okay. *Now* it makes sense. Because, you know, for a second there, with you in that sexy outfit and the fact that it's past midnight, I actually thought you might be here for some kind of late-night hookup."

And as soon as he did, she couldn't stop what happened.

Her face just dropped into shocked realization. Followed by what definitely felt like guilt and horror and about ten other things she knew she shouldn't let show. Now Seth could *see* it. He was looking at it. Oh, and he obviously knew what it meant. He knew so much that he couldn't even be polite about it.

"Holy shit," he gasped. "You're *totally* here for a hookup."

And then it was just a matter of trying not to die of embarrassment. While denying everything in the most dignified way she could muster. "What? No I'm not. That's nuts. Shut up. I'm leaving," she said. Because apparently she no longer understood what dignity was. She even went to do just that. She grabbed the Hoover and turned.

And she didn't feel thankful when he snagged her arm.

When he said, "No no, don't leave, don't leave. Just wait."

After all, it was nice that he did. But it still meant having to face the mess she'd somehow made. And with absolutely zero excuses for why she'd done it, either. She had come here entirely of her own accord. This was all 100 percent her. And sure, she had done it pretty unconsciously. She hadn't really thought about why she really wanted to see him right at that moment in time. But what did that matter? She still looked like a thirsty weirdo, longing for something that could never be real. Like some small, deep-down part of her had really thought it could be—or at the very least hadn't been able to cope with knowing it wasn't.

It was apparently too much sweetness and heat and pleasure for someone who was half-starved to take. So now here she was. Fooling her own mind. And then doing something as humiliating as *throwing herself* at him.

"I can't. I'm late. For never seeing you again," she choked out, pulling against the hand he still had on her. But he held on, he held on, he wouldn't let her escape this humiliation. And oh Jesus, now he was protesting.

"But never seeing me again isn't necessary."

"Of course it is. I just accidentally confessed *that* to you."

"Yeah, but if by *that* you mean you are into doing all of that stuff with me again, then you need to know something," he said, and she turned with her face now blazing, thinking of all the mortifying things he might finish that thought with. All of the remnants of how he'd made her feel in high school—just some dipshit who'd been a fool to imagine she meant the world to him. Then somehow she got him holding his breath. She got him looking at her with all the desperation and desire in the world. And then there were words, oh the words. "I am absolutely into it too. I am madly, wildly, completely head over heels into it too."

And all of them so passionate, so perfect, she almost just went to him.

She could feel the urge like a wildfire, raging through her.

It was honestly a miracle that she managed to push for clarification, instead. To make it clear, absolutely clear, and without a single bit of confusion. "But you're not magically hungry for me, anymore," she said faintly. Half hope. Half mystification.

But god he just looked so pleased. "No, but I am *other* types of hungry."

"Okay. But what other types do you mean?"

"Mostly the ones that involve remembering everything we did. And dreaming about everything we did. And then thinking what I would do differently, if you ever somehow inexplicably gave me the chance to do it again."

Inexplicably, she thought, in a daze.

But it was another word that pushed her to speak. "So it wasn't completely right to you then," she said. "You would change things, somehow, if we went inside and did it right now."

"Well yeah. Of course I would."

"Because you didn't like it."

"Not because *I* didn't like it, Cass. Because *you* didn't."

He said the words so sincerely.

Like that was *obviously* the issue. He didn't even seem to blink about it, so what was she supposed to say then? How was she supposed to explain that she actually *had*? That she had just tried not to enjoy it, to such an extent that he didn't even know it was the case? It sounded even sillier now than it had at the time they'd done it.

Because apparently, he minded her disguising her pleasure.

He wanted full throttle. Way more.

And he was saying this while completely himself.

"Okay, but let's say for the sake of argument that I sort of did enjoy myself, and was just kind of nervous about *seeming* like I did to too great a degree. In case, you know. That was weird, and also maybe like I was taking advantage of a situation you might not really want to be in," she tried. And failed, obviously. His face dropped into what could only be described as *what the fuck*.

"Well, in that case I would say, Oh you can't be serious," he fumed.

Even though that wasn't fair, it wasn't fair at all. "But why not? We never really discussed how much I should be into it."

"Because we shouldn't have to. It should be obvious. And even if it isn't, I actually *did* say. I said I wanted you to have something for you. I told you I wanted to go down on you. I mean, what on earth did you think that meant? I lick your pussy until you experience a moderate, polite amount of pleasure?"

She clenched her fists in frustration. "Now you've made it sound so absurd that I can't say yes."

"You can't say yes because it *is* absurd. My god, Cass. Why didn't you just tell me this? Why didn't you just ask me?"

"It was kind of difficult to at the time."

"But at the time I could have reassured you, and then got you off."

She tried to avoid letting her expression crease in a way that said *oops*. But she could see realization dawning on his face, anyway. And he got there, before she could make it sound any more reasonable than it was. "You cannot be seriously telling me you faked *not* having an orgasm," he said.

"No, I am not telling you that."

"Well, thank god."

"Because I faked not having one multiple times."

Shouldn't have revealed that part, she thought, as he registered what she'd said. Too late now, though. He had his hands in the air, and they weren't coming back down.

"Oh my god. Oh my god. Cassie, do you know how many *I'm so sorry the phony sex we had wasn't great for you* letters I've drafted to you? How many texts I've started, apologizing for being terrible in bed, and then deleted? And you're telling me you were coming all over the place the whole time?"

"Well, not the *whole* time. I mean the first minute was pretty orgasm-free."

"So every minute after that wasn't? Cassie, we fucked for like an hour."

"Oh my god, was it really an hour? No wonder I passed out."

He pinched the bridge of his nose. "You did *not* pass out. Please say you didn't."

"It was only for a second. And in my defense, your cock is very thick, and you have this weird way of moving your hips, and then there were all the noises you kept making and the talking and the lifting. And also I'm pretty sure at some stage I started feeling what you were feeling," she babbled, because it really felt at this point that she should list everything.

And thankfully, it seemed to help. She watched his expression cycle through irritation, and then bemusement, and then what was quite obviously a little bit of feeling pleased with himself. Before it landed on that last part. And then he snapped his fingers. "So *that's* why it felt like I was coming for half an hour," he said, which she had to say was pretty awesome. Because now the subject was steering away from what a fool she was.

And into the fact that he was a bit of one too.

"Honestly I'm amazed you didn't guess," she said.

"Sometimes I think I maybe did. But then talked myself out of it."

"Because it's easier to believe I hated it."

He had the decency to look sheepish. "Yeah," he said. "Or at the very least hated all the things you just said you loved. I mean, god, I would never have known you were into the grabbing and the hips and the noises. They felt like super-weird instincts as I was doing them, in a way I now realize was probably just feeling what you actually wanted."

"I definitely was. Especially when you kind of—" she started to say.

But he got there himself before she could. "Grabbed your ass."

"Yeah, that was the one."

"And then grunted that it felt juicy."

He closed one eye when he said that last word.

Sort of half winced, like he was embarrassed to revisit it.

But that just made it sweeter to reassure him. "Also very, very good. Hell, it's good *now*," she said. And even better, she could do it without a lick of shame or worry. Because he just looked so pumped when she got the words out.

"Really? So you're getting worked up over it, as we *speak*?"

"Just a little bit. Or, you know, a lot."

"So if I said that I want to slide my hands into those tiny shorts right now and get two handfuls of that ass, and then haul you up into my arms, and grind you against my cock until we both come our brains out, you'd actually genuinely like that," he said, but she suspected he knew the answer before she even spoke.

It felt like her whole body lit up like a Christmas tree the second he said slide my hands. So there was no sense denying it. She didn't *have* to deny it. He felt the same as her: that fucking her had felt so good he wanted a second round. And maybe a third and a fourth and a fifth, if his expression was anything to go by when she said: "Both the saying of it and the idea you actually might, yeah."

Though he double-checked after she had.

"And that's just all your own real feelings," he said.

So then she had to fudge a little bit. She had to change the *yes I feel that way about you* to something more about the great sex and her perfectly reasonable reaction to that. But the main thing was: she got there. "Well, I mean, understandably so, considering your super-long tongue."

"Oh my god, I thought you thought that was gross. I almost stopped."

"But you're not gonna stop now, though, right?"

He laughed, and looked away. Then he looked back, and his expression was different. Feral, she thought the word for it was. Hungry.

"Not until you *beg* me to."

CHAPTER TWENTY-EIGHT

She didn't think anything of stripping off once she was in his bedroom. Even though it was freezing in there. The windows were half falling out of their frames; she was pretty sure there had to be a hole somewhere. And the only way to get warm was the bed. The one that she had given him a potion to make, which had apparently made it grow arms.

It tried to grab her as she jumped on.

Naked as the day she was born, not a care in the world.

Because the thing was: she knew she didn't have to have one. He burst into the room, hands full of candles she hadn't been able to obtain the other night, and what looked like a mix tape she had no idea how he was going to play, and a bunch of snacks she was assuming he needed so they could do this all fucking night.

And he took one look at her, all bare and spread out across his bed, and pretty much dropped everything. Candles spiraled under the bed. She got to see that one of the snacks was a pack of Red Vines—still a favorite of his, it seemed—because it fell face up. A can of something definitely burst. She heard it go, even if she didn't see it.

And his expression. It was all eyes, all stunned delight.

Though she couldn't resist pushing him to say it, anyway.

"What are you thinking about?" she asked as mischievously as she could make it.

And sure enough, he didn't even hesitate.

"I'm thinking about what I did to deserve your hot tits and ass all completely exposed to my extremely unworthy eyes," he said,

and with such bemused earnestness she had no choice but to believe it. And even more so when he added, "Okay lemme just—"

Then he simply started yanking off his own clothes in a frantic scramble. He hocked his T-shirt over his head with one hand,
while trying to shove his pants down with another. And as he did
both, he did his best to toe off his socks.

Though one of them still remained, when he got to the bed.
Like he'd forgotten what he was doing halfway through. Which
was, weirdly, one of the hottest things about everything he'd just
done. That eagerness, that single-mindedness—it was a real killer.
It had her pushing her mouth into his before he'd even made it
fully onto the bed.

And not chastely, either.

She went directly to wet and hot and open-mouthed, in a way
that almost felt like too much. Like the other night. But then she
pulled back, and oh, oh. He *followed*. Like a big kid being fed
something super tasty, then fumbling after it the second it went
away. And that was nuts, it was ridiculous, but at the same time it
was so sexy and so sweet that she didn't know how to react.

She wanted to laugh and moan, all at the same time.

In fact, she did. Much to his embarrassment.

"Sorry, sorry, I just wasn't expecting your tongue in my mouth
like that, and it is *ridiculously* hot. Like almost *too* hot. I think I
almost came just feeling it fucking into my mouth like that," he
said, almost as if he shouldn't.

So she kissed him again. "And that would be a bad thing why?"
she asked, archly enough that it left him blank-faced and flummoxed. He had to work up to an answer, while licking her taste
off his lips.

"I have no idea, considering you seemed to hate me taking a
while to get there last time. In fact, at one point I think you practically demanded I finish."

"Yeah, about that," she said, with a rueful look. And he got it
before she even said.

"You didn't actually want me to just finish, did you?"

"Not even a little bit, no. Although you should know, at this point, that I also do not care if you do it fast. Mainly because (a) it's very hot to me that you're so into whatever we're doing here that a kiss can make you come, (b) there are plenty of other options available to us aside from your cock in my pussy, and (c) we both know you definitely do not need to stop at one in a night. Or even five in a night. Or seventeen. I think I remember you saying seventeen was your limit."

"I did, but it was actually more like twenty-seven."

"Jesus Christ, I'm not gonna make it out of here alive."

"Oh no, don't worry, you will. I have lots of rest breaks penciled in, between the five thousand delicious and disgusting things I definitely now think you're okay with me doing to you. And hope you want to do to me."

She thought about the snacks.

The way he'd looked at her outside.

The way he was looking at her now. And proceeded accordingly.

"I'll do whatever you want. Just tell me where to start," she said. Then expected maybe a kiss. Like before, when he had wanted to start out nice and slow. But instead, he took hold of her hand, all tender and sweet about it.

And he put it somewhere that sent a thrill right through her body.

It made her glance down, immediately. Just so she could see how it looked: his bare cock, all stiff and already so fucking slick. Then his hand over hers, urging her to stroke. Though it wasn't as if he had to urge her at all. She started moving almost before he did, every part of her eager to feel that thick, solid thing. To make him moan for her, to make him feel good.

And it worked.

"Oh yeah, just like that," he gasped the second she tightened her grip around his already slick shaft. And it felt so delicious, so exciting, she couldn't resist doing more. She waited, until he was flushed and trembling and practically rocking into her hand.

Then she simply dipped her head. She licked, over that glistening slit at the tip of his cock. Just once, just to see what would happen. And oh, the sound he made. The words he got out. "Ohh-hhh man. Oh that is—that is super intense," he said in a way that definitely told her he wanted more. But she paused anyway, almost entirely for the tease of it.

"So much so that you want me to stop?" she asked.

And got what she'd been imagining.

"God no. No, please just do that again."

"You like it then."

"Like isn't the right word."

"Then what is? Tell me. Tell me."

"Whatever will make you lick me that way a second time."

"Even though I could do more. I could do this instead," she said, leaning down again. Only instead of licking, instead of strok-ing, she let that thick, swollen cock slide all the way past her lips. She took him in, as deep as she could, and then slowly, slowly worked her way back up again.

And oh god when she did. He tried to make a sound, and in-stead almost seemed to choke. One hand went to her shoulder and gripped her there tightly. Like he wanted to stop her or push her away. But of course he didn't do anything of the kind. He just held on, the way a drowning man would cling to a life preserver.

As she did it again. And again. Each time bolder about it. Filth-ier about it.

By the time he got his act together enough to talk, she was working him steadily, hand on all the places her mouth couldn't reach, tongue licking over that now constantly spilling slit at the tip, greedily, so greedily. Of course it was greedily—it tasted too good, felt too good.

And the things he said only made it sweeter.

"Okay, just so you know, I am definitely going to come. As in, I am ten seconds away. So if you want me to do it somewhere other than your mouth—" he started to say, then seemed to stutter to a stop when he realized she wasn't easing up. She heard his in-take of breath—felt the tension in him like someone pulling a wire taught—and went faster. She went harder. She went slicker and sloppier, until that wire snapped. "Ohhhh god, you want me to.

You want me to. Okay, fuck, that's hot, oh you're so greedy for it, oh that's it, oh that's my good girl."

And it almost made her snap too, when it did. She felt the words pour through her, just as his dirty talk had done before. More than they had done before, because now it was truly *him* saying it. This was really how he felt. These were his actual feelings about what she was doing.

And that realization made *such* a mess of her.

She found herself getting sloppy, shaky. She couldn't stop herself rocking—as if he were already inside her, working her into the orgasm she could almost already feel. The beginnings of it burned through her, bright and brilliant enough that she couldn't help making sounds. Lewd sounds, of the sort that would have embarrassed her before.

But how could they now?

When she let out a low, heavy groan, his hand fisted in her hair. His cock swelled in her mouth. Then even better, even hotter—he made sounds of his own. Rich, deep, guttural sounds that seemed to vibrate through him, and into her. They buzzed over her sensitive nipples, her swollen clit, so strongly she wasn't sure she could take it.

She almost pulled back, almost begged for mercy.

But that was when she felt it. The first jerk and swell of that fat cock, too obvious and too delicious to ever back away from. In fact, she found herself working harder, until she got what she was greedy for. That hot burst of come, over her tongue. Just a little, at first. But then so thick and fast she had to swallow and swallow and swallow to keep up.

And it still spilled over her lips.

She looked up at him with it running down her chin. Watched his eyes flash wide and hot to see it. Then she curled her tongue over her lower lip to catch it, and he couldn't seem to help himself. "Oh you like that, don't you," he groaned. Then even hotter: "Here, have some more."

And he took his cock in his hand, and stroked. He worked himself, until another stripe of come coated her lips, her tongue.

She had to open her mouth again to catch it all, then thrilled when he slid that still swollen head back in.

Because God this was Seth, her sweet Seth, and he was doing something so fucking *filthy*.

He was letting her clean his cock of come.

He even said so. He told her she was his sweet girl, for licking up every drop.

So it wasn't a surprise that she was a wreck by the time he was done.

Every bit of her seemed boneless, breathless. She had to take a second to rest her face against his thigh. But that was all right, because he seemed to feel the same. She heard him breathing raggedly. Felt him trembling, one hand in her hair, petting her in a half-reassuring, half-grateful way.

Before he finally got it together enough to speak.

"Okay, that's one of the things I wanted to do down. Now on to the other 4,999. Starting, I think, with running my hands all over every inch of those maddening fucking curves. Unless of course you have any objections?" he said, like some scout leader rallying the troops.

Though, really, he didn't need to rally anything. The moment she nodded, still half pressed against his leg, he trailed a finger over the place where her throat met her shoulder. He said, "Then I'll begin here, at this smooth arch." And just like that, she was lit up again.

"And after that?" she asked eagerly, as he ran his hand further down.

"This sweet groove, between your belly and your hips."

"Because you like that. You're saying you like that there."

"I love it," he murmured. "I dream about it. But not as much as I dream about this."

"But that's just my lower back."

"It's not. It's where you have these two dimples. Just right there an inch away from the starting curve of your ass. Easy to glimpse whenever your top rides up, but impossible to forget once I have. Even back in high school I used to wonder what it would be like, to just—"

he said, and pushed two fingers into those little dents, rubbing and rubbing in a way that made her arch her back helplessly.

Then just as she was wondering if he'd really thought of something so strange back then, he urged her to turn. He got her on her knees, back to him. And he simply went ahead and replaced his fingers with his mouth. He kissed those dimples, hot and wet enough that she bunched the sheets into fists. She made a sound, instead of speaking.

And when she did speak, her voice came out ragged.

"But I'm guessing you didn't think about following it with this."

"No. No, I never let myself think about that," he replied. "Or about doing more after I'd touched them." And then he did just that. He did more. He slid one hand between the legs she hadn't realized she'd spread, and stroked through her slick folds, her swollen clit, and down, down, until he was there. He was working her open, as slow and steady as before.

Only better, because he talked about it as he did. "Or about your liking it. Because I'm pretty sure you are, judging by the way you're rocking into my hand right now and getting it all wet and, oh *yeah*—that's happening because you're gonna come, right?"

He meant because she was clenching around his steadily working fingers, she knew. She could feel it happening, hard enough that he could hardly stroke into her. He had to slow down, and just sort of twist and rub—though of course that only made things worse. Now she was panting, shaking, so flushed she felt as if she was on fire.

And she couldn't stop herself mewling at him for more.

Even though it made him give her less. He slowed, to the point where she had to ask.

"Oh god, why are you stopping?" she managed to squeeze out, and cringed a little over the sound of herself. Until he answered her, that was.

"Because I want to feel you doing it on my cock again. But this time, I want to absolutely know that's what you're doing," he said— and so casually, too. Like it was nothing. Instead of something so hot it made her breath catch in her throat. It made her squirm and try to push back against him, before he'd done a single thing. She had to actually fight to keep herself still, just so she could get every little detail of what he had described.

But it was worth it, when she got that big hand of his on her hip. Stroking, at first, all soft and slow. Then he simply slid his fingers into that cup, between her thigh and her stomach. And he used it to haul her back, back, back, until she could feel it.

The thick head of his cock, sliding through the seam of her sex. Back and forth and back and forth, so steady and teasing she wondered how he could stand it. It was too much for her, and he was barely touching any of the good stuff. He only just grazed her clit with every stroke; her greedy hole got little more than a hint of him.

She almost pushed back, on one of those maddening strokes.

Just fucked herself on him, good and hard.

Yet somehow, it was still a shock when he finally broke. She got a sudden groan, so desperate it had her fisting the bedsheets. Then that thick cock just sliding into her, spreading her, in a way that felt even sweeter than it had the first time. He seemed to spark every nerve ending she had, as he filled her pussy.

Though it was more than that, and she knew it. She could feel it again—that strange echo of whatever pleasure he was experiencing. As if they were still connected in that way, somehow. Like it had left a kind of delicious scar when she'd healed them both.

Only somehow, that didn't seem quite right.

It was something else, she could feel it. But before she could really think about it, he put a hand on the small of her back. He pushed her down, until her belly and breasts were pressed to the mattress. And then he practically rolled into her.

And every thought she had ever had flew out of her head.

All she could think about was the sensations, the feelings, the sweet blooming beginnings of her orgasm, as inexorable as the tide. How much she wanted to tell him she was close, but couldn't quite make the words come. They stuck in her throat, too dirty to speak. Too much, too raw, too like holding back was still the best idea.

But of course he knew, he knew.

"Don't hide it from me. Tell me how good it feels," he said, so soft and full of understanding and reassurance that it would have been enough on its own. Then she felt his hand stroke over her back, and that was it.

She didn't know how to keep it inside anymore.

"So good I'm going to cream all over your cock," she burst out.

And it was worth it, just for the groan she got in response.

"So you like it when I do you like this."

"Yes yes yes, oh god, yes please please."

"And how about now? Hotter or colder?"

Hotter, she thought, *too hot. I'm burning alive and don't want to stop.*

Before she could say it, he got hold of both hips with those big hands. And he hauled her back, onto his cock. Then again, and again, hard and fast and right up against that sweet spot inside her. The one she couldn't reach with her fingers, and hardly could with toys, and definitely never had with any other men she'd fucked.

But he reached effortlessly—and she knew it wasn't because of the way he was built. It was because of that echo, that connection. It had to be, because he shuddered with her every time he got it right. He said her name every time she wanted to say his. And when he reached a hand between their bodies and stroked one wicked finger over her clit, it wasn't just her that lost control.

She felt him buck and grunt and dig his fingers into her hip, the moment he made contact.

Though it was her who got there first. The pleasure just bloomed upward from every point of contact, thick and intense enough that she said his name through gritted teeth. She tried to get away from it.

And she knew she'd made a mess of him. She felt herself spilling all over his cock, felt it coating her thighs and soaking the sheets. Heard him gasping over it, in a way that would have embarrassed her before. But it couldn't here, because she knew what that gasp meant. She knew what everything meant with him now. He had removed all doubt, and replaced it with something better, something sweeter.

She didn't even need him to say.

Though he did, anyway.

"Thank god you brought that potion that cuts the cord between getting turned on and becoming a beast. Because if you hadn't, I'd be mauling you and growling that you're mine, right around now," he panted out between heavy, ragged breaths. Between kisses, god the way he dropped kisses on the nape of her neck.

She couldn't be normal about it.

"I wouldn't care if you did," she replied without even thinking twice.

And got his voice in her ear, breathless, barely human.

"You are, you are, you're all mine," he growled as she felt the first wave of his orgasm running through her. "Say you are. Say you're mine. Say you always will be."

And though his words felt like too much, she didn't hesitate.

"I will, I am, I'm all yours," she gasped.

Then waited for a sense of regret that simply never came.

CHAPTER TWENTY-NINE

The first thing she did when she woke was reach for him. Because yeah, sure, she could tell herself to be careful. She could stop and consider that nothing had been said about what this meant—beyond wanting to fuck the living daylights out of each other, of course. But her semiconscious self didn't really care. It wanted to cuddle up to him. And she didn't really have the wherewithal or even the need to fight it.

She just did it. She was even disappointed, when she found nothing but an empty bed. And an empty, cold bed at that. Like he'd been gone for a long time, even though she was pretty sure it wasn't late in the morning. Gray light filtered through the windows. Six-thirty sort of light.

So she sat up and listened. She tuned herself in to whatever sounds he should have been making. The splash of a shower, the opening of a fridge downstairs. Even though she had no idea if he had a shower, or a fridge. She only discovered that he had one of them when she went to pee in something other than a sex stupor, and actually noticed the shower curtain around the bathtub.

And discovering the other appliance took until she got dressed, and made her way down his death-trap staircase, to the room that passed for a kitchen. Then there it was in the corner, actually humming away. She even found a block of cheese in there and a gallon of milk. A box of Cheerios, too, in one of his cupboards. And bowls, he had bowls, mismatched and one of them chipped, but usable. She got them out and set them on the counter, ready to pour them both some cereal.

And that was when it struck her.

It was kind of weird that Seth wasn't around to eat that bowl.

As in, *what if he went out to get breakfast and they've done something to him?* weird.

And hoo boy, did that thought take her from fuck-drunk to scared in about five seconds flat. She jumped up from the table and went out onto the sagging front porch. Called his name into the early-morning light. But all that replied was birdsong, and the chill fall breeze, rustling the trees.

And it was followed by an even stronger sense that something had gone very wrong. *They shouldn't be able to even see him,* she told herself. But she couldn't help wondering if they'd gotten around her potion somehow. If there was a spell she didn't know about or a trick her research hadn't turned up.

Or if it was something Seth had done.

Because that was a possible thing, she knew. If someone *chose* to be seen, they would be. Though she struggled to imagine why he would. She couldn't think of a single reason he would want to let the Jerks take another shot at him. Why he might see them and think, *sure, let's just stroll up and say hi.*

And she continued to think that, right up until she got back inside, and grabbed her phone from the place she had left it on the kitchen counter, and saw the message waiting for her. A selfie, it looked like, and when she opened it, sure enough. There he was, in 4K.

Only it wasn't the Seth she'd come to know over the last few weeks.

Or the Seth she'd been friends with as a kid.

No, this was a different Seth. A smug-looking Seth, who leered out of the screen at her, fingers curled into an OK sign. None of which would have meant anything to her, if it had just been the photo. But it wasn't. On either side of this brand-new Seth were three similarly amused, smug little faces, bold as brass, and all too familiar.

One of them belonged to Jay. The other to Tyler. And the third was clearly Jordan.

Then underneath, a caption:

Surprise, fatso.
You didn't really think this was a thing, did you?

CHAPTER THIRTY

She tried not to let Pod know anything was wrong once she got back to her place. And with good reason, because the moment Pod managed to snatch her phone from her and figure out what had happened, things went pretty badly. He ran around the house yelling, *murder beefhead*, scooping up weapons as he went. She found herself having a standoff with a raccoon clutching a toilet brush, while the rest of the house seemed to go nuts. All the lights switched on and off repeatedly, as though she were in a very weird nightclub. And the now sentient TV didn't help—it blared one chorus after another from songs that declared death to monstrous liars, cheaters, and thieves.

Most of which were, unfortunately, really catchy. She found herself singing along to Olivia Rodrigo at one point. Fake microphone in hand, dance moves on point, Pod jigging away behind her, as she made her way through the kitchen.

She only stopped when she saw what was on the magnetic notepad, attached to the fridge door. All in careful, slightly shaky handwriting: *I'm so sorry, my darling.* Like someone who wasn't quite there had written it. And of course she knew who the someone was. Her grandmother. Her grandmother, who had seen that she was hurting, even as she danced.

Even though she didn't want to be, anymore. She wanted to be like marble, the way she had been before. Impervious to him and any of his actions, uncaring of what he thought. But of course there was no chance of that now. He'd dissolved all her defenses.

And he'd done it with such precision, such attention to detail, that it was kind of breathtaking, really.

He'd even made sure to go beyond the mating bond.

To say enough to persuade her into confessing her indisputably real desires.

And oh, that thought took the wind out of her. She sat down hard in one of the kitchen chairs, and couldn't seem to get back up again for a long, long time. She just stared into space, until finally Pod dropped the toilet brush. He crept over to her, and put his little hand over hers.

Mom okay? he said.

She couldn't answer, however. Her throat was too full of tears.

SHE DID HER best not to think about it. But thinking about it was all her brain wanted to do. It went over and over everything he'd said and done, trying to piece together the plan he must have had all along. And every time she thought she had satisfied her mind with explanations—*that was done to convince me of this, and this was the reason he tried that*—her mind wanted more.

Worse, it wouldn't let go of the version of him she had grown so close to.

A day later she answered the door to find what looked like a walking, talking coat, scarf, and hat, and her first thought wasn't *what the fuck am I looking at?* It was *God, Seth would find this hysterical. He would say it's exactly like that scene in a movie when the evil gremlins try to disguise themselves as a person.* And he'd have been right.

Although maybe not about the evil gremlins part. Whatever was rustling around inside that human disguise definitely did not seem bad. It seemed soft-spoken and sort of apologetic. "Good day, madam witch," it said. "So sorry to trouble you at this late hour."

Even though it wasn't a late hour at all. It was still morning.

However, she supposed it might be midnight from the perspective of whatever was under the coat. Considering it could be absolutely anything. A being from another dimension, or several beings from another dimension, or a number of talking owls stacked on top of each other.

She couldn't be sure. And it seemed impolite to ask.

So instead she said, "No trouble at all. How can I help you?"

Because help felt like something she could offer. Something that she still had in her, no matter what Seth had taken away. *I am still a whole witch, with a burgeoning desire to care for supernatural creatures,* she told herself. And it was true. She felt it burning anew, the moment the creature answered.

"You very kindly left an offer when you borrowed my essence of dragon scale. And as I find myself with something of an issue, I felt it might be an appropriate time to take your good self up on it," it said, and she grasped what the issue was before it had even finished speaking.

She heard it in her head, clearer than her witch sense had ever been before. *They want a corporeal body that is visible to humans,* she thought. *Instead of having to employ this invisible-man act.* And after she had she realized two things: what was under there wasn't actually a physical being or beings. And the way to fix this was easy.

She would make them a shape to inhabit.

"Would you like to seem human, or like something else?" she asked, then watched as that scarf twitched into something like a smile.

"The former please," they said.

So she stuffed down her heartbreak, and set to work.

She captured some smoke in a vial, and threw it into her biggest pot. Then added some plastic wrap to hold the form, and a little flour to give it body, and a few other ingredients that would make the shape easy to slip into and out of. And finally, she brought the concoction to a boil. A good, roiling boil, until the whole thing made a sound like someone popping bubblegum.

Done, she thought as she grabbed a jar to pour it into.

"At four in the afternoon exactly, open it up and drink," she told the being, once she had sealed it up nice and tight. Then she handed it over. She watched it take what she had made in a gloved hand that wasn't really there.

Before it ambled off her porch, in the direction of the woods.

But just as she was thinking, *well, that was a good distraction*— and that possibly she could distract herself with these sorts of good deeds forever—the creature turned. "Your wolf was right to speak so highly of you. I shall most certainly be recommending your services to the rest of the community," it said.

And then somehow she was right back to square one.

SHE KIND OF thought by the next day she would be past square one. Especially when it became obvious that her last visitor had stayed true to his word. She had another visitor sometime in the afternoon—a troll named, inexplicably, Derek, who kept her busy with a potion for curing spontaneous nipple growth.

Only keeping herself busy didn't seem to matter.

And not just because of what the non-corporeal being had said. Because of other things too, lots of things, weird things that shouldn't have nagged at her, but did nonetheless. Like all of his soft expressions. And the super-sincere things he'd said. And how difficult it would have been for him to fake his kindnesses.

Because of course he must have faked them, if everything had been leading up to some final trap. *But dear god, how?* she found herself thinking, in her weakest moments. And even stranger: those moments didn't feel weak. They felt convincing. Compelling. Sensible.

She just couldn't fathom why. She was used to being skeptical and paranoid and anxious about everything Seth did. To always imagine another prank was coming, or wonder if now was the moment that cool indifference would return.

Because that was what usually made sense.

That was the version of events that had always won out in her mind.

But for some reason, that version was losing. Inexplicably, bizarrely, it was losing. Like he hadn't left in the middle of the night.

Like he couldn't have left of his own accord. Like she'd never seen that text message. Or had seen it, but could somehow get around it.

Impossible, the old part of her brain said.

But for the first time, another part answered back.

You realize it's entirely possible that they faked it, don't you?

And of course she laughed. She told Pod, and he laughed too. Then the microwave and the TV joined in. The latter even played a funny bit from *Friends*, looping the audience laugh track over and over. Which should have pretty much put an end to such thinking forever.

In fact it did, for a little while.

Until she crawled under the bedsheets at far too early a time to sleep. And caught just a hint of Seth on the pillow next to hers. She saw his face in her mind's eye—the moment when he'd turned and looked at her after they'd had sex. That strong sense that he was going to say he wanted to stay, before she'd told him he should probably go.

And it hit her like a lightning bolt.

They didn't circumvent your magic. They used magic against you. They made you see what they knew you're still unsure about, no matter how much you believe you are brilliant and bright and the best: that he doesn't. That deep down, he bought into their bullshit. And it was only a matter of time before he let the truth slip or played a trick or tried to make you feel like high school all over again.

Even though high school is over now.

Though she still had no idea what to do once those electric thoughts were there. She raced downstairs in such a fury that Pod peeped his head out of his cupboard. *What do*, he chittered. *What happen?* While she rifled through the guidebook for an answer.

Something like how to see through an illusion, she thought. But there was nothing, there was nothing—as if illusions like that didn't exist. There was no magical amulet the Jerks could have used, no all-powerful staff that made you see things that weren't real. It was useless, utterly useless, and to the point where she set everything aside. She put her face in her hands, suddenly unsure of the reason she had believed this was anything but him betraying her.

And that was when she felt Pod's little hand on hers.

He tapped her gently. Then pointed at the page the guidebook had fallen open to.

Dad good, he said. *Good good good.*

So she looked, and there it was.

Seth's handwriting, under a bunch of words about how long it took to master flying.

OMG, he'd written. *It only took you a day. You are AMAZING.*

And suddenly her eyes were full of tears, and her heart was running away with her, and all she could think was *you believed because he spent every second of the last month making all your fears unfounded, all your terror of hoping seem so sad, all your worries that something is wrong turn out so wonderfully that you've forgotten what wrong even is. He has tipped the scales back to it being okay to trust in something, singlehandedly.*

And he did without even thinking you would ever see.

Then suddenly she knew exactly how to figure this out. As if it had only been uncertainty that held her back. But now that was gone, and the answer was so clear she didn't hesitate. She grabbed her bike from the hall, pedaled into town, and burst into Nancy's shop like a woman possessed. And she barely even paused when Nancy asked why she was in her pajamas and what on earth had happened and, "Oh gosh, should I call the police?"

She just showed Nancy the image on her phone screen. "Tell me what you see here," she demanded. Heart in her mouth, breath held.

And Nancy answered the only way Cassie knew she could: "I see those three jerkholes from high school with their arms around a department store mannequin for some inexplicable reason I probably don't want to know about." Puzzled, she looked at Cassie and smiled. "Does that help?"

But Cassie couldn't tell her how much it did. She was already furiously pedaling home.

To make some fucking werewolves pay.

CHAPTER THIRTY-ONE

Her first instinct was to create some kind of death ray that she could point at them from space. Maybe while laughing maniacally. But because it had been three days of them doing god knows what to Seth, she thought it was more important to be fast.

So she settled for doing the bare minimum.

First, she needed to figure out exactly how they had taken Seth. Mainly so she could confirm they hadn't circumvented her magic. *You don't want to run in all guns blazing if they have a blazing-gun nullifier,* she told herself as she used an enchanted magnifying glass to go over the Forget Me that hung around Seth's house.

And she found what she was looking for. A sort of warping by the tree line. A tear, of the sort that Seth had definitely made himself. He'd crossed through on purpose, like she'd thought. But for a reason other than joining the wolf pack, quite clearly.

They were on the premises, and up to nothing good, and he saw them and decided to confront them, her mind supplied. All of which fit so well she could hardly believe she hadn't thought of it before. *That* was Seth. Brave and good, but also absolutely ridiculous enough to not even consider that it might be a trap. All he would have wanted to do was rush in, to stop whatever misbehavior was going on.

My big, foolish goofball, she thought. But all thinking that did was to stop her breath. She had to take a second to calm down, hands on her knees, eyes closed. Though she felt no better once she'd straightened.

Now she had to think about where they'd taken him.

Or worse: what if they hadn't taken him anywhere at all? It was perfectly possible that they had killed him. She knew it was, no matter how hard she tried to deny it. Slitting his throat, leaving her forever bereft and thinking she'd been betrayed—it was the perfect revenge. And one that was permanent, even if she figured it out. Because then she would have to live with herself—with the fact that she'd spent three days believing her sweet Seth was an asshole.

And she just wasn't capable of living with that possibility.

It made her periodically groan and clutch herself, to the point where Pod tried to bring her soothing things. Like half an uneaten pizza she didn't know he'd ordered, or his favorite sock, or the TV remote she thought she had lost a week earlier. None of which helped. Nothing helped.

She had to make a Find Me mirror with her heart in her throat and tears in her eyes.

It was really not a surprise when it turned out badly.

All she could see was someone's elbow. Though luckily, it was an elbow she would have known anywhere. *Thank god I mapped out every inch of his body*, she thought, and then laughed. And Pod laughed. And all the lights in the house went on and off again, as if somewhere her beloved grandmother was glad, too.

Seth was alive. Now it was just a matter of making sure he stayed that way.

"Okay, buddy," she said to her furry little companion. "Time to go get your dad back."

And in response, Pod clapped his tiny hands with joy.

SHE KNEW THEY knew she had come. She could feel it crackling in the air, the moment she entered the House That Isn't Here. A kind of tension—the residue of werewolf fear. Plus, there was no golden, glowing hallway to greet her.

All the lights were out, with no discernible way to turn them back on.

But it was okay. She'd thought of that. She'd brewed a potion that formed a glowing blue ball, when she spilled a drop of it into the air. And more: it seemed to guide her. When she stepped to the door of the first room, the orb kept going. It floated all the way to the end of the hall, trailing wisps of light. Then it hovered in front of the door there, waiting for her to catch up.

She had to force herself not to hurry. Because hurrying meant mistakes, and she couldn't afford to make any. These fuckers were wily, and they were mean, and if they couldn't hurt her by tricking her, she knew they'd do it by hurting Seth. So, careful was the name of the game. Cautious. With liberal use of the watch on her wrist, which she'd enchanted to detect threats.

If it buzzed, watch out.

If it stayed quiet, all was well.

Or as well as could be while she hunted a bunch of deranged monsters. Because even with all the protection she was covered in, and the weapons she'd brought along, she knew that was what she was doing. And it was absolutely terrifying on about a million different levels. She had to force herself to creep forward, heart hammering, mouth dry, every part of her shaking.

It seemed to take forever to get to the door at the end of the hall. Then even longer than that to turn the doorknob. Her hand was sweating so much it kept sliding off. She had to wipe it on her jeans and take some calming breaths and think of Seth's sweet face before she could manage.

And finally, finally it gave. The door opened.

But she kind of wished it hadn't.

Because nothing on this earth could have prepared her for what she found beyond. She almost yelled in horror, despite how steely and tough she had wanted to seem. And she only caught herself by remembering that this wasn't real. It wasn't actually the auditorium from high school, appearing exactly as it had when she'd last seen it. It was just an illusion, of a kind so powerful she knew the Jerks could never have created it.

It was the room itself that had done this, quite clearly. She could feel it humming through her whole body—the sense that something in here knew exactly what you were most afraid of. It knew, and then it simply recreated whatever that was, right down to the last letter. And god that last letter was good.

There were banners on the walls yelling about a spring fling. One of the stage spotlights was flickering, just like it had back then. Hell, the magic here had even filled the rows of foldout chairs. A bunch of disturbingly uncanny approximations sat there, staring at the stage.

And every one of them turned to look at her when she stepped into the room.

Waiting, she thought, to laugh at her again.

She almost turned and fled. But then she remembered: they weren't real. And even if they had been, they had no power over her anymore. Truthfully, she was sorry she had ever let them have power over her at all. It seemed so foolish now, so small, like something another person entirely had been bothered about.

Though it surprised her when that thought seemed to make them flicker a little. They took on a faded sheen. And it got stronger, the more she let the idea sink in. *I am not that girl anymore, and all of you were never anything to her anyway,* she told herself. Until somehow, there was not a single face left. Just chairs, the stage.

Jason sat on the edge of it, swinging his legs, like this was all such a blast. "You figured us out. Seems you're not as silly as I took you for," he said in that snotty voice of his. "Still, it was pretty foolish of you to come here at all. I mean, what do you think you're gonna do? Rescue your little boyfriend? When there are ten of us and only one of you?"

Yes, she wanted to snarl. *I'm gonna demolish every last one of you.* But she stayed calm. She shrugged. "Ten, huh? Thought you'd have more," she said, and watched his face crease into unabashed fury, in response.

"It's enough to stop you from ambushing us again,"

"Oh, so that's what happened last time. I just played dirty."

"You fucking know you did, you little bitch. Using that potion."

"You mean the one I can also use to make any of the wolves you've recruited—but who don't really have anything against me—feel a lot better than they currently do?" she said. Then she let that hang in the air for a second, before continuing in the same conversational way. "Because you know, I'm guessing that's why they joined you. You promised them a witch you can bend to your will, and force into helping them. But see the thing is, Jay, I don't need to be forced. If they want to leave you now and come to the little sanctuary I'm setting up, I'd be only too happy to fix them."

There, she thought. Though truthfully, she didn't expect her ploy to work well. It had seemed like a long shot, back when she had dreamt it up. So it was a shock when someone popped up from their hiding place behind the piano in the corner.

"Wait," he said. "You didn't tell us she would seriously just help us."

And that seemed to incense Jason enough to get him on his feet. "Because she's fucking lying. Shut up, Pete, and sit your ass down," he snarled.

But Pete did not. He glanced from Jay to her and back again. Then dashed for the door. Followed by four others, scrambling after him. Including, of all people, fucking *Tyler.*

"You goddamn cowardly little punk," Jay hollered after him.

But it made no difference. He was gone.

Which was good, it was very good, because it meant the first part of her plan had worked. Now she was down to a handful of wolves—and the ones that were left were probably going to panic soon, if Jay was any indication. He paced angrily, and after a moment, gestured to something she couldn't see behind the curtains that lined the wings offstage.

The place where they hid when they did what they did to me, she thought, just as Jordan dragged Seth out on stage. Her Seth, all tied up and bloody and dazed. Like they'd been beating him. Like he barely even knew what was going on.

And okay, yeah, that was a good ploy. It almost distracted her. She took a step forward, heart in mouth, completely unaware of any threat that might come at her from the sides or from behind. But the thing was—distractions didn't matter. It made no difference that her attention was elsewhere.

A wolf leapt at her from the left, and the weapon she had in her right hand—a rolling pin bound to her wrist with a leather shoelace—jerked upward of its own accord, raising her arm with it. Then it came down so hard on the open maw of that lunging wolf, she saw teeth spiral out from the point of contact. She felt the crunch of the blow all the way up her arm. Bones snapped, blood spattered finely over the seats behind them. Then it just landed at her feet in a heap.

Unconscious, she knew, without even looking.

Though she looked anyway. She calmly eyed the crumpled, furry mess.

Before tightening her grip on the rolling pins she had attached to both wrists. The ones she'd heavily dosed with Make Nice just before coming here. The ones that protected her, no matter what. And then she flicked her gaze toward an open-mouthed Jason.

"You didn't really think that would work against a witch, did you?" she said.

But clearly he did, because he tried it again. "Get her," he yelled, at which point several things happened all at once. Seth became sensible enough to understand what was happening and tried to get up. Several full-blown wolves sprang out from what felt like every corner of the room. And the rolling pins did what she had primed them to do.

Only they did it in a way she had never imagined in a million years when she'd done this.

She had assumed they would just block anything incoming. But apparently, that wasn't the only way the rolling pins interpreted their mandate to defend her. They also decided that if two wolves leapt at her at the same time, the best approach was not to try to smack them both.

It was to get her out of their path.

And they did it by dragging her backward. They snapped her arms behind her and yanked. Then she simply went where they moved her. She wound up five feet from where she had been before, staring breathlessly as those two wolves just smashed into each other. They joined the tally of crumpled unconscious heaps of fur.

Astonishing, she thought. But it got even more so, when the pins seemed to realize she was still in danger. Because as soon as they did, one of them hooked itself under the arm of the nearest chair. And somehow, impossibly, incredibly it *hauled her off her feet.*

She performed an honest-to-god cartwheel, a real cartwheel.

Despite never having done a cartwheel in her life. Then before she could catch her breath, or wonder if she'd wrenched her own arms out of their sockets, the weapon in her other hand took advantage of where she had landed—on a chair that was beyond some beast's claws and teeth—and smacked it across the back. She heard the bones of a shoulder blade crack.

Followed by a howl as another wolf crumpled.

But the magic didn't stop there. It didn't wait for her to catch her breath. It turned her, so she could hit a wolf coming at her from the left. Then again when another one came at her from the front. Back and forth, until it felt as if she was constantly moving.

And in ways she hadn't known she could move. She was maneuvered into jumps she wasn't capable of, over wolves so large and terrifying she would never have attempted such a feat on her own. She blocked blows she barely saw coming, whacked chairs into attackers before she even understood they were there.

And best and most incredibly of all: when three wolves regrouped and came at her simultaneously, there was no leaping, no evading. The pins just somehow *twirled* her. They briefly turned her into a spinning top, outstretched arms hitting everything as she spun. And when they did she couldn't help it.

Despite the terrifying circumstances, despite how horrible this all was, it just happened. She felt herself whirling so fast her feet actually left the floor—and she *laughed.* She laughed with pure amazement and delight, face turned up to the ceiling of the auditorium. Like it was the sky, like it was the stars above her, like this wasn't the stifling place that had haunted her memories for a decade.

It was something else. It gave her back her strength.

The whole situation did, she thought, as the spinning slowed, and the pins let her sink back down onto her feet. Because now she could survey the absolute havoc she had wrought, and oh, it was incredible. It was impossible. There were whole heaps of wolves lying all around her. Others fleeing at the sight of what she could do.

Then on the stage, Seth, still on his knees. Staring at her across the auditorium, with so much awe and astonishment and gratitude in his eyes that she wasn't sure how she could ever have doubted his feelings. They were as clear as glass, as air, as anything had ever been to her. She would always know it now.

He belongs to me, and I belong to him, she thought.

Then stalked forward to take out the one last obstacle between them.

Bane of her life. Ruiner of everything. And now just this: some little dipshit, who whimpered "No no no" the second she pointed a rolling pin at him. "You're next," she told him firmly, fiercely, as she climbed onto the stage. Then watched him back away so fast he fumbled over his own feet. He wound up on his ass, scooting away like a kid who'd seen a spider.

"Oh what's the matter, bro? Is it not so fun when you do it to someone who isn't weaker than you?" she asked, as he went. And had the satisfaction of seeing his face crease with bitterness and guilt.

Before he scrambled for a comeback. "You weren't even weak in high school. Look what you did to us," he spat. But there was no conviction in it.

"I didn't do anything to you, you lying little weasel."

"Oh, so being the reason we turned into this doesn't count?"

"You can't possibly be claiming that I turned you into ass-holes," she said, laughing. Though she didn't like the sly look on his face. Or the sound of protest Seth made from behind the gag. The one he tried to get off, as Jay grinned even wider.

He showed his fangs, sharper and meaner than Seth's. "No, I'm not claiming you made us assholes. I'm claiming you made us *werewolves*," he said, and then clearly waited for her face to fall before he continued. "Oh no, did your little boyfriend not tell you? Well, I'm not surprised. I mean, who wants to confess that he got turned into a wolf by his best buddy, and then mauled a bunch of kids for barely any reason at all? We just wanted to stop by and say sorry to the girl we pulled a mean prank on. And look what he did."

He lifted his shirt, on the last word.

Showed her a scar, different from any of Seth's.

This one, quite clearly, had been made by a set of sharp teeth. She could see each separate indentation, obvious enough that you could never mistake it for anything else.

Still, for a second she tried to deny it. She thought of a dozen ways that might have happened, each more plausible than the last. Just as Seth got free of that damned gag and stormed out things she didn't know how to take.

"You deserved it, you lying fuck, don't act like you didn't. Don't act like you were just gonna say sorry, because we all know you weren't. You were gonna keep making her life hell, so I did what I had to do. I put you down, and considering this shit show, I was right to do it. Setting a pack of wolves on her—I swear to god when I get my strength back I'm gonna make the night I savaged the fuck out of you look like a goddamn tea party. And this time? *I'm gonna do it all on purpose,*" he snarled. Like he was doing something good.

But instead it just confirmed her worst fears.

She was the one who had turned Seth into what he was.

Even though the idea seemed impossible, it seemed ridiculous. *I wasn't even a witch then*, she tried to protest in her head. *It was afterward. It was after all of it that I started baking with Gram.* But as soon as she did, she felt the witch part of her laugh.

Wrong, it said. *Wrong wrong wrong.*

And she saw the series of events in her mind's eye. The first moment her powers had manifested. Like Carrie, at the prom. Standing there with her cake—her own creation—smeared down her front and all over her hands. Feeling betrayed and helpless and humiliated. But also galvanized. Like if she really wanted to, she could make them all stop laughing.

And she hadn't. But she *had* done something else. She could see it now, clearly. Her running from the building; Seth running after her. The way he had called her name, how she had turned in a fury. Then she'd shoved him away, and as she had she'd called him something.

You're a fucking beast, Seth Brubaker, she'd yelled.

And apparently that was all it had taken. Just a word she hadn't meant literally, and a potion on her palms that she hadn't even known she'd concocted. Then all of this had followed one event after another, until finally here they were. With Seth looking at her, realization dawning about what he'd accidentally confessed. And her standing there, astonished and crestfallen, over what that confession meant.

While in the background Jay sniveled and whined and swore he wouldn't hurt them again.

Though that, at least, was something she could make sure of.

"You won't be able to," she said to him. "Because you are made of my magic, once removed, and I know it now, so I can command you. And I do so now. You and yours may never lift a hand against me or mine again, Jason Kirkpatrick. I bind you to it, by the weight of the spell I cast against your maker."

And then somehow, above them, thunder rumbled again.

And she knew it was done. She knew it was all over.

CHAPTER THIRTY-TWO

She wanted to say a thousand things to Seth once they were in the relative safety of the Chevy. And she felt pretty sure he wanted to say a thousand things to her. She heard him take a breath, of the kind you did when words were supposed to follow. But no words did.

They flew in almost silence, until they got about halfway back to her home. And even then he only broke it to say, "Stop here a second."

So she did. She landed the car in a clearing in what looked like the middle of the forest. Then got out when he did—despite not having the slightest idea why he wanted to be here. In fact, for a moment she genuinely wondered if this was some kind of punishment for turning him into a werewolf. Like he was gonna pants her, then leave her stranded somehow. Or maybe worse.

I probably deserve worse, she thought.

And doubly so, when he revealed his actual motive: the tree. Their hollowed-out tree. Still with the blue tarpaulin over the entrance, in a way that made her heart clench and her breath catch in her throat. She had to turn away to hide the tears that were in her eyes, immediately, at the idea that he must have looked after the tree all this time.

And then she followed him in, and *oh*.

Oh, they had been right, somehow they had been right.

Because inside, it was *magical*.

It was twice as large as it should have been, and filled with everything you'd ever want to see inside an enchanted tree. There were toadstools for seats, a blanket of stars for lights, a carpet of moss far greener than moss ever usually was. And thicker, too. The second she made her way inside, her shoes sank in almost up to the laces. Each step felt like heaven.

And there was more, so much more. A small stove with a chimney, shelves filled with fantastical-looking books, tiny cabinets brimming with all sorts of things. As she stood there taking it all in, Seth rummaged through one of them. Then finally came up with a jar of jam, and cookies wrapped in wax paper. Some cheese too, of a kind she had never seen before. And a heel of bread that smelled so divine her mouth watered.

She sat down on one of the toadstools before he had even gestured.

Then she watched as he boiled a tiny kettle, and brewed and stewed and sieved. He made her a teeny cup of tea, and handed it to her. And it was only when she reached for it that she managed to stop marveling at everything long enough to speak. "I should be taking care of you, Seth," she said.

But she could tell he didn't get it, even before he replied.

He looked at his filthy shirt and his healed but blood-smeared hands instead.

"Hey, I'm okay. They didn't do anything to me. It was mostly just insults and tying me up and trying to use my blood to replicate whatever potions you gave me. I really don't think they thought through any of what they did," he said.

Because he was a fool. A lovely, lovely fool.

"And that's good, Seth, it's really good, but whatever they did isn't the reason I think so," she explained, and now he winced. Now he looked away.

"Yeah, but I was kind of hoping we could skip right over that."

"We already have skipped over that. For *way* too long."

"And it was working fine. We were best buds again. Everything was cool. In fact, it was so cool that you somehow believed I would never do that thing they said I did to you, despite having photographic evidence that I had."

He looked at her then. Same way he had on the stage—full of

astonishment and gratitude and awe. Like she was something so special and generous. Even though she wasn't at all. She was terrible, and he needed to know that.

"Because you're a good person, who earned my trust."

"So now you don't want to? Now you can't, because I lied?"

"Seth, I don't feel like you lied. I feel like you tried to spare my feelings."

He sighed then. Shook his head. And finally looked at her. Gaze fierce, and more full of warmth than she deserved. "It wasn't about your feelings, Cass. It was about what I knew you'd do once you had them. Because let's be honest, if I had said, after that medicine you made worked and I put two and two together about everything, 'Hey, I think you might have accidentally turned me into a werewolf,' you would *not* have been chill about it. You would have run around doing everything you could to make it up to me, up to and including forgiving me for what I did to you. And I didn't want that," he said.

Though all that did was confuse her. "But you *did* want that."

"No, I really did not."

"Seth, all you've wanted is to be friends again."

"Yeah, the *real* way. The actual forgiveness way. Not some phony thing you only do because you feel bad," he protested, intensely enough that she had no response. She simply let his words sink in, and by the time they had he was calmer. "If we became buddies again, I wanted to *earn* it. I wanted to earn your trust and your love. I never wanted to wonder if that trust and love only existed because you felt you owed it to me."

After which, she still couldn't speak. But now it was for a different reason. Now she wasn't just taken aback. She was being swallowed whole by her own heart. She had to simply live in that love for him, for a long moment, before she could get any words out.

And the first ones she managed were still tear-choked and terrible.

"I did something that awful to you, and all you thought about was making sure I could really believe in you. That if I loved you again, I loved you truly," she said, and shook her head, marveling.

"I don't even know how you did it. How you made yourself that okay with it."

But he just looked bemused. "I didn't *have* to make myself okay about it, Cass. I *was* okay. I *am* okay. It was a fucking *accident*. You never intended to actually turn me into a werewolf. I don't even think the potion was meant to do that. I think it was meant to protect you from harm, because I didn't feel one thing after that. I didn't turn. I didn't show any signs of anything like it. In fact, you know when I did? When I saw that they wanted to keep hurting you. That's when I thought, *If I am a beast, I want to be one who can keep her safe*. And a wolf was what I thought of. And what I became," he said, so earnestly she wanted to accept that. She wanted to feel some relief, that she hadn't been as responsible as she'd thought.

But it still felt impossible.

"All that pain, though. And the fact that you couldn't have sex. And then got forced into a fated-mates, werewolf-sex situation— with the very person who sort of did this to you. Come on, that's at least a little horrible any way you slice it," she tried, face turned away from him as he did.

Then she turned back, and oh. There was such a look, all over his face. A kind of half-sheepish, half-confused look. And she knew some other revelation was coming. It was clear before he even took a breath, and kind of tilted his head to one side. "Yeah, I was kind of thinking you'd probably guessed why that fated mates stuff happened. And that maybe you were just being polite about it. Or trying to spare my feelings. But now I'm starting to wonder if that's true. Now I'm starting to wonder if you really don't know what a coward I was," he said.

But honestly, that only made it more confusing. "You're not a coward, Seth."

"I am. And I'm a fool too. God, I was a fool." He looked away from her again, down at his tightly laced together fingers. So she knew he was struggling to find the right way to say it. And it clearly made it easier, when she put her hand on his arm and squeezed.

Because he took a breath, and began, "Do you know why I

wanted to be someone different? Someone hotter and cooler and better? Because I thought: if I become those things, the girl I love will finally love me. I will be good enough for her then. I'll be like the homecoming king in every movie we loved, mooned after by some sweet girl you're supposed to think is a dork. I will be a prize, golden and glowing and perfect, and she will think so too."

And now she wasn't just confused.

She was frightened. Because part of her knew what he was saying. But most of her didn't know how to accept it. She was still stuck between the kid she had been, and the woman she had grown into, and whoever it was that she could now possibly become. Someone even better. Someone who didn't just dare to trust in the decency and friendship of another person.

But believed in love being returned.

Or at least, believed enough to say it.

To step out over what looked like empty air, and be sure that something safe would emerge beneath her feet. *You'll plummet to your death if you try,* her mind insisted. But somehow she found herself inching to the edge of the precipice anyway.

"But you already were those things, Seth. And if that girl didn't see it, then she was a fool," she said, heart beating like a rabbit's, eyes unable to meet his. Until he touched the tips of his fingers to her chin. He lifted it so she could see his gaze, all full of feeling for her.

"Oh, I think she did agree," he murmured softly. Then more, more, oh there were a million confessions to come. "I think she must have, all things considered. But the problem was, I just didn't know. I didn't understand. And it meant I didn't tell her. It meant I was *terrified* of telling her. That I was terrified of *anyone* telling her. I didn't want her to ever think I was pathetic and lovelorn and not really her friend. So I let myself be taunted into shouting something at a talent show, something ugly, something I only meant as a fumbled, frantic denial of all the things I didn't want her to know. But of course she didn't hear it as that. She heard it as an insult. And it led to us not being friends at all."

She saw it all, the moment he said it.

Everything turned on its head. Everything flipped.

The insult somehow no longer even just accidentally repeated, in anger at them. But accidentally repeated, out of love for someone. Someone she could see now, very clearly. Yet still felt breathless, at the thought of naming.

"So you were friends with this girl," she said, instead.

But he understood. "The best of friends. The very best."

"She was special to you."

"There are no words for how much," he said, as he met her gaze.

And she knew. She knew so thoroughly that she almost couldn't speak what was in her heart. But she made herself, so she could hear it for sure. "Try to tell me some of the things that made her special to you. Tell me what she was like," she said, so faintly she wasn't even sure if he caught it.

Until he stroked a thumb over the tear that ran down her cheek. "Like wild laughter while riding my bike down a hill with her on the front," he said soft, soft. "Like eyes made bright by the movie screen her face is always turned up toward. Like the smell of popcorn and cinnamon and something she baked just for me. Something so sweet, I can hardly stand it."

And when he did, she saw every one.

Felt the wind in her hair.

Saw a movie dancing in her eyes.

Tasted that sweetness on her tongue.

"And is she still those things now?" she dared to ask in a trembling voice. Then got all the wonders she could have ever dreamed of.

"She's more than all of them. I've watched her fearlessly fly into a sky she doesn't know if she's ever going to come down from, just for the love of all that is magical in the world. I've seen her care for someone so much, even while thinking he was her worst enemy. Hell, she thought I *was* her worst enemy again, when she came for me. Fierce as a lightning strike, doing things for me that I could never have imagined getting from someone, in all the horror movies I've ever loved. She is the heroine of all of them, better than all of them, and I'm not afraid to say it. Because that fear was all about me, and how I thought you would see me. When really I should have thought about how *you* deserved to be seen. How you deserve to *know* you're seen. You are the best, brightest, and most brilliant person I've ever known, Cassandra Camberwell. And I love you, I love you, I love you. I love you so much that even though it might cost me to say it, I want you to know it anyway. I want you to know how beloved you are to me," he said.

Then all she could do was look at her own clumsy little life through new eyes.

The way she was, the way she seemed. All the ways he'd told her, and yet somehow she hadn't understood. Because before, he would start to say "love" and change it to "like." He would say he imagined how making love with her might be, then make sure to clarify that he meant now rather than always. He had stepped carefully around an admission that his desire was already there. Held back on confessing his attraction to her. And how many times had he said:

"I mean, not that I do?" . . . "Not that I did?" . . . "Only just?" . . . "Right now?"

So many she should have guessed. She should have guessed over the mating bond. Over the words in the guidebook that she'd always let her eyes skim right over, rather than allowing any of them to go in. *A compulsive connection with a werewolf may only occur if one already exists*, she thought. And oh, the way the witch inside her yelled for that. *At last you ask me*, it said inside her. *Why didn't you ask me?* But of course she knew why she hadn't.

Her entire view of how things were had stood in the way.

Just as his had stood in the way for him.

He hadn't thought he was enough.

Even though he was everything, he was everything, oh god she could finally tell him how much he was. "Oh, love. How could you ever think it would cost you anything at all, when all I ever wanted was to hear you say one-half of what you just said, one-tenth of it, one-millionth? I used to lie awake at night dreaming of just that tone in your voice," she said.

And once she had spoken—once she saw the light in his eyes change from dark to shot through with lightning, once she saw his frown smooth and his lips part—she couldn't stop. She let out all the words she'd always wanted to.

"Every love song I loved I sang at the top of my lungs while alone, thinking of you. My heart used to come close to bursting, with the hope that you thought of me too. It's the reason it crushed me so completely when you went away, because the thing was, it wasn't just losing my friend. It was losing the whole idea of the way life could be. The idea that sometimes things turn out the way you most long for, sometimes things will be okay, sometimes you are the heroine at the end of the movie, who takes a chance, and it goes the right way. The amazing, brilliant, perfect-just-as-he-is nerd she loves chooses her, the moment she says."

After which, it was his turn to be speechless. She saw his lips form words, then stop, and start again. And again, and again. Until finally he managed to get them out. "And you're saying that's what this is. That this was always it, to you."

"With all my heart, it was, and still is, and always will be."

"But you never let it show, not ever."

She shook her head, half laughing. "Do you know how many things I did to make sure it didn't? The amount of times I would wait to text you back, or pull faces when you hugged me, or sign birthday cards with just my name so you would never know. So you could never guess," she explained, and oh, the laugh he let out when she did. The delight in it, the ruefulness. The way it spurred her on. "It's why I can't ever be mad at you for fearing looking lovelorn and pathetic. Because I was terrified of the same thing, too. I used to think *if he did, he would say, if he did, he would say, if he did, he would say.*"

"And all along I thought the same."

"I guess so."

He shook his head. "Boy, we really made a mess of things, huh?"

"I'd say yes. But nothing has ever felt less like a mess to me than this."

"Even though we wasted all that time, and suffered all that agony?"

"It's a small price to pay to feel my heart soar like this. To know, finally, that I can put my hand over yours, and you will turn your hand and fold it around mine, just like you are doing before I even say it," she said, because sure enough he was. And so instinctively that he looked down in a wondering sort of way. Like he could hardly believe it was true.

That this was how things were now.

They were love, all love, no holding back or trying to pretend.

"God, yeah. You're right," he said, after a moment of letting that wash over him. "I'd pay that price a thousand times over again, for this feeling. Even being alone, even being a monster, even longing for you the way I did, I would."

And then she offered what she had known she would, the moment the truth about what she had done had hit her. The thing she could give him, as one who had made him what he was. "I can turn you back, you know. I can give you back everything I took," she said as he looked at her again. As he met her gaze, steady and so full of love it was like being held.

Then he spoke, softer than ever. "You already have. You've given me what I always wanted. To be like this, to be the beast from the kind of movie you saved the day in. But with a better ending than anything like that beast gets. I am all the magic of a million things we watched together, and none of the agony, at the end," he said. And as he leaned in to kiss her, he whispered one more thing. "Because now we get to live out our happily ever after, forever and ever, amen."

EPILOGUE

Cassie had told him that she could just use magic to install the sign. But Seth had insisted on making a contribution of his own, and so had Pod. And so here they were, him halfway up a ladder leaning against the porch roof, Pod trying to pull him up there by his hair, her giving directions from the grass.

"A little higher up on the left," she said. And of course he went too high with it. So she waved a hand down. Then he went too low. Really, she was just going to have to face the facts: the Sanctuary for Supernatural Creatures was just going to have a slightly crooked sign. And if she was being honest, it kind of felt better that way.

It gave the whole place character. It made it seem welcoming.

Not that they needed to be more welcoming. They were already busy all the time now. Yesterday they had fixed a vampire's ingrown tooth. The day before, they had treated a fairy's damaged wing.

And then there was Nancy. Nancy, who was almost certainly the witch Cassie had suspected she was. She had seen this very sign laid out on the grass, ready to be put up. Even though Cassie had covered it in magic. So of course, Cassie had explained a few things. Pointed her in the right directions. Watched her be amazed by all the wonders of the world, before setting her off on her own journey toward something better.

Just as she had for the wolves who had turned up, too. Even though she was pretty sure one of them had been Tyler, wearing a disguise. He had slunk up looking for a cure, sheepish yet not exactly sorry. Though she hadn't said anything about it. She didn't have to.

The wolves knew they had no power over her now. Nor would they ever again. "We're the ones who won," she said to Seth when he grumbled about them.

And they had too, in all the ways that mattered.

On Sundays, they went to the farmer's market, and wandered around holding hands. Like every couple they never thought they'd be. They went to the movies twice a week, just like they used to as kids. But now with a lot of kissing, to make up for all the times they never could.

And those were just the ordinary dates.

There were others, more magical than anything they could have managed before. They parked the Chevy in the sky, and listened to a riot of old songs with their arms around each other, and their raccoon child in the back. Raced through the trees, her flying and him on foot.

Then him on all fours.

Often it ended with him on all fours. And he would find her, and pounce, and roll with her through the green and the black and the brown of the forest floor, until they were breathless. Until she was buried in his fur, so deep it felt like she would never get back out again.

She didn't want to ever get back out again.

She was here now, in their wonderful world of love and magic.

And all was well.

ACKNOWLEDGMENTS

When I was a kid dreaming of being an author, the thing I always thought I would write was almost exactly what you're holding in your hands right now. I wanted witches, and werewolves, and vampires, and demons. Flying Hoovers, sanctuaries for supernatural creatures, raccoons that talked. I swear, some form of this very story has been in my head since 2004. And so to say that getting to write this book was a dream come true is an understatement.

Which means I now have to thank everybody who made it possible. My agent, Courtney, who had hardly any idea what monster fucking was, but got onboard with this book anyway. My editor, Eileen, who was as excited as I had always dreamt of someone being over my werewolves and witches. And gleefully sold it to everyone at Macmillan, when it had the word "horny" in the title.

You're the best, Eileen.

And then there's Kelly Wagner, for the Christopher Pike–looking cover I've always longed for. The design team, for their endless patience with my fussing over every detail. Kejana and Hannah and the rest of the marketing and publicity bods who work so hard to get my books out there and in everybody's ears and eyeballs.

My wonderful family, my lovely friends.

My doggo, who is my own personal Pod.

And finally, I want to thank my readers. The way you showed up for *When Grumpy Met Sunshine* is something I will never forget. Taking photos with it in stores, showing me library wait lists, excitedly reviewing . . . I am very lucky. Thank you for sticking with me.

I won't ever stop, again.

ABOUT THE AUTHOR

Elizabeth Baker Photography

Charlotte Stein is the RT- and DABWAHA-nominated author of over fifty short stories, novellas, and novels, including entries in *The Mammoth Book of Hot Romance* and *Best New Erotica 10*. When not writing hilarious, deeply emotional, and intensely sexy books, she can be found eating jelly turtles, watching space wizards fight zombies, and occasionally lusting after hunks. For more on Charlotte, visit www.charlottestein.net.